The vha'attaye hissed, and an icy wind rose in the *b'dabba*, and began to swirl around the warrior and the child. The wind shrieked with deadsoul anguish, spun and clattered the hanging drumsticks against the drums overhead. Cold, wet ghostflesh hands gripped Medwind and Kirtha, shook them, slid cold dead fingers from living arms to living throats —

Kirtha shrieked and hit at the huge ghost hands with her tiny ones. She struggled against them for only an instant, then closed her eyes. "Go away," she howled.

Power surged from the child, uncontrolled and unchecked.

The wind died with a "pop." The hands vanished. The vha'attaye disappeared — not the gradual melting of line and form they chose for themselves when returning to the dark places between the worlds, but with a loud, sucking, tearing sound, and so suddenly that they might never have been.

In the sudden silence, the last clicks of swinging drumsticks overhead made Medwind jump. She exhaled and shivered.

Kirtha looked at the suddenly bare bones and shook her head slowly from side to side. She stared into the face of the Hoos warrior again and pursed her lips.

"Uh-oh," she said. "All gone."

"Uh-oh," Medwind agreed, staring at the child. The sensation of wild power that had banished the vha'attaye still clung to Kirtha. A feeling very like the vha'attaye's icy fingers played up and down Medwind's spine. Kirtha's mother, at the age of nineteen, ~~had~~ ~~a~~ stone village to mo~~~~er mother's daughter.

BONES OF THE PAST

Holly Lisle

BONES OF THE PAST

Copyright © 1993, by Holly Lisle

A Baen Books Original

Baen Publishing Enterprises
P.O. Box 1403
Riverdale, NY 10471

ISBN: 0-671-72160-7

Cover art by Larry Elmore

First Printing, March 1993

Distributed by Simon & Schuster
1230 Avenue of the Americas
New York, NY 10020

Printed in the United States of America

DEDICATION:
To Chris,
best friend, lover, colleague, husband.
And to my fellow writers in Schrödinger's Petshop,
who helped this book happen.
And to Misty Lackey, who not only got me started,
but also saved my life once.
Heinlein said you don't pay back —
you only pay forward.
So I am.

ACKNOWLEDGMENTS

This story came into being because Micky Hart and Jay Stevens' wonderful book *Drumming on the Edge of Magic* left drums in my dreams that woke me one night too many—

And because, after failing miserably at growing my own bonsai, I wondered at what sort of people could grow really big bonsai—

And because my editor, Toni Weisskopf, didn't want to read about anyplace cold.

SOUTHEAST TRILLING

WEN TRIBES
1 Allwater 4 Blackstone
2 Pennifish 5 Firemountain
3 Smoke

ARHEL

DELMUIRIE'S BARRIER

PENNAR CHAIN

AMOTIC ISLE

BÓSÉLEIGH BAY

SAG SEA

Wennish Jungles

PUNDAK OCEAN

CUMBLEY SEA

Klaue Ruins

Omwimmee Trade

Wen Tribes Province

Treaty Line

Ono Bay

Little Tam

Big Tam

Cumbley Bay

Maisee Cliffs

FEY PLATEAU

Hak

Bonton

Forest Province

Gunnit

ARISS

Fey Province

BOOAR MTS.

Bright

Willowlake

Dumforst

Otwoch

Swom

Sairefe

Bonwite

Branch River

Fey River

Kele Bay

KÉLE SEA

Belldote

Fisher Province

Punce

Caille Pass

Chak River

Rabeoline Province

Braxille

Chak

LITTLE SOUTH SEA

Huong

Hoôs Domain

Stone Teeth

DELMUIRIE'S BARRIER

¤ PROLOGUE

Throughout Ariss, the first bells of morning began to sound. The heavy fog that shrouded the city muted their clamor — still, they were loud enough to warn the whores who plied their trade in the street beneath Roba Morgasdotte's window their night's work was done. They were loud enough to rouse the musician who lived in the next apartment; through the thin walls, Roba heard him shuffling about the room, then out and down the hall to the communal water closet. After a few moments, his door slammed again and he began sawing away with great energy but little skill on his violetto. The poor instrument's squeals and shrieks and coughing stutters set Roba's teeth on edge. She clenched her fist around the pen and wrote faster.

The sheer incompetence of the violettist next door didn't bother Roba as much as her suspicion that he was making more money butchering music than she was teaching. *He'll still be killing Mambrinsonne's "Apprentice of Dherolg" long after I've starved to death and blown away to dust*, she thought, and glared at the wall.

She had no more time to polish the student's paper. Her landlady rose with the bells. At any moment, the woman might arrive at her door and begin bellowing like a fishwife after the money Roba still owed her — and then Roba would have to climb out her window and down the stone-and-daub wall again to avoid the harridan.

No thanks, she decided. *I nearly broke my neck last time.*

She shoved the paper into her bag, grabbed her cloak, and swung it haphazardly over her shoulders as she ran for the door. If she were lucky, she'd get out before Madame Greldene caught her; if she were really lucky, she would find the student whose paper she'd edited before *antis.* The four copper hidaros he owed her would buy an entire loaf of two-day-old bread, a flask of watered wine, and a small pot of fish-paste — awful fare, but enough to keep her on the right side of starvation for another day.

And tomorrow, she thought, as she crept down the rickety wooden stairs to the first floor, *tomorrow I attend the secret meeting of the Delmuirie Society. If afterward I don't get thrown out of the city for being a subversive, maybe Thirk will give me that raise he mentioned.* She was nervous about any association with the Delmuirie Society — from her department head's whispered comments, she gathered that it was dangerous to be a member — maybe even to associate with members. *I don't care anymore, though. I'll be a subversive if it gets me enough money to pay my rent.*

Two whores, hard-eyed and thin-lipped, swung into the dark, narrow hall from outside and headed for their room. Roba gave them both a polite, silent nod of greeting. The first merely nodded in return.

The second, with a malicious smile, yelled, "Ho, Teach-er! Madame said if I saw tha' I was to tell tha' she wants her money by th' morrow — or she will take tha' rent out in trade. If tha' canna pay her, tha' can stand onna corner with me, Teach-er!"

Behind Roba, Madame Greldene's door flew open with a crash, and the landlady roared, "I want mah money now, you! Today — or I'll throw you into the street!"

Roba didn't waste time looking over her shoulder. She could hear the woman's thundering footsteps behind her. She bolted.

¤ Chapter 1

Seven-Fingered Fat Girl tested the soothing hush of wind through the trees, the soft murmur of a nearby brook, and the restful whispering of leaves — and found the jungle a liar. Jungles were never gentle. Thick loam on the woodland floor muffled the measured tread of big maneaters like roshu and koriu — the pleasant rustle of leaves covered the hiss of leather-winged dooru as they stooped to kill. Delicate greenery gave hiding places to smaller assassins; sometimes the greenery was the assassin. Prickling hairs on the back of her neck told her the jungle was hiding something now.

She had the point, leading the band of tagnu far from its last trade stop at Five Dots Silk. They were upland and deep in unknown terrain; and here, in a valley with the bony spines of mountains rising on either side, the trees were shorter, of smaller girth, and farther apart than those around the villages where they traded. The underbrush was heavy; the canopy above thin and in some places nonexistent. Everything about this place conspired to expose them to the things that hunted humans. The band roved in a pack, wary.

Seven-Fingered Fat Girl fought to slow her ragged breathing. She tightened her grip on her dartstick and shifted her dart packs to a more accessible position. "Myed on the right," she snapped at her followers. She trotted around the coils of vine draped over the branches ahead, bare feet padding noiselessly.

Whitened bones gleamed from beneath the myed's glossy leaves and told a truth the gaudy, sweet-scented flowers would have hidden. But the myed was merely a little danger to those who remembered to watch for it. The bigger dangers were not so easily avoided.

And with that thought still fresh in her mind, she heard it again — a subtle click, a near-silent cough more nerve-wracking than the most violent face-to-face confrontation. Without a doubt, something was stalking them.

Behind her and to her left, Dog Nose pulled a hurlstick from his carrier and twisted the rawhide thong in a spiral to the middle; he picked up the pace of his lope. "They're on both sides."

"Ya. Close in — weapons ready." Seven-Fingered Fat Girl shoved a poisoned dart into her dartstick, never missing her stride. Her nerves stretched taut. Behind her, all six companions moved closer to her and to each other. The tagnu increased their pace to an easy run, eyes scanning everything.

At that moment, she could even have welcomed the hated tree-paths of the Silk People, Fat Girl thought. If the tagnu had been on such a tree-path, there would have been only one direction from which the skulking tagnu hunters could have attacked — impenetrable walls of trees would have guarded their sides, and the villages of the stinking Silk People would have protected their backs.

Ahead, the trees thinned further, and the underbrush became sparser — and in a beacon of sunlight, she spotted a point where the ground rose perceptibly into an artificial-looking mound. This mound was less overgrown than the surrounding terrain. She knew from experience that it was better to fight from high ground, so she nodded sharply in the direction of the rise, and the band, swarmlike, shifted and reformed and surged forward on its new course.

From both sides, the jungle echoed with the scurrying of heavy feet. Underbrush cracked as the unseen hunters maneuvered to cut off their prey. Then one of the stalking beasts emitted a low, rolling trill, followed by a bass hiccup. Fear hit Seven-Fingered Fat Girl like a gut-punch.

"Kellinks!" Toes Point In gasped. "Oh, Keyu, we're going to die!"

"Blast Keyu!" Fat Girl yelled. "Run faster!"

Any of a handful of predators *could* have been after them. That kellinks were the beasts on their trail, however, was an evil omen. Seven-Fingered Fat Girl cursed Keyu and her stupid ambition and sheer bad luck — bad fat. Four Winds Band could have stayed on the cleared paths — they had nearly enough to eat most days, and they probably would have scraped by without new trades. They didn't have much chance to scrape by against kellinks, however. The six-legged beasts were fast and tough and mean. They inhabited the deep jungle, ran in packs large enough to surround the herdbeasts they favored, and killed by darting in at their prey one at a time, nipping and snapping.

One bite was all a kellink would need against them — its spittle was deadly to humans. Seven-Fingered Fat Girl got her name because she once scratched her hand on a thorn on which a kellink had drooled. If Dog Nose had not sliced off three of her fingers with his dagger the day they turned red and started to swell, she would not have lived to run with Four Winds Band. *For all the good it will do now,* she thought.

Runs Slow made whimpering noises and stumbled along at the back of the pack, losing ground. Laughs Like A Roshi dropped back with her and urged her on. They would have made easy targets for their scaled-and-fanged pursuers — but kellinks corralled their prey. *If they weren't herding us into a trap,* Fat Girl thought, *those two would be dead already.*

Fat Girl ignored the stabbing pain in her left side and the breath that burned her lungs and whistled through her pursed lips. The mound was close, almost within reach. She quit pacing herself and bolted. If she could just get to that high ground — but to her right, a sudden flash of sunlight dappled a kellink's green-gold scales as it charged in to cut her off. She saw the beast and put her dartstick to her lips and blew.

The dart, like a deadly bird, homed in on its target and landed silently. The kellink roared. She caught a glimpse of the beast twisting, trying to bite her missile out of its shoulder. Then the poison hit the creature's bloodstream, and every muscle in its body went rigid. The dead kellink crashed to the ground just as she reached the slope of the mound.

She found the going steeper than it had looked from the distance. The mound was a rubble of scree and square-cut, massive, tumbled stones. She scrabbled her way up, using the sparse, scrawny trees that grew among the rubble as handholds. Rock shards scraped her knees and the palms of her hands, while big stone blocks tripped her and bruised her shins. She loosed miniature avalanches of whitestone talus with each upward move, and as often as not, she slipped down a span for every two upward spans of progress she made. At the top, she turned and crouched and panted. Below, the rest of Four Winds Band scrambled behind her, still alive. All her people might yet survive — kellinks could run forever, but the beasts couldn't climb.

Dog Nose had kept up with her and was near the top of the rubble mound. Fat Girl reached down from her perch and gave him a hand up. He, in turn, assisted Three Scars and Spotted Face to safety.

The four tagnu at the top pelted the kellinks while the last three tagnu climbed.

Dog Nose muttered something as he buried one of his hurlsticks in the chest of a big kellink.

Fat Girl reloaded her dartstick. "What?"

"I said Runs Slow is going to get us killed one of these days." He launched another throw into the swarming kellink pack, and the nearest of the monsters roared and snapped at the hurlstick. Fat Girl hit that one with a dart, and after an instant, the beast fell to its side, arching its spine and foaming around the mouth. The rest of the kellinks edged backward toward thicker cover.

"Na!" Fat Girl snapped. "She's going to get *herself* killed — and maybe take Laughs Like A Roshi with her. But you shouldn't complain about her. She hasn't slowed your feet." Seven-Fingered Fat Girl refused to dwell on Runs Slow's unfitness to be tagnu. It was a problem that would resolve itself eventually. In the eight or nine season cycles Fat Girl had been tagnu, every original member of Four Winds Band — except herself and Dog Nose — had been killed. Most of the fresh recruits the band picked to replace them were also dead. Runs Slow was simply one of those people Fat Girl didn't intend to get to know very well; there wasn't much point.

She blew a series of hard, short puffs through her dartstick and a stream of tiny red missiles skimmed over the heads of her band. Three kellinks bucked and died, and the rest edged just out of range and started up a hideous keening shriek that made Fat Girl's teeth hurt.

Meanwhile, the last three tagnu made progress. Toes Point In, who was a poor climber, was finally near the top. Laughs Like A Roshi had braced against a huge block of stone halfway up the mound; he threw his hurlsticks at any kellinks who ventured too close, protecting Runs Slow, who climbed and cried at the same time.

Finally even Runs Slow was out of danger. Fat Girl whistled shrilly, and the tagnu held their attack. *No sense wasting ammunition,* she thought. The kellinks dropped out of sight in the underbrush. They would crouch there, waiting, until the dead kellinks began to rot — or until the tagnu grew unwary or desperate for food and ventured within their reach. The big beasts snarled and trilled, and Fat Girl frowned. The kellinks would wait a long time for her tagnu.

Runs Slow reached the top, puffing and sobbing, with Laughs Like A Roshi right behind her. "I want to go home," she wailed. "I want my mommy! I want my daddy!" Tears rolled down her round, pink-flushed cheeks.

Seven-Fingered Fat Girl felt a long-festering wound reopen in her soul, but she refused to pay it any attention. "Tagnu don't have mommies and daddies," she said. She tucked her dartstick into the waistband of her myr and made a show of counting her remaining darts so she wouldn't have to look at Runs Slow. If Fat Girl just didn't have to look at the younger girl, her own tears would stay safely hidden. "You're tagnu now," she snapped.

"I don't want to be tagnu! I want to go home!"

Don't we all? Seven-Fingered Fat Girl thought, feeling a swell of old bitterness. *If we just had a home to go to.*

All the tagnu sat on the top of the rubble mound, breathing hard, looking like they were trying not to hear what Runs Slow had just said. The tagnu had an unspoken code that prevented anyone from talking about the days when they had been real children, before they became tagnu. Runs Slow had violated that code in the worst way, by reminding each of them of the best of all they had lost.

Seven-Fingered Fat Girl almost wished the rest of the band could feed the child to the kellinks. Instead, she looked more closely at the pile of stone on which she stood. She bent down and ran her finger along the straight, square shapes, still recognizable in spite of moss and obvious weathering. She looked along the top of the mound, which became less a pile of rubble and more of a stone causeway further back, and split in two directions. A few interesting white bulges showed over the line of what seemed to be a very high wall.

Dog Nose watched her, then nodded in the direction of the kellinks. "Wonder why they ran us right to a spot where we could escape." Like Fat Girl, he'd been studying the scree, but with a different purpose. He took his cutter out of his pack and tried the various kinds of rock in the rubble against it. He found a bit of glossy brown stone that was to his liking and chipped at it carefully, working it into a stone head for a hurlstick.

She was surprised by the kellinks' behavior herself, but she had an idea. "They probably run most of their prey against this wall to trap it. Not many herdbeasts can climb."

Dog Nose put the unfinished hurlstick head into the rawhide bag at his waist and dug through the scree for more of the brown stone. The other, younger tagnu watched him, then imitated his actions.

"Ya," he finally said, and pouched a few more bits of stone. "Good fat for us. You saved us again."

Fat Girl shrugged. "Maybe. Or maybe I have trapped us between kellinks and starvation. We need to see where this wall goes. We may be stuck here a while."

At her signal, the band left off stone hunting and stood, brushing hands on skinny thighs or rough-woven myr — the ragged loincloths that were their only clothing. They waited and watched her. She turned without another word and paced cautiously along the top of the wall. Behind her, the tagnu followed single file.

Away from the rubble mound, the top of the wall became wide enough that her whole band could have walked side by side. Time or careful cutting had smoothed the whitestone blocks until they felt like frozen silk beneath Fat Girl's bare feet. The gentle incline carried her slowly up, until with a start she realized she

could see the tops of trees falling away to either side of
her, and the ragged bones of the earth that broke free of
the hated trees to soar toward the sky, and the sun, and
Keyu's Other Eye. It had never occurred to Seven-
Fingered Fat Girl to wonder what the world might look
like from above the treetops.

She turned slowly, taking in the odd view. In the valley beneath her feet, the treetops falling away down the
steep hill were as rumpled and mussed as her own thin
blanket when she woke in the morning. *Great Keyi's
blanket*, she thought — then she shuddered. That was a
bad image. It made the Keyu seem even bigger and
more frightening. As she continued her turn to the left,
she saw that the rest of the tagnu were as taken by the
strangeness of the view as she was. They, too, stood and
gaped. She saw them point, speechless, at the mighty
stone mountains. She heard their whispers of, "Look at
the trees," and "Oh, look at the sky," and she smiled.
Her good fat had won them this view. They would be
grateful — later.

She walked to the edge of the wall and peered down.
Scattered piles of sun-whitened bones, some with
shreds of flesh still attached, lay like drifts of snow at the
point where the causeway joined the main wall. No
doubt the kellinks had been herding the band of tagnu
toward that same spot — their killing field. Lucky for
her and her people she had seen the rubble mound
first. She spared the boneyard another quick look, then
shrugged. Most of the bones were of kree and hrod-
haggu. A few bones looked human — but none of them
were her people. So Four Winds Band could afford to
be even more grateful. She wordlessly pointed out the
evidence of past massacres to her followers; only when
all of them had seen did she turn away.

Fat Girl walked onward. The stones beneath her feet
were smooth and cool. They were far removed from
the tree-walls and tree-walks of the Silk People — as far

removed as Earth from heaven. Who made such a giant wall? she wondered. Marveling, she reached the intersection of the causeway with the main wall. She clambered up a step nearly as high as her waist, and then another, and stood at last atop the main wall. The other tagnu followed her lead.

Seven-Fingered Fat girl was vaguely aware that the tagnu had stopped whispering. The silence from her band echoed her own awe.

Beneath her, giant stone buildings and the broken remains of buildings sprawled like the bleached bones of monsters. Buried in vines, worn round and smooth by time and weather, they reminded her of the kellinks' boneyard on an impossible scale — and each white-stone bone carried with it whispers of a long-dead past. Seven-Fingered Fat Girl crouched on the lip of the wall and stared.

Nearest her, tens of pairs of domes that curved like women's breasts jutted from the grass, their roofs flat nipples. Beyond, higher up the side of the mountain, the remains of soaring arches and spires and towers stretched broken fingers to the sky. White roads traced patterns through grass and weeds and scrubby brush. There were no people, no animals except the birds and hovies that swooped and soared and fluttered through the clustered ruins. The silent city lay like the broken promise of something wonderful, and Seven-Fingered Fat Girl felt the pang of its breaking.

Toes Point In asked the question foremost in Fat Girl's mind. "I wonder who lived there — and who sent them away."

Dog Nose was more practical. "I wonder how we can get down there. I don't see any way in."

Fat Girl looked along the wall in both directions. "The people who lived here had to get in and out. We'll walk along the wall until we find the place they used."

"Which way?" Three Scars asked.

"That way." Runs Slow pointed left and downslope.

Toes Point In glared at the younger girl and immediately pointed right and upslope. "That way would be better, I think."

Fat Girl gave Toes Point In a hard look and led the tagnu left.

Seven-Fingered Fat Girl was sure that there would be some simple way to get down off the wall, but after a long hike, she began to believe she was wrong. When the party came to a broken spot where the stones formed another steep talus slope, she was willing to admit there probably were no easier entries. It would be the talus slope or nothing.

"Wait," she told her comrades. "I'll go first to make sure it's safe." She crept down the jumble of rock.

It was farther down than she had guessed — and the buildings were bigger than she had imagined. When she looked back at her band, they were nothing but specks at the top of the wall. They waited for her signal.

She turned once in a full circle to take in the grandeur of the city, and hugged herself to hold in her growing excitement. *There is no one here but us. This could all be ours,* she thought. *A base — a roof over us at nights, a safe place to keep the jungle beasts away. Maybe a home.* It had been a long time since she'd thought of anything in terms of "home."

Keeping her excitement to herself, she waved her band down.

The water-drums and slit-gongs outside the temple prayed tree-prayers to the far reaches of the winds. Inside the temple, the Yekou, the attendant-clergy of the Keyu, donned their best and brightest silks. They raced from branch-room to branch-room, pulling out their best ribbons, readying their censers, finding drumsticks and headcloths and good slippers. To Choufa, now twelve cycles old, all this activity was

worrisome, because this time, it involved her. Between
spurts of finding their things, the priests readied
Choufa's group of temple children for the Tree-
Naming ceremony.

Choufa had allowed the priests to strip her and paint
her green and braid flowers in her hair, but only because
Doff kept saying she must. This was an important night,
Doff repeated — over and over. It was Choufa's Tree-
Naming, when she would cast her baby-name aside and
become Keyunu, one of the Tree-People, if the Keyu so
declared. Doff, the ancient, skinny Yekoi who was the
only mother Choufa had ever known, insisted that this
was the day when the Keyu would choose the fates of all
their children "for the best."

So Choufa, excited and impatient, fidgeted as the
bright green paint dried on her skin and started to
tighten and crack.

"It itches," she whispered to Thasa, her temple-sister.

"Ya. Looks stupid, too." Thasa ran her fingers nervously through the alloa blossoms she carried in her
clay basket. "Doff told me I had to give this to Great
Keyi. She give you something to give Great Keyi, too?"

"Beads." Choufa unfurled her clenched fingers long
enough for the other girl to get a quick glimpse of shiny
reds and blues and yellows.

"You want to trade?" Thasa asked, eyeing the bright
colors.

Choufa didn't miss the undertone of envy in the
other girl's voice. Thasa loved pretty things. Like the
rest of the temple children, she had so few of them.
"Na. I like my —"

A crop cracked on the backs of Choufa's legs.
"Silence and reverence, *ibbi*," snapped the slender
priest who had appeared out of nowhere. She lashed
Thasa once, too, before she swooped past the girls with
her silks fluttering and her ribbons dancing behind her
like butterflies in a high wind.

Choufa was a veteran of the crop across the back of
the legs. After twelve cycles with the Yekou, nothing
short of a solid beating fazed her anymore. She
grinned as that particular Yekoi pranced down the
branch to take her place beside the other silk-clad
adults. Her Tree-Name was Woman Of Great Grace,
but until two years ago, she had been a temple child
just like Choufa. Choufa harbored visions of winning
her own silk and coming back to this tree in honor —
maybe with a name like Most Beautiful One — and
thrashing the skin off the backs of Great Grace's legs.

Then she glanced over at Thasa out of the corner of
her eye. Thasa looked like she was envisioning
revenge, too. Choufa nodded in Great Grace's direction and whispered, "She's just jealous of us because
she has a face like a tree-frog."

Thasa grinned. "And a voice like a screeching hovie."

"And a temper like a tube-snake," Choufa
elaborated.

The other temple-child got into the spirit of the
game. She whispered with a conspiratorial wink, "And
breasts like big, rotten marshmelons."

Choufa giggled. She'd just gotten her own breasts,
and no one was going to compare them to anything as
large as marshmelons. Scrub-apples, maybe. She
started laughing and trying to cough to cover up her
laughter at the same time.

Her struggle infected Thasa, who began to sputter and
giggle, too. Then Choufa heard, overhead, the insults
being quoted down a line of younger temple-children who
sprawled along the arching branches, taking everything
in. The giggles spread further.

A sharp command cut the good humor short.

The Yekou were all in line below, adorning the main
branch like a flock of harlequin hovies. Suddenly the
senior priest, the Mu-Keyu of the temple, brought his
drumsticks high overhead with a loud crack and

slammed them down onto his ceremonial drum. He rolled out the rhythms of the first prayer — "Oh, Keyu, We Come to the Naming."

Choufa's stomach churned, and she felt a little shiver of fear. She had seen the first part of this ceremony at regular intervals all her life, sprawled in the upper branches of the temple-tree like the children who watched her at that moment. But now the drum-prayer was for her. "Be serious," Doff had told her. "Be brave and pure, because the Keyu punish all those who are not serious and brave and pure. Win a good name and a good silk from the Keyu, little Choufa — because after this night, nothing is ever the same again."

I'm brave, Choufa thought. *I'm not very serious, and I don't think I'm very pure — but I'm brave.* She tried to think serious and pure thoughts as she and Thasa marched behind the Yekou, down the main branch and out into the darkness, onto the first of the connectways that led to the Keyu. She hoped that would be good enough.

She had never seen the Keyu before. No children saw them. That was the privilege of the Tree-Named, the grown-ups. Doff said they were very frightening; old and huge. Doff said they knew what everyone thought, always. Choufa wished that she could see them for the first time while she wore patterned silk and ribbons, instead of bare skin covered with dry, cracking green paint and garlands of stupid flowers.

She gripped her beads harder. What would Keyu want with beads? she wondered. Or a basket of flower petals? Then she reminded herself not to wonder. The Keyu were not to be questioned, Doff said. The Keyu knew what was best. Choufa concentrated on thinking pure thoughts — or at least what she felt the Keyu would think were pure thoughts, which mostly consisted of promising Great Keyi that she would never again commit the many pranks she routinely inflicted on her

fellow temple-waifs. The connectways soared up, dipped
down, crossed and meandered, and she concentrated for
a while on thinking pure thoughts *and* not falling off the
tree-branch paths. She was conscious of other silk-
garbed adults taking places behind her and of other
green-painted children walking with them.

Abruptly the path dropped steeply, all the way to the
ground. The drumming grew louder, and the Yekou
began to sing. The procession marched across grass,
the tree-priests' closed clay lanterns flickering in the
darkness like a necklace of tiny suns; they filed into a
huge circle of bare earth surrounded by the ugliest
trees Choufa had ever seen.

The trees squatted like fat old men, glowering in at
the Tree-Named who gathered there, and at the *ibbiu*
— the postulants — who came to earn their Tree-
Names. In the shadows cast by the lanterns, the
hideous trees seemed to shrink, then swell, moving
back and forth in their places around the circle. Their
leaves were yellow and stunted and sickly looking.
Their gnarled branches dipped near the ground and
twisted and spread into little fans of diseased-looking
twigs, covered by growths and funguses. Thick, shiny
white growths spread out from high on the sides of the
trunks and trailed down into the grass, glowing faintly.

Those white things look like whole nests of keyudakkau,
Choufa thought, and shuddered, remembering her
one sight of the blind white flying serpent the Tree-
People held sacred. She had once — only once — spied
on the Yekou as they prayed and had seen the snake
then. The Yekou were kneeling and chanting in the
hollow of the temple tree. The air was white with
incense, and the drums throbbed. Choufa had lain on
her belly, squeezed under two supporting branches
high above them, and watched through a tiny space
where the wood of the temple tree had split. The chief
priest, the Mu-Keyi, had danced and drummed and

shouted in the center of the circle of Yekou. He threw his head back and screeched, spinning and stamping his feet in a manner totally unlike the stuffy behavior he displayed to the rest of the world. The ceremony had fascinated Choufa. When the drums stopped, a streak of white shot through the temple from out of the darkness, and settled on the shoulders of the Mu-Keyi. All the Yekou sighed as this miracle occurred. They whispered that the Godtrees heard their prayers; that this was a sign. Choufa's skin had prickled and her stomach had begun to churn. She had not liked the greasy white keyudakkai that coiled over the shoulders of the priest as he drummed and prayed — and she did not like the trees. She shuddered again. The trees felt evil. They felt *hungry*.

The drums rumbled away into silence, and the procession halted in the exact center of the tree-circle. Choufa peeked over her shoulder and gasped. Behind her, a long line of people trailed back clear to the connectway. There were, she guessed, at least fifty adults, and perhaps fifteen or twenty more children. She had not had any idea so many others would share her Tree-Naming with her.

A single drum began again, this one whispering, "Oh, Keyu, we are here — we are here — we are here — oh, Keyu." To the soft pittering, the Mu-Keyi walked back along the line and separated out the children from the adults. Choufa was finding it much easier to be serious in this grim and frightening place. She did not share any secret smiles with Thasa now. She could not find anything to smile about. In her mind, the conviction that the trees were hungry grew stronger —

The Mu-Keyi led all the naked, green children to one side of the circle, while the adults spread out along the other side. Choufa wanted, suddenly and completely, to skip the Tree-Naming and go home.

"*Ibbiu* — who will be from this night forward be *ibbiu*

no more" — the Mu-Keyi intoned — "You are in the presence of the Keyu. *Show honor!*"

Doff had drilled her in this part of the ceremony. Along with every other child, she threw herself facedown onto the hard-packed earth. Then she lay there, frozen motionless — too scared even to take a deep breath.

The chief priest raised his voice and chanted over the heads of the *ibbiu* at the adults. "You have raised them, you who are named and who know honor in the branches of the Godtrees. But only Great Keyi knows the worth of the seedlings you bring. If they are strong seedlings who will grow to be a glory to the forest, all will know today. If they are weak, Great Keyi will show us. If they have filled their souls with hidden rot, Great Keyi will make us see it."

The chief priest fell silent and let the silence build. The ground felt hard and cold and unforgiving under Choufa's hands and belly. It pressed against her nose and bent her toes back at an uncomfortable angle. *Pure thoughts,* she reminded herself frantically. *Think pure, brave thoughts.*

In the silence, the creaking of the branches of the ugly trees sounded like the crunching of dried bones. A deeper rumble started, and Choufa realized with horror that it came from one of the trees. "Begin," the rumble commanded in the Drum-Tongue.

"Stand, *ibbiu!*" roared the Mu-Keyi.

The *ibbiu* leapt to their feet and huddled together, round-eyed and breathing hard. The adults across the clearing shifted and fidgeted.

I want out of here, Choufa thought frantically.

The chief priest knelt facing the largest of the trees, a colossus so broad twenty men could have knelt side by side in the circle in front of it with room left over. His ribbons hung limply, and his glorious silks spread out in a fan over the hard-packed dirt. He drummed back,

"We are your servants, Great Keyi. Make these, our children, your servants too."

The drum echoed into silence. No one moved.

"Give me first my gift," the tree thrummed.

Immediately, the chief priest responded, "We obey."

All the drums pounded into life, thundering, "Blessed be your gift, Great Keyi, and your people who gift you."

Four men in matching green-and-gold silks marched forward, carrying something between them. That something struggled, then screamed, "No! No! I did what you told me to do! You promised! You promised! Let me go-o-o-o!"

The voice belonged to a girl.

The girl struggled violently, and one of the men carrying her stumbled. Choufa got a brief look at her. She was as naked and green as the *ibbiu*, but striped and decorated with hideous pictures and words that formed patterns on her skin. She was bald and soft and pudgy-looking, with big sagging breasts and a round, shapeless belly. She was ugly beyond anything Choufa could have ever imagined. Each man held onto her by ropes wrapped around her wrists and ankles. They carried her a few inches above the ground and made a great show of never looking at her.

Choufa self-consciously fingered her long brown hair and tried to imagine what force could have created the ugly creature that the men carried to the greatest of the Godtrees. The other *ibbiu* were obviously having some of the same thoughts — they stared at the girl with frightened loathing or disbelief written on their faces.

I wonder, Choufa thought, suddenly distracted by a minor detail, *why we're all the same color green she is.*

The drums pounded louder and faster, "Bless this gift, bless this gift, bless-this-gift-bless-this-gift —" and all the while the men hauled the girl closer to Great Keyi. The girl screamed and pled, but most of her

pleading was buried in the pounding of the drums.
The men dumped her at the very roots of the Keyi, and
backed off — fast.

For a moment, all the world seemed poised on the
point of a very fine needle. The girl lay shaking at the
foot of the giant tree, the drums crashed and roared,
the *ibbiu* stared with indrawn breath, and Choufa
clutched her beads and prayed, *I am brave, I am pure, I
am brave, I am pure.* The sense of waiting for something
to happen — to *really* happen — filled the grove.

There was no warning when it did. One minute,
everything hung in that horrible state of anticipation.
The next, the white palps that grew in profusion from
the sides of the tree whipped out and around the
crumpled, sobbing girl. Great Keyi split his bark open
from the roots to the base of the first branch, and his
slimy-looking white tentacles flung the ugly girl into his
black maw.

As fast as it came, the horror ended.

The drums stopped. In the hush, Choufa realized
that all around her children were crying. It took her a
moment longer, however, to realize that she cried, too.

"Send them to me now," the tree drummed.

The Mu-Keyi bowed and drummed his brief "We
obey" again; then he and the green-and-gold-silk men
briskly grabbed the children and pushed them into a
line. Choufa occupied the fourth place. Thasa was
somewhere behind her, unseeable. Tears streamed
down Choufa's cheeks. "Nothing will ever be the same
again," Doff had told her, and she knew now that Doff
had been right. These were the Keyu, the almighty
Keyu, the ones to whom she had said prayers morning
and night all her life. These hulking, lurking, awful
trees were the gods she had asked to help her with her
recitations from the Sacred Songs, and to make Massio
stop bothering her, and to watch over Doff. In her
prayers, she had imagined the Keyu as bigger versions

of the friendly orchard trees, that gave fruit in season and let the temple children climb them. Nothing like these trees had ever entered her prayers.

The men in gold-and-green silks stood on either side of the long line of children. Choufa stared up at them, and knew that she and all the children with her would be thrown to Great Keyi. When the Mu-Keyi said to the first child in line, "Go forward and take your Tree-Name," Choufa saw the boy's knees sag. Then one man on either side of him took an arm and propelled him forward.

The boy knelt — rather, he stumbled and landed on his knees — and his offering fell out of his hand to land at the base of Great Keyi. One man placed the boy's hand on the bark of Godtree, where the giant tree-mouth had split open to swallow the striped girl. Choufa pressed her clenched fist into her teeth to keep herself from screaming. Now Great Keyi would eat him.

But the tree stayed motionless. A single drum began a count. One — two — three — four, and the two men moved forward and lifted the boy and walked him away from the tree, toward the line of waiting adults. The oldest of the Yekou, the priest-woman Fine Fingers, bowed in greeting him, and draped a simple red silk robe over him — the robe of the new initiate, of the newly Tree-Named. "Welcome, keyunu, brother of the People of the Three Flames Silk, Tree-Named," she intoned.

She then addressed the waiting adults. "Give him his name."

The boy's father stepped out of the crowd wearing a big smile, his eyes still wet with tears. "We name him First With Courage."

"You are so named. Go." The Yekoi made shooing motions with her hands, and First With Courage, newly minted, raced into the arms of his father and mother.

"Go forward and take your Tree-Name," the chief priest commanded to the next *ibbi* in line. The girl walked forward under her own power, though two of the gold-and-green-silk men walked by her sides. She held her head up and carried her gift as if it were the most valuable thing in the world. Choufa watched her kneel and place her offering on the ground and her hand on Great Keyi's mouth. The drum beat. One, two, three — four. Then the men tapped her and she rose, brave and graceful, and walked over to the waiting adults. She got her silk and her name; Heart Of Fire.

The boy in front of Choufa, a cycle or two younger than the first two, walked forward as bravely as Heart Of Fire. He knelt and placed his gift with the others and the drum began to beat. One, two, three —

On the third beat, one of Great Keyi's shiny white palps whipped out and lifted the boy's gift from the ground, and threw it far into the jungle. From the middle of the crowd of waiting adults, someone sobbed in despair. The men lifted the boy, whose eyes were white-rimmed with fear, and dragged him to the Yekoi. They dropped him on the ground in front of her.

The Yekoi clenched her hands into fists, and her mouth tightened into a thin line. She stared down at him, and Choufa, who knew Fine Fingers' rages, saw one coming. "You shame us," the thin old woman hissed. "You — who would dare pretend to be worthy of our kinship — have shown your unworthiness. Great Keyi has seen the blemish in your soul, and has declared you not one of ours. You will never be keyuni, a person of the Godtrees. You are tagni, not human. You have no Tree-Name. You have *no* name." She spit that out like a curse.

Choufa thought the Yekoi grew taller as she snarled down at the boy. She lifted one skinny old arm and pointed at the pack a green-and-gold-silk man held in his hands. "Because we are kind, we will give you parting gifts — food and a weapon and a blanket, that you may find life elsewhere. But you will never enter the ground made sacred by the presence of Keyu and keyunu again, on promise of death. Take our gifts, tagni, and leave."

The boy stood uncertainly, then stumbled toward his parents, who clung to each other in the crowd. "Mommy?" he asked, voice high and pleading. "Daddy — please, Daddy?" The man who held the pack grabbed the boy and shoved the pack in his hand. "Please, Mommy — Daddy, please don't let them make me go." The boy's mother, crying harder, squeezed her eyes shut and held her hands over her ears. Her shoulders shook from her silent cries. The father, his face streaked with tears, gave his son an agonized look, then took his partner and led her from the Tree-Naming ceremony. He hung his head as he walked away.

"Mommy!" the child shrieked. "Daddy! Please don't go. I love you —"

Fine Fingers slashed one hand down, a sharp, chopping motion. The man who held the boy, now struggling to get away and run after his parents, nodded and picked the child up. He carried the kicking, screaming boy down the path — taking him away from the village.

They eat people, and take children from their parents, Choufa thought. *These cannot be the same gods Doff told me about — the ones who loved us so much.*

"Go forward and take your Tree-Name," the Mu-Keyi intoned, and Choufa snapped back to attention. It was her turn. *At least,* she thought with a bitterness that surprised her, *Great Keyi can't take me away from my parents. I don't have any.*

She walked forward, shaking inside but on her own power. She knelt and put her beads with the other gifts, and with trepidation rested one hand on Great Keyi's rough bark. She heard the first beat of the drum, but not the second. A sudden alien whisper inside her head drowned it out — an exultant voice that murmured,

<You! I want we want you are ours I want you!> Great
Keyi's tentacles wrapped around her, cold and moist
and slippery and incredibly strong, and pressed her
hard against the rough, scratchy bark of the trunk.
Choufa screamed, a wordless howl of pure terror,
curled into a limp ball, and closed her eyes tightly. Inside her head, the hungry, nasty, awful other voice kept
crooning, *<Mine you are mine I love we love you MINE!>*

Rough hands pulled her away from the tentacles.
Choufa looked up and found that the men in green
and gold had saved her. She tried to smile at them, but
they carried her as if she were something disgusting
and dirty. Both of them averted their faces from her.
She sprawled in front of the Yekoi when they dropped
her — *threw* her — down.

The Yekoi shook her head in disbelief. Choufa
looked up at the towering, silk-clad figure and found
the woman's eyes hard with a hatred Choufa had done
nothing to earn.

"We raised you," Fine Fingers said. "We taught you the
goodness of life in the branches of Keyu, protected you
from the evilness of your parents — and yet you have
taken our goodness and made wickedness of it. You are the
worm at the heart of good fruit, rot in the core of the strong
tree. Yours will be a life of penitence and punishment —
the keyunu do not leave the rot in the heart of the tree."

I didn't do anything wicked, Choufa thought. *I didn't.
This is all a lie!*

The Yekoi seemed to sense her defiance. "Your
mother was sharsha. Your father was sharsha. And
now, in spite of all we have done for you, you are sharsha — sharsha you shall be called, and nothing more."
The Yekoi threw her hands in the air. "So be it. The
keyunu prune you from our branches." Fine Fingers
directed her attention at the burly men in gold and
green silk. "Take her."

The same men who had saved her from Great Keyi

now looped a rope over either of her wrists and used those ropes to pull her down the path between the trees. As she stumbled along between them, she looked back at the adults. No one, not even Doff, wept for her.

Sharsha, she thought. *My mother and my father, two people I never met — never even heard anyone mention before — were sharsha. Now I am sharsha.* She shuddered, remembering the screaming green-striped girl the Keyunu threw to Great Keyi. *Sharsha.* It was an ugly word. It meant "sacrifice."

Medwind Song woke to arrhythmic, head-throbbing pounding that rolled down over her from the jungle to the north. She hid her head under Nokar's pillow, but the pillow didn't help much. After a few moments of allowing herself to realize just how much it didn't help, she sat up and sighed.

Damn, damn, damn! What time is it this time? she wondered.

She crawled out of bed, careful not to wake Nokar, pushed open the shuttered window, and looked out. It was still dark. Of course. And the racket was the Wen—again. She'd always thought the Stone Teeth Hoos were pain-in-the-ass neighbors — which just went to show how little people appreciated life when they had it good. She decided she'd rather have Stone Teeth Hoos trying to steal her goats any day than listen to another early-morning all-drum no-rhythm concert by the goddamned Wen. It was a regional hazard nobody had mentioned when she and Nokar and Faia packed up shop and fled Ariss for the politically safe wilds of Om-wimmee Trade.

She wished some brave soul would venture into the forbidden jungle long enough to introduce the Wen to rede-flutes or violettos, or something else with a bit less carrying power. Or even the simple concept that days were for being noisy and nights were for sleeping.

Three cheers for the mysterious Wen, Medwind thought. *May they all roast in the sajes' hottest hell.* Behind her, Nokar rolled over on the mat, wrapping the blankets completely around himself. Medwind grinned and watched him sleep. *As if the sajes could agree which one that was.*

Nokar, ex-librarian, history fanatic and dirty-old-man extraordinaire, was her most recent husband. He was also superbly talented at sleeping through anything. Medwind didn't think that was fair, but she didn't see where waking him up to complain would get *her* back to sleep. The drums thundered and rumbled on, and she groaned.

Then she snapped her shoulders back and nodded sharply, once. There were things that could use doing, even in the middle of the night. Due to the press of deadlines and production schedules, it had been several weeks since the last time she'd called up her vha'attaye. The spirits grew restless and bored when they didn't get the homage they required from the living. If not paid sufficient attention, sometimes they became capricious, lying when called upon. Sometimes they became angry and cursed their attendant with ill fortune. Worst of all, sometimes they got the spirit wanderlust and simply drifted away. Medwind imagined herself calling up her vha'attaye — and getting no response. She shivered.

She pulled the shutter closed and slipped out of the room. She didn't bother with clothing, just padded down the breezeway and out into the central garden. She'd pitched her *b'dabba* against the back wall, where it crouched, looking a great deal like a small, dark, hairy animal in the garden — thoroughly disreputable next to the big, rambling, breezy house she and Nokar had bought when they'd arrived in Omwimmee Trade. It was hard to remember that not only she, but at one point all her husbands, had occupied that cramped *b'dabba* — and sometimes, when it was cold, the human occupants had shared their space with the most valuable of the livestock, as well.

No, she amended silently, as she ducked into the waxed-felt tent and inhaled, *it isn't all that hard to remember that once nine sweaty young men, two horses and a few goats shared this space with me. One deep breath brings it all back.*

She took her bag of quicklights down from the hook high overhead — (*gods forbid Faia's cat-from-the-hells should get hold of them and incinerate the compound*) — and lit the pots of incense that sat on either side of her altar.

The goat-and-boy reek died down a bit. Medwind, her nose pampered by twelve years of keeping company with people who used soap, decided this was an improvement. She bent over the low altar and lit both fat, herb-scented candles. The *b'dabba* began to smell even better.

I'm spoiled by too much clean living, she thought. *I'd have a hell of a time going back to the Hoos Plains now. How odd, that when I left, I intended to change the world. The world is still pretty much the same — but I'm so different I don't know that I could ever go home.*

She shrugged that melancholy thought away. *Life is change. If you want things to stay the same, Medwind, die.*

Faia's cat Hrogner — one of the progeny of Flynn, the Mottemage's handed cat — sat watching her light the candles, ears pricked forward and tail twitching. He had that smug air about him that always annoyed Medwind — the air of knowing something she didn't know. She didn't appreciate the attitude in humans and despised it in small furry animals. She gave him a hard look, and realized he held something gold and gleaming in his stubby furry fist. It was her favorite *sslis,* which had gone missing three days earlier.

Medwind lunged at the cat. "Give me that, you *schkavak!*" she yelled.

The cat darted out of reach and scurried into the forest of drums, still clutching her *sslis.* "I hate cats," Medwind growled.

She glared into the drums after Hrogner, then plopped herself on the thick cushion in front of the altar. She touched the heads of her *sho*, the two-headed drum that was reserved for calling the vha'attaye.

The candles cast a yellow sheen over the bone and sinew candleholders and the Ancestors and Advisors who sat on the altar. Medwind took a handful of incense cones out of an apothecary jar and reverently placed and lit one on each of the tiny bowls that rested inside the skulls' jaws. Smoke began to issue from between the skulls' teeth — more from between the filed teeth of Troggar Raveneye, best enemy and Advisor. She moved slowly down the line; she touched the skulls of her grandmother's grandmother, her enemy, her comrade, her father's grandfather. Her heart raced; blood throbbed in her fingertips. "May the incense and honor please you, fearsome dead," she whispered, "so that you will not hunger for my life."

When she got to the last, she rested her hand for a moment on the cool, smooth bone and closed her eyes. "Aaiee!" she whispered. She traced the bright patterns on sharp cheekbones and empty eyesockets with one finger. "Have you forgiven me yet, Rakell? Will you ever?"

Her stomach tightened, and she took a deep breath. The vha'attaye waited — always waited. She had her duty, as Huong Hoos, to honor the spirits of those who lived and died honorably.

Medwind inhaled the tendrils of incense that swirled around her and began a five-beat rhythm with her left hand. With her right, she overlaid seven beats to the five and felt the magic build in a spiral, patterns chasing each other around, meeting suddenly, then darting in different directions. The soft, intricate rhythm washed away the Wen pandemonium and drew her deeper and deeper into its complexities. She hummed and breathed, steadying herself, settling into the comfortable shadows of the *b'dabba*, letting herself drift with the soothing flight of the drumbeat and the nasal tickle of her humming, until her body felt it had become another shadow. Her eyes drooped, heavy-lidded, and the twin flickers of candle flame smeared into huge, blurred balls of light.

She called up the song easily then, the old Huong Hoos song to revive the vha'attaye. Husky-voiced, deeply entranced, she sang:

> "Mekaals-koth dla-aavuaba'kea
> Ten-thoma etrebbo'kea baa ya yi?
> Kea'aakashall dre-kashe-keo
> Faha ydroomee-keo hoosando-ni!
> Kea fa'oatado-thoma.
> Koth'po-shompo!
> Koth'po-tyampo!
> Koth'da-dvaapo-kea-di —
> Kea'dli-nerado po!
> Keo'vha'attaye byefdo tro!"

> (For what shall I have let you die
> When life ran hot and full in you?
> You had not fought your best battle
> Nor loved your last lover.
> You are not done with life.
> I declare it! I demand it
> I announce this to you
> So you may be sure of it!
> Your spirit is still needed!)

She sang the song through a second time and then a third, increasing pace of song and drumming. Between the hazy twin lights from the candles, a pale, glowing fog grew, drawing form from the smoke of the incense and the damp of the night. The fog descended, separated, shaped itself into little balls of woolly light, and settled into the skulls of Inndra Song, matriarch; of Troggar

Raveneye, enemy; of Rasher the Hunter, comrade in battle; of Haron River, grandfather's father; of the Mottemage Rakell Ingasdotte, friend. And the mist smoothed hazy impressions of flesh over the sculpted bones. Foggy eyelids opened, and beneath them, green lights brighter than the candles gleamed. Ghostly lips formed shapes, the very real bones of jaws creaked, hard-edged whispers scuttled forth like spiders from their drybone lairs. Medwind ceased her drumming and waited.

From behind her, the cat Hrogner hissed and snarled, and when the ghost-figures remained, vacated the *b'dabba*. "Wakened . . ." the skulls whispered. "Wakened . . . alive . . ." The row of glowing green eyes fixed on her, and Medwind, who had first met some of these same vha'attaye as a small child brought before her mother's altar to honor them, still felt ice down her spine. Her hair stood on her arms and the back of her neck, and her mouth went dry.

Inndra Song asked, in a voice that was every night-creak, bone-scrape, gooseflesh sound in the dark, "What would you have of us, distant daughter's daughter?"

"I come to honor you, revered ancient mother's mother," Medwind said, pressing her forehead to the floor in ritual greeting.

"We acknowledge that," the bonevoice whispered. The rustles of other vha'attaye blended with Inndra Song's words, a general agreement, temporary appeasement of the dangerous dead.

"This is no honor," whispered one skull. Medwind rose from her deep bow and stared along the line of bodiless heads that watched her unblinking from the altar. The bones beneath the ghostflesh gleamed along the line; ivory teeth, empty eyesockets, painted bones softened and obscured by the faint fur-sheen of light, but not gone. "I am dead," the bonevoice of the Mottemage Rakell Ingasdotte whispered from her place in the far corner, "Let me die."

Tears damped Medwind's cheeks, and she said, "I cannot. You are my best friend. I need you."

"If you are my friend, let me go," the bones said, and the ghostlids shuttered down over the green-lit eyes, and the eyes guttered out and went dark.

"Rakell!" Medwind cried, and clenched her fists so tightly her nails dug into the flesh of her palms. She hung her head.

When Rakell was gone, Rasher the Hunter spoke. "That one is weak, Hoos-warrior. She fears the things that hunt between the worlds. She cowers in the cold darkness and does not bear the suffering of the vha'attaye bravely. She cries out — she begs for the light, and for life, and sometimes for release."

"She shames herself, and shames us," Troggar Raveneye whispered. "Not even I begged for the soul-death, I who am your enemy, and not your people."

Inndra Song said, "You profane vha'atta. You give this gift to a coward, a weakling. We do not welcome her. We do not want her. Take her away."

The other bones rasped and whispered, and Haron River, grandfather's father, said, "We have had enough of the cryings of the outlander vha'attaye. Girl, your heresies compound. You brought to the spirit realm a woman unworthy to join us — not brave, not willing, and not Hoos. This would be dishonor enough for anyone — but not for you." The bonevoice grated louder and the green flames in Haron River's eyes burned brighter. "Though you keep your *b'dabba* and honor us as you should, and though your husband brings incense for us on the sacred days, your husband is not Hoos. Do you think the eternal valleys of Yarwalla wait for one of his kind? A worshiper of a pantheon of petty, squabbling godlets who has never ridden into single combat — who is unblooded? But that is not all — not even that. Always, we wait and wait for the children. Where are the children who will honor us in the next generation? Why don't you bring them to us?"

Medwind looked into the cold angry glitters in her grandfather's father's eyesockets, and tensed. "I still have no child to bring."

The bones hissed. "Our shame . . . our shame . . ." and Grandmother Song asked angrily, "How is this, then? Are we to be abandoned, barren one? Left without honor at your death? Who will light candles and incense for us when you are gone?"

Medwind grew angry. "I'm trying to get pregnant! I just haven't yet."

Around her, the hissing grew louder. "Get a younger husband," some of the voices demanded. "Kill that old *makcjek*," Troggar Raveneye urged. A small drum, a shempi, suddenly leapt off the hanging rack and flew past her, almost hitting her.

"Stop that!" she yelled.

The hissing stopped. The vha'attaye glared at Medwind.

"Don't throw things at me," the mage said.

Inndra Song whispered, "Then honor us as you should. Destroy your unworthy vha'attaye. She shames you and shames us. She has not earned the long passage of vha'atta. And bring a child for us to teach, a child who can honor us when you are gone."

"And if I cannot do these things?" Medwind asked.

The bonevoices rose again in grating wails— soft, horrible echoes that mimicked living voices — but stripped of all humanness. Teeth clacked and gnashed, eyesockets blazed bright, ghostflesh contorted in shapes of remembered rage. The vha'attaye did not answer her.

Medwind asked again, "If I cannot do these things?"

Inndra Song spoke over the rest of the voices of the dead. "Then we will not know you — and when you ride to the gates of Yarwalla, you will be turned away. Living, you will have no people — and dying, you will have no home. That shall be our curse."

¤ Chapter 2

Roba Morgasdotte shivered on the cold stone seat in the damp, draft-ridden subbasement and pulled her cloak tighter around her. Her mask was wood and heavy, with a featureless circle with slits for her eyes and a very minor and uncomfortable depression for her nose. It slipped a bit, and she shoved it impatiently into place. Around her, on rows of equally awful stone benches, about thirty other scholars huddled, rubbing their hands or fidgeting with their masks. A few of them scratched on wax tablets with tiny stone styluses, then passed their notes around.

So this, she thought, *is the mighty and blasphemous Delmuirie Society, huh? For this I got up before the crack of dawn? Without even a nice hot cup of coffee? Bleh! I had better secret meetings than this when I was eight.*

It was funny that her boss had made such a big deal about the Society. She grinned beneath her mask. That was Thirk Huddsonne all over though, once she thought about it. He made fusses about the oddest things. She leaned over and patted him companionably on the shoulder. "So when does this meeting get going?" she whispered.

He threw his finger over the blank mouth-region of his mask in a melodramatic fashion and bent down to scrabble around under the bench. He came up with another wax tablet and stylus. In big letters, he wrote, "It's already underway. Haven't you been reading?!"

Oh, please, Roba thought. *They get up before dawn on a*

workday morning so they can wear stupid costumes and sit in a cold dark room passing notes? I'd rather do the university's seasonal inventory by myself.

Still, once she was aware that the notes she'd been passing were for everyone to read, she gamely perused them. Most were benign — and exceedingly dull; memos regarding upcoming secret meetings, suggestions for festivals honoring the great Edrouss Delmuirie, a sketch suggesting a new mask design (it had more room for a nose, and Roba voted in favor.) There were also some heated protests over the contents of the last issue of the Faulea University *Campus Informer*. Some student humorist had published a satirical piece called "Delmuirie Lives: Paternity Suits Prove It!" in the University press sheet. There were any number of fraught little editorials decrying that. *These people have no sense of humor.* Roba shook her head sadly, reading those. *"Delmuirie Lives . . ." was hilarious.*

One memo brought up the recent news of the Ariss Historical Society's decision to cut out all funding of Delmuirie-related research, declare Delmuirie an apocryphal figure, and proclaim the recently discovered *Delmuirie Diaries* a fraud. Roba, who read Thirk's copy of the translated diaries at the time she got her job, thought the AHS was on the right track with the diaries, even if it might have gone too far with its other decisions. Nobody got laid as often or as variously as "Delmuirie" claimed to and still got any work done. But the *Delmuirie Diaries* were apparently damned-near sacred texts to DS'ers. And as for cutting funding —

"I move that we infiltrate the AHS," read one memo, "find out who voted in favor of the Delmuirie revisions, and neuter the reprobates."

"Duly seconded," was scrawled underneath, and someone had drawn a tally with votes FOR and AGAINST.

Roba noted that votes were running about three to

one in favor. There was even a little block drawn on the bottom where volunteers could write in their secret society name, offering to take on this essential mission.

She shielded the tablet with one arm, bent over it, and made a little mark in the AGAINST column. Then, grinning behind her mask, she rubbed the wax smooth over everything except the initial motion and the second, and scrawled in, "I move that the above motion be tabled as unworthy of the generous spirit and upstanding ethics of Edrouss Delmuirie, for whose honor we meet."

She passed the tablet to the person on her left and noted that the woman read her note, nodded, and scrawled "Duly seconded" under her own motion.

But that was the high point of the excitement, as far as she could tell. The Delmuirie Society huddled on its benches and wrote its little notes until the bells for *antis* began clamoring through the city; then one by one, and with a great show of cloak-and-dagger secrecy, the members crept out.

"Wait for me by the Sargis Crustery and we'll get *antis*-fare," Thirk wrote. Roba nodded, and when her turn came, marched into the anteroom, tucked her mask into her carrybag, and strode out into the last damp curtains of Ariss' morning fog.

She waited a block down the street, outside the huge double doors of the Sargis Crustery, surrounded by the rich aromas of wood smoke and hot spiced meat pies and fresh breads that wafted from the shop. If she thought about it, she also noticed the barnyard smell of the road and from somewhere down the Way, the stench of a tannery as well. So she tried not to think about it. Instead, she watched the goings-on of Six Round Way.

Ariss traffic always left her in awe. When in the city, she didn't drive, she didn't ride, and she didn't fly — and the reasons why were in the street in front of her.

Traffic was still light — it was, after all, very early — but
the flat paving stones of Six Round Way already rang
with the iron-shod clatter of horses' hooves and the pit-
ters and clunks of herds of goats and sheep and cattle,
all bellowing. To these, Ariss drivers added the rattling
wheels of huge wooden transport carts, the swish of
light two-wheelers pedaled furiously by suicidal riders,
and the rumbles and low growls of the lean, fast,
demon-powered horseless carts. Bells and horns and
voices all demanded right of way; the bad-tempered,
long-horned bovines mostly got it. That was road traffic. Above the road, fliers of airboxes and carpets and a
menagerie of exotic winged mounts swooped and dove
and screamed at each other to make way.

Even on the walkways, the traffic was hectic —
walkers tended to be fast and rude, while the rollers in
their faddish new wheelboots were bloodthirsty
maniacs. Pedestrians like Roba, who found the pace
too exciting, kept to the walls and tried to think thin.
Still, collisions happened. Those who got hit swore in
three or four languages that Roba recognized and a
score she didn't, while those doing the hitting swore
back, mentioning "mudcrawlers" and "slugs" about as
often as not. Roba found it all, perversely, very entertaining.

In the outer rim of Ariss, housing was cheaper and
foreigners from other provinces were common. She
noted three Huong Hoos — pale, black-haired, blue-
eyed — their faces cat-patterned for battle, pacing
majestically forward on their lean, bell-bedecked war-
horses while traffic parted and surged around them
like water around rocks. A flock of ebony-skinned Ral-
ledines from Punce dropped their light flier to eye
level, watching for someone or something on the
ground. Stone Teeth Hoos pushed past, and she backed nervously. One of the young men flipped his long
gold hair out of his face and grinned at her, and she

smiled back, faintly. The sharp points of his filed teeth glittered in the pale sunrise.

Someone tapped her shoulder and she jumped. Thirk grinned up at her, his round face beaming.

"People watching in this part of town always has that effect on me, too. You know not to show your teeth when you smile at a Stone Teeth Hoos, right?"

"Ah, no." Roba tried to remember how much she'd smiled. "Why don't you show your teeth?"

"Big toothy smile means you want to have sex with him. It's a very blatant form of making a pass."

Roba let that thought percolate for a moment. Finally, she muttered, "Why, that little shit." Then she thought about it further and burst out laughing.

Thirk crossed his arms in front of his chest and tipped his head to one side. "What's so funny?"

Roba headed for the doors of the Crustery. "I'll bet those horny little cannibals are disappointed a lot here in Ariss."

It was Thirk's turn to laugh. "Probably not as often as you'd think. They have a reputation as legendary lovers."

"I didn't know that. I might have given him a nice big smile if I had."

Roba stepped inside and inhaled. Behind those heavy doors, the food smelled even better than it had outside. And once the doors swung shut, the riot from the street was muffled. She closed her eyes for a moment, appreciating the atmosphere.

Thirk said, "That's fairly common knowledge among Arissers — but you aren't actually from Ariss, are you?" He pointed out the items he wanted to the Crustery's shopkeeper. "Get whatever you like," he added. "I'm buying."

Roba ordered a small loaf of blackbread and hard cheese, a mug of coffee, and a slice of the still-steaming mutton pie that sat on the counter. While Thirk paid, she carried both of their trays to one of the low tables next to the window.

"I'm actually from Gornat Wilds," she admitted. "It's a fishing village not too far from Big Tam."

Thirk raised an eyebrow. "Not a very cosmopolitan area," he said between bites.

"Indoor plumbing came as quite a shock."

Thirk laughed. "I bet. At least that explains why city traffic puts you in a trance. And why you didn't know about the Stone Teeth Hoos."

"I knew a Hoos once —" Roba sliced a thick slab of cheese with her belt knife and ate it with the tough blackbread. She washed it down with the scalding hot coffee and sighed happily. "*Huong* Hoos."

"Oh?"

Roba sawed another hunk of blackbread off the loaf and piled the cheese on. "Medwind Song. Student at Daane University, way back then — very strange girl. She kept a collection of skulls on the worktable in her room. We took a lot of classes together and hung around with each other in the evenings, even roomed together one year. We still stay in touch."

Roba broke off her reminiscences and smiled, remembering with amusement some of the long-ago adventures she'd shared with Medwind.

Thirk nodded, clearly not interested. "I know some Hoos jokes," he said. "What do you get if you cross Huong Hoos with Stone Teeth Hoos?"

Roba shrugged. "What?"

"A warrior who can't decide whether to talk to his dead victim's head or eat it. What do you take to a Stone Teeth Hoos feast?"

"I don't know — what do you take?"

"Weapons. Why are Huong Hoos girls lousy at sex?"

Roba narrowed her eyes and said, "I don't know, but I'm sure you're going to tell me."

Thirk laughed. "Yeah. They'd rather drum on your

bones than come on your bo —" He faltered, catching Roba's expression, and winced. "What? You don't like jokes?"

"Tell you what —" Roba started packing her leftovers into her daybag. She decided she would have them for lunch and save her meal money for the next day. "I'll tell those jokes to Medwind the next time I see her, and tell her you told them to me. We'll see if she likes them. No telling when she went headhunting last."

"Never mind. I didn't realize you'd get huffy about it. I just won't tell you any more of my jokes."

Thirk stared out the window, arms crossed over his chest.

"Med's a friend of mine who happens to be Hoos. I don't like people making jokes about my friends."

"I'll remember that." He stood to go, still obviously annoyed. He left the remains of his meal on the table. Roba eyed the leftover food wistfully, then stood as well.

Outside the Crustery, they headed toward Faulea University, not talking.

Thirk moved off Six Round Way at the first opportunity, down a curving little side street that ran along a small stream. Traffic thinned and, as they worked their way deeper into the residential area, nearly disappeared.

"I'm sorry I offended you." Thirk muttered the apology so softly Roba almost couldn't hear it.

"It's all right."

They walked again in silence, but at least, Roba thought, it wasn't angry silence. Finally, with no one in earshot, Thirk leaned over and whispered to her, "So what did you think of the meeting? Pretty exciting, huh?"

Roba kept a straight face. "Thrilling," she agreed.

"I'm glad you thought so. It's important that you be a part of this, Roba. The Society is poised on the threshold of change; signs and omens of change are everywhere. We

need scholars with vision to piece together the truth about
life in Delmuirie's day — we need facts and plenty of them
before we make our move."

Roba nodded.

Thirk's expression went from intent to rapt in one
instant. His eyes gleamed with a zealot's fire. "We are
going to win Edrouss Delmuirie the place in history he
rightly deserves," he whispered. "It would mean a lot
to know we could count on your support — a lot to us,
and a lot to you. Are you with us?"

The assistant professor considered her job — and
the raise Thirk had hinted might be forthcoming if she
were to become "one of the *farsighted* scholars of Ariss."
The raise was more than a luxury at the moment — it
was something she had to get, one way or another. And
if joining up with flakes who were sure to keep her
presence secret was the price of that raise, she was willing to pay.

She met his eyes and put on her most sincere face.
"I'm with you," she said.

"Good. I have to warn you — well, you saw for yourself
this morning — we're very subversive. But, Roba, this
city needs to be shaken to its roots — and the Del —" he
glanced around again, just to be sure no one was spying
on him. Satisfied, he nodded and continued, "— The
Delmuirie Society is set to make its statement. Edrouss
Delmuirie will get the honor he deserves, and his followers will change the face of all Arhel."

You can bet your last dari *on that,* Roba thought. *Ariss will
stand up and salute Delmuirie when the sajes' Seven Ugly Gods
walk from the hells to bring me birthday presents.* Inside her,
mirth bubbled like the racing water of a mountain stream.

"I'll do everything I can to make sure he gets *exactly*
the honor he deserves," she told him gravely.

He reached out and clasped her shoulder in the
Arissonese gesture of warm affection.

"Then welcome, friend and fellow."

* * *

The sharsha, who had been named Choufa, wished she could beg passing keyunu for water or food as she had done the first two days of her captivity. But her mouth was too dry. She lay on the packed-earth floor of the thorn-tree cage, eyes closed, listening but no longer waiting for rescue. She knew, finally, why she had never seen a sharsha when she was a temple child. The keyunu let them all die.

The morning dew, which she had licked off the leaves and bigger spines of the wall of thorn-trees, had long since evaporated. The sun was directly overhead, and in her cage there was no longer any shade. The sun burned into her skin, made her tongue a dry, swollen rag, and caused the sky to spin dizzily above her. She watched the heat mirages rising from the cage floor. They looked like water. She wished with all her forsaken soul that they were.

I must have been very bad, she thought. *I don't know what I did, but I'm sorry. I'll do anything they want if they won't be mad at me anymore.* She would have sworn her apologies to anyone who would listen if she could have —

She heard clacking and scraping from the far side of the cage. She moved her head a little, enough to see one section of the thorn-spiked cage wall being pulled away. A keyunu entered — a young woman with lovely long red hair and an expression of disgust on her face. The woman carried a cup.

"Water," she said, shoving the cup at the sharsha.

The child propped herself on one arm with difficulty and clutched the cup. She took one deep draught and realized instantly that she'd been lied to. Whatever the bitter, horrible stuff in the cup was, it wasn't water. But it was wet, and she was so thirsty — she drank it anyway. If it was poison and the keyunu wanted her dead, that would be fine with her.

The woman took the cup away from her when the

last drop of liquid was gone, and stood. She stared at the child with hatred glittering in her eyes.

The child stared back from her propped position until, unaccountably, she began to feel weary. She let her arm slide from under her and lay in the dirt. She continued to stare back at the woman.

Abruptly, the keyunu said, "On your feet, sharsha, and come with me."

The sharsha tried to push herself to a standing position but the air seemed to have turned to water. It pushed down on her, holding her to the ground as if she were pinned to the bottom of the river by invisible rocks. She whimpered. She could not talk. Her mouth tried to form words, but it got tired from the effort and wouldn't go on.

The woman smiled. "Good. Holds Flame! Leaf Wisdom! This one is ready now."

Two of the green-and-gold men came in with a strip of rough cloth stretched between two poles. They put their litter on the ground, tossed the sharsha on it as if she were a bag of rotted fruit, and hoisted her into the air between them.

"We have only two more of these to take to the circle before we're done for the day," the woman commented as the group trotted along the aerial connectways. "Let's drop this one off the connectway and save ourselves some time."

The men laughed, and the one in the back, whom the child could see, said, "That's a good idea." He dropped the poles he held. He caught them again immediately, and the three keyunu laughed, but in that split second when the poles were in the air and she thought she was going to die, Choufa, the sharsha, tried anything she could think of to get her traitorous body to respond — and failed. She was awake, she knew and understood everything that was happening, but she realized that she was completely helpless —

completely at the mercy of the keyunu. And as she had already seen, the keyunu had no mercy.

She was afraid — as afraid as she had been when she knelt in front of the Great Keyi, as afraid as she had been when the Keyi had pulled her into its slimy embrace and claimed her as its own.

The keyunu took her to the tree-circle. The sun glared through the opening in the canopy of leaves; down at drummers who talked anger and righteous-ness on their drums; down at priests who chanted and danced and burned their incense; down at men and women who crouched around the bodies of small naked children, jabbing needles into them. The Keyu squatted in all their ugliness, muttering along with the drums. The very air in the circle was skin prickling, charged with wrath and driven energy.

The sharsha saw all of that for an instant and heard the hungry thoughts of the Keyu as she was brought into their presence again. Then the green-and-gold men dumped her into a vat of liquid, and someone else pulled her out by her hair. She gasped and choked on the bitter stuff, which burned her eyes and her tongue and filled her nose with its pungent scent. No one seemed to care whether she could breathe or not. The stranger who pulled her out of the fluid laid her on a table, took a brush and scrubbed the last remnants of itchy green paint from her hide — scrubbed so hard Choufa was sure her skin was peeling off. Then another stranger took a long blade and shaved away her long, soft hair. He cut her several times with his shaving blade, so that she would have screamed if she could. He didn't even seem to notice. When he finished with her and her hair and eyebrows were gone, he passed her to yet another stranger.

Tears ran from the corners of the child's eyes, but she could not cry. *I must really be bad,* she thought. *I must. No one would do these things to a good child.*

A burly, ruined-faced nightmare of a woman slung her over one shoulder and trotted to a bare patch of earth. The woman flopped Choufa on a coarse, reed-woven mat that covered the dirt and squatted beside her. A priest joined them.

The woman asked him, "What do you want the legend on this one to be?"

The priest thought a moment, templing his fingers in front of him and staring off into the distance above them.

"Yes . . ." he said at last, and a cold smile crossed his face. "This one was one of the temple children. She was destined to be a Song of Keyu before she desecrated the sacred places. On her, put, 'This is excrement not worthy to feed the least tree. This is the broken song, and the spirit that covets corruption.' "

The ugly woman nodded. "Partial *mashoru*? Or more?"

"Dear artist, please!" The priest looked scandalized. Full *mashoru*. Even the eyelids and the soles of the feet. Those who are raised in the heart of Keyu and who still choose the ways of malignancy must suffer most of all."

The woman nodded. "As you will."

The woman picked up a fine brush, cocked her head to one side and studied the sharsha for a moment, then began painting lines on the child's body. She chewed on her lower lip as she worked, hummed absently and far off-key, and occasionally stepped back and squinted at her results. Choufa felt the damp lines the woman's brush left on every fingers' breadth of her body.

The longer the artist worked, the more the child began to fear. They'd cut her hair off, and the woman was decorating her like the saggy bald girl who'd been sacrificed to the trees. They were going to feed her to the trees as soon as the painter was done — Choufa knew it. Tears streamed down her cheeks again, and the woman, when she looked up from one of the sharsha's legs and noticed, slapped Choufa across the face.

"Stop crying. You're making my paint run, and they'll do a bad job on you that way."

Do a bad job of what? she wondered. Nevertheless, Choufa made herself calm down.

Finally, the ugly woman was done. She called the priest over, and he stared down at Choufa. With one toe, he rolled her from her back to her stomach, so he could look at the painting the woman had done on her back. He left Choufa lying face-down on the mat. She heard him say, "Good work. Call them, and let's get her done today. That will give us two days for purification before we go to the river."

Choufa could make no sense of that. The woman was calling for "tabbers" though, and the sharsha didn't have time to puzzle it out. Suddenly she was surrounded by men and women in short, pale blue silks. The painter, like the priest, pointed out parts of the designs drawn on her, and again like the priest, rolled her over with one point-toed shove.

She looked up at them. She counted nine, all grim-faced, who stared at various parts of her body.

"I'll take the left leg," one said finally.

Another nodded. "Well enough. I shall do the legend and the belly."

"I'll finish off the head," a third volunteered.

Choufa lay and listened while the keyunu divided her up like bits of a roasted hovie. She tried to move her arms and legs, or even to turn her head or force her lips to form words. The drug the first woman had given her still held her in thrall. Whatever these people were going to do to her, she was helpless to prevent it.

They crouched, and a drummer came and stood beside them. The priest lit a bowl of incense, and a group of chanters formed behind the drummer, singing the drumwords in steady cadence — building

power. The tabbers each picked up a pot and a needle
— the needles were thorns of the giant thorn-tree, half
an arm long and shaved to deadly sharpness.

The chanters and drummer increased their pace
until they pulsed their way through a fast, hypnotic
song with a dark, edgy, frightening beat.

On the beat, at some predetermined signal, the tabbers knelt.

On the beat, the dipped their huge needles into their
pots.

On the beat, they pulled their green-dripping needles out of their pots and aimed them at the sharsha.

On the beat, they drove their needles into the sharsha skin.

The inside of Choufa screamed and begged mercy.
The outside lay like one dead. And as the pain and fear
overwhelmed her, Choufa dropped into the painless
nothingness of unconsciousness.

She dreamed of fire — and drifted on the beat of the
drums. In her dreams, the Keyu danced and beckoned
to her, and their mouths gaped in horrid invitation.
The ugly fat girl with no hair leaned out from one of
the mouths, struggling to escape. Choufa noticed suddenly that the fat girl had no head — and as soon as she
realized that, strangers in green-and-gold robes came
and cut her own head off and carried it to the Keyu.
Terrified, she struggled to wakefulness and felt her
body respond. She screamed and flailed around — and
immediately, a hand clamped over her nose and
another cup of the burning liquid poured down her
throat. Strong arms held her down. After a moment,
her body when limp in spite of her, and after another
moment, the searing pain of the needles returned.

The stabbing started on the palms of her hands and
along the crease of her eyelids, and she fell back into
welcome darkness.

When she woke again, her body ached and throbbed.

She was alone, and the long, hot day was past. Keyu's Eye rode high in the sky, throwing pink light into the deep shadows of the jungle around her new, tiny prison. Her face was pressed into a mesh of woven twigs, while her knees jammed into her chest and her back crowded another woven wall. She lifted her head, and it throbbed and pounded as if the drummers of the day had moved inside her skull. Carefully, she moved one arm and then the other forward to pull herself straight — she thought perhaps she could get up.

But the sight of those arms — stranger's arms — stopped her. They bore hideous designs, black against her pale skin in the light of Keyu's Eye. She stared at the designs. Keyudakkau spiraled around each arm, their wings wrapping over her shoulders and their heads biting at her neck. Their tails entwined with the symbol of Keyu's Eye on the back of her hands. On her palms, the keyunu had drawn the bleeding mark of sharsha.

She couldn't see the rest of her body — and she didn't want to. Without looking, she knew that she looked like the sharsha she'd seen fed to the tree. Every ache on her body indicated another mark. No place on her body didn't ache.

Hopelessly, she licked the palm of one hand. The marks did not come off. She lowered her face to the dirt and sobbed.

I'm bad. I'm evil, and I'm bad, and now I'm ugly, too. No one will ever want me.

A day and another and yet a third, Seven-Fingered Fat Girl and her band of tagnu scavenged through the ruins of the giant city, searching for food. They listened to the warbles and howls of the kellinks that fought and ate their own dead outside the city walls. At night, huddled in one or another of the huge, domed buildings, they told stories to cover the groans of the wind

through the abandoned streets and the growls of their
empty stomachs. The city was dry-bone bare, foodless.
Only birds, hovies, and a few small rodents inhabited it
—only grass grew in the spaces between the stones. No
one could live forever on grass and rodents and hovies.

"We will have to leave," Seven-Fingered Fat Girl told
them on the dawn of the fourth day. "We must get past
the kellinks and return to the paths of the Silk People.
If we stay here, we will starve."

Dog Nose, gaunt and weary, said softly, "We were
starving on the paths of the Silk People. That is why we
left." He fingered the arrow points he'd chipped from
the local stone and looked thoughtful.

"We are starving faster here."

"Dead is dead." Dog Nose straightened and walked
to the entryway of the round-walled building and
looked out. With his back to the rest of the tagnu, he
said, "Sooner or later, the kellinks will finish eating
their own dead and go off hunting for new meat. When
they do, we can go over the wall and bring down beasts
for ourselves. We can make good arrows in this place,
and you can find enough thorns and feathers and
raouda poison to make your darts."

He turned and faced them. "It is not a good place,
but it is better than the paths of the Silk People. Here
we do not sleep in the rain. And no Keyu grow here."

"A city with walls to keep out the gods—it is a beautiful dream, and I must rip my heart in half to let it go."
Fat Girl stood, and, eyes almost on a level with Dog
Nose's, said, "Do you think I haven't seen the good
stone? Do you think I haven't thought of a roof over
our heads when the great rains fall. But hard cold
comes to the high stone mountains, and when it does,
the birds and hovies will all fly to the lowlands. All the
squirrels and chervies will hide away. Ice will fall from
the skies like rain and bury the ground. And what will
we eat then? Each other?"

"Maybe we could steal the trade goods of the Silk People," Toes Point In offered.

Seven-Fingered Fat Girl nodded. "Yes. And the Keyu would send monsters from the jungle to eat us. The Keyu love the Silk People."

"I won't go back down there," Laughs Like A Roshi said. He tightened his arms over his thin chest and glowered. "I won't let Runs Slow go there either. This is a better place."

Fat Girl sighed. "Your remmi is going to be your death, Roshi. You might survive on your own — but not with her."

Roshi lunged toward Fat Girl as if he would strike her, then stopped himself. He face was flushed. "She's not my remmi!"

"No? Then what would you call her?"

"My sister."

Fat Girl froze. She looked from the tall, long-haired blond boy to the little girl with the short yellow curls. Then she hung her head. She'd often wondered what had happened to her own sister, who had become tagnu, and therefore unspeakable, two cycles before her. And she wondered about the house full of children she'd left behind. She had not been as lucky as Roshi and Runs Slow. She had never found any of her own family.

"Oh," she whispered.

She looked at her comrades. Around the room, she saw her own thoughts mirrored on tagnu faces. Wistfulness and pain and envy mixed in all the other eyes.

If she could, she would give them this place. Nothing had hunted them since they crawled up the wall. They had slept warm, and dry. The Keyu couldn't see them — she felt sure of that. Hidden from the sight of the gods, they could become real people again.

If only there were food.

"The keyunu dig in the dirt and food grows out of it.

I remember," she said, looking around at the rest of Four Winds Band. "Could we make food grow out of the dirt?"

"The Keyu make the food grow," Dog Nose said. "They wouldn't do that for us."

"That's right," some of the others agreed.

"Maybe. But I've visited the places of the peknu, and food grew out of the dirt for them. The Keyu hate the peknu."

Roshi looked intent. "Could the peknu show us how to grow food from dirt?"

Fat Girl became excited. "If we could pay them — they'll trade anything. We could tell them they have to trade us the gods' dirt-trick." Her smile faded as she realized the flaw in her plan. "But we have nothing to trade."

"What do they want?" Toes Point In asked.

Spotted Face snapped, "What does it matter what they want? We have nothing!"

Runs Slow looked up at Spotted Face and shook her head until her curls bounced. "There are things here. I saw some."

Fat Girl nodded slowly. "You're right," she told the little girl. "There might be things here we could take." She squatted and thought. "We carried little pot drums and silk and incense from Five Dots Silk to the peknu sea village. We carried back beads in lots of colors and fine skins for special drumheads — some strange things, too."

Roshi asked, "What should we look for?"

"Anything we can carry." Three Scars broke his silence and grinned. "I went to the peknu village the very last time Fat Girl made the run. I walked through their trading place — those peknu are strange."

"Good plan." Seven-Fingered Fat Girl rose and assumed her stance as leader. She led them down the passage and outside.

The tagnu stood at the very pinnacle of the city, looking at the sprawl of white buildings below. Fat Girl pointed out sections. "Roshi and Runs Slow, start with the buildings below us and work to the big lake. Three Scars, Toes Point In, and Spotted Face — hunt from that stone pit over to the big tit-houses along the far wall. Dog Nose and I will take the little bowl-houses right below us and all the buildings with the monsters watching the doors."

Along the cliff-wall to her back, the dark opening of a cave mouth with carved stone at the entry beckoned. She could hear the tinkle of water from somewhere inside of it. The city was pocked with similar openings. She had looked inside of one and had been confronted by wide, dark tunnels that twisted off in all directions.

She gave her tagnu a hard look. "Don't go into the caves. We will find something in the places on top of the ground, or we won't. But don't go under the ground."

"But what if they left all their good things in the caves?" Spotted Face asked.

"Then we won't ever find them." Seven-Fingered Fat Girl crossed her arms so that her mangled left hand lay clearly in view. "Those caves are danger, and I say nobody dies today."

She uncrossed her arms and hooked her thumbs into the strap of her loincloth. She smiled and saw her tagnu relax. "Besides," she told them, "we'll find something we can trade above the ground. I'm sure we will. Meet back here at high-sun, and bring what you find."

The others smiled and laughed. Their faces bore expressions of excitement and hope. Even Fat Girl herself found she could not suppress the hope stirring inside. She didn't believe their search would do them any good. After all, she felt certain that when the people had left their city, they had taken all their good things with them. But the hope would not die.

The three teams split off. She and Dog Nose worked

their way down the mountainside toward the nearest of a mass of small round white half-spheres.

Up close, the buildings towered over the two tagnu — but they were smaller in scale than anything else in the city. The lacked the curved tunnel entrance that the larger, double-domed buildings all possessed. Instead, Fat Girl and Dog Nose entered through an open arch. Inside, the building was disappointing. The floor was lowest at the edges and rose toward the center, and at the very center, had the same circular depression as the buildings the tagnu had slept in. But where the floors of the larger buildings were pieced together in complex patterns of brightly colored stone, this floor was gray, smooth, and ugly. On the insides of the big domes, stone-chip murals of imaginary beasts flew or charged or swam. These walls were plain white.

The building was empty.

"These places may not have anything good in them," Dog Nose said.

"But there are so many of them. Maybe this is the only bad one."

Fat Girl had assigned herself the little buildings because there were more of them than of any other type of construction in the city, and they were all clustered together. She was sure there would be something worth trading in many, if not most, of them.

"Let's go on to the next, then." Dog Nose was already at the entryway. He cast one disgusted look around the inside of the building, though, and snorted. "I don't think you should have picked these places, though. I'll bet the good things are in the buildings you gave to everyone else."

Fat Girl shrugged. A dozen buildings later, however, she was ready to admit he was probably right. Every one of the little buildings was plain, and ugly, and empty.

After the twelfth disappointment, Dog Nose sighed. "We're wasting our time."

Seven-Fingered Fat Girl leaned against the cool, curving outside wall and nodded. "I know. Dog Nose, I don't think there is anything here to find. Not just *here*, in these little places, but anywhere in the whole city. No one would leave trade things behind."

Dog Nose came over and leaned beside her on the wall. His arm felt warm and comforting against hers, and she pressed closer to his side.

"You were right to make everyone look," he said. "We have to at least try to get away from the Silk People. The peknu were kind to us when we carried the Silk People's trade-packs to them. They gave us a lot of food. I think you had a good idea."

He rested his arm lightly across her shoulders, and in spite of his warmth, she shivered. "Even if we find nothing?" She looked up into his face.

He was staring at her with an expression on his face she didn't understand. Or perhaps, she thought, she was afraid to understand. He pulled her to his chest and held her and stroked her hair. No one had held her like that her since her mother, on that long-ago Tree-Naming Day. Then, her mother had looked at her so seriously, and hugged her, and stroked her hair — and her mother had cried. Fat Girl, at that time still Aredne, had been confused and a little frightened; her mother, wordless and inexplicably sad. Her father had taken her to the ceremony. She'd never seen her mother again.

Remembering, Seven-Fingered Fat Girl cried, too.

Dog Nose backed away and looked worried. "What's wrong?"

Fat Girl shrugged and moved back against him and wrapped her arms tightly around his waist. She saw him smile and felt his body go hard against hers. He shivered and whispered, "Want me to be your remmi?"

Her breath quickened, and she felt her pulse pound in the veins of her neck. She nodded her head "yes," but said, "Not yet. We have to go through the jungle to get to the peknu village. The jungle kills remmu tagnu. You've seen it."

"Maybe. Maybe the remmu just got careless."

Fat Girl pulled away from him. "You may be right — but what if we get careless, too? We can be remmu when we're safe back here and we have the gods' dirt-trick. With that, we'll never have to go back to the jungle again. Then if we're careless, it won't matter."

He looked disappointed, but nodded agreement. "Let's look through the rest of the buildings, then. If I have to wait until we're back here for us to be remmu, that means we have to find something to trade."

Fat Girl grinned. "Yes. It does. So let's go."

They continued their search — silent with each other in a suddenly awkward way. She watched him when she thought he wasn't looking, and he turned to catch her eyes on him. Her face burned; she glanced quickly away. She searched the small buildings; felt him watching her; caught him staring. The excitement of being near him, of knowing that she could touch him, even though she didn't, made the constant swings of hope and frustration as they searched building after empty building bearable.

Finally, though, Dog Nose threw up his hands in disgust.

"There's nothing here. Why don't we go back to the meeting place and wait for the rest of them? Maybe they found something."

"We still have both monster buildings to go through." Fat Girl twisted the braided rope of her dart pouch between nervous fingers and looked down the hill at the two giant buildings just beneath them. Huge carved-stone monsters crouched in rows on either side of the entryways to both buildings — gape-jawed and many-fanged, with half-furled wings and glaring eyes. From where she stood, the entryways were hidden;

both buildings faced away — downhill and north. But the worn, moss-patched monsters were plain to see from where she stood — as they were from almost anywhere in the city.

When the tagnu had hunted for food, they had crossed the paths of those big stone beasts — once. Once only. By unspoken accord, they had, after that time, always chosen another way to walk from one place to the next, a way that did not carry them in front of the glittering black eyes set into the white stone heads. Those eyes had *watched* every move the tagnu made — and Seven-Fingered Fat Girl put no stock in the fact that those eyes rested in the bodies of stone beasts. If trees could eat people, so could stone monsters.

Dog Nose stood beside her and stared down the hill at the monsters, too.

"There's probably not anything to trade in either of those buildings," he said finally.

"I know," Fat Girl agreed.

"The rest of the tagnu have probably had more luck than we had," he added.

"I know." Fat Girl twisted harder at the rope that held her dart pouch. The big winged monsters waited on their stone pillars. They looked very hungry. She wondered if the reason the city was empty was that they had eaten everyone in it.

"We could say we looked inside," Dog Nose whispered.

"I know."

They studied each other in long, painful silence.

Fat Girl took a deep breath. If she wanted Dog Nose, she braved the monsters. There was no other way.

She wanted Dog Nose.

She started down the hill. He'd evidently reached the same conclusion an instant before her. He was already working his way down the steep grade. She eased her way down the slope after him.

The monsters waited. When Fat Girl and Dog Nose reached the the point where the stone path branched off to both the monster buildings, they faced a hundred black, watching eyes — patient, wily, crafty eyes set high on lean, long-muzzled faces that bore a variety of toothy grins.

Fat Girl swallowed hard. Her mouth was suddenly dry, but the palms of her hands sweated.

"We could each take one building," Fat Girl said. "That way we could get done faster."

Dog Nose looked at her as if she had eaten white fern and was babbling in the throes of fern-madness. "I don't think so," he finally answered.

She felt relieved. "Which building first, then?"

He held out a closed fist. "Rocks, bones, and roots — winner picks."

"Yes. That will work."

"Ready?" Dog Nose looked away for an instant, into the flock of grinning stone faces, and cringed visibly.

Fat Girl held out her own closed fist. "Ready."

"Rocks break bones," they said together.

"Bones dig roots.

"Roots crumble rocks — one — two — three!"

Seven-Fingered Fat Girl held her hand outspread.

Dog Nose displayed a closed fist. He grinned. "Roots crumble rocks — you win."

"Well enough. That one." She pointed to the larger of the two buildings, the one on her right. Best, she thought, to get the worst over with first — it left less to worry about.

Dog Nose nodded and took her hand. "Fast," he said in a suddenly low, hoarse voice.

"Yes," she agreed, and tensed. "Now!"

They bolted down the path, between the towering ranks of monsters. Fat Girl imagined she felt the huge beasts' breath on the back of her neck and ran faster. Dog Nose paced her, neither in front nor behind. The two of them practically flew up the ramp and between the carved stone pillars into the huge, dark interior of the building. As one, they flung themselves against the closest wall and crouched, breathing hard.

Slowly, Fat Girl's eyes adjusted to the relative darkness inside. At first, it seemed that she had led the two of them into another entrance to the caves — what appeared to be paths split in front of her in a handful of directions. But as the darkness became less confusing, she realized the paths were rows of huge shelves like the ones that grew inside the trees of the Silk People. But these shelves were stone, carved with strange, twisty designs on the sides and decorated with little slashes and dots along each base. Slabs of some sort rested edge-on from the floor to the ceiling, filling every available nook.

There were no big monsters inside the building — at least, not that Fat Girl could see from her limited vantage point against the wall.

"What is this place?" Dog Nose asked.

Fat Girl laughed. "I don't know. What do you think?"

Dog Nose shook his head and spread his hands out, palms up.

"Then let's see what's stacked on the shelves."

They crept to the nearest shelf, trying to watch in all directions at once, wary of creeping monsters. Fat Girl tugged and struggled with a slab. It came loose suddenly, and she staggered back. It was lighter than she expected, but bulky and awkward — almost as long as her torso, and somewhat wider. The slab was hard as stone, but thin, with a silky texture — smooth and white. When she tapped it with her fingernail, it rang slightly. She held it up to the light that worked its way in from the high, slit openings in the wall. She could see the shadow of her hand through the slab.

"Take out another one," she told Dog Nose.

He worked loose a slab from farther down the line, and held it out to her. She compared the two.

Both were covered with slashes and dots carved in
rows on one side — but the patterns were different.
She compared the marks to those carved into the
shelves and picked out many that matched.

She put the slab she held down and wrapped her arms
around herself, hugging herself and bouncing slightly on
the balls of her feet while a broad grin spread across her
face. Her whole body tingled. She wanted to shout, or
scream, or run in circles until she got dizzy and fell down.

"What is it?" Dog Nose asked.

"It's something we can trade." She gave in then to
her delight and flung her arms around Dog Nose, and
pressed her nose against his scarred one. "We can trade
two or three of these for enough food to feed us for a
whole winter. And look — there are enough here to last
forever. We won't even need the gods' dirt-trick."

Dog Nose pulled away and stared at her. "Why? Why
would anyone give us food for these?"

She laughed. "I don't know. But in the market in the
peknu village, I saw an old man with a long beard and
braids almost down to his feet, who gave a man *three
bags* of grain and a goat for a little square with symbols
on it. I asked him what he got, and he said it was —" she
paused, fishing through her memory, for the right
words, "— *beck . . . bhak . . .*" She sighed. "I don't
remember now. But he said it was a thing of great
power to those who knew how to use it. He showed the
thing to me. It had little marks in rows all over it, just
like these." She laughed again. "But it was very small.
These are much bigger. We will take some of these to
him, and we will make him give us so much food we
could feed a whole city full of tagnu."

Dog Nose looked at the white slab doubtfully. Then
he looked at Fat Girl, and his expression of doubt was
replaced by one of trust. "We will carry these things to
him, then. You're good fat will make us all fat." He
hugged her, and pressed his nose to hers.

Her pulse picked up again, but her excitement was no longer because of their wonderful find. She gave in to the urgings of her body, and pressed herself against the boy, and ran her hands over his warm, smooth skin.

"Let me be your remmi now," he whispered in her ear.

She wanted so much to say yes, but she shook her head "no" instead. "When we get back here. When we never have to go near the Keyu again." She pressed her body hard against him, and added, "Soon."

¤ *Chapter 3*

Medwind shivered and shook herself out of the trance. The vha'attaye were once again nothing but gleaming, lifeless bones. She put down the sho, and carefully blew out the altar candles.

Noises of cattle and vendors and laughing, shrieking children from outside the compound told Medwind she had been in the *b'dabba* too long. She felt drained, bled dry — almost as if she would crumble to dust in the first slight breeze. The vha'attaye always left her tired — but this time was worse than usual. She felt they'd tried to suck her life away.

The Hoos part of her life was falling into ruin — dying. She'd failed her people; the vha'attaye; even her gods, Etyt and Thiena. She'd failed to keep the promises she'd made.

For a moment, she was twelve again, standing in the darkened sacred place, at the moment of the choosing of her gods. She stood, head high and shoulders thrust back, and to the pale and ghostly presences of the vha'attaye who questioned her, she demanded to present herself to the service of the gods of warriors. And the vha'attaye had accepted her choice and had given her their burden. The onus of Etyt and Thiena, gods of war, whispered by the waking dead, echoed again in the corridors of her memory:

"So say the gods, your gods —
'You, who ask our bounty,

Wear our mark on you.
In all things, live large.
Not one child, but five;
Not one lover, but ten;
Not one enemy, but a hundred.
In battle, wear bones at your waist,
Drum on the skins of your defeated foes,
Drink from the skulls of your slain.
Fuck merrily,
Fight heartily,
Never die in bed.' "

She thought it more than she could endure, to be abandoned by such jovial gods as those.

Barren. She looked with loathing at her flat, empty belly. She had to face the fact that she would never have a child. She'd had ten husbands, countless lovers — and never even the hope of a pregnancy. It was time to find another way to satisfy the gods and the vha'attaye, before she lost them both.

She might be able to pacify the vha'attaye with an alternative. Perhaps Faia would let her train her daughter Kirtha in the Hoos Path. The gods would not accept a child who was not Medwind's own, but the waking dead might. After all, anyone who could call them would guarantee their immortality. And Kirtha was two years old — more than old enough to meet the waking dead and begin learning the language.

Medwind went to dress, then walked from her own room to Faia and Kirtha's.

The door was open — Faia and Kirtha were already up. Faia sat cross-legged on the woven-rush mats that covered the floor of her main room, her daughter seated on her lap. A basket rested at their side, and a handful of small, round red fruits — shaffra — spilled across the woven reed mats. Faia and Kirtha were concentrating on something Faia held in her hand. The hill-girl looked up when Medwind entered, and the intent expression vanished from her face. She grinned.

"Hai, Medwind, you will not believe this. Watch Kirtha."

She shifted and positioned herself and Kirtha so Medwind could see the fruit the two of them held together. It was bruised, rotted, far beyond edible. The tiny child looked at her mother, waiting. Faia nodded. "Go ahead, Kirthchie. Fix it."

The child laughed and closed her eyes, and Medwind felt stirrings of power — subterranean rumbles so tiny, and so like the first terrifying rumblings of an earthquake in both sensation and import that the mage leaned against the nearest wall to keep herself from falling.

After an instant, Kirtha opened her eyes and reached out for the shaffra, smiling brightly. Her mother handed the fruit to her. It was perfect, unbruised, fresh.

Two years old, Medwind thought with a barely suppressed shudder, *and possessed by more magic than most adults will ever have. Precocious — but then I should have expected that. Kirtha is more than her mother's daughter. She's the result of the first mage/saje union in over four hundred years. Her mother was the strongest wild talent anyone ever saw. Her father was a promising saje student.*

And magic runs in the blood.

Medwind closed her eyes, as if doing so could make the situation go away. When she opened them, Faia was watching her with silently laughing eyes.

"Impressive, do you not think?"

Medwind bit her lip. "Impressive, agreed. But possibly not well thought out. Have you considered the consequences of teaching her to tap the magical energies when she's so young? A two-year-old — Faia, she's as incapable of taking responsibility for her actions as . . . as. . . as a cat! What if she decides to 'fix' something besides fruit? One of the village children, for instance. Someone who annoys her —"

Faia waved away Medwind's objections with a flick of her hand and a lithe shrug, and Medwind's ire rose. The apparent indifference wasn't Faia's entire response, however.

"I caught her setting fire to the flowers in the garden by looking at them," the hill-girl said, voice dry and eyebrow arched. "I thought perhaps training was better than no training, under the circumstances. She may have the ethics of a cat — but even a cat can be taught the meaning of 'no.' So now I am teaching her the things she is permitted to do with magic."

Medwind swallowed hard and felt her mouth go dry. "How did she learn to start fires?"

Faia's bemused shrug spoke volumes. "For that matter, how did she learn to make books fly across the room? She saw one of us do something similar and figured it out, I suppose. So long as she has not given the handed cats wings, I will not worry too much."

"Kit-ty kit-ty?" Kirtha asked. She leaned back to look up at her mother and smiled, red curls pressed against Faia's chest, bright baby teeth gleaming.

"No kitty," Faia said with maternal firmness.

Medwind winced. The idea of the already intolerable handed cats sprouting wings was too much for her. "*Absolutely* no kitty," she added fervently. Then she took a deep breath, and changed the subject. "I have a favor to ask of you, Faia. Please don't say anything until you've heard me out — it's a big favor. It concerns Kirtha."

Faia shooed Kirtha over to the side of the room she'd set up for Kirtha's toys. The little girl quickly occupied herself with her favorite rag doll, and the younger mage returned and settled gracefully onto a low, carved stool. "Problem?"

"Yes." Medwind felt her nails digging into the

hardened flesh of her palms, but couldn't seem to unclench her hands. "Big problems."

It took her a while to explain. Faia had once asked about the *b'dabba* and its contents — and at that time, Medwind had informed her that it was sacred space to the Hoos warrior, and taboo for anyone not Hoos to enter. Nokar had been an exception because he was Medwind's husband, and even then only on the sacred days. Medwind would not make exceptions for friends. Faia had, with decorum and propriety worthy of a Hoos ambassador, avoided the topic — and the *b'dabba* — from then on.

So Medwind found that she had a lot of ground to cover. She also discovered that her friend was dismayed by the idea of the existence of vha'attaye and horrified that the Mottemage of Daane University had become one.

But Faia was a bright young woman, and tough — she acclimated quickly to the idea that Medwind kept a ghost collection in the hairy hut in the compound yard. She was less certain about Hoos training for Kirtha.

"I don't want her to grow up to be a headhunter, Medwind," she said, when the Hoos mage had finished her explanation.

Medwind sighed. Even the very best and closest of her non-Hoos friends insisted on thinking of her as a reformed headhunter. Most of the time she even encouraged the misconception — it had its uses. But it was going to be inconvenient in this situation, she could tell.

"Kirtha would have to choose her gods when she came of age — she wouldn't have to choose Etyt and Thiena, though. If she chose a Hoos god and your gods, that would work."

"I do not know how the Lord and Lady would feel about sharing Kirtha's affections with Hoos gods. But another thing concerns me even more. Your ghost-skulls —"

"— Vha'attaye —"

"— yes, that is what I said — are threatening to harm you. You say they threaten to curse you, they throw things at you — so why do you think they will not harm Kirtha?"

"They want a child to teach and to guarantee that they will have someone to care for them when I die." Medwind pressed her hands together into her lap and leaned forward. "And I don't think they really intend to harm me. I think they only intend to make me miserable until I give them what they want."

"How noble of them." Faia stood and stared down the hall to the room where Kirtha played, unseen. When she spoke again, her voice held a distant, wistful quality that Medwind found startling coming from the usually blunt hill-mage. "I see all life as the work of the Lord and Lady. I always believed that every part of life — everyone else's religion, all the good and all the bad things that happened — was simply a different view of Them. Even your strange, outlander ways seemed to be just another side of the Lady's and Lord's odd humor. But I learned what I believe from my father and mother — and I always thought Kirtha would learn her beliefs from me. If she becomes partly Hoos, and worships Hoos aspects of Them —" Faia's voice faltered. She turned and looked at Medwind, eyes searching the warrior for a glimpse of something that seemed to be inside, yet very far away. "I cannot make her a part of Bright — because my village does not exist anymore. Everything in it is dead and gone. But I had always thought I could make Bright a part of her. There was nothing Hoos in Bright."

Medwind started to stand, nodding slowly. She was disappointed — but she could understand.

Faia waved her back to her seat. She said, "That was not my answer. That was me trying to find my way to an answer." She paced across the rush-woven mats. "We hold on to the past, for ourselves and then for our children. I try to make myself believe, I suppose, that if Kirtha is just like the children I grew up with in Bright, Bright will live on — and everything I loved as a child will not cease to exist."

Medwind started to stand again. "I understand, Faia. I really do. You don't have to explain."

Faia's expression became bleak. "Medwind, Bright died long ago. Pretending it did not will not give Kirtha the childhood I knew and loved. It will only give her lies." Faia hung her head and stared at the floor. "It is better that I give her a future than a past."

Silence hung in the room between the two friends. Medwind waited, unwilling — or perhaps unable — to say anything.

Finally, Faia looked up. "Teach Kirtha your Hoos ways. She can have both — your beliefs and mine. It will make her stronger."

Medwind found herself at Faia's side without being precisely sure how she got there. She hugged the hill-girl fiercely. "Cursed with barrenness — but blessed with friends," she whispered, and felt tears — strangers to the eyes of a Hoos warrior — burning down her cheeks.

Roba Morgasdotte flipped through the bound sheets of the next student proposal and swore creatively. The student had chosen *Ariss: The Magic of the Circle City* at the topic for his research project. Of the seven proposals she'd already checked, five had been on some variation of that theme. She'd seen *Ariss as a Center of Magic*, *Ariss: Magical Hub of Arhel*, *Major Schools of Magic in Ariss*, *Hedge-Wizardry in the Walled City*, and the extraordinarily narrow-minded *Ariss — Home of Real Magic*.

"There is," she wrote for the sixth time, gritting her teeth and pressing so hard on the tough green sheets of drypress that it tore slightly, "an entire world outside the walls of Ariss!" (*You moronic, parochial little twit*, she thought, but did not add.) "Choose a topic that will expose you to somebody else's philosophy regarding magic!!!"

Thirk peeked through the door of her office, and grinned. "How're they coming?"

Roba bared her teeth in a snarl, then smiled sweetly. "Why don't you come in here and ask that?"

"Nah — I get the feeling it wouldn't be good for my health. How many on sex magic this year?"

She sighed and brushed her hair out of her eyes. "Only two so far — they were the bright spots in the stacks. Everyone seems to have chosen Ariss as their topic."

Thirk laughed. "Sure — it's a nice broad topic and easy to research. You be ruthless with them." He shook his head and grinned. "By the way, don't let the kids do papers on sex magic. Ethically, Faulea University cannot condone or acknowledge research into that area for undergraduates. The parents would have our hides."

"I already figured that out."

"Oh, good." He took one step into the room. "Can you take a breather for a minute or two? I have a surprise for you."

"Forever, if I can escape *Ariss, City of Stupid Students*."

He laughed and stepped back into the main hallway. Roba followed him and found herself facing both Thirk and a stranger; a gorgeous young man in graduate robes — redheaded, with freckles, and the warmest brown eyes she'd seen in years.

Gods, she thought, *what I would give to be a few years younger* — She smiled politely, and said, "Hello." Her voice never quavered.

Thirk inclined his head toward Roba and said, "Kirgen, this is Roba Morgasdotte, my department assistant and the professor of Mage-History. Roba,

Kirgen Marsonne, graduate student majoring in Historical Studies, with an emphasis on the First Folk. I'm trying to shift him into Delmuirie Studies, but so far he hasn't budged. He's your new assistant. You can make him read undergraduate papers until his eyes fall out if you want."

Roba's breath caught in her throat. She held out her hand to take his shoulder, and he reciprocated.

I'd love to see you out of those clothes, were the first words that crossed her mind, but she decided they weren't quite suitable for an introduction. "Delighted," she told him, unable to come up with anything more appropriate.

"I know," he said. He flushed, and pulled his hand back. "No. That isn't what I meant to say. I mean — yes — I mean — so am I." He took a deep breath. "Pleased to meet you, I mean."

By the time he'd sputtered to a stop, Roba had her composure back. She grinned. "Once you've seen what I have in mind for you, you won't be."

He flushed again.

Her eyebrows rose. "I'm going to turn you loose on undergraduate research proposals." She smiled wickedly, and Thirk burst out laughing.

"You are a cruel woman, dear mage!"

"This from the man who stuck me with the bedamned things in the first place!"

Amusement danced across Thirk's face and sparkled in his eyes. "Ahh," he said cheerfully. "But *I* am a cruel *man.* I will do whatever I must do — and in this instance, I had to get rid of those asinine papers before they drove me to madness." He smiled as the other two laughed. Then he said, "Now, Kirgen, if you will wait in Mage Morgasdotte's office, I must explain to her why she warranted an assistant."

Kirgen, with skills honed by years as an undergraduate, made himself scarce.

Thirk waited a moment, then peeked through the doorway. "Good," he said softly. "Your assistant is looking over the undergraduate papers. We can talk."

"An assistant seems lavish," Roba commented.

"He won't. I want you to have enough time to do research in our — ah — other line of interest."

"Research?" Roba experienced a sudden stab of doubt about her wisdom in joining the Delmuirie Society. "What sort of research did you have in mind?"

"Delmuirie vanished — seemingly just fell off the face of the planet. His diaries end with him taking off on what he described as a secret mission — as far as we can tell, he never came back. There might be more diaries somewhere — or at least some information on where he went. Right now, we have no idea what sort of research he did before developing the Delmuirie Barrier — if there are more diaries, perhaps they can tell us that. Now we have no Delmuirie, no real direction —"

Roba stared at Thirk in disbelief. "And you want me to figure out where some possibly nonexistent diaries went? Or where Delmuirie went? Why, all of that took place hundreds of years ago —" She bit her tongue to keep from blurting out the second half of the sentence, which was, "— *if it ever happened at all!*" She didn't say that, but it was a near thing.

"I don't expect you to single-handedly solve the Great Mystery —"

— Roba heard him capitalize "great mystery" when he said it —

"— but I do want you to come up with some possibilities for where and how he might have disappeared — or what he could have done with the last diaries. You're familiar with the history — having learned your version from the mage side of the city, you may be able to come up with some avenues the sajes haven't explored." He looked up at her and grinned again. "I have to tell you — after the Mehevar War, when mages started coming to Saje-Ariss, I couldn't see any good in it. But I'm starting to see possibilities in women's magic — and in mages."

Roba smiled politely and refrained from making the sharp retort that immediately occurred to her. "Good," she said instead. Thirk had less tact than anyone she had ever worked with, but as far as she could tell, he didn't mean to be insulting. He just had a bad case of what her mother had always called Dung Tongue. Everything that came out of his mouth offended.

"Then it's settled. Teach your classes, but let your assistant do all your slog work. In your free time, re-search the Delmuirie Disappearance. Try to have a new slant on the problem in writing by Wuenday four-teenth." He leaned against the wall and stared down the hall at a transfer student — a mage in the skin-tight dyed leathers that served as public wear for Daane University students.

Roba followed his gaze and wondered if she'd ever looked that overtly sexy in her school uniform. Then she shrugged. Even if she had once looked like that — and she doubted it — she didn't look that way anymore. Getting older hurt. Men looked at the young, pretty women, and women her age got pushed to the sidelines and ignored.

So tell the wind it blows too hard. Complain to the sea that it's too wet. She turned her attention back to the problem Thirk had presented. A new slant on the Delmuirie idiocy by the fourteenth?

She frowned. "Thirk, the fourteenth is only two weeks from today. Ten days isn't very long —"

"And I don't expect you to have solved the problem by then." His eyes stayed fixed on the transfer student, who was stopped in front of the directory down the hall, comparing a note against the writing on the sign. "I just want something. Get yourself the new annotated copy of *Delmuirie's Diaries*, and spend some time in the library — she's heading toward *my* office —" he said suddenly. "I need to go see how I can help that student," he told Roba and, without further comment, trotted down the hall.

Thirk owned the maker's mark on rude. Roba shook her head, bemused, and went back into her office.

She'd forgotten Kirgen.

"So I'm to do your slog work while you do secret research?" the saje student asked. He grinned at her and waggled his eyebrows.

"Sort of." Roba tried to keep any hint of derision out of her voice.

"Sorry I overheard — I really wasn't eavesdropping — but Saje Huddsonne and you did get a bit loud."

Roba laughed. "He has that effect on me."

Kirgen chuckled along with her. "He has that effect on everyone. I had him for some of my undergrad stuff — my roommates and I used to discuss different ways of killing him off. He's not as bad as some of them — but he does have his . . . ummm . . . obsessions."

"Delmuirie." Roba leaned against the wall, shoved her hands into the pockets of her tunic, and rolled her eyes.

"Yah."

Roba watched him digging through the stack of report proposals on her desk. He had nice hands, she decided.

She said, "I'd noticed that obsession. So." Her next class was due to start. The bells would be ringing any instant. Yet she found she wanted to stay in her office and make inane conversation with her new assistant much more than she wanted to go teach Mage-History. She couldn't, but she wanted to.

"You mind staying here and checking over the rest of those proposals?" she asked. If he would, that might keep him busy for a long time — easily long enough for her to get back from her class and see him again.

"Consider it done," he said, and smiled.

The smile was incredibly sexy. "Good," she said. "Veto sex magic and 'The Magic of Ariss' in any form. Give the go-ahead to anything that looks remotely interesting. And put aside whatever you aren't sure about — I'll look at those when I get back." She smiled at him, suppressing wistful, lustful thoughts. "And thanks."

"I'll see you when you get back," he told her. He was staring at her. She realized it the same instant that he blushed and began furiously shuffling through the students' proposals. Her smile broadened as she hurried to her next class.

I'll be damned and bespelled, she thought. *If I didn't know better, I'd say he was interested in me.*

Seven-Fingered Fat Girl checked the knots in the harness Dog Nose had made for himself. They were tight enough, and they held the single tablet firmly to his back.

"That will do," she finally said. "Can you still throw a hurlstick?"

"I spent the last half day retying the knots until I could. I don't want to be kellink food any more than you do." He stretched and studied her so intently she was almost afraid to breathe. "Let me check yours," he finally suggested.

She turned her back to him, and felt him tugging at the knots at her back as she had his. Then he moved closer, and one of his hands crept around from her back to cup her breast. She laughed. "That feels good."

She turned so that his arm circled her and pressed her chest against his. "I like you, Dog Nose," she whispered. She ran her finger down the scar that went from his forehead to the top of his upper lip, the one that split his nose into two ugly halves. "I'll make you feel good." Impulsively, she wrapped her arms around him and squeezed.

They stood holding each other, until Fat Girl pulled away and pointed to the east. Pink tinged the horizon, and the whispers of the rest of the tagnu grew louder.

"First light," he whispered in her ear. "Let's run."

The tagnu had their finds ready. Toes Point In wore a heavy, deep green circle of carved stone around her neck. Three Scars and Spotted Face each had flat disks of carved stone tied to their waists — they'd found an entire room stacked with similar disks. Laughs Like A Roshi had opted not to carry trade goods. Instead, Runs Slow was going to ride on his back part of the time, so the band could cover more ground each day.

"Tagnu —" Fat Girl said, loud enough to get their attention. "Time to run." She raised her fist in the air, and added. "This time we run for us."

"For us!" Four Winds Band shouted, raising their fists. They trotted to the broken part of the wall and scaled it. Then they hurried upward along the wall to the very top of the city, and clambered down the side of one of the whole towers on a length of vine.

Fat Girl had decided the band would be better off staying in the mountains above the treeline until they got too hungry — she wanted to keep them out of the trees as long as possible. They found the moss-covered, broken remains of a stone road that ran along the ridge, marked every so often by worn standing stones carved with the faces of monsters. They followed the road for three days, running hard, heading south. When the road veered east, they abandoned it. When the mountain ridge veered east, they reluctantly abandoned it, too, and moved down, into the scraggly semicover of twisted, windswept shrubs and evergreens — then lower, into the true jungle.

The air grew warmer and moister. Runs Slow spent more time perched on her brother's shoulders, frightened by the things that moved through the undergrowth. Spotted Face and Three Scars had a big fight over something — Seven-Fingered Fat Girl missed everything but the outcome; they both pressed so close afterward to Toes Point In that the girl got angry with them and started running at the front of the pack.

South and west the tagnu fled, and with every step, the weight of the jungle seemed to pile itself heavier on Fat Girl's shoulders.

Laughs Like A Roshi put Fat Girl's feelings into words one night as the band crouched around the remains of a kret Dog Nose had killed. "It feels like it's been waiting for us," he whispered. "Like it's angry with us."

Fat Girl nodded slowly. She had never felt the anger of the trees so clearly.

"Keyu are bad," Runs Slow added in a hushed voice. Her eyes were huge and scared.

Fat Girl pressed her finger to her lips. "Don't ever say that *here*," she hissed. "Don't even think it. The Keyu don't like it when someone says things like that."

Dog Nose nodded his agreement. The other tagnu stared at Runs Slow, horrified by her careless words.

Then the jungle began to pulse — a thing felt before it could be heard.

"Drums!" Seven-Fingered Fat Girl cocked her head to one side, and froze.

Four Winds Band stilled. In the silence, the arrhythmic throb of distant drums grew louder. They rumbled and faded — and answering drums from somewhere nearer boomed in response. Fat Girl jumped. She hadn't known they were so near a settlement of the Silk People.

She waited, while the drummers passed their riffs back and forth. When they finally fell silent, she frowned and rose.

"Pack up. No sleep tonight," she told the tagnu.

The drums carried bad news. Big Fangs Band, rival

tagnu, were in the area. Unknowingly, Seven-Fingered Fat Girl had led her band near their Paths — and if they discovered the presence of Four Winds Band, Big Fangs Band would kill as many of the invading tagnu as they could. Any secure tagnu band would. Tagnu suffered to find dependable food and a steady trade route. They didn't dare permit even accidental interlopers.

Keyu's Eye was dark — Seven-Fingered Fat Girl would have considered that a good omen, except without the pink light the Eye cast, the jungle darkness seemed a thing alive. Hisses and clicks and coughs filled the night air. Every step she took, she expected to feel the dry, rough hide of a merth under her foot. With each whisper of wind through the trees, she expected the weight of a keyudakkai on her shoulders, and the sting of its fangs in her neck. The band pressed together, beside and behind her, weapons ready. They were tired, and frightened, and Fat Girl had no comfort to offer.

We have a home, she kept thinking. *A safe place, waiting for us in the mountains. We have good things to trade. Just a few more days — that's all we need. Then the Keyu won't be able to hurt us, the tagnu won't be able to find us —*

Her fingers wrapped tight around her dart stick, and she pressed her shoulder as close to Dog Nose's as she dared. He pressed back, and she bit her lip. She had always had Dog Nose — but every other friend she'd ever had was dead. The jungle ate all of them, one way or another. If the jungle ate her, it wouldn't matter. She wouldn't know. But what if it ate Dog Nose? She didn't want to think of a world without him in it.

Four Winds Band crept through the darkness, through the tangles of undergrowth, all of the children touching each other for comfort and protection. They stumbled, and huddled. Fat Girl had never felt closer to tears. Tagnu camped at night — they never, never ran.

How could they see myed vines that spread their traps so skillfully? How could they avoid the darkhunters?

But somehow, they did.

"Light," Fat Girl whispered, hours later. She could finally see the outlines of trees, darker and lighter shadows — everything was still black and gray, but dawn was coming. She sagged against Dog Nose, relieved beyond words.

"Water ahead," he said. "Listen."

It was a thundering rumble, muffled by trees and distance, a muted roar. Seven-Fingered Fat Girl knew it. "The wild river. On the other side, it is only half a day's hard run to the peknu places." For the first time in days, she smiled. "Let's run."

Her enthusiasm infected Four Winds Band. The children raced over the tangled roots of trees, flew like stags over fallen limbs, galloped around boulders, homing in on the pounding growl of the river. They ran in complete silence, but their feet shouted their happiness.

At the river, they halted. They stared over the cliffs into the ravine, at the careening surges of dark brown water that pounded against huge white boulders.

"How do we cross?" Roshi asked.

"There are bridges — we'll walk until we find one." Fat Girl looked east and west, along the banks. She could see no bridges nearby. "West," she decided, and trotted along the cliff edge.

Seven-Fingered Fat Girl, in the lead, was the first to sight the bridge. She stopped everyone and pointed it out. Two ropes, one over the other, were strung across the river from a massive tree to a boulder on the other side.

"The ground in front of the bridge is cleared. It's part of a Path." She frowned, unhappy with that.

"Whose Path?" Spotted Face asked.

"We're out of Big Fangs territory — I have never

run on this Path," Fat Girl said. "I crossed the river farther west, on the bridge we hold. I don't know who holds this."

"Should we try for our bridge?" Dog Nose asked.

Laughs Like A Roshi shook his head vehemently. "We can be in peknu land just after midday if we cross here. I want to make our trades as fast as we can. We have a safe place for Runs Slow now — I want to get her there."

Toes Point In frowned. "We could go east and try to find a bridge that way."

Fat Girl bit her lip. "No. The other bridge could also be on a Path — and like Roshi, I want to get out of here as fast as possible."

Dog Nose had been scanning the trees around them. "I don't see watchers. And we would have to cross the Path to go on to our bridge, and maybe one or two more on the way. I say we cross here."

Three Scars said, "Me, too. I'll go last to guard your backs." He pulled a hurlstick from his carrier and made a great show of hefting it. Then he smiled at Toes Point In, who smiled back.

Spotted Face glared at Three Scars. "*I'll* go last and guard your backs." He looked quickly at Toes Point In, then pulled out a hurlstick of his own.

Fat Girl frowned at both of them, and then especially hard at Toes Point In, who was clearly encouraging the conflict. "Both of you can cross last — and Toes Point In will cross right before you. I'll go first, then Dog Nose, then Roshi, then Runs Slow —"

"I want Runs Slow to cross before me," Roshi interrupted.

"And I want you to cross before her so you can cover her from the other side of the river. Then Toes Point In, then Spotted Face, then Three Scars. I say it will be that way, and it will be that way. Of all Four Winds Band, only Dog Nose and Three Scars and I have crossed the river before. So you do it how we say." She crouched down, and with a bit of twig, drew out the curves of the rope bridge, the line of the far side, and the anchor tree on the near side in the dirt. "When I am in the middle of the rope, Dog Nose will start across. When Dog Nose is in the middle, I will be on the other side, and I will kill anything I find on that side. If something kills me, turn back." She looked up from her crouch into the faces of her band — serious, intent faces. "You run west to our Path, and you cross our bridge, and you take your trades to the peknu that way — if you live."

She waited, and after an instant, her tagnu nodded their understanding.

"Good. So if nothing kills me, you come across like I told you. Hold the top rope with both hands, keep your feet pointing out, and never look down. You understand? Never look down. Never look back. Don't stop, no matter what happens. Yes?"

"Yes," they whispered, one at a time.

She stood and stretched. "Dog Nose, still no signs?"

"None." He watched the canopy above them with worried eyes. "Not anything."

"Right. Then we go now."

She led the rest of the band up to the edge of the clearing, then waited while they found concealed positions and readied their weapons. When they were all well hidden and prepared, she bolted for the bridge, grabbed the top rope, swung her feet onto the bottom rope, and started across, keeping her hands and feet moving at an irregular rhythm. The tablet strapped to her back chafed and interfered with the free movement of her arms. She felt awkward. She felt trapped. She fixed her eyes on the far cliff and locked them there.

The rope was damp, and slimy, and very coarse. Patches of moss grew on it — her hands and feet encountered them and automatically slid forward to spots with better traction. Every time she had to move her maimed left hand forward, her breath caught. The hand was strong — but with just the thumb and one finger, it didn't grip the way her good hand did. And the ropes swung — just a little at first, but more and deeper the further out she got. Mist from the pounding water beneath her slicked her skin; wind that blew down the river channel chilled her. On the bridge, she was completely exposed and completely helpless. It was a horrible feeling. Dooru or keyudakkau could see her and attack at any time. Enemies from either bank of the river would find her a vulnerable target. She could fall so easily. Her imagination painted the river beneath her as a gaping maw, waiting to gobble her up.

Her pulse pounded in her ears, louder than the crash of the current below. Then she felt wobbling pressure beneath her feet and in the palms of her hands. *There*, she thought. *Dog Nose is on the rope. So I'm halfway.*

She kept her pace irregular — rhythm was even more important with two people on the bridge. If they could stagger their paces, it decreased the swinging of the rope. If they moved at the same time, it made the swinging worse. Dog Nose knew about timing — she felt every step he took counterpointing her own. The arcs of the swinging ropes became smaller and less horrifying.

As she neared the opposite cliff, she began scouting for movement in the treetops or the underbrush. The clearing was empty, and the jungle seemed still. She held her breath the last four steps, not really aware she was doing it — until her feet hit solid ground again and she gasped. Then she was running, dartstick at her lips, dart loaded — looking for anything that threatened her tagnu. There was nothing. The jungle was still.

She took a position under cover at one side of the clearing to get a clear field of vision and waited for Dog Nose.

Dog Nose touched the center, and right on time, Laughs Like A Roshi moved onto the bridge. The ropes swung in deeper and deeper arcs for a few difficult moments as he tried to keep pace with Dog Nose. Then he caught the trick of keeping his movements random. He made the center of the bridge just as Dog Nose reached Fat Girl and took up a defensive position with his back to hers.

The two of them kept their weapons ready, and Fat Girl watched Roshi making steady progress across the bridge. Dog Nose checked over his shoulder from time to time. Laughs Like a Roshi crossed the center of the bridge . . . then moved steadily beyond it. "Where's Runs Slow?" Dog Nose asked.

Fat Girl studied the other bank and muttered a curse at the gods. "I don't see her — no, wait. There she is."

Both Fat Girl and Dog Nose tensed. The little girl had moved out of her hiding place. She stood, in plain sight in the clearing, with one hand on the top rope of the bridge. She stared down at the cliffs and the river, frozen.

"Oh, no," Seven-Fingered Fat Girl whispered.

She became aware of soft muttering at her back, and then of the words muttered. Dog Nose was chanting under his breath, "Come on, come on, come on, come on —"

Roshi was almost on the other side. His face was blank with concentration. Fat Girl knew he was aware of nothing right then but the rope and the movements of his hands and feet. But that would change as soon as he saw Runs Slow still poised on the other side of the river, unmoving. When he realized she wasn't coming across, he would do something stupid. Fat Girl could feel it coming.

She whispered to Dog Nose, "I'm going to wait by

the bridge. When Roshi gets off, I'm going to grab him, tell him to be quiet — maybe get him to wave Runs Slow across. Cover me."

"Yah."

She kept as close to the undergrowth as she could, moved without sound, watched as many directions at once as her eyes would take in. Roshi came off the bridge, unaware that she was beside him. He let out a long breath, and grinned — and Fat Girl grabbed him and said, "Quiet. Your sister won't cross the bridge. Wave her over here without making a sound or we leave her on the other side."

"I'll go back —"

"If you try, Dog Nose will spear you. We don't have time for this. The rest of the band still has to get across."

Laughs Like A Roshi jerked around to where Dog Nose crouched. Dog Nose's hurlstick pointed right at him. He turned back to stare down at Fat Girl, and she could see the whites around his eyes, and the trembling of his upper lip. Without another word, he moved to the point where the rope bridge crossed over to solid ground. He stood there, in plain view of anyone on either side of the river, held his arms wide, and began to beckon for Runs Slow.

Fat Girl retired to her hiding place and told Dog Nose, "He wanted to go back across to get her. I told him we'd kill him if he did."

Dog Nose whispered, "No! Roshi is good tagnu." He pivoted and grabbed her shoulder. His fingers bit so deep, she felt as if they cut to the bone.

She shook him loose and rubbed her shoulder angrily. Her eyes narrowed. "That's what I told him. I want him to believe it. A dooru could fly overhead at any time, or the Keyu could notice us and get angry at us and send a keyudakkai, or kellinks could scent us — we've been here too long already."

"But would you kill him if he went back?"

Fat Girl bit her lip. "No. I don't think so. But I don't want him to know that."

Then Runs Slow moved onto the bridge, and Fat Girl relaxed.

She was the big problem, she thought. *The rest of them will be all right now.*

Runs Slow kept her eyes on her brother and moved forward at a slug's crawl. Seven-Fingered Fat Girl tensed again. *Too slow,* she kept thinking. *Too slow.* With every tiny step the little girl made forward, Fat Girl felt her muscles knot tighter.

Then there was a full-throated scream from the other side of the river. Fat Girl's stomach soured, and her fingers clenched around the dartstick. *Ah, Keyu,* she thought. *Now we die.*

Dog Nose shifted to cover the bridge — his arrows would be more accurate across it than Fat Girl's darts. She covered the clearing. From her position, she could no longer see the river, and the bridge.

She heard no more screams. But suddenly, Dog Nose cried, "No! Too soon! Tell her it's too soon."

"Tell me what's happening!" Fat Girl yelled.

"Toes Point In is already on the bridge. Runs Slow isn't to the middle yet — and Toes Point In is going too fast. She's making the bridge swing — Runs Slow has stopped — she's screaming —"

Fat Girl heard shreds of the thin child-screams above the roar of the river.

"No! Toes Point In is trying to catch Runs Slow — I think she's going to throw her off the bridge — oh, no! —" Fat Girl heard horror in Dog Nose's voice. She forced herself to keep watch. "What?" she whispered.

Dog Nose's voice was ragged. "Oh, gods, oh Keyu, someone shot Toes Point In. A smallspear hit her, and she lost her hold — she's fallen into the river. There are tagnu moving on the other side of the bridge — more than our two —"

She felt Dog Nose's pull away from her and heard the soft hiss of his hurlstick taking flight. "That's one," he growled. And an instant later, "Good. She's moving again. Faster this time."

"Runs Slow."

"Yah. She didn't fall. She's coming now, but Roshi is still out there."

Fat Girl, who had not sincerely prayed to the gods since the gods made her tagnu, prayed then. *Anything you want of me,* she promised, *I will give you — if you will let my people live. I won't go back to the mountain city — I'll stay on the Paths and be tagnu forever. Just get my tagnu across the river safe.*

Dog Nose let out a sigh that was almost a sob. "Runs Slow is here," he said. An instant later, Roshi and Runs Slow were under cover with the two of them. Fat Girl detailed them to guard the Path. She turned in time to see one of the stranger tagnu fall with an hurlstick through her chest.

"Good," she yelled. "Kill them all, Three Scars, Spotted Face!" The distant tagnu wouldn't be able to hear her over the noise of the river, but she felt better for cheering them on. As she watched, another stranger tagnu died. Fat Girl was proud of her people — they held their positions, they did just what she'd told them to do —

The clearing on the other side of the river was still. Dead tagnu sprawled on the packed earth; Spotted Face and Three Scars were still out of sight. Long moments passed while the tagnu band waited for any sign that the enemy still lived. There was no such sign. Peace descended on the jungle, and the warmth of the sun trickled down to the places where Fat Girl and Dog Nose hid. Fat Girl relaxed. Toes Point In was lost — and the band would grieve her — but she would have lived if she had followed Fat Girl's orders.

Finally, Spotted Face leapt out of hiding, swung onto

the rope bridge and crossed to the middle easily. Three Scars took his place on the ropes and followed.

Fat Girl smiled. They moved well across the bridge, staggering their steps, avoiding swinging the rope much —

Inexplicably, Three Scars stopped moving. He hung on the rope, an expression of horror on his face. Then he crumpled slowly, and toppled from the bridge, and spun, end over end, through the air to the boulders and raging currents below. A smallspear protruded from his back.

Spotted Face screamed as a red spot appeared on his chest, and became a thin red line that coursed down his chest and belly. Another red spot bloomed beside it. Dog Nose, hurlstick ready, searched the far shore with frantic eyes, looking for the assassin. Seven-Fingered Fat Girl watched the far cliff, too.

The boy pulled himself the last few steps across the rope, then fell to the ground. He lay there, gasping, with tears in his eyes. Two long, red-fletched smallspears pierced his back.

Fat Girl ran to his side, keeping cover between herself and the invisible killer. She stroked Spotted Face's hair.

He lay very still, gasping for air. Blood bubbled from his lips, and his skin was white and sweat-slick. "I'm sorry, Fat Girl," he mumbled. "I didn't see them."

"No one saw them," she told him. "They kept still and waited until you were helpless on the bridge. You did the best you could."

He nodded, seemingly satisfied with that, then closed his eyes. He gasped several more times, then stopped.

Tears streaked Fat Girl's cheeks. *But you could have saved them!* she raged silently at the gods. *Foul Keyu, you could have saved my tagnu — but you didn't. You let them die instead. I swear, I will be death to you now!* Her fingers clenched into fists.

On the other side of the river, drums thundered to life. "Come to vengeance," they rumbled. "Kellinks-Fear-Us Band, answer our call."

Dog Nose and Seven-Fingered Fat Girl exchanged frantic glances. Kellinks-Fear-Us was a big band that split into several smaller units. They took pleasure in their viciousness; they stole territory; they ranged over more of the jungle than any other band. Fat Girl had lost people to them before. Four Winds Band was doomed unless she could figure out some way to stop them.

At her gesture, the remains of her band ran to her side behind the rock that anchored the bridge and clustered around her. They were all crying. "They'll have more tagnu here soon," Seven-Fingered Fat Girl whispered. "If any of their band is already on this side of the river, very soon. Three of us plus Runs Slow won't be able to win if Kellinks-Fear-Us Band is already here. But if they aren't, we have to stop them, or at least slow them down."

"How?" Laughs Like A Roshi wiped tears from his eyes and sniffled.

Fat Girl took a deep breath to calm the racing of her heart. "We have to cut the rope."

Dog Nose and Roshi stared at her, stunned. "But we can't," Dog Nose said. "The Paths are sacred to the Keyu. If we destroy a bridge on one, the Keyu will hunt us down and slaughter us."

"Maybe." Fat Girl nodded and grimly pulled the stone knife Dog Nose had made for her from its place at her hip. "But if we leave the bridge, the other tagnu will kill us for sure."

"You are our fat," Dog Nose said, and rested one hand on her shoulder. "I will cut the rope with you."

Roshi nodded. "For Runs Slow — so will I."

Runs Slow looked at the other three. "I have a knife, too. I will help."

Fat Girl sawed on the bottom rope. "I don't think I
have any more good fat," she said. "But we still have to
cut the rope."

Runs Slow cut with her. "I got scared," she
whispered to Fat Girl. "The water was so loud, and I
was afraid I would fall. I'm s-s-sorry." She stopped cutting at the rope and sobbed, covering her eyes with
small fists.

Fat Girl kept sawing away at the rope. She made
headway, as did the two boys working on the upper
rope. She tried to ignore Runs Slow's anguish, but as
hard as she tried, she couldn't keep blaming the child
for the deaths of the three tagnu. "It wasn't all your
fault," she finally said. "You're too little to be tagnu."

"I didn't have a Tree-Naming," Runs Slow admitted.
"Mama and Papa wouldn't let my big sister go to be
Tree-Named. So the priests took all of us away from
them. They said my sister was sharsha. They made me
tagnu."

Fat Girl stared at the little girl. "What happened to
your parents?" She couldn't imagine anyone defying
the priests or the Keyu.

"I don't know. The priests were really angry. Do you
think they did bad things to Mama and Papa?"

Fat Girl was almost certain they had, but she didn't
want to say so. "Probably not. Maybe the priests don't
do things to big people. Just to kids."

Runs Slow looked thoughtfully at her hands, then
nodded. "Maybe."

The boys were nearly through their rope. Only a few
strands held it in place.

"Stop," Seven-Fingered Fat Girl told them. "Leave it
that way."

She sawed on her own rope until it was equally
frayed. "Maybe one of them will die when they try to
cross it," she said. Let's run, while we still have time."

The four remaining members of Four Winds Band

took off, running south and west, off the Paths. The sounds of the wild river faded and disappeared, and the other noises of the jungle replaced them.

"They'll wait," Fat Girl said suddenly, while they ran. "They'll — wait because we might still — be there. Won't want to — be the first to — cross the bridge."

"Easy targets —" Roshi said, and his eyes were dark with pain.

Fat Girl bared her teeth in a not-smile. "Yah."

"How long — will they wait?" Roshi asked.

Dog Nose snorted. "Not long enough."

As if to prove him right, the drums roared to life again. "Bridge destroyed, bridge destroyed —" they raged, over and over. Then the drums fell silent.

Ominously, the jungle hushed. The animals froze and flattened; the air stilled. Fat Girl felt the jungle grow somehow darker, though no clouds covered the sun. Bad things were about to happen. Every particle of air, every leaf on every tree, every hovie hidden in its stump-hole, shivered with the presentiment.

"Faster," Seven-Fingered Fat Girl urged her tagnu. Unreasoning fear crushed her. Her heart bludgeoned against her ribs; her throat constricted until she feared the air in the jungle was gone. "Run faster," she croaked.

All four tagnu broke from their steady lope into panicky, headlong flight. They wouldn't be able to keep it up, Fat Girl thought, and at the same time forced herself to run even faster. The fear had a life of its own — it came from outside of her, and drove her. She could not argue with it, could not reason herself out of it. So she flew, raced, galloped.

Low thunder rolled through the jungle; the voices of the Keyu called out their promises of vengeance. "You who violated our Path, know that you will die," they thrummed. "You cannot escape us — the enmity of your gods is forever."

"Faster," Fat Girl urged.

Laughs Like A Roshi controlled his own panic long enough to stop and pull his sister onto his back. She wrapped her legs around his waist and clutched at his neck like a drowning swimmer. With his added burden, he began to fall behind.

Fat Girl heard low, muttering murmurs off to one side. Then a soft cough, a bark, quick hisses that came from behind her and in front of her — something flapped its wings and shrieked high overhead.

Now we die. She didn't say it out loud — she didn't have the breath. She veered in the one direction from which no predator sounds came. Dog Nose followed her; Roshi ran a bit to one side.

The sounds kept coming from behind her and to her right and in front of her, no matter how much she turned. Her fear grew with the abrupt realization that the jungle was driving her, forcing her to run toward its destination instead of her own. *No!* she thought. *No! She might die, but she would not die easily.* She readied her dartstick and veered back toward the peknu lands. She would face her attackers — not flee them. Not this time.

Dog Nose matched her, both in speed and direction. He pulled out his dagger.

Roshi followed them, but fell further behind.

The animal noises stayed in front of Fat Girl and behind her and at her sides, but never grew any closer. She squinted, trying to make out the moving forms of the hunting beasts she knew had to be there, but in the moderate underbrush, she could not see anything that moved.

The tagnu came over the top of a slight hill, and in front of them the underbrush grew suddenly thicker. Fat Girl looked for a way through — directly in front of them, the thicket became abruptly and viciously impassable. Gleaming thorns tangled and wrapped over each other. She veered west.

Roshi screamed.

The scream was awful — a lost soul, mournful, dying animal plea for mercy — pain made human, begging for release. That scream jerked Fat Girl to a complete stop more effectively than all the thorns in the world could have. She looked back.

The boy was wrapped, from foot to neck, in glistening green vines. He lay on the ground, struggling weakly against the tentacles. His sister stood just out of reach of the vines, her hands pressed to her mouth. She was filthy, covered with humus and dead leaves. Fat Girl could see where Roshi had thrown the girl. The furrow in the jungle floor where she'd landed was clear as a fresh scar.

Seven-Fingered Fat Girl looked at Laughs Like A Roshi, then at Runs Slow, and then at Dog Nose. She started back toward Roshi as a slow walk, clutching her dartstick.

"Get Runs Slow," she told Dog Nose. "Go west; south and west as soon as you can. Don't — don't stop. Don't look back. Run. I'll catch up with you if I can."

Dog Nose bit his lip and nodded. He ran to Runs Slow, pulled her away from the place where her brother lay, and carried her, kicking and screaming, off into the jungle.

Fat Girl walked as near as she dared to Roshi and the myed vine that trapped him. He looked up at her, his eyes glazed with pain. She looked at him; looked at her dartstick.

"Take . . . care of . . . Runs Slow." His eyes pleaded for release.

I wish it were Runs Slow in the myed vine instead of you, she thought. She stared at Roshi, doomed Roshi, and wanted to kill every living thing in the jungle.

He begged, "Promise . . . me . . . Fat Girl. Promise."

I don't want to, she thought. "I will," she told him, wishing he had asked anything else.

He screamed again, as the plant dug more of its root-lets into his flesh. The tentacles contracted and relaxed, contracted and relaxed. With each contraction, he screamed again. Finally, at the relaxation point in the cycle, he gasped, "Do it."

She couldn't save him. The myed had destroyed him the instant it caught him; impaled him with its tiny rootlets. Even if she could have destroyed the plant, Roshi would be dead. And this myed was huge, with hundreds of tentacles still waiting. Some were buried under the leaves, some sprawled around the ground near her. She could not save him. She could die with him — but that would not help him, nor her.

She could only do what he asked. If she just left him, he would not die for a day or two — and he would suffer while the plant slowly ate him. Her tagnu would not die like that. She held her breath, tried to steady her shaking fingers, tried to hold off the tears for just another moment. "Goodbye," she said, or tried to say. The sounds strangled in her throat — Roshi couldn't have heard them anyway. The myed tightened its coils again, and he was screaming.

She put the dartstick to her lips and blew. The little red-tufted missile shot out of the stick. It buried itself in Roshi's belly. He twitched once, and stopped scream-ing. His body went limp. The horrible rictus of agony left his face.

"I would not have killed you on the bridge, Roshi," she whispered. "I would have let you get your sister."

Fat Girl turned away. She ran — west, then west and south, running by feel, her eyes blurred by tears, her feet stumbling as she sobbed.

She ran through the worst of the thicket — it tore ribbons of flesh from her arms and chest, and she didn't even care. On the other side, the jungle ended. A rolling, treeless plain spread in front of her. On a hil-lock, Dog Nose and Runs Slow sat and waited.

¤ Chapter 4

"Gods, you look even more bored than I feel. What does he have you doing?"

Roba looked up from a dull, badly written treatise on Edrouss Delmuirie and sighed. "You don't want to know," she told Kirgen, who had finished the student papers a day ago and was hanging around her office grading tests.

"Sure I do. Maybe I can help."

Roba snorted. "I don't know if I should tell you. What I'm doing is supposed to be a deep secret. You see —" She got up and looked out into the hall to make sure Thirk wasn't about to drop in on her. Then she closed her office door. "Thirk hinted that I'd get a raise if I joined the Delmuirie Society. So I joined."

"Did you get the raise?"

"Yes."

"Really?" Kirgen's eyebrows and voice rose together. "Can I join?"

"Oh, I'm sure —" Roba laughed. "Not that you'll get a raise. But I don't think you'd want to. I'm doing something worse than counting grains of sand in a desert — at least I could find sand in the desert to count. But I have to come up with a theory on where Edrouss Delmuirie disappeared, and why. And I don't really think there ever was a Delmuirie."

Kirgen started to laugh. "That's what he has you doing? You're kidding."

"I wish I were."

"Well, in that case, I *can* help." Kirgen launched himself onto her desk, where he sat, grinning down at her with cheerful camaraderie. "You can't possibly prove that the theory you come up with is correct, right?"

"Obviously."

"Sure." Kirgen smiled. "It doesn't even have to make sense, so long as it's different and you can cite sources. I happen to be great at this kind of stuff. I can turn cow flops into poetry —" He chuckled. "If you don't believe me, I'll show you some of my papers on speculation into the nature of fire elementals. They're great reading."

"So you're saying not to bother trying to come up with something rational —"

Kirgen made chopping motions with his hands. "The whole premise is irrational. Just come up with something that sounds really big and impressive. And new. It ought to sound new."

Roba smiled for what felt like the first time in days. "What a wonderful idea. I guess you can help."

When the keyunu came for Choufa, they came singing. Women priests traded off lines with men priests, calling and responding; the hard, fast song they sang matched their movements. Hand over hand, the priests worked the ropes that lowered the sharsha in their baskets to the ground. Choufa, shivering in the raging downpour, listened to the words of the song they screamed over the howling of the winds. The words chilled her far more than the rain.

"Heyo, rains are falling,
Winds are rising, ho-heyo!
Ho! The sharsha
For the Keyu
To the river!
Ho! Heyo!

"Heyo, Keyu calling!
River rising, ho-heyo!
Ho! The sharsha
Feed the Keyu!
Holy river!
Ho! Heyo!

They came to her basket, and lowered her to the ground. One took a blackglass knife with white eyes and teeth on the sides of the blade and cut the withes that held the cage front shut. Another tipped the cage forward, and Choufa sprawled on the ground.

"Up, sharsha," a gold-and-green-clad man yelled over the storm and the singing, and kicked her to make his point.

With all the other sharsha, Choufa wobbled to her feet. The cold, pouring rain soaked her skin and left her shivering, teeth-chattering, bone cold — but it washed the accumulated filth of days from her body, and she was grateful for that.

Above the jungle canopy, towering thunderheads rose, crackling with fire and growling with the voices of angry gods. The cloudgiants had nudged and jostled and fought until they pressed so close together the sky was blackened beneath them, and the sun and Keyu's Eye vanished.

The season of rains had come — sacred season of the Keyu. Choufa knew all the holy songs of the rain festival and all the temple rituals going on at that very moment under the silk canopies. What she did not know and wished she did was what would happen to her. She could still feel the Keyu. They were no longer dreaming their slow tree-dreams. As the Festival of Rain began, they came fully awake, and their hunger grew.

The priests dumped the last of the sharsha on the

ground, and got them all standing. Then they waited: nine sharsha, two hands of priests, and two hands of the big men who wore green and gold.

A thin old woman priest Choufa didn't know clapped sharply. All the keyunu burst into an awful droning song, full of words about duty and sorrow and sanctification and pain. Choufa suspected that they were the ones who would get credit for the duty and the sanctification, but the sorrow and the pain would be hers.

Then the keyunu began a stately march in the direction of the river. Along with the rest of the sharsha, Choufa stood and watched them. She felt too weak to move — she hadn't eaten in days, and her legs were so weak from being cramped in the tiny basket cage that she was having difficulty standing.

"March!" one of the green-and-gold men snarled.

The sharsha all looked at him stupidly. Choufa took a few tentative steps, lost her balance, and fell in a heap in front of the man who had kicked her before. He kicked her again, and when she could not stand, snarled, grabbed her by the back of the neck with one hand, and jerked her to her feet. He shoved her toward the other sharsha.

She stumbled into the huddle, and the other children caught her and held her up. As weak as she, they leaned on each other, and with difficulty, began the journey toward the river.

Choufa was no longer frightened — she found she didn't care very much what happened to her anymore. She didn't think there was anything else the keyunu could do to her that could frighten her. She wished all the pain and the awfulness would end, and she thought soon it probably would. That would be fine with her. Dying would solve a lot of problems.

She watched the other children as they tottered along together in the wake of the priests — ugly nearly bald stick figures covered with green designs. The fuzz of their hair growing out made them look hideous as newly hatched birds. Choufa wondered if she looked as bad as they did. *Probably*, she decided. She discovered it no longer mattered. Once they fed her to a Keyi, who was going to notice?

That thought struck her as funny, and she giggled.

<*Laugh-laugh, oh yes-yesss laugh. We can-we can do much-much do much with one who-one who laughs,*> Keyu voices whispered into her head. The thoughts were cold and probing, horribly inhuman — laced with insatiable hunger. <*We will-yesss will love-love you. You will be-yesss beautiful-will be to us. (Mine! She's mine!) You will come-come to us yes-yesss-come to be a part-be part of us forever. (No! She's mine! All mine!) How pleasant-yesss how happy-you/we (MINE!) will be.*>

She felt them inside her, the Keyu — rummaging around in her *self*, poking and fondling with obscene delight. And she felt their hunger — their blinding, lusting hunger. For an instant, she was back at the Tree-Naming ceremony again. That awful Keyi's gelid white palps wrapped around her, and it gleefully claimed her, screaming "Mine! Mine! Mine!" into the core of her mind.

She whimpered. All her courage and all her strength disappeared. The Keyu waited for her. They wanted her. And they were going to get her. She found that she could still be frightened after all.

After that, everything became a meaningless blur to her. The keyunu held a ceremony at the river, poured sickly sweet oils over the sharsha, and stood them in the muddy water in a slow back eddy. Choufa did what they told her to. She knelt, rubbed the sweet oil into her skin, then struggled back to her feet. Most of the other sharsha did the same. One of the boys, however, moved into deeper water, suddenly dove under the surface, and swam out into the main current. Choufa watched with detached curiosity as he was swept into the racing stream, smashed against boulders, and drowned.

How lucky for him, she thought, and felt a dull stab of envy.

At his death the Keyu roared in frustrated rage. Their voices outboomed the thunder, and the keyunu blanched. *Deprived of one of their meals,* Choufa thought, and wished that she had been clever enough to drown herself. But the green-and-gold men were herding the sharsha out of the water, and the priests were separating the boys from the girls.

The green-and-gold men half-marched, half-dragged the boys away from the riverbank. Choufa felt the Keyu, wherever they were, begin clamoring for the treats that were coming to them.

My turn next,, she thought. She would have prayed as she'd been taught — prayed for deliverance, or at least peace. But how could she, when the gods she would have to pray to were the gods from whom she hoped to be delivered? So she did not pray. Instead, she wept.

The girl who stood next to her hugged her. Choufa put her arm around the stranger's waist, and the two of them stood, crying in the pouring rain, waiting to be fed to the Godtrees.

The priests were singing another of their songs, this one about glorious gifts to the gods and what wonderful things the gods would do for them because they were so good and holy. When they finished, one of the Yekoi swaggered over and stood in front of the girls and lifted her arms.

"Consecrated are you now to the holy purposes of the Keyu, and though you are evil beyond measure, yet will your lives serve Keyu and keyunu for the good of all."

She lowered her arms, the keyunu sang again, and then the Yekoi spoke.

"Sharsha girls, listen to me carefully. You have been

consecrated to the Godtrees, and to them you will go like the boys who were consecrated with you, unless you leave your evilness behind you. Your are fortunate — we are giving you a chance to repent. We will take you to the sharsha-house, and there you will stay until the Keyu demand you."

The priest wrapped her arms in front of her and glared at the little flock of girls.

"If you purify yourselves daily, however, and bring forth a child — which is the duty of every keyuni — the Keyu will refuse to swallow you when you are brought before them. And if they refuse to swallow you, you will rejoin the keyunu, and we will rejoice that one of our children has been reborn to us."

One of the sharsha, braver than the rest, asked, "How do we purify ourselves?"

The priest glared at her. "Only you know why the Keyu would not permit you to have names. Repent of those evils, and the Keyu will forgive you. Otherwise, you will die."

Then, in the distance, the slit drums rumbled, and the Keyu began to speak. Choufa heard, not only their sound-voices, which demanded sacrifice, but also their thought-voices, which rejoiced in the coming of new food. And she heard, by thought-voice only, the moment when each boy who had been marched away became one with a Keyi. She heard each individual scream of horror — for the briefest of instants, she felt the pain. Then the boys' voices were — swallowed, perhaps, or drowned — and the larger swell of the Keyu overcame them.

Choufa looked around at her three fellow sharsha, to see if any of them shared her terror at what had happened. Their faces held only relief that they would not be sacrificed that instant. Choufa wondered if they had not felt the boys being sacrificed, or if they simply didn't care.

Then the drums rumbled, "The Keyu are honored, praise the Keyu!" and the priests prodded the girls along the dirt track back to the village. They stopped again in front of a large, twisting tree grown all around with heavy thorns. The silks that draped the tree were dark and sad-looking. Choufa knew the place well enough — she'd walked past it on the days when it was her turn to get water. She had never known who lived there or why they draped their silks so tightly, and she had never found anyone who would tell her. "It doesn't matter, little one," the keyunu always said, and looked at the tree and shook their heads.

Now she knew. It was simply a bigger cage for the sharsha. The priests unwove a gate in the middle of the thorn thicket, pushed the four girls through the narrow passage they created, then wove it shut again. Choufa stood on the inside, staring out.

"Keep yourselves from sight," the Yekoi told them. "You are a stain and a shame, and if you flaunt yourselves, you will be first to feed the Keyu."

Choufa looked up into the curving, interwoven branches of the tree. From behind the draped silks, faces stared down at her — the ugly, green-scarred faces of other girls. Some of the sharsha above were nearly as bald as she was; some had longer hair. Hands beckoned urgently; whispered voices urged her up into the tree. "Hurry," the strangers called. "You must come hide."

The new girls struggled up the twisty connectway into the aeries of the sharsha-tree somehow. A girl a little older than the four of them waited in the first aerie, just inside the draped silks. Her hair was short and silky, pale bright yellow. Her eyes were as green as the tattoos on her face. She must have been pretty once, Choufa thought. She had soup for them — pale thin broth not much stronger than water.

" 'Loa," she whispered, and smiled shyly, and hugged

each girl in turn. "You're safe now. Drink this slowly. Those *skeruekkeu* never feed the new sharsha —" She reached out and pulled the gourd of soup away from one of the children. "Not too fast — if you drink it too fast, you'll be sick."

Choufa looked at her, wonderingly. The gentle sound of the girl's voice shocked her — and no one had smiled at her for so long, she'd forgotten how it felt. She slurped her soup, trying hard not to drink too fast. While she worked on the soup, the girl brought thick, rough towels, and dried off each of the new sharsha.

"I'm Kerru," she told them. "You may call me that unless the keyunu are here — if they come in, we all call each other sharsha and keep our eyes on the floor. You must look very sad when the keyunu are here."

"I *am* very sad," one of the sharsha said.

"You won't be. We've made this a good place for us. There are some bad things here, but not so many. Just remember — be very quiet and never let the keyunu see you. Now tell me your names."

"We don't have names anymore," one of the sharsha said.

All four girls looked at Kerru earnestly and nodded their heads.

"Bah! You have the same names you always had. Don't let those *skeruekkeu* make you think you don't."

The four little girls looked at each other, eyes round and surprised.

"Dathji," the dark-skinned brunette said first.

"Allia," said the youngest.

"Choufa."

"Kano."

Kerru smiled. "I may not remember all your names today, but I'll know all of you soon. Now, if you're feeling a little better, come with me. I'll show you where we live and sleep."

It's a safe place, Choufa thought, and hugged herself

with happy relief. She followed as Kerru led them
across a silk-draped connectway into an upper aerie.
Kerru says this is a safe place.

"Hey, Roba —" There was a loud sneeze from somewhere further down the Daane library aisle. "Gods eat
this damned dust! I just found the manuscripts you
were looking for. They were misfiled."

Roba stretched from her crouch and winced as both
knees crunched. She took a minute to rub the pain out
of her legs, then ambled down the aisle to find Kirgen.

He looked over at her and grinned, and proffered a
stack of thin, dust-coated tubes. "These haven't seen
daylight in years."

"Centuries," Roba agreed. She took one tube,
rubbed the dust off the catalog mark and sighed. "Ah,
how lovely. Prodictan Era histories. The script will be
illegible, the language archaic, the writing flowery and
pompous — and the authors will give the full weight of
fact to every myth and child's tale. *Nobody* studies the
Prodictan Era histories anymore."

Kirgen grinned. "In other words, in the midst of all
that nonsense, we ought to find some really special
nonsense to make Thirk happy."

Roba shook her head ruefully. "If you say so."

They took the pile of manuscript tubes to the head
librarian and signed them out.

Medwind sat cross-legged in front of the
reawakened vha'attaye. Kirtha squirmed on her lap.
The vha'attaye, minus the Mottemage, who had
appeared, then vanished in a faint green puff of disgust, blinked and stared at the little girl.

None spoke, until the silence in the dark, spice-
scented *b'dabba* grew unbearable. Then, with a
creaking hiss, Inndra Song asked, "Has it then been so
long, child of my children's children? And are you so

ashamed of us that you did not present us to your
newborn at her birth?"

"I am not so faithless," Medwind said. "This is Kirtha
— daughter of my friend and comrade."

Kirtha looked up at a Medwind when she heard her
name, then resumed staring at the vha'attaye.

The vha'attaye hissed. "Not your flesh and blood?"
the matriarch whispered and her jawbones clicked.
"Then you have adopted her?"

"No. Her mother still lives."

Bone-creaked murmurs skittered spiderwise in the
darkness — slow, brightening green glowed from the
ghostflesh faces — and the bones snarled, hissed,
snapped in growing, building anger. "Not satisfactory,"
Troggar Raveneye said for all of them. "The child must
be bound to you, and only you, so that we may be sure
she will bear your burdens after you are gone."

Medwind snarled back at them, "So do you expect
me to steal a child?"

The vha'attaye quieted. Haron River said, "That
would be acceptable. It has been done before."

"Well, it won't be done by me!" Medwind broke a
drumstick and hurled the pieces over the heads of the
vha'attaye.

"Uh-oh," Kirtha whispered.

The vha'attaye hissed, and an icy wind rose in the
b'dabba, and began to swirl around the warrior and the
child. The wind shrieked with deadsoul anguish, spun
and clattered the hanging drumsticks against the
drums overhead. Cold, wet ghostflesh hands gripped
Medwind and Kirtha, shook them, slid cold dead
fingers from living arms to living throats —

Kirtha shrieked and hit at the huge ghost hands with
her tiny ones. She struggled against them for only an
instant, then closed her eyes. "Go away," she howled.

Power surged from the child, uncontrolled and
unchecked.

The wind died with a "pop." The hands vanished. The vha'attaye disappeared — not the gradual melting of line and form they chose for themselves when returning to the dark places between the worlds, but with a loud, sucking, tearing sound, and so suddenly that they might never have been.

In the sudden silence, the last clicks of swinging drumsticks overhead made Medwind jump. She exhaled and shivered.

Kirtha looked at the suddenly bare bones and shook her head slowly from side to side. She stared into the face of the Hoos warrior again and pursed her lips.

"Uh-oh," she said. "All gone."

"Uh-oh," Medwind agreed, staring at the child. The sensation of wild power that had banished the vha'attaye still clung to Kirtha. A feeling very like the vha'attaye's icy fingers played up and down Medwind's spine. Kirtha's mother, at the age of nineteen, had accidentally reduced a stone village to molten slag. Kirtha was very much her mother's daughter.

Kirtha hadn't destroyed the waking dead — Medwind was certain of that. Annihilation of a soul was a work of extreme effort and terrible malice. The child had neither the strength nor the depth of hatred necessary to destroy the Hoos ancestors. But the child had sent them somewhere — and Medwind had no idea where among the places of the dead they might have gone.

It didn't matter, though. She was both guardian and servant of their souls, and as such, she was going to have to find them. She was going to have to enter their realm.

She remembered a fragment of an old ballad.

Onto the paths of the dead I ride,
Seeking ghosts who have not died
With hell's hounds hunting at my side.
And if I falter, if I fear

The dead who mock and the ghosts who leer
And the hounds that hunt will hold me here —

Such a pity, she thought, *that I don't know any comforting ballads about traversing the paths of the dead.*

First, she needed to get Kirtha out of the way.

Medwind picked the little girl up and carried her back to the house and her mother. Faia was explaining the details of a house-guard system to a customer in the public room. She waved to her daughter and Medwind as they came in, but continued with the villager.

"No," Faia was saying, "this guard will *not* kill your intruders. It will decide how much threat the intruder poses, and react according to that. You do not have to kill thieves to make them stop stealing from you. Believe me, you will not have any problems once word gets out that you have this."

Faia gave the man a reassuring smile. He smiled back uncertainly — then his eyes flicked from Faia to Medwind and Kirtha, and back to Faia again.

"What if one o' my family comes in late?" he asked.

"That will not be a problem. The guard will always recognize your family. And it will not harm any friends you bring into your home. If your friends, or anyone else, try to sneak through your windows in the middle of the night, though, it will change them from men into women, or women into men. If they persist, it will give them long fur. If they still will not stop, it will turn their arms and legs into tentacles that cannot support their weight." Faia grinned at Medwind.

The Hoos warrior gave her an impatient grimace.

Faia said, "With you in a moment. I want to know how it went," then returned her attention to her client. "If they are armed, or the guard senses malice toward you or your family, it will immediately turn them into tentacled mice. You can scoop them up and take them to the town hall in the morning.

The man smiled broadly. "I like it. But the effects are fully reversible?"

"I can reverse them. If I am not available, then whoever you have caught will have to spend some time as whatever they become."

The man chuckled and looked down at his gnarled hands. "No more Warreners stealin' me blind —" He glanced up at her, and pulled a battered leather pouch from his belt. "I want it. How much?"

They finished their dicker, and the villager left.

"Turning thieves into mice seems excessive," Medwind remarked.

"The villagers wanted something that would turn them into little smears of ash on the floor. This was the best compromise I could manage."

Medwind sighed. "The villagers will simply kill the mice, you know. Or their cats will."

Faia shrugged. "So this will add an interesting element of risk to armed thieving. I do not see anything wrong with that." She finished tallying the new money into the account ledger and closed the book. "How did your ancestors like Kirtha?"

"Not too well, but that wasn't the real problem."

"Really? There was a problem?" Faia frowned.

"Kirtha didn't like my ancestors. She disappeared them."

Faia stared at Medwind, eyebrows rising. "She did *what*?!"

Medwind put Kirtha down, then leaned on the worktable. "The vha'attaye got upset — they want someone who's bound to me, who can be forced to serve them."

"That sounds unreasonable."

Medwind shrugged and idly fingered the corded fringe of the drop cloth on the table. "I guess your perspective changes when you're dead. Anyway, they got angry, and Kirtha told them to go away. No. Let me rephrase that. Kirtha *made* them go away. The vha'attaye don't do anything they're *told*."

"I do not imagine you will want to have Kirtha back in your *b'dabba* again?"

Medwind snorted. "No, I don't think so. They were angry with me before; I can't imagine how they're going to be once I find them again."

"Bad mans," Kirtha said, and frowned, and tossed her red curls. "All gone."

The Hoos warrior arched one eyebrow and studied the child out of the corners of her eyes. "Your daughter," she told Faia, "scares me. A lot. Much worse than you did, in fact, and you nearly scared the life out of me."

"As family traits go, I think I will keep that one. Being able to scare a Hoos headhunter seems useful to me."

In spite of herself, in spite of the fact that she was once again without a child to teach for the vha'attaye, in spite of the sure anger of the waking dead when she brought them back — assuming she could find them — Medwind laughed.

"I have to go after them," she told Faia. Her smile faded.

"Go after them?"

"Go to the place between the worlds. My ancestors and enemy will be there somewhere. I have to bring them back."

Faia's eyes lost their laughter. "The living do not belong in the spirit realm."

"I have no choice. This is my duty."

"Then let me come with you. Let me help."

Medwind smiled slowly. "Thank you — but I cannot. The place I go is sacred to the vha'attaye. It is a Hoos place. I have to go alone."

Faia shook her head. "They demean you, they despise you, they treat you terribly, they demand things, and they are completely unreasonable. I would leave them wherever Kirtha lost them, if I were you."

Medwind started to get angry, then forced her anger out of the way. The hill-girl did not understand the depth of commitment a Hoos took on who vowed service of the Ancestors. She did not understand that the bonds of the vha'attaye were the prime bonds of Hoos family — that a Hoos who served the vha'attaye served them first before husbands and children and parents. She took a deep breath. "Faia," she said, "Kirtha is your responsibility, no matter how she behaves. Yes?"

Faia tipped her head to one side, then nodded. "Of course."

"Of course," Medwind said. "You ask no questions — you simply accept the burden. In that same way, the vha'attaye are my family and my burden."

She looked around the big, friendly room for a moment and sighed. "If I have not come out by tomorrow, please bring Nokar and come into the *b'dabba*. Nokar will know what to do with my body." She turned and walked out without waiting for an answer.

She left mother and daughter standing in the workroom and stalked back to her hut. Perhaps the hill-girl would understand. It would have been easier to be self-righteous, though, she decided, if Faia's suggestion hadn't been so tempting.

She knelt in front of the abandoned skulls and offered up a solemn prayer to Etyt and Thiena. There were those among the living who had travelled to the place between the worlds, but only for compelling reasons, and never happily. She knew this, and knew as well that many who left never returned. She offered up her soul to the hands of her gods. Death in the service of her vha'attaye was honorable; she would face it as a warrior.

She was ready. Chanting and drumming, she drove herself into a trance, into the place where her soul could disentangle from her body. She reached into the cold, dark emptiness between the worlds — stretched her soul into that aching otherness. Her vision darkened, sensation faded, and sound was replaced by the pressure of dark and empty infinity, by an expanse of nothingness so immense the weight of it pressed her into despair. She was alone in that void — the only living thing.

She stretched into the vast nothing — tried to reach out a hand, and had no hands; tried to walk or swim or fly through the oblivion, and discovered herself legless and armless, yet she moved. She saw without eyes, heard without ears, glowed warm as a tiny sun in the screaming nothing that was the kingdom of the dead.

Things approached. A few ghostgreen shimmers tendrilled against her, touching like the barest of breezes — strangers. Not her Ancestors. Medwind held her fear close to her and pushed a question at them, formed in the familiar shapes of her waking dead. *These — have you seen them? Where are they — my Ancestors, my enemy, my friend?*

Missing, the strangers seemed to tell her. She felt suggestions of the abruptness of the parting, of a rushing wind, great force, surprise. The thing that overcame her ancestors and her enemy was a novelty to the spirits of the waking dead.

They did not fall to the things that hunt the waking dead? Medwind shaped the thought, touched the ghostgreen strangers with it, and felt a flush of fear, and the recoiling of the soulfingers that touched her mind.

No. Something other. Something new. The ghostminds rolled the memory among themselves — they showed curiosity at the phenomenon, but no fear.

It was only Kirtha's doing, then. Perhaps she could stop worrying.

A different strain of ghostthoughts touched hers mind. *So you've come. Good. Look around this hell you've thrown me into.* This new vha'attaye was familiar, angry

— but Medwind felt her own spirit soar in spite of the other's anger.

Rakell! She swirled around the greenlit spirit in formless embrace. *I'm so happy to find you!*

I wasn't lost. I left before those bastard Hoosghosts of yours got blown across eternity. The Mottemage's thoughts felt smug.

But where are they?

Gone. For good, I hope.

Medwind felt herself drowning in anguish. *No!* She pled with the dead Mottemage. *Help me find them. They're — my family. You are. I need all of you.*

The cold green shadowshape that was Rakell withdrew to the very edge of Medwind's touch. *I don't want to be needed. I want life, or true death — and whatever comes after.* She separated herself from Medwind and retreated, a swiftly receding glimmer of light.

The other waking dead crowded around Medwind, touching with their cold dead souls the bright, shimmering essence of her life. Then, without any warning, they set up a keening and scattered like dim stars fleeing a monster bent on swallowing the sun.

She felt something — embodied hatred or embodied hunger — coming at her from a distance. It shot toward her; fast, ravenous, unreasoning, malevolent. She saw nothing, but sensed, somehow, its displacement of the nothing-stuff that formed the place between the worlds. It was massive.

She bolted, and it came on —

Panicked, terrified, she flung herself off the paths of the dead, and fell — through sounds and sensations that built toward a roar, eye-searing light, invisible fire that burned every cell of her body at the same time, tastes and smells that became a miasma so thick for a moment she couldn't breath. Her skin seemed to bubble and shift while meaningless colors and shapes swirled in front of her eyes and a pounding wall of noise assaulted her ears. Air felt liquid — her body was hot, then cold, then hot — and gasping, heaving, she crumpled into a ball on the floor of the *b'dabba* and retched and cried.

She shivered, struggled with a body that twitched erratically, tried to push herself up, fell on her face instead.

She lay on the goatskin rug — and gradually the incomprehensible attack on her senses resolved into understandable smells and tastes and sights. Her drums hung above her, her candles flickered in front of her, guttering low, and the sound of rain hissed and drummed against the outside of the *b'dabba*.

Alive, she thought. *Thank Etyt and Thiena, I'm still alive.*

She lay still, staring up into the forest of drums. The place between the worlds waited in her future — if she became someone of importance to the Hoos, she would become vha'attaye. She would be a revered Ancestor, watched and guarded and kept for generations on a table, asked for advice, honored as the voice of wisdom. And in between moments of honor, she would wait in the eternal, terrifying darkness.

The places of the dead were not for the living. With the charge of the soul-eater still fresh in her mind, she wondered if they were for the dead, either.

Fat Girl kept the tagnu to an easy lope. Even Runs Slow maintained the pace without difficulty. The three of them skirted the edge of the jungle, staying well out of its reach, moving west. They ran in a no-man's-land — too close to the jungle for the peknu, too far from it for the tagnu and the jungle beasts. The ground was grassy and rolling. Mornings were dry and easy — but by early afternoon every day, the sky broke under its burden and heavy, pelting rains began.

Three days out of the jungle, still running west, Fat Girl noted a change in the terrain and in the plants that grew on the grassy plains. Thick tangles of shrubs bent away from constant salt-tanged wind. The leaves of plants were thicker, and all, when licked, bore a faint flavor of salt.

Late the fourth day, in drenching rain, the tagnu topped a rise. Below them sprawled the peknu place they sought, filled with houses of wood and stone, surrounded by high log walls. Beyond it the Big Water reached to the horizon.

Fat Girl and Dog Nose readjusted the uncomfortable tablets in their harnesses. Seven-Fingered Fat Girl had been to this same peknu place twice before. It frightened her — it was dirty and noisy and stinking and full of far too many people.

"We find the old man who trades for *becks*, we get our god-dirt and our food, and we get out of that place," she said.

The other two nodded their agreement silently. All three tagnu took deep breaths. Then they went down into the lair of the outlanders.

The pretty girl at the gate stared at them and clucked her tongue. In Hraddo, the trade tongue, she said, "Declare you trade-stuff."

Seven-Fingered Fat Girl knew the routine. She showed the girl her tablet and Dog Nose's. "That all."

The girl wrinkled her nose. "That good-stuff not. That junk."

Fat Girl shrugged. "We lose good-stuff in jungle," she lied. It was to her advantage if the gate guard decided she was only carrying junk. Somewhere in the peknu town, there was an old man who would trade a lot for *becks*. But that was her secret.

The girl made scratch marks on a flat green pad, asked for the names of all three tagnu, made more scratch marks. "You have pay tax when leave Omwim-mee Trade."

Fat Girl eyed the gate guard. "I know *that*. I here

before. You mark value this junk now." When they left Omwimmee Trade, anything they took in over the girl's valuation of their goods would be pure profit — tax-free.

"Ten rit each," the girl decided.

"*Ten rit!*" Fat Girl shrieked. "You say this junk, I never make ten rit! I have pay more what I make for tax. It worth five rit both. No more."

"I give you eight each." The girl started to scratch on the pad again.

Fat Girl rolled her eyes and put her hands on her bony hips. "Too much. Who pay me eight rit each this stuff — you tell me? Six both."

"Six each. Best I can do." The girl spread her hands out and shrugged.

"We lose all good stuff, you rob us for junk. Is bad world this." Fat Girl turned to Dog Nose and Runs Slow and in her own language said, "She doesn't know how much these are worth. I think we can get ten tens for each of these — but she's almost down to nothing. Runs Slow, you cry hard. Dog Nose, hug Runs Slow, look at the guard like she's bad tagnu, then turn around and walk away. Don't look back."

Fat Girl turned back to the guard. Behind her, Runs Slow began to sniffle, then to sob. Dog Nose made comforting noises. The noises began to retreat.

"We pay tax someplace people not try steal we eyes. We come long way trade here, we have bad luck." Fat Girl felt tears welling up in her own eyes when she said that — she let them slide down her cheeks. "We friends die. She brother die." The tears began falling in earnest. She started to turn away.

"Little girl brother really die?" The voice at Fat Girl's back was soft and concerned.

Fat Girl hated herself for using Roshi — but in a way, she thought, what she was doing was for Roshi. The money they made would feed Roshi's little sister. She turned back. "Yes," she whispered. It was truth, and it rang as truth.

"Six both," the guard at the gate said. "Go in. I hope you make lot money on you junk." The girl scratched on her pad, and handed a wooden square with marks painted on it to Seven-Fingered Fat Girl. Fat Girl dug a string of twisted vine from her pouch and strung the square on it. She put the makeshift necklace on.

The guard stared at her left hand, the hand with the missing fingers, then looked away.

"Thank you," Fat Girl said. She turned and called back Dog Nose and Runs Slow. The three of them hurried into the peknu town — they slipped through the gate and trotted down the high walkways to the market before the girl at the gate could change her mind.

The city seemed almost deserted. Fat Girl had only seen it before in the dry season, when the streets thronged with people and the skies were filled with flying people on carpets and winged beasts and in odd-made things. Now the roads had become rivers, full of swift-running, muddy-brown water that swirled into holes beside the walkways and vanished with a roar. The sheeting rain stung her skin, while the damp cold left Fat Girl's teeth chattering. The skies were empty except for the low, gray-black clouds.

Two sodden travellers drove their cart toward the market — the miserable beasts waded through the current that pulled at their legs and hung their heads in soggy misery. Fat Girl and her tagnu loped past them on the highwalk. An icecart driver heading in the other direction stared at them from the dry, covered perch of his cart. Fat Girl stared back.

Light spilled from the windows of the houses the tagnu ran past onto wet grass and rain-slicked cobblestones — warm yellow light that shimmered in the rain and cast gleaming reflections in the puddles. Fat Girl wished for an instant that she could be behind those windows, in the dry places where the peknu lived. She wished for a thick grass-thatched roof over her head, for a house built from the bodies of dead trees. Then she smiled. She didn't need that. She had a stone city, her own city, where no tree dared grow. She'd bargained well on her taxes. Now all she had to do was find the old man.

The outer market was empty, desolate, the square deserted except for a few hardy travellers selling wares out of their covered carts. Those seasoned peddlers recognized the tagnu as unlikely prospects and let them past unchivvied — they saved their strident calls for people less obviously hungry and less poor.

The inner market, however, was as lively as the outer market was barren. Tables overflowed with a riot of things to buy — with fruit and shoes and flowers, bread and pastries, tools and weapons, woven hammocks, live chickens, roasted pigs; with fish frozen on huge blocks of green ice packed in sawdust; with folds of cloth in colors and patterns that dazzled the eye, and caged birds that preened and shrieked and cackled. Pots and hammocks and baskets and slaughtered beasts hung from the rafters. Smoke wafted up from a hundred cookfires — hawkers screamed after the tagnu in a babble of tongues, crying, "Try! Taste! Buy! Look at this!" The languages might have been different, but the words were the same — Fat Girl knew the hustlers and the peddlers and the thieves, no matter what they said.

People stared at them. Old women looked from Dog Nose's scarred face to Fat Girl's maimed hand, and their tongues clucked. Vendors glared at them, obviously suspecting thievery. Bored young men who leaned against the stalls, whittling at sticks with their big knives, ogled Fat Girl's body with expressions that frightened her — they called after her, words she didn't understand in voices she didn't like. Their laughter behind her felt dirty and dangerous, and made her want to hide. Women with painted lips and painted eyes watched her pass, and studied her skinny, scarred, half-naked body, and tipped their heads in mocking salute.

The scent of cooked meat wrenched her stomach into a tight fist. Runs Slow pointed at a spitted suckling pig roasting over a brazier, its juices sizzling in the low flames, and said, "I want that, Fat Girl."

"Later. We have nothing to pay with yet." Fat Girl wished she could ignore the wonderful roasting-pig smell. She wended her way through the tight, twisting aisles. She stopped to admire bright red beads at a jewelry stall, then studied a leather carry-bag with a keen eye — she'd copy the design as best she could later. Always she kept part of her attention on the people around her — on the swarthy, brightly clad young children who offered to direct customers to the merchandise they desired for a fee, on the hard-eyed merchants who stared after her distrustfully, on the pickpockets and cutpurses who cruised the aisles in search of prey. Fat Girl's dartstick rested on her hip, tucked into the thong of her myr — but one hand always hovered over her dart-pack. The first person to try to steal from her would feel the prick of her dart and die.

Dog Nose moved ahead of her, drawn by a gleaming display of metal knives. Fat Girl followed — and noticed two men with long metal-banded braids and beards staring at the tablet on her back. The men leaned their heads close together. One nodded, glanced at her, and slipped out from behind the stall where they stood, selling amulets. They looked rather like the man she sought, but she did not like the expressions in their eyes. Fat Girl tapped Dog Nose. "Move on," she said, her voice low and flat. "Turn right, then left, then left again."

Dog Nose made no sign to show he'd heard, but he

turned as she'd directed. Runs Slow followed, and Fat Girl brought up the rear. She watched for the man with the braids and the long, gaudy robes — she looked for his reflection in baubles that hung in the jewelry stalls and watched out of the corner of her eye as she stopped to admire kittens and puppies and silver-scaled lizards in wooden crates.

There he was! He came around the corner of the third turn, caught sight of her, and immediately stopped and pretended to be looking at the wares of the cloth vendor nearest him. He talked with the merchant, held up a piece of fabric to the light — and when Fat Girl moved on, he moved with her.

She caught up with Dog Nose and Runs Slow. "There is a man following us," she whispered. "Get around the fruit stall, then run." She backed off — tried to make her quick footsteps look casual. All three tagnu eased into the tight side corridor, then through it, then walked calmly in the opposite direction. Behind them, someone shouted incomprehensible syllables, and someone else yelled in Hraddo, "Stop, thief!"

Hands reached out to grab them. Fat Girl bolted, bit at the grasping fingers, clawed at eyes and faces — escaped, ran faster. Dog Nose kicked the fat merchant who tried to block his way. He squirmed through a tiny space between two stalls. Runs Slow followed him. Fat Girl brought up the rear, sidling sideways, feeling the tablet on her back drag along the rough wood planks.

Ahead of her Dog Nose darted right, into a less congested aisle, with Runs Slow at his heels. Fat Girl got out of the tight cut-through in time to see a huge puff of green smoke billow up in front of him. The man with the braids and robes stepped out of it and reached at him. Dog Nose yelled, turned, and bolted in the opposite direction. The man chased after him. Fat Girl snatched Runs Slow's hand and raced behind him. As she passed a stand on which chickens and turkeys sat with their legs tied underneath them, she shoved. The table overturned, the turkeys and chickens went up and over in a flurry of squawks and feathers, and marketgoers and merchants alike began to shout.

"Left," she yelled at Dog Nose. "Go left."

All three tagnu raced down a short aisle where competing rug merchants screamed in Hraddo and half a dozen other tongues that their carpets flew faster or longer or better. If she'd had any idea of how to make it work, Fat Girl would have stolen one. But she didn't have the time to even ask. The cloud of green smoke burst into existence at the end of the aisle.

"Right!" Fat Girl yelled, and the three tagnu jumped over a pile of rolled carpets, sent the standing rolls tumbling, and left the rug merchant screeching in their wake.

"Faster!" Dog Nose called. "Out!"

They were near an exit. Through the opened door, in the deepening gloom, Fat Girl saw a forest of tall, straight wood and draped cloth — *Silk People!* her mind screamed, even as she realized what she saw were the masts of ships. And beyond them was the vast, dark line of the Great Water. The tagnu were trapped.

Their pursuer yelled in Hraddo, "Thieves! Catch them!" and four old men looked up from a table where they pushed colored stones back and forth. From either side of the aisle, merchants rushed out of their stalls to capture the tagnu. A giant, dark-haired man grabbed Dog Nose; a woman in red caught Runs Slow and held her, squirming. Fat Girl saw the way ahead was blocked, looked over her shoulder, saw the man with the bearded braid and long robes right behind her, looked ahead again just in time to see one of the old men from the table stand. He also wore long, brightly colored robes, and like the man who chased her, his white beard and long hair were braided and ornamented with gold bands. Seven-Fingered Fat Girl screamed. The old man held out his hands to catch her, she tripped and fell into the board and sent the multitudes of tiny pieces flying, and the dark-bearded man clamped a sharp-nailed hand around her wrist.

"You come with me," he told her. "You thieves come with me." Then, in a different tongue, he talked to the merchants and the old men. The merchants pushed Runs Slow and Dog Nose toward him. Fat Girl kicked and struggled and tried to get her hand to her dart pouch.

"Wait," the old man said in Hraddo. He was staring at Fat Girl's hand, at Dog Nose's face. "Wait, wait. I know these children. They not steal. They good children — Wen traders."

Fat Girl looked at him closely and recognized him as the man who had told her about *becks*.

"Yes!" she yelled. "I bring you *becks*, old man. We find these *becks*, we bring them you, you trade us good!" She got an elbow into the belly of the dark-bearded man and he snarled something and tightened his grip on her wrist. Then he grabbed onto the tablet tied to her back, and she felt a sort of wrenching, twisting sensation. Green smoke enveloped her.

Then the dark-bearded man was gone, and with him, her tablet.

"My *beck*!" she yelled.

The old man was looking at Dog Nose. "You have other *book*, yes?"

Dog Nose nodded.

"Then no problem. We find that *beck* and that *saje* thief later. Now you come my house, get good food. We trade good." He turned Dog Nose around, looked at the tablet on his back, and smiled — a tiny, secretive smile. "We trade good-good," he added.

The merchants let the tagnu go, and all three of them followed the old man out of the market, and down the windy, drying streets.

Fat Girl wanted to cry at the loss of her tablet. After everything her tagnu had suffered, now they only had one thing to trade. One *beck*. Could they buy their freedom with that?

But the old man seemed happy. Maybe one *beck* would be enough.

Kirgen snickered, and Roba looked up from her manuscript to see why.

"I think I've found what you need."

"Let's see."

"No, just listen." Kirgen assumed an oratorical pose, one hand pressed against his chest. He translated as he went and declaimed in sonorous, rolling syllables:

" 'Once, it has been said, the First Folk ruled the Northlands. They were cruel masters, exacting tribute from the honest peoples of the South. They built their cities of gold wrung from the sweat and blood of their helpless victims, and demanded half of all jewels, all grains, all fine woods, all fruits and all herdbeasts that each town and city brought forth in every year. And also, they demanded in tithe the fairest and most perfect of the youths of the Southlands, for —' "

Kirgen paused, a puzzled expression on his face.

"Don't stop now," Roba said dryly. "This is delightful stuff."

"What's *temrish*?"

"Oh." Roba closed her eyes and thought. "That's an old, old term. Bondage of some sort — contractual, I think."

"Fine. That makes sense." Kirgen continued.

" '— they demanded in tithe the fairest and most perfect of the youths of the Southlands, for *temrish*, for sport, and for their feasts, which they held in honor of their bloody gods on the day of the mating of the Tide Mother with the Sun. The fairest of the fair the First Folk served up on platters on that day, to sate their abominable hunger.' "

"They *ate* them?" Roba squeaked.

"Looks like," Kirgen said.

"Ye-e-ech!"

"So anyway — 'The people of the Southlands, weary of oppression, heartsick at the lost of their loved ones, impoverished, but great in spirit, rose up, and in a mighty tide, stormed to the very lairs of the First Folk, intending to demand their freedom by treaty, or do battle. Long this great army was absent from its home, and long did the patient rulers and councilors wait for word of the battle. Then at last came back one man, crying that all the army were slain, but that the First Folk also were no more. And so saying, he fell to the ground and died, and the rest of the tale died with him. And from that day to this, there has been no call for tribute from the North, and all believe the First Folk to be vanquished, or well and truly dead.' "

"What a happy story. Simply charming." Roba sighed. "So — the story is that somewhere to the north, there's a city made of gold, a First Folk city." She spread her hands and shrugged. "So what?"

"So —" Kirgen said. "Imagine this. Delmuirie was in the army that went to the north. He rode into the First Folk city, single-handedly conquered the First Folk, and died a mighty hero, after erecting Delmuirie's Barrier so that Arhel would be safe forever after." Kirgen crossed his arms over his chest and jutted his chin.

"Sorry. I don't buy it."

Kirgen winked and laughed. "*You* aren't supposed to."

"Oh." Roba leaned back in her chair and stared up at her young assistant. She couldn't help but think what a pity it was that he wore all those bulky saje robes. She imagined him in the short fishermen's breeches and light tunics worn by the men in her part of Arhel, and decided even that was more than he needed to wear. "Fine. So we tell Thirk this marvelous little tale — then what?"

"Then he rewrites our theory, puts his name on it,

and claims the scholarship for himself — which in this case is a very good thing. You wouldn't want your name on this tripe."

"True." Roba stood and gave her assistant a warm smile. "Well, Kirgen, you're as good as your word. You've solved my problem for me. Let's find a few more quotes. If we're lucky, by tomorrow morning, I'll be able to write this up and present it to Thirk — and he'll pat me on the head and tell me I don't need an assistant anymore." She shook her head slowly. "That's a shame, too. I think I could have gotten used to having an assistant."

She looked away. When she glanced back, she discovered Kirgen was studying her with discomfiting intensity. "I can think of an advantage in not being your assistant."

Roba noted that, irrationally, her pulse sped up. "Really?" she said, fighting back the huskiness that crept into her voice. "And what would that be?"

"I could tell you how beautiful I think you are — if I weren't your assistant."

Roba shoved her hands into her tunic pockets. She could feel the heat in her face. "You could," she agreed. "Of course, if you weren't my assistant, I could tell you how very attractive I find you."

She saw Kirgen tense. He slipped off the desk, moved away from her. With his back to her, he said. "I could also tell you, if I weren't your assistant, that I've watched you every minute I've been with you — and I've never seen anyone as intelligent as you, or as sure of herself. I could tell you I've never found anyone I wanted to be with as much as I want to be with you."

Roba's whole body tingled — she felt as though she might stop breathing and explode and catch fire, all at the same time. She walked over to him and rested one hand on his shoulder. She leaned over to whisper in his ear — felt the heat of his skin against her cheek, breathed in the musk-and-soap scent of him — and said, "Tell me that anyway."

He turned and her hand fell away. The smallest of distances separated them — they were not touching at all, yet Roba's body sang at the promise of his skin against hers.

"I want you." He whispered it. His upper lip trembled when he spoke.

She wanted to reach out and touch that trembling lip. Instead, she avoided touching him at all — somehow, she felt that any move in his direction would be irrevocable, would throw her completely out of control. "I want you," she echoed. "Come home with me tonight."

He nodded.

Very close but not touching, they left her office together.

✿ *Chapter 5*

Medwind carried the last of the abandoned skulls into her workroom. She stroked the painted suture line at the top of the skull of Troggar Raveneye, best enemy, and sighed. *Where are you hiding, you old bastard?* she wondered. *Are you safe somewhere? Or have the things that hunt between the worlds gotten at you?* She stared off into space, the chill of too-recent terror raising the hair on her arms. *I hope all of you can find your way home. I won't go back looking for you again.*

The front gate slammed shut, and Medwind jumped.

"Med! Hey, Med! You won't believe what I found at the market!"

Found? Medwind wondered. It was Nokar's day off. He was supposed to be sitting in the geezer corner of the market playing Three-and-One with his cronies, not shopping. Certainly not spending money. Nokar had appalling ideas regarding what constituted a good buy.

Expecting to be confronted with yet another stuffed kellink-foot drypress-holder or tacky imitation-Proageff tapestry of pudgy nudes on horseback, she hurried into the breezeway.

He brought home skinny naked kids? She studied the strangers in her hall with surprise and shook her head slowly. *Well, that's a change.*

"You found kids?" she asked, looking at them. They were pitiful. Skinny was only the start — the boy's face was scarred from forehead to upper lip; his nose split down the middle. The girl was missing the last three fingers on her left hand. All three wore bruises, scrapes, cuts, and the thin pale scars that spoke of more of the same in their short pasts. Their loincloths were torn and filthy. The boy wore a harness of twisted vine — raw spots on the older girl's skin showed she'd worn one, too. They carried their weapons with a sullen defensiveness and stared at her with untrusting eyes. "Wen kids," she added, and sighed. "I think I'd rather have had another tapestry."

She'd seen Wen kids in the market from time to time — always trading or dickering. They were tough little traders and meaner than the sajes' lowest hell. The older ones always looked like they'd been run over by a cattle stampede, then threw themselves off a cliff after-wards to mess up anything the cattle missed. She'd never seen an adult Wen.

But Nokar was shaking his head and grinning like a lunatic. "The kids aren't what I found — well, they are, but look, Med. Look what the boy has on his back." In Hraddo, he told the kid to turn around. The boy did, and Medwind got a good look at the tablet he'd strapped there.

She stared, then moved closer and looked harder. It was a rectangular tablet of something stonelike, luminous off-white, slightly translucent, glossy, and covered by some achingly familiar script that she couldn't, at that moment, place. She knew that she had never seen anything similar. "What is it?" she asked, fascinated by the odd white material and by the long rows of dots and slashes impressed into the surface. "I know I've seen the script before, but where?"

Nokar cackled and rubbed his hands together. "Think bigger."

He was excited — Medwind couldn't really remem-ber seeing him so obviously thrilled about anything before. His cheeks were flushed, his eyes shone, he seemed to dance without moving.

Bigger, she thought. **Bigger?** *Bigger what? Bigger tablets, or bigger script?*—

And suddenly she knew. The slashes and dots . . . carved on stone pillars topped with the carved heads of monsters, left in strangely inaccessible places — it was the same script. "Oh, by the gods," she whispered. "By the *kranjakken* gods, that's a First Folk artifact. Oh, sweet Etyt, Nokar, that's a *hruni*ng First Folk artifact."

Everyone knew no portable First Folk artifacts existed. None. The First Folk left the giant carved pillars, a few broken stone domes built high in the mountains, occasional carvings on the sides of rocks — when they vanished into the murky mists of prehistory, they carried everything that could be carried with them.* So said conventional wisdom.

Now here was something that made conventional wisdom appear wrong. "Do you think the tablet is genuine? Is it old — or new? Are these kids First Folk?" Medwind frowned, concentrating. "Did the First Folk become the Wen?"

Nokar laughed. "I don't know — and right now it doesn't matter. There's more. One of the Tethjan sajes was chasing these kids through the marketplace when they ran into me. He grabbed the tablet the older girl had strapped to her back, and vanished with it. I expect he went to the University — gods know, a find like this would make a scholar's reputation forever."

"Then, if he's going to claim the find before you, why are you laughing?"

"Because he may have a tablet, but I have the kids who brought it."

Medwind sensed that she wasn't going to like the direction the conversation was taking. "And . . .?" she asked.

"And with these kids, we can go into the jungle and find the source — maybe a living First Folk village,

Med. Maybe a ruin that still has artifacts in it to show us how the First Folk lived." His voice dropped, became a whisper. "Whatever we find, it will be a link to our real past, to the history we lost in the Purges."

"Well, where do they say they found it?"

Nokar grinned at her. "They won't say — yet. But I'm going to find a way to get them to tell me."

In Hraddo, the girl interrupted. "Where food? Old man say you got food."

Medwind arched an eyebrow at Nokar. "You told them we'd keep them?"

"I told them we'd feed them. I want them around at least long enough to find out where they found the tablets. What if there are more of them, Medwind? What if we could decipher more than the few numbers and symbols we know — if we could truly *read* the language of the First Folk, think of all we could learn."

Medwind felt herself becoming caught up in his excitement. She'd always loved the past. At Daane, history had been a minor subject, overridden by such practical things as research and development, agricultural and livestock sciences, and other current concerns. Medwind's tendency to bury herself in history books had earned her some derogatory nicknames and had probably been partly responsible for the difficulty she'd found being accepted. In Nokar, she'd discovered a kindred soul — someone else who saw that past as other than dead and dusty.

"Don't dig up the bones of the past, old man," she'd said more than once, repeating an old Hoos proverb, "— for the past is not dead, and it resents being buried." That proverb was a joke between them. The living bones of the past called to her as seductively as they did to him.

"First Folk," she whispered, and smiled carefully at the three Wen kids. In Hraddo, she told them, "You come-follow. I feed. Later-later we talk trade."

Excitement pushed her worry about her missing vha'attaye temporarily to the back of her mind.

Choufa curled on a palmetto mat and looked up at the dark arch of the tree above her. The rain had stopped, and the night echoed with the throb of message drums — nearby, tagnu traders negotiated their right to approach a village for trade goods. Farther off, a village passed along the word that no one had found the rogue band of tagnu who desecrated a sacred path of the Keyu, then vanished into the peknu lands.

Choufa listened, only mildly interested. Her stomach was full, and she was dry and warm — clothed in coarse ragweave, but clothed, and that seemed good to her. The Keyu were silent, somnolent. Her friends slept around her. The gentle rocking of the tree's branches lulled her.

She dozed, only to snap awake, aware that something had changed. Her heart pounded and she froze, eyes still shut, listening. She heard nothing out of the ordinary — the creak of the tree's branches, the wind through the leaves, drums and animal sounds from the jungle, the steady breathing of the other sharsha nearby —

— And quicker breathing, very close. A faint, slight shuffle right beside her — her eyes opened as a hand clamped over her mouth.

"Quiet," someone whispered. A boy's voice.

There aren't any boys here, she thought. She swung her legs up at him and kicked him in the face. He grunted, then pressed harder on her mouth. She bit him, and he yelped and swore and jerked his hand away.

"Damn, damn, damn-all! That hurt. I didn't hurt you. I just told you to be quiet." He managed to bring his voice down to a whisper. "You new ones are always the same — and now the rest of them are awake. I hate it when they're awake."

His hand was away from her mouth, and he hadn't actually hurt her. She whispered, "What do you want? Who are you?"

"I'm Leth. I live here."

She could make out few details about him in the darkness. He was a tall boy, very thin, with hair as long as hers had been before the keyunu cut it off. So he had been sharsha a long time.

A female voice asked, "What's going on?"

A much younger voice said, "Someone's here."

"It's only me," Leth said. "Go back to sleep."

The darkness rustled with girls shifting, the new sharsha asking questions, the older girls reassuring them. "Leth is sharsha," one said. "Just like us. He's supposed to be here, so you can go back to sleep. Everything is fine."

The sharsha nest settled down. When it was quiet again, Choufa asked Leth, "Why did you wake me up?"

He was silent a long time. Finally he told her, "I had to. I have — um, things I have to do — or, um, the Silk People will feed me to the Keyu. I don't want to die."

"No," Choufa said. "Me neither." She sat up and wrapped her arms around her knees. "What kind of things?"

She could see the boy lower his head. "Bad things," he whispered. He fell silent again, but Choufa waited. After long, uncomfortable minutes, he added, "I have to put babies in the girls' bellies."

Choufa didn't like the sound of that. She couldn't imagine why anyone would want babies in their belly, and she was certain she didn't want one in hers. "Does it hurt?" she asked.

"Um —" He crouched and rocked back and forth, slowly. "No . . . not really. Well," he amended, "maybe the first time, a little. But after the first time, the girls seem to like it — and it feels good to me. I guess the babies are really little. They get bigger after they're in there a while."

"You have to put a baby in *my* belly?" Choufa eyed him warily. "How will it get out?"

"I have to. The boy who was here before me stopped doing what the keyunu told him to do. They fed him to the Keyu and made me watch." Leth shrugged. "I don't know how the babies get out, though. The keyunu know when they're ready. I guess the trees tell them. The keyunu come and get the girls, and most of the time the girls don't come back. After the babies come out, the keyunu say the girls get to be keyunu. The Keyu forgive them and give them names."

"Do you believe that?"

"Do you believe anything the keyunu say?" The boy snorted softly. "But I know they come and get the girls who are here a long time and don't get babies in their bellies. They feed them to the trees on Naming Days. They always tell us about it."

"Oh." Choufa thought about that. She looked at Leth, who crouched beside her. "I guess you'd better put a baby in my belly."

Leth seemed uncertain. "Are you going to bite me again?"

"No."

"Not even if it hurts?"

"Will it hurt as bad as when the keyunu stuck their needles in me?"

Leth hissed, a quick intake of breath through his teeth. "Nothing like that."

"Then I won't bite you."

Afterwards, Choufa stretched out on her stomach on the mat, eyes searching the shapes of the darkness. She was sore, but not terribly so. She felt odd, but thought the feeling would pass. She wondered, laying there in the darkness, if she had a baby in her belly. She wondered about a lot of things.

* * *

Roba and Kirgen put the finishing touches on their report only a few minutes before Thirk arrived. When he came bounding into Roba's office, gold bands in his beard and hair clacking against, the two of them were on opposite sides of the room, innocently rummaging through manuscripts.

"Well?" Thirk asked, looking from Roba to Kirgen and back. "What did you need me for? I just got your message."

Roba grinned. "I've got your paper, and your theory."

Thirk looked startled. "You're early. I wasn't expecting that paper for several days —" He took the stack of dull green drypress she offered and flipped quickly through the pages. "This is *original* research? Not just a rehash of somebody else's work."

"It's a completely new theory," Roba assured him. "I guarantee it. I enlisted my assistant, and the two of us have spent every free minute putting this together." She laughed. "I'm so far behind on my classwork right now, my students are going to start rioting. But you'll have plenty of time to go over this and verify our work before the next Society meeting."

Thirk's face went gray. His eyes darted to Kirgen, then fixed on Roba. "That's a secret," he hissed.

"He wants to join," Roba said. "He believes in the cause."

Thirk looked dumbfounded. He stared at the graduate student, and his expression indicated he wouldn't have been more surprised if Kirgen had sprouted wings and flown out of the office. "You're joking."

"I want to join," Kirgen seconded from his place in the corner of the office. "I want to be a part of the great things I think will be happening in Ariss. I think the Delmuirie Society has important things to do and say. I

believe there are changes that must be made, and I
believe the Delmuirie Society is the group to make
those changes."

"Funny, but I don't remember you having any great
love for Delmuirie back in your undergrad days,"
Thirk said. He watched Kirgen suspiciously. "As a matter of fact, I remember you being deeply involved in a
few incidents in my classroom —"

"I've grown up since then," Kirgen assured him. He
stroked the downy fuzz of his saje beard with con-
templative seriousness.

Roba would have laughed had she dared. Instead,
she dropped her gaze to the clutter of junk on her desk
top and pretended to be looking at something important.

"Well and good, then, young Kirgen," Thirk said at
last. "If Roba Morgasdotte will vouch for your
behavior, I'll see that you become a member."

Roba kept her eyes fixed on her desk and said, "He's
as dedicated to the cause as I am, Thirk. I promise and
swear it."

Thirk smiled then, a broad, happy smile. "I'm going
to go to my office and look over this. In the meantime
— Roba, do you feel that you still need an assistant?"

"Desperately," Roba said, looking up into Thirk's
eyes and attempting to project heartfelt sincerity.

Thirk was still thumbing through the presentation.
"Hmmm. I suppose so. It looks like the two of you have
put a great deal of time into this. I see things in here
I've never seen before." He looked up and nodded.
"Kirgen, you want a permanent position as Roba's
assistant? — it would help fund your graduate classes."

Kirgen studied the ceiling with a thoughtful expression. "Well, yes, sir. A job like this would mean a great
deal to me. Especially once I get to my independent
study."

"Then it's yours." He smiled a fatherly smile at

Kirgen, bowed slightly to Roba, and swept out of the office at a stately pace, with the new Delmuirie Disappearance theory clutched in his hands.

Kirgen kept silent only an instant. Then he said, "I'll bet he started to run as soon as he stepped out the door."

"No—"

"Let's look."

Both of them peeked out the doorway. Roba stared down the hall, then started to chuckle. Thirk was indeed running, the skirts of his robe flying, braids swinging wildly — he was the antithesis of dignity.

"You owe me," Kirgen said, as Thirk vanished into his office like a snake down a hole.

"I never bet you."

Kirgen slipped up behind her and nibbled gently at the base of her neck. "Yes you did. And I want to collect."

Roba shivered, then gently pushed Kirgen away. "I don't doubt it. But I have a class on mage/saje comparative history, and after that the Evolution of Magical Practices lab. Then I have all those tests and reports to grade —" She waved glumly at three giant stacks of drypress. "And I'm sure there's *something* you're supposed to be doing, too."

He laughed. "I'm sure there is, but I'd rather be with you. If you don't want to stay and play, though, I suppose I could make an appearance at all those classes I've been skipping. . . ."

Roba sighed and picked up her notes. "Come over to my apartment tonight — will that be soon enough?"

"I suppose it will have to be."

The Wen kids had, after considerable debate among themselves, accepted sleeping mats — which they had then unrolled under the eaves in the central garden. They would not sleep in the house, no matter how

Nokar and Medwind tried to reason with them. They ignored the rain, and refused to come inside. When Medwind checked on them early the next morning, the rain had stopped again, and they were pacing around the enclosed courtyard, pointing at various plants and flowers — and Medwind's *b'dabba* — making quiet comments in their odd, musical language. Kirtha had joined them and was trying diligently to communicate with the little blonde Wen child.

"You gots no shirt," Kirtha announced in her high, piping voice.

The Wen child said something to the bigger girl, who, in Hraddo said, "She no speak you words. You speak Hraddo, I tell she what you say."

Medwind watched without calling attention to herself. Kirtha, at two, didn't know Hraddo any more than she knew whatever language the Wen kids used among themselves. The Hoos woman was interested in seeing how Kirtha would solve the dilemma of not being understood.

"You gots no shirt," Kirtha said to the older girl, in loud, firm Arissonese.

"Talk Hraddo," the older girl said. "I no talk you words."

"I gots shirt." Kirtha lifted the skirt of her tunic and showed it to both girls. "I gots nice shirt."

All three Wen kids conversed, and the older girl shrugged. "I no understand you talk," she told the child patiently. "You no talk Hraddo, I no talk you talk."

"You take my's shirt," Kirtha said, and pulled her tunic off over her head and handed it to the older Wen girl. "I gots lots."

The Wen girl took the tunic, her eyes wide with surprise. Medwind shared her amazement. Kirtha had never shown any inclination to share — was, in fact, territorial about her possessions to the point of blood-thirstiness.

The girl looked at the tunic, and after a moment's thought, put it on the little Wen kid, saying something vehemently at the same time. The blonde girl looked like she might resist, but, after a glare from the older girl, allowed the foreign clothing to be pulled over her head.

The arms and skirt of the tunic were too short, but the Wen child was terribly thin. It was no tighter on her than it had been on Kirtha, who surveyed the results with evident delight.

"Pretty. Good shirt," she announced, and smiled broadly, and hugged the smallest Wen child, who was still a head and a half taller than her, vigorously. Then, without another word, she strode across the garden — her baggy peasant pants tucked into her little boots; her fiery red hair swinging; bare as the day she was born from the waist up.

Medwind smiled. Kirtha was a constant source of surprises.

She waited until the little girl had banged through the garden door and stomped down the breezeway to the room she shared with her mother. She waited yet another moment until she heard Faia exclaim, "Kirtha, what did you do with your shirt?!"

Then Medwind walked out into the garden.

The Wen kids were instantly on the defensive.

"She no steal that," the older girl said, pointing to the little one. "Red-hair girl give her. You want back?"

"We have more clothes," Medwind said. "You want for you? I give you shirt, pants."

The kids looked at her warily. "Why?" the boy asked.

"You need. I give you."

The two older kids exchanged suspicious glances, and the girl asked, "Why you give?"

Medwind looked at the three scrawny, half-starved kids and said slowly, "Because you need. You want?"

"This is trade? You say give, you mean trade, yes? We

no trade *beck* for shirt. We trade food only. Many many food." The girl crossed her arms over her chest and glared fiercely. The boy, with the First Folk tablet still strapped to his back, hooked his thumbs into the thong that held up his loincloth and nodded his agreement.

Medwind sighed. "Give. I say give, I mean *give*," *you suspicious little brats*, she added silently. "Come," she told them, and went into her *b'dabba*. The kids followed her inside. She knelt and rummaged around in her kit bag, and pulled out two old *staarnes* and two worn pairs of blue-dyed leather breeches — clothes that had seen better days. "Take these," she said, and turned.

The kids weren't looking at her. They were looking, instead, at the huge assortment of drums hanging from the *b'dabba*'s bone struts. They took the clothes she offered, but their eyes never left the dangling instruments. All three of them exchanged whispers, and at last the older girl turned to Medwind. "We touch?" she asked.

So they like drums. "Yes," the Hoos woman said, and watched as they carefully pulled down several of the smaller drums. They exchanged excited comments, pointing out structural details, trying riffs with their fingers, and cocking their heads to listen to the varied sounds. They finally settled on a *shopo*, a tunable drum with a musical, carrying sound. Each of them took turns pattering away on it — irregular Wen drumming exactly like the noises that kept Medwind awake at night.

Let me strike a blow for cultural harmony, she thought. She took the drum away from them, sat cross-legged on a pillow, and said, "No. Play drum this way." She set up an easy four-beat rhythm with her right hand, then added a six-beat rhythm with her left. The drum sang, and the shifting, melding patterns filled the goat-felt hut. When she finished, she handed the drum to the older girl. "You try like that."

The girl stared at her, baffled. "Why? You say nothing. You just make lot noise."

It was Medwind's turn to be bewildered. "What you mean — 'say.' I make music."

The older girl made a deprecating noise through pursed lips and sat with the drum. "This drum talk," she said. "Like this."

"*Tagnu fnaffigglotim — fnaffigchekta hekpeknu.*" She said the words slowly, and drummed an irregular riff.

Medwind caught her breath. She noted similarities in the pattern of the girl's speech and her drumming and formed a theory about the Wen drumming. "Do again," she said.

"*Tagnu fnaffigglotim — fnaffigchekta hekpeknu,*" the girl repeated, pronouncing each syllable precisely. Then she drummed again. Each drumbeat mimicked a syllable of the girl's speech.

Medwind was stunned. She could hear it clearly — things the girl did with her fingers made the drum seem to talk. The mystery of the rhythmless Wen drum concerts was solved. Medwind had been eavesdropping on long-distance conversations and hadn't even known.

"What those words mean?" she asked.

The girl grinned. "I drum-talk — trade drum with you."

"You want drum?"

The skinny kid nodded vigorously. "I want. I trade. It good drum — loud."

"What you trade?" Medwind would have given the kid that drum — it held no particular meaning for her. But she was curious what the kids thought the drum was worth. They had nothing, at least that she had seen, but their First Folk tablet.

And they had already made it clear they weren't taking anything but food — and lots of it — for that.

"I give you shirt," the girl said, offering back the *staarne* Medwind had just given her.

Medwind just barely kept herself from laughing. The situation was both funny and pitiful. The kids had nothing — absolutely nothing. But they wanted that drum.

Medwind pretended to consider the offer. "Why you want drum?" she asked.

"Other *tagnu*, he have us drum. He fall in river. Dead. Drum gone — we need."

Medwind wanted to ask them more about their friend with the drum, but Hraddo simply didn't allow the complexity of real communication. It was a trade tongue, nothing more.

She had an idea. "I trade for drum," she told them. "I make good trade. You teach me drum-talk, I give you drum."

The Wen kids stared at her as if she had started frothing at the mouth and howling at the Tide Mother. They huddled, muttering in their rapid-fire speech, looking up at her from time to time. Finally the girl said, "You trade drum for drum-talk. That right?"

"That right," Medwind agreed.

"What you get for drum?"

Medwind tried to figure out how to explain the value of knowledge in Hraddo and gave up. "I get words," she told them.

"That trade you want?"

"Yes."

"We take — you no change trade, understand?"

Medwind nodded solemnly. "I understand."

"We take." The girl took the drum and handed it to the boy, then shook her head and stared at the Hoos warrior with a worried expression. "You no smart. We get drum. You get nothing."

"I get words," Medwind said. "I need lot words."

Both Wen kids were busy putting on the hand-me-down Hoos garb. They didn't say anything out loud, but their eyes told the Hoos warrior they thought she was out of her mind.

She smiled at them — a reassuring smile. Let them think she was crazy as long as they would. The words were good — understanding the Wen drum speech would be a wonderful asset. But that was nothing compared to the time she'd bought — time for Nokar or her to find out where that tablet came from.

That was even better.

Seven-Fingered Fat Girl, swathed in her peknu clothes, fingered the drum the peknu woman had traded her. It didn't make sense to her that the woman would give her the drum in exchange for words. Nothing that had happened since she walked into the market made sense to her, though.

The old man wanted the tablet — but instead of trading Fat Girl food for it and sending her on her way, he brought her to his house and insisted on feeding her and her tagnu. His mate gave them clothes and good drums and made terrible trades. Fat Girl thought the peknu woman would have starved long ago if she'd had to live by her trading skills.

Fat Girl munched on some *bread* — a peknu food the people of the house kept giving her. She liked it. It filled her stomach, and she looked around, trying to figure out what kind of plant *bread* grew on. She wanted to get some of those plants in trade.

While she munched, she wondered how long it would take to teach the peknu woman drum-talk. She wondered if she could drag it out until the end of the rainy season, so that when she and her tagnu crossed back into the jungle, they could do so without having to fight the swollen, deadly river and the horrible flash-floods.

She decided she could probably count on free food and a place to sleep for at least that long. Anyone stupid enough to trade a perfectly good drum for nothing would take a good long time to learn her nothing.

*   *   *

One cycle of the Tide Mother later, Seven-Fingered Fat Girl was forced to revise her estimate. While the worst of the rains were over, they would still come and go for at least another cycle — but Medwind Song and Faia Rissedote and Nokar Feldosonne were drumming their way intelligibly through simple messages. And they spoke Sropt, the True Language. Not well, but better than Fat Girl had learned their tongue in the same length of time. She could barely understand the demands of little Kirtha, while she suspected the three peknu followed the better part of her conversations with Dog Nose and Runs Slow.

The peknu made her uneasy. She liked them, and this worried her. She sat in Medwind's *b'dabba*, drumming the odd rhythms the peknu woman favored, trying to understand the peknu, and what it was they wanted from her.

Dog Nose peeked into the *b'dabba*. "I want to talk."

Fat Girl nodded toward the cushion not already occupied by Hrogner, the compound's thieving, fire-starting cat.

The boy leaned over on his way past and kissed her, a peknu thing he had learned watching Medwind and Nokar.

She grinned at him and stopped drumming.

"I think we need to trade our *beck* and get away from here," Dog Nose said.

Fat Girl closed her eyes. Her grin died. The journey that lay ahead of them, back through the jungle, through the domain of the Keyu, unrolled in her imagination. She was afraid to go back into that green-roofed hell — more afraid with every day that passed. And the reward at the end of the trail became less tempting as well. The cold, sere city perched atop the mountains waited in her mind's eye. It would be lonely without Spotted Face and Three Scars. There would be no Toes Point In to dance from house to house, telling stories about the pictures on the walls. Laughs Like A Roshi's wild laughter would never fill one of those empty rooms again.

"What if we didn't go back?" she said.

Dog Nose sat back on the pillow and stared at her. "What?"

"I've been thinking." Fat Girl rolled the ends of the drum's hide wrappings through her fingers and stared down at her feet. "We could stay here."

Dog Nose made a disgusted noise. "I knew you were starting to think that. You're getting soft, Fat Girl. You're acting like these peknu will let you stay." He leaned forward, palms pressed flat on the *b'dabba* floor, and stared into Fat Girl's eyes. "The Keyu didn't want you. Your own parents didn't want you. And when these peknu decide they don't want you anymore, either, they will make you go away. You will have forgotten how to live in the jungle, and the Keyu will kill you."

He averted his eyes and whispered, "And then I will be alone."

Seven-Fingered Fat Girl looked down at the drum nestled in her lap. *That's what has been bothering me about the peknu*, she realized. *Something inside me knows they will make me leave — but I didn't want to believe it.* She listened to the noises emanating from the big house. Faia was laughing, telling some story to a man who'd come to buy the things she made. Kirtha yelled, "Medwind! Medwind! Look'a me! I'm tagnu," in her shrill, piping voice, while Medwind said, "Hush, monster. I'm working. And put your shirt back on." Nokar whistled, busy in his workroom.

All the peknu would gather in that same workroom later to trade drum riffs and tall tales with the tagnu. Kirtha would climb on Fat Girl's lap and play with her hair. They both had the same color hair, a coincidence that delighted the peknu child.

Since the day Nokar brought the tagnu to his home from the market, nothing had hunted them. No strange men had chased after them. They had not needed to watch for the traps the jungle set to catch them. They had enough to eat. They could wash themselves in a huge tub of hot water — a privilege Fat Girl found so delightful she'd taken to bathing twice a day. They kept no night watch.

And the peknu were kind to her. Medwind Song, struggling to master the Sropt tongue, told stories of her days as a Hoos warrior and scary tales about the places of the dead. Faia, only a little older than Fat Girl, reminisced about her long-gone village and boys she used to know. Faia understood about Dog Nose and told Fat Girl the secret of not having babies. Fat Girl — thinking of the hardship a baby would be in the mountain city — paid close attention. Nokar gave them sweets and read to them from his *books*. And Kirtha followed them around with a worshipful expression on her face and tried to act just like them.

Dog Nose was right. She was getting soft, and the jungle would eat her if she didn't get out of the peknu place soon.

She sighed and put the drum down. "I'll give the peknu three-four more days to learn drum-talk. Then we'll make our trade and go."

He was naked, and that was even better than she'd imagined it would be the first time she saw him. He stood in front of her mirror working his hair into the banded braids of a saje — still silver-banded, until he earned his graduate degree and his professional robes. Red hair — she liked that red hair — and a scruffy red beard that was still too short and too thin to braid. His beard frustrated Kirgen, and that made Roba laugh.

A million things about their relationship made her laugh — the laughter was warm and tingling, and it bubbled up inside. The month since he'd become her assistant had been a wonder. Roba woke with him at her side every morning, and fell asleep, usually exhausted and sated, with him in her bed at night. Between waking and sleeping, they worked, roved Ariss together — and laughed. In all her life, she'd never had so much fun.

She sat for a long time and watched him dress, liking the freckles on his back and the way his muscles slid over each other when he moved.

"What a shame you have to wear clothes," she said.

His reflection grinned at her from the mirror. He adjusted his robe over the loose shirt and breeches he wore underneath. "I don't think Thirk would forgive me for showing up naked at his big day, even if I did it to please you." He pulled a plain black tabard over his best blue robe — the tabard indicated that he was a graduate of sajery, but black indicated that he was still a graduate student. He'd end up with some terribly gaudy and frightfully meaningful bit of cloth to wear when he was accepted into the Society of Sajes — and like Thirk, he'd probably keep tacking on new ornaments and awards for the rest of his life, until he looked like a whore's junk sale.

Roba shook her head ruefully at the thought and changed the subject. "I'm still surprised how well his paper went over at the Delmuirie Society meeting." Roba got off the bed and went over to fix the back of the tabard, which had gotten twisted when he belted it into place.

"It was supposed to go over well. If you tell a bunch of fanatics the man they adore was secretly the hero who saved the world, of course they're going to believe it. I just can't believe the Delmuirie Society voted to have Thirk present the paper at the Saje Scholars' Conference. The scholars are going to slaughter him."

Roba checked her own reflection in the mirror. The

plain blue leather of her fitted tunic and pants looked nice enough, and the silver bracelets at her wrists and over her baggy blue boots added an elegant touch — but Kirgen was definitely the fancier of the two of them.

She brushed a few fly-away curls into place with annoyance and sighed. "That's as good as it gets, I suppose."

Kirgen laughed. "Don't even start. You look fabulous."

"Do you really think the scholars will tear Thirk apart?"

Kirgen rolled his eyes. "There are two possible reactions. The first is that they'll publicly shred him. The second is that they'll laugh him out of the building."

"No chance they'll just quietly ignore him?"

"You haven't been to a Saje Scholars' Conference before, have you? If any of those guys can get ahead by ripping somebody else to pieces, they'll do it. And with the crackpot theory we cooked up — it will be a bloodbath."

Roba played absently with her bracelets, so that they clinked softly. "I feel guilty about putting that paper together."

"Don't. He asked for it, he put his name on it, and he's going to walk up in front of all those people today and claim he wrote it. He's had plenty of time to go over our sources and see that we only quoted old dead guys and crackpots." Kirgen picked up his staff and wrapped an arm around Roba's waist. "Hells, maybe he'll come to his senses and back out before he presents the paper."

Roba favored him with a derisive snort. "Thirk?!"

"Yeah, well. Not much chance of that, I suppose."

"Not much."

"Maybe he'll be lucky. Maybe there will be somebody there with a paper stupider than his."

Roba raised one eyebrow, but said nothing. She

couldn't imagine a stupider presentation than the one she and Kirgen put together.

The Basin was only about half full when Kirgen transported them in. They arrived in a cloud of green smoke, and Kirgen immediately grabbed Roba's hand and dragged her at a run away from the center of the arena. The two of them climbed the stone risers, found a comfortable seat about midway to the top, and sat down. "The Basin won't be full today, so we might as well get close enough to see the presenters," Kirgen said. "It won't be anything like it was during the Conclave before the Mage/Saje War."

"You were here then?"

"I was a student," Kirgen said. "I was much more involved in that mess that I would have liked to have been."

"Really?" Roba was fascinated. Kirgen had never mentioned having any part in that very-short-lived war. "What did you do?"

But Kirgen didn't answer. Instead, he pointed to a big, brawny, blond man in the most hideous saje attire Roba had ever seen. The robes were an unfortunate mixture of purple, orange, yellow and black. "That's Ruenif Burchardsonne, Speaker of the Assembled Sajes. He's a pretty nice guy, really."

"I'm sure he can't help being color-blind," Roba remarked.

Kirgen laughed. "That robe has the blessing of more than four hundred years of tradition."

"Mmm-hmmm. And it needs all the blessings it can get."

Burchardsonne raised his arms, and the assembled sajes and interested onlookers quieted.

"Welcome to the last day of the annual presentation of papers by members of the Saje Scholars' Conference. Our four scheduled speakers today are Tamridn Dakurst, Otwoch independent scholar, who

will present 'Practical Applications of Nude Spellcast-
ing;' Elin Praniksonne, Tethjan Sajerie, who will
present 'First Folk Artifacts and the Unveiling of the
Current Whereabouts of Their Makers;' Thirk Huddsonne, Prembullin Sajerie, who will present 'The
Delmuirie Disappearance — A New Hypothesis;' and
finally Srokley Outell, Ralledine independent scholar,
presenting 'Seven New Uses for Fifth-Level Smoke
Demons.' "

Kirgen groaned.

"What's the matter," Roba asked.

"It's going to be worse than I thought. I didn't realize
they'd scheduled him for crackpot day."

"Crackpot day?"

"Oh, yes. Every year, there are a few sajes — usually
independent scholars, but sometimes not — whose
papers are just too weird to believe. And the scholarship committee has to let them present their papers —
that's in the rules. But they schedule them all together,
so that the serious scholars don't waste their time. The
audience for this is always the worst one you could
imagine. There will be a couple of guys here who are
serious scholars. They'll stick around so that if there's
anything important in a paper, they can transport out
and get the rest of the saje academics. But the rest of
the sajes here today came for laughs."

"Oh, no."

"Well, it will at least limit serious debate — which in
Thirk's case is a good thing. About the worst thing that
will happen to him is that he'll get a few vegetables
thrown at him."

"The sajes wouldn't do that."

"The sajes would do much worse than that. They
dragged one fellow off the dais and transported him
out and threw him in the Polvene River. He washed
halfway to the swamp before anybody fished him out."

A dumpy Otwoch saje in full provincial ceremonial

garb had taken the stand and was reading his paper in a high, droning voice. Roba tuned him out. She had little interest in nude magic — except, of course, the brand of magic she and Kirgen cooked up.

"So why did they throw the saje in the river?" she asked.

Kirgen leaned close to her and whispered, "He presented a paper on turning women into these historical oddities he called — 'seamaids' . . . 'fishmaids' . . . no, I remember now. 'Mermaids.' He said there was a historical precedent, that the ancient ecology of Arhel actually supported women who were half-woman/ half-fish. He thought we ought to be turning women back into these sea-creatures and restocking the oceans with them."

Roba glanced down at the portly man in the center of the Basin, then back at Kirgen. "Good gods, why?"

"Both the Prembullin sajes and the Tethjan sajes were celibate before the Second Mage/Saje War. The Tethjan sajes still isolate themselves from women — that's one of the reasons you don't have any Tethjan students in your classes. Anyway, I take it women were starting to get on his nerves. He figured if they were all out in the ocean, they couldn't tempt him."

"Thoughtful of him," Roba remarked.

"Not enough sex will do that to a man." Kirgen gave her a cheerful leer. "Brain damage."

Hoots from the audience distracted both of them. The plump saje on the dais was shedding his clothes, evidently preparatory to some sort of demonstration. Immediately, a few ripe redfruits and rotten squashes arced through the Basin. Two landed on target, and the audience laughed and yelled. The saje began redressing in haste.

"That's bad," Kirgen said. "They're hard to get calmed down once they get started. I feel bad for the next reader."

The pro-nudist saje cleared out of the Basin in a puff of sulfurous yellow smoke, and Burchardsonne retook center stage. He waved his arms and waited, and the audience finally gave him attention. "Fellow sajes, honored guests, I ask that you refrain from any such displays of contempt unnecessarily. Please give each speaker a good hearing. Saje Elin Praniksonne will now present his paper. I ask that you give him all due respect."

"That should help," Roba said.

"Not really. Burchardsonne only asked for all due respect. If this reader is as hopeless as the last, the audience will figure a redfruit bath is all the respect he's due."

Roba folded her hands in her lap and looked around at the sajes, many of whom, she now noted, carried bags of produce. "I wish I hadn't dressed up to come to this."

Kirgen nodded. "I know what you mean."

A lean, scowling, dark-visaged saje took center stage and immediately held up a glossy white tablet. The audience started out loud and mocking, still wound up from the last presenter — but they quieted as each person tried to get a good look at the tablet. Then the saje muttered a few words, and the air around the tablet seemed to bend. Each member of the audience was granted the equivalent of a close-up look at the thing he held.

Roba realized that she could suddenly see the details of the tablet perfectly. "Hey," she whispered. "That looks like First Folk script."

"Yes, it does. But I thought First Folk script was only used for inscribing monuments. What's the tablet made of — stone?"

"No — you can see a bit of light through it, but it doesn't look grainy — and the indentations have been pressed, not carved." Roba found the white material of the tablet fascinating. "Pottery of some sort?"

"Maybe," Kirgen agreed, "but I've never seen pottery come close to that degree of whiteness."

The murmurs of the audience told Roba that the rest of the crowd were impressed with the tablet, as well. Perhaps it was a genuine First Folk artifact, she thought. It looked real — although it certainly wasn't like anything scholars had found before.

Multicolored puffs of smoke from around the Basin caught Roba's attention, and she pointed them out to Kirgen.

He nodded. "I told you if anything interesting happened, they'd go get the other saje scholars. This is certainly interesting."

Elin Praniksonne, holding up his artifact down in the center of the Basin, had spotted the smoke, too. He moved aside — prudently, Roba realized. An instant later, the center of the Basin was alive with bearded men in gaudy robes who appeared out of the air in the center of the dais, then ran like the very hells to get out of the way of the next wave of latecomers.

"Sit close," Kirgen said. "It's going to get tight in here."

He was right. Within moments, the Basin was packed. Praniksonne waited for the smoke to clear from the dais, then stepped out in front of the audience again. "Thank you," he said, "for your kind attendance. I apologize for keeping my artifact to myself until this unveiling — I realize I might have gotten a better spot on the program if I had —"

The audience laughed, and he gave them a tight smile and continued.

"I got this book from two First Folk children —"

The noise level rose again in the Basin — this time from gasps of astonishment, disbelief, a few catcalls and scattered shouts of derision.

Praniksonne waved down the shouts. "I confess this sounds unlikely — but I have proofs. I shall now present those proofs."

He began to read from his paper. He described his discovery of three children in Omwimmee Trade who spoke an unknown language, who were all strangely deformed and in the garb of no known people — primitives, he called them. But each carried a tablet, and once he had made himself understood to them, they traded him one of their tablets for a few trinkets and baubles. He then described how, after he gained their trust, they led him into the jungle, and into their village — also primitive, he said, full of deformed lizard-worshipers who shrank back in fear at the sight of someone as tall and straight and healthy as he obviously was.

In the middle of this presentation, Kirgen leaned very close and whispered, "Look at Thirk."

Roba spotted the saje down in front of the assembly. He was frantically scanning the audience — she realized he was looking for them. When his gaze moved in her direction, she began waving.

It took him a moment, but he finally saw her. He crept out of his seat and began climbing over and through the audiences.

Meanwhile, Praniksonne was telling about the lizard-headed monuments he'd found in the jungle — new, just made by the ugly, inbred descendants of the First Folk. He described their degenerate culture, that held only echoes and imitations of its former glory. He described the books — used as plates or building materials, many broken, none read — and he sadly hung his head. "They've lost any memory of the greatness they once had," he said. "And they're destroying the remnants of the ancient First Folk civilization."

Someone asked him, "Saje Praniksonne, how did you survive in the Wen jungle? Is it not death for any not Wen to enter?"

"For any normal human who is not Wen — surely. Even my trip was fraught with perils. But for a saje of my power and skill, those perils can be overcome. You could not think mere primitive could stand against magical power like mine."

Thirk made it to Roba's side. He nodded to Kirgen, then pushed between them and sat down. He leaned close to Roba. "This is it. I can't believe it, but this is confirmation — if we can find that village, and the rest of those tablets, we might be able to find Delmuirie's final resting place. We have to go now."

Roba felt her hands clenching into fists, automatically, as if they weren't a part of her body. "Now as in — when?"

"Right this minute. We have to get to Omwimmee Trade and find someone who knows how to find that village."

Roba was getting a sick feeling in the pit of her stomach. "What about presenting your paper, Thirk?"

Thirk gaped at her. "Are you insane?" he sputtered. "Then everyone will beat a path to the jungle — and I want to get there first."

"No —" Roba said, shaking her head. "No — no, I don't think so. You should go ahead and present —"

"No. We have to go."

"But what about my students?" She heard her voice developing a whining edge that she didn't like, but she seemed powerless to stop it. "What about my *job*?"

"I hired you — and they'll find a sub for your students. When we get back — after we've found that village, and vindicated Delmuirie's name, you'll be able to have any job you want. This is the proof that your paper was right, Roba. Proof!"

"No. Oh, no," Roba whispered.

☿ Chapter 6

It took a full day for Roba, Kirgen, and Thirk to gather supplies for an extended jungle expedition; Roba loathed shopping for rugged clothes, ugly snakeproof boots and light-but-tasteless no-spoil foods. She hated paying rent and apartment protection in advance. She despised leaving her classes. She abhorred the idea of abandoning a perfectly good civilized city for someplace that wouldn't have hot and cold water or Ralledine restaurants.

That day was followed by another full day spent flying in an unscheduled airbox to get from Ariss to Omwimmee Trade. Roba spent most of the airbox trip looking out the glassed-in side at the changing cloud-terrain beneath, wishing she could have thought of some compelling reason for not going. Kirgen, in the seat facing hers, slept. Thirk, beside her, fidgeted and wrote notes to himself and referred incessantly to the paper she and Kirgen had concocted.

Thirk was excited, tense, and frequently chatty. "Praniksonne will be able to transport," he fretted. "Even if his expedition left after us, they'll still get there before us."

"Those tablets have waited out the Purges, the wars and the gods only know what else." Roba pulled her gaze away from the window. "They'll wait for you. Besides, Praniksonne can't possibly suspect another group will go after that First Folk site." *Why should he,* she thought. *He's the first person in recorded history to cross into the Wen Territory and live to tell about it.* She hoped to the gods he wouldn't be the last.

"I don't care about the tablets," Thirk snapped. "I care about finding Delmuirie's final resting place — and vindicating him and winning him the respect history owes him."

Roba pressed her cheek against the cool, wavy glass and closed her eyes. *I'd be happy to know we were going to survive.*

"Praniksonne is going to subvert this whole thing to his own ends," Thirk muttered.

Focusing an expedition on actual scholarship instead of your personal obsession — now that's an interesting definition for subversion, Thirk. Roba sighed. With her eyes still closed, she said, "Well, at least the two of you aren't fighting for the same discoveries."

"No. But I want to be able to make mine first. I don't want the important discovery buried under a mound of trivia."

Trivia, he calls it. It galls him the way the scholars flocked around Praniksonne — the way they made much over him, and ooohed and ahhhed his discovery. It infuriates him that they begged and pleaded to accompany the great man into the jungle, to be present at his find — that they would not take "no" for an answer, even when he warned them again and again of the dangers. He knows the scholars would have made no such clamor over his paper — not even if he'd marched Delmuirie himself in front of them.

Roba forced herself to breathe deeply and regularly and pretended sleep. She knew there was no way she could actually sleep — her multitude of falsehoods, hanging over her head like storm-filled clouds, left her stomach churning. The pending Delmuirie fiasco was going to destroy her career. Thirk would come to his senses and realize the sources she and Kirgen had used to create their "Delmuirie Disappearance Hypothesis" were nothing but ludicrous old myths . . .

. . . She would be publicly discredited and removed

from her position, Kirgen would be thrown from the University . . .

. . . And Kirgen . . . what about him? Thirk didn't realize the two of them were living together. He wouldn't approve — he had made his own interest in Roba clear from the time he hired her . . .

. . . Worrying about the theory or her future or Thirk's reaction to Kirgen were all wastes of time. None of that would matter. She was going to die in the jungle, along with Kirgen and Thirk and all her hopes for the future. None of the three of them had any idea where the First Folk site was — and Praniksonne wasn't going to tell . . .

. . . But if they did make it to the First Folk site, Thirk would *kill* her. He wasn't going to find Delmuirie — what he was likely to find was Delmuirie had never been anywhere near the First Folk site. . . .

Thirk, Kirgen, Delmuirie, the First Folk, the jungle, the University, humiliation, exposure, despair, death. With her mind looping endlessly around its multiple tracks of worry, Roba fell into exhausted, nightmare-ridden sleep.

The Keyu stirred and roused with sudden intensity — their thought-voices snapped Choufa out of deep slumber.

<*Coming — something coming for us (ME) us we want it wantitwant! Peknu is it peknu yesssss! Peknu (BRING IT HERE) we must call it (HUNGRY) I/we are all we are so yesssss! HUNGRY!*>

The thoughts slid greasily through her mind, not aimed at her — not, she suspected, intended for her. Perhaps the Keyu didn't know she could hear them whenever they spoke. Would they hurt her — eat her — if they knew? *What is out there?* She wondered. *What could they want so much?* She shivered, feeling pity for whatever it was.

The Keyu clamored. <*Falling we must make it fall (I WANT IT) bring yesssss! bring it here I/we want *no, send it away* what?! (FOOD — DO NOT SEND FOOD AWAY). Ignore don't mind that one that one — it is stupid new it is new is new here. Wait listen I hear they fall them falling (YESSSSS! NOW SEND THE BEASTS) oh, yesssss! the beasts *not them* the beasts can bring will bring them to us can *no the beasts will eat them* catch them for us.*>

Choufa shuddered. She hated the Keyu and hated being privy to their hungry, hateful, nasty thoughts. Her gods were evil gods, who set their monsters to bring down people — who hungered for the death of people.

Not people — She corrected herself. *The Keyu hunt pekņu. Nothings. I should not worry about them.*

And then the irony of that ingrained habit of thought struck her, and she bit her lip. She was a nothing. Sharsha were as low as pekņu but trapped in tighter bonds.

And then the thought-voices of the Keyu clamored in excitement, overriding her own thoughts. Unable to fend the Keyu off, she became absorbed in the thrill of their hunt.

<*Here they are they come are coming (BRING THEM INTO THE CIRCLE) the beasts chase they run chase them into chase into the circle, YESSSSS! they run, closer they are coming closer I want we want (SEND THEM HERE) one for me/we want I WANT *no don't eat them* I hunger we hunger give us one!*>

There were no pictures in Choufa's mind — there were only the words, the slippery, whispery, everywhere voices of the Keyu and the sense of something being forced toward the hungry trees that squatted in their deadly circle. She could feel their guiding thoughts, that drove the beasts in the jungle to chase the pekņu-who-were-food. She could almost understand — could almost feel through her fingers and toes (branches and leaves?) — the manner whereby she could drive the beasts herself. The sensation tingled through her body, and then the beasts gave the peknu into the hands of the Silk People, and the minds of the outlanders fell silent.

When, later, to the pounding thunder of the drums, the Silk People offered up the wakened captives to the Keyu, the anguish of their embrace — mind-screaming bone-shattering flesh-rending horror — ripped Choufa into and out of treemind trance and left her shivering and scared on the branchwoven floor of the sharsha tree.

Medwind, Nokar, and Seven-Fingered Fat Girl sat to dicker. The faced each other across the broad table in the public room — behind Fat Girl stood Dog Nose and Runs Slow. Behind Medwind, Faia and Kirtha waited.

Medwind was prepared for a big argument between Nokar and the kids — she knew they wanted a lot for their tablet, and after all they'd been through, she wanted them to get it. Nokar, however, was infamously tight with his trades. She would have preferred to handle the trading, but Nokar said he was the one they'd been looking for, he was the one who had spent years archiving the First Folk reference collection in Faulea's library, and *he* was going to be the one to dicker.

Medwind didn't trust him. He had about him the air of a man hiding something — and he wouldn't even tell her what.

So they waited, with the tension at the table growing.

"We trade this *book*. What you trade?" Fat Girl opened in Hraddo.

"I have come ready to offer you wonderful things," Nokar smiled and said in the girl's language.

Medwind realized that by dickering in the girl's own language, Nokar had won a tactical point — *he* could use a different tongue to discuss details of the deal with his colleagues, but Fat Girl had no fall-back language.

The old man continued. "I'll give you two bags of grain, two bags of sweet-roots, and a bag of journeybread."

"*WHAT?!*" the Wen kids yelled.

Medwind turned to him and, in Huong Hoos, a language that, of those present, only they spoke, muttered, "Are you crazy? That's *nothing*, Nokar. That tablet is worth a hundred times that, and you know it. And they know it."

"Yes, of course," Nokar murmured, also in Hoos. "How thoughtless of me."

Seven-Fingered Fat Girl stood. "You are trying to steal from us," she said. "We will take our *book* to someone else."

Nokar switched to the girl's language. "Medwind tells me I have offered you not enough. So I will pay you two tens-of-tens bags of grain, two tens-of-tens bags of sweet-roots, and one ten-of-tens bags of journeybread."

"Saje god and demons," Medwind muttered in Hoos. "Now you're going to break us."

Fat Girl sat down and smiled. "That is better." She looked to her colleagues, and they smiled, too. "We also want the secret of the dirt-trick, which you must show us, and some of the magic dirt that makes food grow."

"Of course," Nokar agreed. "How many bags of the magic dirt do you want?"

The three Wen kids huddled, and Fat Girl came back to the table a moment later. "We have to feed us for the cold season in the mountains. So you tell us how much food one bag of magic dirt makes."

Medwind told them, "You could grow enough tare-grain from one bag to last you a season — and tare-grain stores well. That goes for beets and onions and calley, too."

"Then we want ten bags of magic dirt," Fat Girl said.

Nokar told them "fine" before Medwind could even begin to dicker. "So do we have a trade?"

The Wen kids looked at him warily. They conferred again. "Yes," Fat Girl agreed when she returned to the table. "We will trade."

"Good." Nokar rose. "Then we trade you five tens-of-tens of food and ten bags of magic dirt here tomorrow. How you going to carry it all?"

The kids stared at each other, then at the old man. They wore horrified expressions.

Nokar crossed his arms over his chest and said, "I no think you and Dog Nose carry more than two bags of food at one time. Little Runs Slow maybe — maybe — carry one. Even then, you no can run very fast."

"But that is not enough for our *book*." Fat Girl stood again. Her eyes shone with unshed tears. "We must have *much* food — we must so that we can go to our city —"

Her eyes widened as she realized what she'd said.

Nokar didn't let the comment pass. "City?" he asked. "You no say anything about city. You say Silk People throw you out of their villages. You say you live on paths between, and no have any home. So what city?"

Fat Girl's face went gray. "There is no city," she said.

Medwind felt her heart beginning to race. Fat Girl was lying. "What city, Seven-Fingered Fat Girl?" she added in Sropt. "Did you find tablet in city?" Over the past month, the kids had neatly changed the subject anytime the question of the origin of the tablets came up. They wouldn't say whether there were any more tablets, or how they found those. When questioned, they suddenly couldn't understand a word anyone said to them, or they looked off into space, or remembered a word of drum speech they hadn't taught yet, or noticed Kirtha or Runs Slow doing something they weren't supposed to. They'd guarded their secret for all they were worth.

A city — Medwind thought. Her heart pounded wildly. *That's quite a secret to hang onto.*

"Is it a city made of stone?" Nokar asked. "Does it have stone monsters in it? Some buildings shaped — like so?" He described a dome with his fingers — put into Sropt his descriptions of the only First Folk artifacts anyone had ever found before.

The Wen kids stared at each other, then at the old man. They wore their shock on their faces.

That's it! Medwind thought and clenched her hands together under the table.

"It is exactly as you say." Seven-Fingered Fat Girl hung her head. "I didn't know you knew the city. I thought only we knew it."

Medwind Song and Nokar exchanged glances. In Hoos, he said, "They've found one, Med. They've found an actual First Folk city." And to Fat Girl, he said, "Yes, we know this place. Tell me, how many other *books* you find there?"

Fat Girl looked at him and shrugged. "Tens of tens of tens. Too many to count. We were going to keep trading them. We would have been very rich."

Medwind thought her heart was going to pound out of her chest. "A library, Nokar," she whispered in Hoos. "They sound like they've found a library."

Medwind saw Nokar's fingers grip the table edge. His knuckles turned white, but his voice stayed calm. "I offer different trade, then," he said. His Sropt was slow and careful. "You take us to city and show us *book* place. In trade, we carry your trade goods to city, and we teach you work dirt-trick to grow food. We stay in city, and you stay in city — there place enough for all you and us. What you say?"

For several moments, no one said anything. Fat Girl did not confer with the other Wen. She merely sat very still, staring at her hands. Then she took a deep breath, and looked up, and slowly nodded her agreement.

* * *

The airbox landed outside the massive log palisades
of Omwimmee Trade. While Roba and Kirgen got out
and stood ankle-deep in the mud and unloaded their
supplies, Thirk started giving directions.

"We're going to spread out and find out what we can
about First Folk who've come in to trade. I'll take the
indoor market. Kirgen, you take the outdoor market.
Roba, why don't you come with me?" He gave her a
broad, encouraging smile.

Roba noted the smile, and caught the deeper
implications immediately. Thirk figured with Kirgen
occupied elsewhere, he could cozy up to her. She shook
her head. "I have a friend who lives here now — the
Huong Hoos woman I told you about once. I'm going
to stop in and visit her —"

"You want to waste our time paying social calls?"
Thirk's expression changed to disbelief, then became
barely contained fury. "Praniksonne will beat us to the
find!"

Roba glared him down. "We've discussed Praniksonne as much as I want to. Medwind Song lives here
— maybe she's heard something. Besides, I haven't
seen her in years. I'm not coming all this way and then
not even stopping to say hello."

Thirk snarled into his beard and turned his back on
her.

From inside the palisade, a single bell began to ring,
calling the hour before *nondes*.

Kirgen came up beside her and smiled. "Nothing
compared to the pandemonium in Ariss, is it?"

Roba picked up her travel pack and slung it over her
shoulder. With one finger, she activated the airfloat that
carried the rest of her supplies and beckoned for it to
follow her. "I'd prefer the pandemonium," she
remarked.

Kirgen looked surprised and a little hurt. "Don't let

him upset you. Go visit your friend — and cheer up. This could be fun."

"This would be fun if somebody besides Pranik-sonne had ever made it out of the jungle alive."

Kirgen shrugged. "I'll bet people do it all the time — but nobody thinks to mention it." He sighed. "Hell, Roba, it's a forest. Trees, you know? What could possibly be so threatening about that?"

Tromping through the town on her own, trying to find either Fair Road or North Street, or especially the place where Fair Road met North Street, where Medwind said the house was, she decided Kirgen was probably right. It seemed ludicrous that people would live so close to a jungle — surely full of game animals and wild fruits — and never, ever, go in it. The tales of the inviolate Wennish jungles were probably distortions, like the unbelievable stories she'd heard spread about herself when she became one of the first mages to take a teaching position in a saje university. That exchange program had fostered some ludicrous tales — but experience had proven the truth to her doubting students. Things were rarely as strange as people made them out to be.

She smiled and relaxed a bit.

The houses had ceased to be rush-walled slums a block or so back. Now, trudging through heavy drizzle along the ludicrously named Fish Street, she noticed that the buildings were becoming distinctly good. They were large and sturdy, and looked warm and inviting with the yellow glow of lamps and a few ghostlights spilling out onto the streets. She found Fair Road, figured out which way north would be, and turned to her right, hoping that whoever had named the streets had a practical mind.

He had. North Street was the last one before the town backed up against the palisade again. The house directly in front of her, a colossal white one-story with tall, gabled, thatched roofs, had two massive, carved, wood gates. On one of them hung a sign painted in six languages.

The sign said:

"Qualified, Certified-Safe Magics — Guarding, Transporting, and Livestock Our Specialties. Also Historical Research. We Buy Books! Private and Group Lessons Watterdaes. NO LOVE SPELLS!!!"

"Livestock?" Roba muttered. "What by the gods have they come to, mucking about with livestock?" She rapped on the carved stone knocker and listened to the crash that echoed inside. *That doorknocker would drive me insane,* she thought. *I don't know how Medwind stands it.*

She waited, with the rain pissing merrily on her head. It was picking up force; she half-suspected this was because the bloody weather knew she was stuck out in it. She gritted her teeth and stuck her hands into the pockets of her travel cape and determined not to notice.

After a moment, she heard footsteps coming toward her. "Coming, coming," someone yelled, and then a small door inside the gate flew open, and Roba confronted the oldest living human being she'd ever seen. He was a saje, with fabulous long white braids bound in gold. He had his official robes on — evidently he'd been working. She looked at his chest for the usual ribbon-salad of awards, guilds and other frippery the sajes loved to confer on each other and was surprised to discover the busy mess wasn't there. Where it would have been, the old man wore a single featureless onyx sphere, circled with a narrow rim of smooth yellow gold.

Roba had been in the saje side of Ariss long enough to recognize *that* award. It was the *Eye of the Infinite* — the highest, and rarest, award the sajerie offered. Roba had been given to understand that the only plane of existence higher than "Wearer of the Eye" was god —

and not one of the minor demi-gods, either.

The old man grinned at her. "You're wet," he said.

"It's raining."

"Yes, it is. But you're a mage — why the hell are you wet?" He was still grinning — and standing in the rain, she was still getting wetter.

"I'm wet because it's raining."

The old man laughed, and did something, and suddenly, standing there in the pouring, rapidly-becoming-sheeting rain, she wasn't wet anymore. "See?" he asked. "If you don't want to be wet, just think dry." He moved out of her path and beckoned her inside.

He looked up at her from under his bushy brows, and his expression became mysterious. The pitch of his voice rose, while he stared through and beyond Roba, and his eyes half-closed, and he began to rock slightly from side to side. "Roba, mage, you have come to visit Medwind Song. Your mission takes you far from your home. Your two friends should have come with you, though. I suspect we could have found for them the things they sought."

Roba felt chillbumps rising on her body — neither from the rain nor the weather nor from anything else of the sort. The old man was scary.

"Ummm, yes," she agreed. "So, ah, is Medwind here?"

She stepped past him, into the huge public room, and realized that one solitary room was bigger than her entire apartment. The whitewashed plaster walls and soaring ceiling that rose into a dark tangle of mortise-and-tenoned beams and roof thatching would have been cozy in a smaller place. *Like home*, she thought and shook her head. But in this place, they were rather grand. Primitive, but grand.

Then she heard other, faster footsteps in the passage. *Good*, she thought. *Maybe somebody normal* — A moment later, she confronted an ageless, fierce-looking Hoos woman with ice-blue eyes and glossy white hair. Roba thought, *Her face is so young, but . . .*

A trick of the stranger's movement caught her attention, and Roba gasped. "Medwind?"

The Hoos woman grinned. "None other. But you needn't look so surprised. You've changed as well, Roba Morgasdotte."

"If I've changed so much, why did you recognize me?"

"I know only two women with your height. The other lives here. With those odds, I had a fair chance of being right. So, what brings you to the backwater hells of Omwimmee Trade? I thought you'd sworn never to leave the comforts of civilization again."

Roba laughed. "I fell among evil companions who led me astray."

Medwind linked arms with her. "As have I. This is my husband, Nokar Feldosonne, once Chief Librarian of Faulea University, now out in the sticks hedge-wizarding for love of me. He seduced and corrupted me."

Roba had barely enough time to nod politely before Medwind was dragging her back through the house. Her old roommate's last line finally registered on her ear when the two of them were halfway along an enormous breezeway. She stopped and looked at her one-time roommate and snorted. "*He* seduced and corrupted *you*? What about those nine young husbands you were forever going on about when we roomed together — and the men you used to sneak into the room, and — ?"

Medwind waved Roba's objections away with a delicate sweep of her hand. "*I* seduced and corrupted *them*. There is a difference. It's subtle, but it's there."

Roba laughed. "Ah, Medwind, yours is like the tale of the randy bellmaker seduced by the village virgin — very little rings true." She chuckled and leaned on her friend's arm. "You are as full of bilge as you ever were."

"Very possibly," Medwind agreed, and grinned, and opened a door. "This is the workroom. Best room in the house for just visiting, as far as I'm concerned. Have a seat."

Roba dropped herself cross-legged onto a large, soft cushion, and sighed. "So what in the hells happened to your hair? I swear you look younger now than you did when we roomed together — but last I saw you, your hair was black as the inside of a demon's heart."

Medwind arched an eyebrow at her. "Interesting analogy — I'll try not to take it personally." She sat on another cushion, and shrugged. "I went Timeriding — it has some side effects. This," she brushed a hand through her hair, "was one of them. A bit of physical un-aging was another."

Roba was fascinated. "I heard a rumor of your Timeride. You were involved in the Second Mage/Saje War. You went over to the saje side of the city . . . there was some talk at the time of you being a traitor."

Medwind leaned back on several extra pillows. "Indeed. To some of my colleagues, feelings ran deeper than talk. After that brief war was over, I found it easier to leave Ariss. I feared the Council might decide to try and sentence me — it was easier to go voluntarily into unofficial exile. I didn't mind too much. Unlike you, I never had any great love for the City of Fogs and Bogs." She gave Roba a bemused smile. "That's why I never understood why you left after you took your master's. I know the mages would have found a teaching spot for you — probably even reserved you a room in their tower."

Roba smiled and stroked a cat that climbed up on her lap. "I stayed with city life. I didn't want to teach; I didn't want that responsibility. I wanted to be free to spend all my time learning — so I accepted a position as a civic mage down in Braxille. I lived in the archives at night."

"Gods, Braxille's not a city. It's an iceberg!"

"If you spend all your time indoors, it doesn't matter."

Medwind gave her friend a disbelieving laugh. "I suppose not. Still, I think I'd rather be dead than in Braxille."

"Ah, yes." Roba nodded wisely. "The motto of the Fisher Province. I think they've even stamped it on the money now." She grinned and shrugged. "Anyway, I did get tired of the cold and the dark. For about the last year, I've worked on the saje side of Ariss, teaching mage history and historical mage-applications of magic. I've pulled a lot from the Fishers, and a lot from Daane University — and besides, it's one mighty library that old man of yours left behind in Faulea."

Medwind leaned forward, curiosity stamped on her face. "And that brings us to what you're doing here, in the far reaches of hot, steaming nowhere."

"Ask your husband. He knew my name, how I got here, why I'd come — he's very, very good at farsight. And very spooky."

Medwind sputtered and inexplicably threw herself back on her pile of pillows. She was laughing, Roba realized — silent convulsions that became big, gasping roars of laughter. Tears rolled down the Hoos woman's cheeks. "Nokar good at farsight!" she howled. "Nokar — good — at farsight!"

Roba leaned forward and told her old friend, crisply and with cold precision, "That was what I said. Would you mind letting me in on the joke?"

Medwind caught her breath and made herself quit laughing. Wiping tears from her eyes, she said, "Nokar couldn't farsee past the end of his nose. He bribes the town urchins to bring him news — pays them in sweets and the occasional copper rit. They come running up to the window of his workroom and tell him anything they think he'll be interested in — every once in a while, they even bring something he can use. But then, when he thinks he'll get away with it, he does this big farcical mystical act —"

Roba remembered her awe of the old man. She wasn't convinced by Medwind's denial of his talent. "He fooled me."

"Yeah, well — he's had lots of practice. He has the fishermen around here so nervous they tack trinkets on our gate before they go out to sea, thinking to appease the mighty magician Nokar with them."

"But," Roba protested, "he wears the Eye of the Infinite. He must be brilliant to have earned that."

Medwind sighed and scooted back to an upright position. "He's one hell of a fine librarian," she agreed. "Superb researcher, too. Pretty decent linguist. And he can transport himself and a roughly equal mass simultaneously without ending up in the middle of solid objects —" The Hoos woman shrugged and made a dismissive gesture. "That's about it."

Roba wanted to be more impressed. "He can keep rain off someone."

"So can a rainjacket."

Roba gave up. Obviously, she had been duped. "All right. So — I was suckered, and I was spied upon by snot-nosed village kids."

"So you were. It happens." Medwind tossed her rows of braids back out of her face. Her pale eyes flashed and the dangling bit of gold she wore in her nose jingled. "And still you haven't told me what you're doing in this hole at the end of the universe."

"Chasing after frogs by trying to walk on water, I suspect."

Medwind laughed. "That sounds frustrating."

"Mmmm-hmmm. Worse, since I suspect all I'm going to get out of the ordeal is a soaking — a soaking, I might add, I richly deserve."

Roba quickly told Medwind about Thirk's fascination

with Edrouss Delmuirie and her decision to join the Delmuirie Society so she could get a desperately needed raise, and finally, about the fiasco with the cobbled-together hoax of a new Delmuirie theory she and her young lover had devised. As she described Praniksonne and the tablet, however, and the events that led up to her hurried flight to Omwimmee Trade, she sensed a shift in Medwind's mood. It only made sense, she supposed. Medwind had always had a place in her soul reserved for ancient history, just like Roba. It was part of the reason they'd remained friends.

But Medwind was suddenly on her feet. "Pranik-sonne," she muttered. "I don't know that name, but —" Her attention shifted to Roba. "Come look at this," she said, and beckoned Roba to a workstand draped with cloth. "Is this anything like what you saw?" She pulled the cloth back, and Roba looked.

The University instructor felt the world beginning to shift and spin around her. The tablet lay gleaming and white, seemingly suffused with a light of its own, impressed deeply with the First Folk script. She reached out and stroked it lightly, almost afraid, at first, that it might crumble to powder at her touch. It was cool and smooth and beautiful. It looked newly made, but had about it the feel of great, patient age. "Yes," she whispered. "That's it. So you also have found these deformed offspring of the First Folk? You have seen the things Praniksonne spoke of?"

She knew she sounded hopeful and probably childish in her yearning after the things of another time. But she couldn't help it. Perhaps Thirk Huddsonne was leading her on a fool's race — but that didn't change for a moment the fact that there were *real* wonders to be found at the end of the race.

Medwind shook her head, though, in firm negation. "That isn't what we found at all." She grinned then, and in that grin, Roba could see the bared fangs of a hunter.

"Praniksonne lied. He stole that tablet. I have the kids who brought both of them out of the jungle here in my house." The Hoos woman's grin became broader, wilder — Medwind's teeth flashed in the reflected light, and Roba saw traces of the barbarian and the warrior the Hoos had once been. "And I hope that when the sajes find out Praniksonne stole that tablet and lied to them, they rope him to the bell tower at midday and set fire demons to dancing under his skin."

"Could happen," Roba muttered.

Softly, Medwind added, "We have everything ready — we're going after the *real* city of the First Folk in the morning. You were planning on going into the jungle anyway — do you want to come with us?"

There was no question in Roba's mind but that she would be going along..

Seven-Fingered Fat Girl twisted an end of the heavy braided belt she'd tied around her waist. She knelt inside Medwind Song's *b'dabba* beside Dog Nose and Runs Slow and Kirtha. Dog Nose was tense and unhappy.

"They're going to take our city away from us. It won't be our place anymore — it will be their place, and when they get tired of us, they'll make us leave."

"No," Fat Girl said. "We told them it was our city — that we would let them come to the *book* place, but they could not stay. They agreed." She leaned closer to Dog Nose, her body taut with the uncertainty she felt. "They *promised*."

"And what is that worth? — the promise of peknu. As much as the promises of the Silk People, who say they will trade us good silks for the meat we bring, and then trade us dyed ragcloth?"

Fat Girl made a rude noise. "These are not the Silk People."

Dog Nose sat straighter. His face was angry, his lips

tight. "You are our fat. Your word is our word — the word of Four Winds Band. But, Seven-Fingered Fat Girl, remember that your life rests with us as ours does with you." He stared pointedly at her maimed left hand, and forced her to recall the debt she owed him. "Remember who your band is."

He stood and stalked out of the *b'dabba*.

Kirtha looked at Seven-Fingered Fat Girl and Runs Slow with concern. "Dog Nose mad at?" she asked in Arissonese.

Fat Girl bit her lip and nodded to the little girl. In the peknu tongue, she said, "Dog Nose mad at. It not matter. His mad go away."

"*Kyadda*," Kirtha said, crossing her tiny arms over her chest.

Fat Girl winked at the little girl and forced herself to smile. "*Kyadda*," she agreed. That was a Hoos word, one that Fat Girl had picked up quickly. It meant "everything is as it should be." With Dog Nose angry at her, she didn't see how everything could be fine — but Kirtha looked happier thinking it was.

Runs Slow and Kirtha raced out of the *b'dabba* to play in the garden — Fat Girl sat in the lonely goat-felt tent after they were gone and drummed softly. Maybe she had been wrong to lead her tagnu away from the Paths. Maybe their villages would have started giving them better trades. Perhaps, if she had stayed, the rest of her tagnu would still be alive.

Were these new people, these peknu, her friends? — or were they, like all the people she'd ever known (except her tagnu, she thought), just waiting for a chance to take away from her whatever little bit of goodness she got for herself?

She quit drumming and rested her face in her hands. How could she know what was right? she wondered. How could she be sure she made the right choices? She had no answers.

* * *

Choufa sat in the swaying upper branches of the sharsha tree with several of the older girls. With their mottled green-on-tan skins, they blended into their surroundings like jungle snakes and hunting hovies; they lurked high in the treetops, imagining sending down deadly thunderbolts on the Silk People they hated.

The air was cool, the sun was setting — visible for a few moments under the heavy clouds, and the girls were as somnolent as the just-fed Keyu. Choufa swung her legs off the branch and chewed on a leaf stem.

Thedra, a much older girl, whose hair fell to her shoulders, and whose belly was round as a marshmelon, pointed down at a Silk Woman who walked on the dirt below them. "I can make her drop that basket," Thedra said.

Choufa was surprised. "Really? By shouting at her?"

"No. Watch." Thedra pointed one slim finger at the woman, and closed her eyes.

Choufa could suddenly "hear" Thedra, the same way she could hear the Keyu. The girl was telling the basket to fall, as the Keyu had told the jungle beasts to drive the peknu toward them. She seemed to be touching the Keyu with her mind — for a moment, she seemed to be one with the Keyu. Choufa "saw" how she did it and wondered if she could do the same.

And the basket fell. The fruits, gifts of the Keyu to their people, splatted into the dirt or rolled away in all directions — and the girls up in the branches laughed softly.

"Oh, that was good," Maari said. "How did you do that?"

"She talked to the Keyu," Choufa said. "Didn't you hear her?"

"No." Maari, a stocky girl with stubby black hair, shook her head. "That isn't the thing I can do."

Thedra said, "Most of the time, I wish I couldn't talk to them, either."

"Me, too." Choufa wrinkled her nose. "They think awful things. They ate all those peknu —"

"*Peknu*," Maari snorted. "It could have been worse. It could have been us."

"It will be us," Thedra said, her voice flat and hard. She grimaced and pressed her hand to her belly, and Choufa, fascinated, watched ripples roll across the tight-stretched skin.

"The baby — ?" she asked.

"It *kicks*," Thedra said.

"Leth put a baby in my belly," Choufa offered.

Maari shook her head. "You haven't been here long enough to be sure."

"What do you mean?"

"You have to miss your bleeding to be sure — do you bleed yet?"

Choufa felt her stomach turn. "Do I do *what*?!" She thought of all the awful things that had happened to her — apparently there were a few she'd missed. "I *don't* do that! I don't want to, either."

Thedra laughed. "It doesn't have anything to do with the Silk People. You just have to do it before you can make a baby — so you probably don't have one in your belly yet. It's not so bad." She looked down at her own round stomach and sighed. "I wish I hadn't gotten one so fast. As soon as you have it, *they* take you away and feed you to the trees."

Choufa bit her lip. "Are you sure?"

"I can hear the trees."

"I didn't believe the Silk People when they said they let us go after we had babies," Choufa admitted. "What are you going to do?"

Thedra's laugh was flat and lifeless. "What can I do? Tell the trees not to eat me? I think the reason they want us is because some of us can talk to them."

"Why do they want me?" Maari asked. "I can't talk to them."

Thedra rocked on her branch, rubbing her fingers in round circles on her stomach. "I think I know," she said slowly. "There is a — a kind of fuzzy feeling — I get from each of us sharsha. When I close my eyes and 'look' at one of us, I can see a sort of glow — and I can't see it from any of the Silk People. I think the glow is what the trees want."

"Oh!" Choufa shook her head in admiration. "How did you think of all of that?"

"I didn't." Thedra pressed her lips in a thin line. "My best friend, Larria, noticed the glow first. I think she was the best of all of us at seeing that."

"Larria?" Choufa thought hard. "I haven't met her yet."

"You won't." Thedra looked away. "They fed her to the damned trees. I heard them do it."

Choufa saw the tears that glittered down the other girl's cheeks. "There has to be some way we can get out of here," she said. "There just has to be."

"No one ever has before."

"Well, I'm going to find a way," Choufa said. "That's what *I'm* going to be best at."

Thedra looked back at the younger girl. Her eyes gleamed with tears waiting to fall. "If you do, Choufa —" She paused, and looked down at her swollen belly and pressed her lips together.

Choufa waited, but the other girl remained silent. "What?" she finally asked.

"Do it soon. That's all. Just do it soon."

Roba saw the two of them halfway down the street, waiting for her at the main entrance to the indoor market. Thirk scowled. His arms crossed tightly over his chest, except when he gave in to quick outbursts of visible temper and pounded on the market's doorframe. Kirgen stood as far from Thirk as he could, pretending not to know him.

Oh, no, she thought. *What now?*

They spotted her walking toward them in the deepening gloom and both charged into the thin drizzle to meet her.

"Praniksonne's been here and gone," Thirk snarled, "and took every great saje and scholar he could lay finger to with him."

"It doesn't matter," Roba told him, but he ignored her.

"They transported in yesterday morning — *yesterday morning!* —picked up supplies and a convoy of flying carpets and took off before the sun was even fully up. He had Telrondsonne with him, and Mards from Dumforst — both of the Ralledine Bentlee's — Craysonne — gods, the list reads like a dream guest list for the Sajerie's Condrene Awards." Thirk's fist smacked into the open palm of his other hand as he talked, over and over again. "That robe-kissing Tethjan bushsaje in the market nearly bepissed himself telling me about it. *He* wasn't invited. He wasn't mighty enough."

"It doesn't matter," Roba said again.

"By the cursed bell of Conclave, woman, it *does* matter! How can it not matter? He has every brilliant mind in or out of Ariss drooling over his expedition — and who do we have on ours? The three of us. *How* can we get any respect with an expedition like that?"

Roba smiled, feeling very like the cat who gobbled the goldfish. "Praniksonne lied," she said. "He stole the tablet and led 'the most brilliant minds in or out of Ariss' on a giant snark hunt. When they find out, they'll have his hide for shoeleather."

Kirgen gasped. "You jest!" he whispered.

Thirk gaped. "It can't be. He had the tablet. He confirmed our theories."

Roba sauntered. She swaggered. She wished she

could think of a particularly noxious way of rubbing Thirk's nose in her discovery. She decided blunt was best. "I found the people who found the tablet. They are setting out for the true ruins of a First Folk city in the morning. We're invited."

"How — how — ?!" Thirk stuttered to a halt.

"The kids who found the tablet are living with my old roommate and her husband — who just happens to be a wearer of the Infinite Eye." *How's that for important?* she thought. "I told her I was traveling with two sajes. She said if we pack our own supplies, and the two of you help transport the trade payment for the kids once we get there, all three of us can go along."

All the way to Medwind's house, Roba couldn't help but notice that Thirk kept repeating, "Praniksonne lied. Praniksonne *lied.*" He varied that with, "His credibility is *gone* — hayh!"

Nokar met them at the door, and Kirgen, an expression of disbelief on his face, said, "Sir! I was led to believe you'd died in the war! I haven't seen you since — well, since the swamp."

Roba stared at her young lover, startled. Nokar apparently recognized Kirgen, too, for he pounded the younger saje gleefully on the shoulder. "Kirgen, lad! — you look better than the last time I saw you! Then you had mud to your ears and were sure as death the world was about to end."

"We all thought so at the time, sir."

"Didn't we? But I didn't die. I got proposed to instead — a lifetime of celibacy, and I get proposed to by the most gorgeous dying woman I've ever seen — when I'm almost too old to enjoy the sensation." He waggled his bushy eyebrows and cackled. "But not quite. Not quite, boy. And she's a good Hoos girl into the bargain. You know about Hoos girls, don't you, boy?"

"Well, ah — not from experience —"

"Take my advice — you ever get the chance to marry a Hoos girl, you take it. What they don't know, you aren't interested in anyway."

Thirk looked like someone had walked up behind him and hit him on the head with a paving stone. "You *know* him?" he asked Kirgen.

"We were in the war together —"

"We were *all* in the war," Thirk said stiffly.

Nokar said, "Even so, but this boy and I were in the war *together.* But come on back. You're just in time for *nondes.* We have hovie stew and a mess of heathen foods a man with my digestion shouldn't even have to look at. Hummph! Hovie stew!" he snorted. "As if scaly, six-limbed fliers could be fit food for human consumption!"

Nokar set off down the breezeway at a remarkable clip, and the three of them chased after him.

Roba found herself wondering what part Kirgen had played in the war, to be friendly with someone of such rank and importance as Nokar. She wouldn't ask again — she always had the feeling his memories were ones he would have been happier without. But curiosity was eating her.

They marched into the dining room. She was last through the doors. She saw all the people she'd encountered earlier — Medwind, the three Wen kids — and two more she didn't recognize. The first was a tall, lovely young woman with long brown hair and freckles, who wore Kareen peasant garb as if it were the robes of a Council great. She was cutting meat for a fiery red-headed child of perhaps two or three, who had stopped herself in mid-tantrum to stare at the newcomers. The Kareen woman looked over at them, as well — began to smile politely — and froze.

She was staring at Kirgen, and Roba felt a sudden surge of jealous possessiveness.

The girl said, "Kirgen?"

He nodded, and Roba noticed how pale he looked. "Faia?" he whispered. And tipping his head toward the little girl, he asked, "Who — ?"

"Kirtha," the girl named Faia said.

Roba felt her world beginning to tilt. Kirtha was the feminine of Kirgen. The child looked just like him. Still, it might all be coincidence.

But Kirgen couldn't be satisfied to leave well enough alone. He asked Faia, "Ours?"

And the woman nodded.

The information blindsided Roba. Like his old war stories, Kirgen had kept any stories of previous lovers strictly to himself. Roba had considered his youth and his association with the sajery, and the long hours he spent in study, and had come to the conclusion that he might not have had any previous loves.

Which was apparently as nearsighted of me as assuming he didn't do much in the war because he never talked about it.

She stared at the woman and the child and Kirgen, who was looking from one to the other of them without ever turning his eyes to her. Her heart felt as if it were about to burst.

Yes. His child. Their child. And where does that leave me?

Roba stepped back, so that she could lean against the wall without being too obvious. She felt sick. She wished she could leave the room, but that was a childish reaction. She was beyond such behavior. She found no satisfaction in the fact that most of the people in the room, including Kirgen, looked as surprised as she felt.

It was the disaster with Janth all over again. She'd loved him with all her heart at fifteen and been sure he was in love with her, too — until he ran off with the healer's daughter. In retaliation, *she* ran off to join a bunch of lonely celibate women in the Daane University magerie.

While she was off in the cold southern wastes, someone had changed all the rules. She came back to Ariss to find she was free to seek love again.

And like a fool, I did, she thought. *I ran out, and found myself another handsome young Janth. And now I'm going to get my fool heart broken all over again.*

Well, that's what I get for loving him.

The atmosphere around the *nondes* table was tense enough to give Medwind indigestion. She'd seen Roba with Kirgen when they walked through the door and had realized the same man Faia identified as Kirtha's father was also Roba's lover. She could feel trouble brewing, though she was unsure where the outburst would come from or when it would come. The suspense made the fried hovie in her stomach slide around perilously until she regretted even tasting it. She watched the interplay of glances and glares between Kirgen, Faia, and Roba, by turns morbidly fascinated and appalled — and she waited.

Kirgen had seated himself across from Faia and Kirtha. Faia occupied herself feeding the little girl, who didn't want or need to be fed — the hill-girl didn't eat anything herself.

Roba looked miserable sitting beside the too-talkative saje who was her department head. When prodded, the mage delivered a few one-word comments on scholarship and the search for First Folk artifacts and, with a wince, Delmuirie. She played with her food, but Medwind suspected she swallowed nothing but her tears.

Kirgen stayed silent throughout the meal, and Medwind noticed he ate little. She suspected his stomach was probably in the same shape as hers. She could just imagine long days and nights in the company of these same people, and weeks of sitting to table together playing out the same delightful mealtime rituals.

I ought to be back down to my fighting weight in no time, she decided. *On the other hand, it doesn't look like the added mouths are going to require many more supplies than we needed before*. She wished fervently that she hadn't invited Roba and her associates on the trip.

When Kirgen finished not eating, he sat, fumbling with his dinner knife. He started to speak several times, but faltered. Finally he blurted out, "Have you — um, both of you — been well?"

Faia traced spirals in her remaining food with the point of her knife. Thirk and Nokar's noisy discussion of library politics at Faulea, drifting from the other end of the table, covered the awkward silence. Finally, the girl said, "It is hard sometimes, but my friends help." She looked up at him and smiled carefully. "We have enough to eat, a place to sleep, and I have work I can do — we are both well."

He smiled back, but when his glance drifted from Faia to Kirtha, the smile faltered. "I didn't know." He stared down at his hands. "I wish I'd known."

"I am sorry. I did not know myself until after the war — until after I left the city. Then, I did not dare try to find you, and I was not sure you would even want to know." Faia sighed. "Nokar told me to the best of his knowledge you had survived the war — I thought perhaps some day I could risk going back to the city to show her to you. But I am not truly welcome there — you understand?"

He nodded. Medwind watched him and noted that he could not take his eyes off his daughter's face. "She's very beautiful," the young saje said softly. "She looks like you."

Faia blushed and laughed. "Your red hair, your freckles, your brown eyes, and she looks like me? Hardly."

At the other end of the table, Nokar bellowed, "You don't mean that twittering ass Virven Sharsonne is up for the head librarian position?!"

Thirk laughed. "Practically uncontested. He's claiming he was your heir apparent — and after

Timmesonne tried to launch an open-to-the-public policy, the reactionaries are willing to believe him."

"Virven's a ninny."

Kirtha yawned, and Faia turned her attention to the child. "Sleep-time, Kirthchie."

"Not sleepy!" Kirtha protested.

"Ha! That is what you always say." She scooped the little girl into her arms and rose. "I plead pardon." She excused herself and headed for the room she and Kirtha shared, then stopped in the doorway. "But maybe your da would like to help put you in bed tonight?" Her face was a picture of doubt, and her eyes focused on Kirgen.

The young man gave her an uncertain smile. "Could I?"

"Of course."

Kirgen made his own excuses and disappeared into the breezeway after her.

Medwind returned her attention to the other guests. Roba sat at the far end of the table, her face a mask of indifference. Her eyes, though, glittered suspiciously bright.

Thirk, next to her, sighed. "Isn't it wonderful," he said, "that the two of them have found each other after all this time. Ah, young love." He elbowed Roba. "Not the sort of thing you and I are ever going to have to worry about again, is it?"

Medwind gritted her teeth and wondered if the man was always so insensitive — or so blind.

Roba handled it better than the Hoos woman expected. "Apparently not," her old friend said stiffly. "Apparently not."

Conversation shifted to the expedition that would start in the morning. The Wen kids, Medwind noted, looked unhappy to be including anyone else in the trip to their city. Nokar had introduced the Ariss scholars to the Wen children, and both Seven-Fingered Fat Girl and Dog Nose had been cold and aloof.

The Hoos woman thought she understood. The Wen kids found the city, and decided it would make a good home for them. According to the stories they told Medwind, their own parents had thrown them out to fend for themselves in the dangerous jungle. They'd seen friends die, and spent years unwanted by anyone. A place that was theirs alone must have seemed like a haven — and Medwind and her colleagues were crowding that haven.

Not for long, though Medwind thought. *We'll get the information we want, and move on, and leave them to their city.*

Then she considered what a find like a First Folk city would mean to the rest of the scholars of Arhel. No one had ever found a First Folk library before. No one had ever located a genuine city, even if the city were small. No one had ever found portable First Folk artifacts before. And once the First Folk site was publicized, no matter how good her intentions, or Nokar's, the Wen kids were going to be betrayed.

Scholars won't abandon a find like that. Once the city is common knowledge, there will always be some mage or saje with a reason to be there — and the claim those kids have on the city will always be less important.

She stared off at nothing, saddened. It didn't take farsight to see the shape of unhappiness in the making.

¤ Chapter 7

"You cannot seriously mean to include children in this expedition," Thirk said.

Medwind stood outside the house in the predawn cold and stared him down. "You were invited to join *us*," she said. "Do not think you will dictate who may go with us and who may not."

Thirk looked disgusted. "Mothers and children. Scruffy heathens. What kind of serious scholarly journey would include them? Think what the history texts will say — that the expedition that proved the Delmuirie Hypothesis included three little jungle rats and a baby. No one will take us seriously!"

"I suppose the histories could leave off your name if you prefer."

He glared. "Think of the danger. A helpless mother and her tiny babe—"

Medwind broke into disbelieving laughter. "Helpless!" she sputtered. "Helpless? Do you have any idea who that poor helpless mother is?"

Thirk frowned. "Faia something-or-other. Some girl Kirgen knew."

"Faia Rissedote," Medwind clarified. "The same woman who bested the Wisewoman Sahedre and brought the Second Mage/Saje War to an end. She can take care of herself."

The Hoos warrior had her own doubts about Kirtha's presence on the trip, but Faia had been adamant. The hill-girl was sick of Omwimmee Trade, and bored, and lonely, and she craved the adventure a trip into the forbidden Wen jungle promised. Faia promised she would keep Kirtha from burning down the jungle or the First Folk city. Medwind, who could understand the girl's wish to *do* something, kept her opinions on Kirtha's probable behavior to herself.

There were no further arguments, and, with everyone boarded and the gear packed at last, the air-box lifted silently into the still-dark sky. It banked around and soared toward the Wen Tribes Treaty lands. Within an instant, it was over the lush jungle canopy.

Medwind leaned back against the padded leather seat of the airbox and stared out the window as the bright crescent slash of the Tide Mother rose on the horizon with its cup of purple, red, and orange tipped. *To spill the blood,* she thought, and bit her lip with annoyance at her own irrationality. Hoos legends said when the Tide Mother tipped its cup to Arhel, it spilled blood on the battlefield. Medwind reflected that, since one Hoos looking cross-eyed at another Hoos was enough to spill blood on the battlefield, the old legend stood good odds of being right *somewhere*.

But, all the same, she wished the damned planet were hanging straight in the sky. A heritage of Hoos superstition sent tingles down her spine in spite of all her knowledge.

Edgy — that was the word. She felt it. They all felt it.

The two older Wen kids were fighting in the seats to her left. They were whispering very fast, and in Sropt, so she only caught snatches of the conversation. "— too many peknu —," "— they *might* steal our food —," and "— do not like these flying things —" seemed to make up the gist of the argument.

They didn't like leaving their loot behind, in spite of Nokar's patient explanation that it would be easier to transport it all after they arrived than to carry it with them the whole way. His explanation of the relation-ship between mass, energy, and magic had not interested them. They were decidedly cranky.

Kirgen and Roba were on the outs.

It's all that Gornat fisherfolk morality of Roba's, Medwind thought. *Gods, among the Huong Hoos, you have to parent a child before you can marry within the tribe. And to Faia's hillfolk, marriage is nothing but a kiss and a promise, anyway — if you tire of each other, off you go. No shame in parenting a child without the promise — and no promise made if you parent a child.* She shook her head and studied her friend, who sat stiff-backed on the other side of the airbox. *But to the Gornats, the gods ordain, and mortals refrain. If she ever sees reason again, the poor man will be fortunate.*

Medwind had seen Kirgen well after *nondes* the night before, trying to smooth things over with Roba. He hadn't been doing well — and from results that morn-ing, she figured his luck hadn't changed. He was in the eagle-seat at the moment, copiloting the airbox with Nokar, avoiding both Roba and Faia. Even so, the ten-sion between them was thick enough to walk on, and Medwind heartily wished them to the other side of the continent until they worked their problems out.

Thirk, sitting next to Roba, was oblivious to the mood in the car. He rattled on, and on, and on. "— and just think, Roba, you and I will finally be able to destroy the conspiracy that has kept Edrouss Delmuirie from his rightful place as the hero of all Arhel —"

Medwind rolled her eyes. *Perhaps,* she thought, studying the horse-faced saje, *I gave up headhunting too soon. Not that his head is a specimen I'd want to keep — but I think I'd like it better if it were separated from his body.*

He'd told her a handful of Hoos jokes the night before after *nondes*. They were obnoxious, and one was even crude. She'd smiled politely, then reciprocated with a quick translation of the one about why Arissers made lousy drumskins. A slow smile crept across her face as she thought back to that — Thirk had gotten very quiet and decided after a moment that he wanted to tell Faia all about Edrouss Delmuirie.

Medwind was glad to be on her way — but the farther the exploration team travelled, the more she wished she and Nokar were going alone.

Fat Girl quit snarling at Dog Nose long enough to look over at Medwind, then point to the canopy of green below them. "That is our territory down there," she said. "Look down next to the Path we follow. You can see the four white stones — they mark Four Winds Band's Path. Our bridge across the river will be ahead."

Medwind looked down. A tiny thread of a path meandered through a natural outcrop of whitestone — the trees were thin enough near the outcrop that she could see the jungle floor. The whitestone boulders became more prevalent, and the trees thinner, until suddenly the airbox was over a gorge, through which an ugly river raced. The river was thick and swollen and muddy brown from the rains, and she could see its treacherous currents and white-water runs from the air.

"I didn't see the bridge," Medwind said when the river dropped away behind them.

"No," Seven-Fingered Fat Girl agreed. "I did not see it also. But from here it is very small. *Everything* is very small. It is a good bridge, though. Three-strand vine rope — very strong."

Medwind considered that. The Hoos had rope bridges — sturdy knotted contraptions with wood-slatted walkways and high basket sides. The most valued Hoos horses were those that would edge across them without balking. But she would have been able to see a bridge like that from the air. "What sort of bridge is it?" she asked at last.

Fat Girl's forehead creased with bewilderment. "Rope," she repeated.

"No — how is it made?"

"Oh!" Fat Girl smiled, and a look of understanding crossed her face. "You have to soak the vines — green vines work best — and pound them with rocks until they are soft. Then you twist three —"

"No." Medwind interrupted, and shook her head. "I know how to make vine rope. I meant, how was the bridge made?"

Fat Girl's expression let Medwind know she'd asked an unbelievably stupid question. "One person ties the rope to something strong on one side of the river. Another person ties it to something strong on the other side of the river. One rope to walk on, and one or two ropes to hold on to. We have a good-good bridge. It has three ropes."

Very few things frightened Medwind Song. But when she imagined crossing that ugly, deadly river walking on a single line of rope, her stomach churned more wildly than the river's rapids had.

She was still thinking about the rope bridge when Kirgen muttered something to Nokar. He said it softly, but a sharpness in his intonation caught Medwind's attention. She tensed and leaned forward in her seat, trying to hear better.

Nokar was answering. "— energy fade (mumbling) trace the lines back, but not forward (more mumbling) —"

There was a brief silence.

She heard Kirgen clearly. "I don't find anything."

Nokar muttered something else. "— try bringing in earth energy —"

The airbox began a gentle drift rightward.

"Bring it back on-line!" Nokar snapped. "Don't lose your concentration!"

"I didn't!" Kirgen's voice got louder.

The airbox moved back to the left — then drifted rightward again.

"Damn all to Grum's hell, what's going on?!" Nokar roared.

The passengers fell silent as they became aware of the struggle at the front of the airbox. They watched the two sajes directing their flight, frozen in poses of anxiety.

Thirk cleared his throat. "Might I be of assistance?" he asked. "I've done quite a bit of piloting —"

"We don't need another by-the-gods-damned pilot — we need power," Nokar snarled.

The magicians in the airbox exchanged puzzled glances. Medwind thought she'd misheard. "You need what?"

"Power," Kirgen said. His face was pale. Sweat beaded his forehead and glistened beneath the thin furring of his mustache.

That was what Medwind thought he'd said. She closed her eyes, and mentally reached out to touch the energy of sky and earth —

And came up dry. As impossible as it seemed, the ley lines that crisscrossed Arhel were absent over the jungle. She felt some form of energy nearby, but, oddly, it wasn't in a form she could touch — or perhaps she didn't know how to use it.

The airbox veered more to the right and began losing altitude.

Seven-Fingered Fat Girl gripped the back of Nokar's seat. The girl's knuckles were white, and her fingers dug into the leather. "Turn now," she said. Her voice was raspy and frightened.

"We're trying, dear," Nokar said.

"You do not understand. You must turn now. 'Trying' is not to be good enough." She leaned forward again. Her voice shook when she spoke. "You said this was safe way to travel — that if we go in airbox, we not have to worry about hunting-beasts or Keyu. You said the Keyu not bother us if we fly." The girl was breathing fast, and her body was rigid.

"We didn't expect problems," Medwind said. She

watched her husband, and felt the talons of fear scrape along the back of her neck.

Nokar gripped the pilot's brace and chanted, trying to draw in energy from anywhere. The airbox slid slightly leftward, then jerked hard back to the right.

The airbox was flying directly into the rising sun, forty-five degrees off the direction in which they'd been traveling.

"Something's pulling us!" Kirgen whispered. He strained against the invisible opponent.

Fat Girl stared out the window at the trees below and shuddered. "Silk People village is that way," she whispered. "The Keyu pull us to them."

Medwind barely refrained from snapping at the girl. It wasn't time for superstitious nonsense — the Hoos woman shook her head and turned her attention to her colleagues, hoping that one of them might have succeeded where she'd failed. Like her, Faia, Roba, and Thirk had all been searching the earth and the sky for usable power. Roba and Thirk had given up. They looked from her to each other. Their eyes reflected the horror of their situation.

Faia tried longer. She closed her eyes and formed her hands into the shape of a ball. Her fingertips glowed faintly blue, and for a moment, a thread of blue light traced its way from the ball of power she'd collected to the pilot's brace. When it did, the airbox righted its direction. But the light grew paler almost as soon as she'd drawn it, and after only a moment it faded and disappeared. Her forehead creased with concentration. The airbox swung back and forth, with Nokar and Kirgen directing it and Faia supplying a steadily decreasing stream of power. Finally, though, the airbox resumed its eastward course, and Faia dropped her hands to her sides and looked up. "It's gone," she said. Her voice was hollow, edged with fear. "The magic's gone."

Nokar leaned heavily against the useless pilot's brace and stared straight ahead. "I know," he said.

The airbox flew on, right toward the village of the Silk People, losing altitude all the while.

Into the horrified silence, Roba Morgasdotte asked, "How is the airbox still flying?" Her hands twisted the leather straps of her pack, and her fingers trembled. "How can it fly with no magic?"

"I don't know," Nokar said.

"It's the doing of the Keyu," Seven-Fingered Fat Girl answered in her own tongue. "We have angered the Keyu, and now we will all die."

Medwind translated for Roba, Thirk, and Kirgen. "She says we made the trees angry, and now we're going to die."

"No," Fat Girl said, switching to Arissonese. "We not angered *keyu* — trees. We angered *Keyu*. Gods." She pulled her dartstick from her belt. Then she stood and lifted her clenched fist until it touched the ceiling of the airbox. "*Kyadda*. We die now — but we die like tagnu. All you — get quicklights out. Do what I tell you. Damn-damn Keyu going to pay this time."

"Brace yourselves!" Nokar yelled. "We're going to hit!" He gripped the pilot's brace and gasped, and Medwind looked past him, into the jungle. They dropped below the canopy, and she caught a blurred glimpse of a dozen airboxes — and then they skidded across the deep jungle loam and bounced to a stop. The nose of their airbox came to a halt against the gouged-open door of an orange rental airbox.

The air filled with cries and groans.

Even though she'd braced, that final bounce threw Medwind into the back of the seat in front of her. She'd felt her nose crunch, and blinding white-hot pain shot straight through to the back of her head. She tasted blood. Others among her companions swore softly, and both Runs Slow and Kirtha began crying.

Kirgen got to his feet and worked his way through the compartment, checking to see that everyone was safe. He bore a few cuts and scratches, but otherwise looked fine. When he came to her, Medwind held her bleeding nose and waved him on.

By the time the world quit spinning, Fat Girl was at the airbox door, listening. "Stay! Quiet!" the Wen girl snarled. She shook her head in frustration, cracked the door open a tiny bit, and froze in position again.

"Nothing there now," she said with satisfaction. "Everybody out, get dry stuff, put it up against trees, and start fires."

"What? Why?!" Thirk said. "The jungle will be too wet to burn — and even if we could start fires, we might burn ourselves in them."

"You are peknu," the girl said. Her expression was cold. "You in Silk People land, with big Silk People village right over there." She pointed off into the trees. "When Silk People catch you, they kill you. Fsst-fsst." She made an unpleasantly abrupt gesture across her throat with her fingers.

Medwind winced. If their magic were intact, she wouldn't be worried about the Wen. Faia was a potent weapon — a natural talent more powerful than any trained magician Medwind had ever come across even when she was untrained — and now that she had training, possibly unbeatable. The rest of the party combined varying degrees of natural talent with years of schooling and experience. Nothing could have hurt them.

Except that they had no power from which to draw their magic. They were as dependent on whatever physical fighting skills they possessed as the magicless Wen kids.

Medwind pulled her waterproofed packet of quicklights out of her pack. "Get tinder from those other airboxes," she said. "Start the fires. It will at least give us a diversion so we can escape."

Fat Girl laughed bitterly. "We not escape. The

Keyu make sure of that. We die now — but we take the gods with us."

Kirgen and Seven-Fingered Fat Girl and Dog Nose pushed all the downed airboxes except their own together, while Roba and Thirk and Nokar piled the dry contents into a heap in the central one. They lit a fire; then, when it began to blaze, tossed clothes, books and other items from the airboxes into the heap. Medwind tore the contents of the airboxes into shreds and piled the shreds inside the middle airbox.

Faia watched, holding Kirtha and Runs Slow.

Medwind lit the tinder. It caught and began to blaze. Then the fire went out.

She lit it again, and again it started to blaze — and again, some unseen force snuffed it out.

"Keyu." Fat Girl had been watching the progress of the flames. She stared around at the trees and muttered, "They not like fire so close to their places."

Medwind tensed. *They're watching,* she thought. *The Wen — or whatever guards the Wen have set to protect themselves.* She shivered involuntarily and peered into the canopied gloom around her. She saw nothing but trees, but the feeling of eyes on her never faltered. *Watching us from somewhere out of sight.*

She snarled. *Come out and fight, sheshrud, cowards, drinkers of goat-piss,* she thought. *Come out and die.*

A muffled exclamation drew her attention to one of the outer ring of airboxes. "Heya!" Roba yelled. She emerged from the ripped door and held aloft something large and white. "Look what was in this airbox!"

It was another First Folk tablet — surely the same tablet Praniksonne had stolen from the Wen kids in the market. Which meant that all those downed airboxes, with the doors gouged open and huge clawmarks scarring the painted wood sides —

Impossible, Medwind thought.

— Praniksonne's expedition, full of Ariss' great

thinkers and doers, which went out only two days
before them —

Preposterous.

An expedition made up of the greatest sajes of the
age, caught in the same trap . . . ? She couldn't believe it
— she wouldn't consider it.

Roba carried the tablet past her to their own useless
airbox and placed it carefully inside.

Hope lives in the most foolish places, Medwind thought,
and tried one final time to light the fire. Again it burned
only to die.

Suddenly Seven-Fingered Fat Girl waved her hands
over her head to catch everyone's attention.

"Quiet," she whispered. She froze, head cocked to one
side. Then she swore — softly but with deep feeling.

"The gods, they get us now," she said. "Listen."

At first, Medwind heard nothing. When she did,
what she heard made no sense. Laughter — chittering,
screeching, high-pitched laughter — tittered at the
very edge of audibility. It touched the base of her spine
like the point of an assassin's dagger, scraped up
between her shoulderblades and along the back of her
neck — left the tiny hairs there standing on end. It
grew louder, and shrieked and sawed along her nerves
until she couldn't think clearly. It was a crazy sound —
depraved and deadly . . . and it was coming nearer.

"What in all the hells — ?" Nokar muttered.

"Roshu," Fat Girl said. "One roshi is really bad, but
that not one roshi. That a lot roshu — from one-two-
three different directions. They big — big teeth, very
hungry. And very fast."

"Then we had better run," Thirk said.

"Where?" Seven-Fingered Fat Girl looked at him, eyes
dark with cold calculation. "You got someplace to go?"

"The jungle?"

"Nothing to keep you from their claws. They did
that —" she pointed to the rows of hand-deep gouges

in the airboxes' doors. "Off the Path, nothing will save you from them."

"Well, then the Path —"

"You not Silk People, big man," she said with scorn. "The Silk People, they got no need for peknu. They throw their own kids out to make food for the roshu — what you think they want with you?"

Nokar cut Thirk off. To Fat Girl, he said, "You know this place. What is best to do?"

She snorted. "Not much choice. We die now by the roshu or die later by the Keyu. Which you like better?"

"Later," Nokar said firmly. "There is always a chance that 'later' may be postponed indefinitely."

Seven-Fingered Fat Girl shrugged and slipped a dart into her dartstick. "I don' know 'pose-poned in-def-in-lee,' but if you want 'later' we got to run like wind now." She trotted away from the roshu noises, snapping orders in Sropt at her two fellow Wen.

Runs Slow moved to Dog Nose's side and he lifted her to his back, where she clung. Faia swung Kirtha up onto her shoulders.

Medwind ran back to the airbox and shut the door. Her vha'attaye were in there, or what was left of them. She couldn't run with them and survive, but she couldn't just leave them unprotected. *As silly a gesture as Roba and her First Folk tablet,* she thought. *Not much chance we'll make it back, but . . .*

They ran — Fat Girl in front, Dog Nose in the rear, and Medwind and the rest of the outlanders packed in the middle.

"This is to the village," Fat Girl called. "The trees get closer soon. We on a big Path right now. Maybe they let *us* run on their Path without good trade stuff — but not you peknu. And we brought you — so they sure will kill us, too."

The Wen kids drew ahead of the rest of the party — even Dog Nose with Runs Slow outdistanced them.

Nokar was struggling to keep up. Medwind dropped back with him, while the rest of the group passed them. He was gasping, and his skin was gray-tinged and waxy.

"I'm — too — old," he gasped. "I can't — do this."

"Yah — you look bad, old man," Medwind agreed. She put two fingers to her mouth and whistled — a piercing, high-pitched shrill that caught the attention of the rest of the party. She waved her arms and yelled, "Kirgen! Here!"

The young saje stopped, then turned and raced back. He pulled up in front of her, breathing hard.

"You're strong and fast. Help me here. We have to carry him — or he won't make it."

"Both — of us? How?"

"Hoos trick. We carried injured warriors this way when we weren't raiding on horseback." She glanced at her husband. "Act like you're sitting in a chair," she told him. To Kirgen she said, "We each lock one arm around one of his legs, and he puts an arm around each of our shoulders. Got it?"

Kirgen nodded.

"Then on three. One — two — three!" They lifted the old man and ran. The rest of the band was well ahead of them, the roshu sounded close, the drums pounded louder. "Just make sure you — don't go left when — I go right," Medwind told Kirgen between gasps.

Kirgen snorted once, his laugh disbelieving.

Medwind shook her head. "I mean it. We ripped a — warrior's hip — out of its socket once. Damn near — took his leg off. You all right — Nokar?"

"I've been better," the old man said. "I would have been a lot better if I hadn't known about the warrior—"

"You could have — been a lot worse — if Kirgen didn't know."

"There is that." The voice above her head was thoughtful.

The depraved laughter of the roshu grew louder. Medwind looked quickly over her shoulder, swore, and yelled, "Faster, Kirgen!"

She didn't want to think about the things that chased them, but she couldn't help herself. There were several of them; three for certain, and maybe more — big, armor-plated brutes that seemed, from her vantage point, to have been predominantly teeth. She ventured another quick glance, and bit into her lower lip. The things *were* all teeth.

"Faster," she urged again.

Kirgen made a face. "If I could — sprout wings — I would have by now!"

The character of the jungle had changed, Medwind noticed with a start. In that part of the forest, someone had planted the trees in rows — tight rows that had grown into palisades. The trees on either side of the three of them were too closely grown for even one person to squeeze between.

I've let myself get trapped, Medwind thought. *Of all the damned stupid —* She might as well have waited in a corral for the roshu to come get her. She'd been thinking too much about carrying Nokar, and not enough about what she and Kirgen were carrying him into.

She suddenly realized she couldn't see the rest of the group. *Where is everyone else?* she wondered.

The walls of trees on either side of her had been narrowing — she realized that she was having to slow down and squeeze in to avoid hitting the trees.

— Narrowing —

"Yes!" she shouted. She laughed.

Kirgen glanced over at her, surprised.

"It's too — tight in here for — the roshu! It's almost too —tight for the three of us — side by side."

She looked back. The roshu were well behind them again and not moving any closer. They chittered and howled their twisted laughter at the sky;

puffed and tore at the ground with their clawed forelegs; shook their ugly heads. Their huge yellow eyes glowed like fires in the gloom of the narrow tree-path. "Kirgen, we made it," she said.

They stopped and lowered Nokar to the ground.

Kirgen faced the monsters and grabbed his throwing knife.

Medwind put out a hand to stop him. "Don't waste a weapon," she said. "We may need it ahead."

He glared at the roshu, then sighed. "Right. I wasn't thinking." He turned back to Nokar. "Can you walk now?" Kirgen asked the old man.

Nokar still looked gray and weak, but he nodded firmly enough. "The magic is thin here — that's bad for me, but I suppose I'll do well enough. Where did the rest of the group get to? I lost sight of them."

"They have to be further along the path," Medwind said. "They can't possibly have gotten off it."

"It looks like the trees grow into a solid wall just ahead," Kirgen said. He stopped and sniffed the air. "Odd smell," he noted. "Smoke —"

"Somebody cooking midden." Medwind cut him off. "The path must curve on ahead" It was a relief to be able to walk instead of running. She stared around her — up along the tall, straight trunks to the branches that met in peaked arches hundreds of *eashos* over her head. The corridor of close-growing trees with its oddly symmetrical, precise structure reminded her of the soaring Temple of Time in Ariss — but not even the Temple could compare with the slender spires and the sparkling green canopy that filtered light down to the leaf-carpeted jungle floor at her feet. Incredible beauty — and still the feeling of eyes — eyes everywhere.

The three of them walked on.

"Maybe we ought to wait here for the rest of the group to come back," Kirgen said.

Medwind stopped walking. "Perhaps you're right.

Seven-Fingered Fat Girl didn't want to go into the village. Perhaps if we just wait on the path until the roshu get tired and go away, we can get our packs and start back for Omwimmee Trade. Everyone will realize we haven't caught up with them and turn around soon."

"Yes," Kirgen said. "Soon."

"Certainly," Nokar agreed. "We will wait."

"They'll be fine," Medwind said.

"Of course," Kirgen agreed.

"We'll just sit down right here and wait," Nokar said. They sat down in the soft leaf mold.

"Roba and Kirtha and Faia are up there," Kirgen remarked suddenly. He stood and looked down the path. "You two go ahead and wait here. I think I'll just catch up with them and tell them what we're doing."

Nokar said, "I don't like the idea of splitting up."

"No. But I want to make sure they're safe."

Medwind stood. "They may need our help. Let's keep going."

Nokar stood too. "Yes," he said, "I think really that will be the best thing to do."

He looked so frail—so very, very old. Medwind said, "You follow Kirgen and I'll bring up the rear."

Perhaps, she thought, she would shout for some of the group ahead. It would save Nokar any further walking — but then, perhaps not. The roshu were no longer laughing behind her. They crouched at the mouth of the path, yellow-eyed nightmares, and waited in silence. The Wen drums had fallen silent, though when she thought about it she couldn't remember when. In the whole of the jungle, she could hear nothing but leaves rustling in the breeze and the soft thuds of her footsteps and those of her companions. The idea of shouting into that silence made her skin crawl. They walked single file, forced to follow each other because of the still-narrowing passageway between the trees.

"I wish we could hear them," Kirgen said. His voice was swallowed up in the silence.

Time stretched as they walked. Or perhaps the path stretched. There seemed no end to it — the gloom, the tall, rough-barked trees, the unnatural hush.

The smoke from the Wen village had an uncanny reek to it, Medwind thought. Odd — but she couldn't place it; she had no idea what they were cooking to make that stink.

The path narrowed more — curved to the left, then to the right.

Bad! Bad! Medwind's nerves screamed. Kirgen moved around one of the tight twists, momentarily out of sight — Nokar followed. She pressed on. Even the sound of their footfalls died away, swallowed by the twin walls of trees. At the end of the line, wending along the twisty maze, she only caught brief glimpses of Kirgen, though she never lost sight of Nokar for more than a second.

Bad! Bad!

She knew it. She felt it. But her friends were ahead. The only way on was forward.

The last semblance of daylight died. The living walls of trees pressed in so tightly only the faintest ghosts of light reached the ground. Kirgen and Nokar ahead of her dissolved into shadows, darker against dark. Medwind looked up to reassure herself with the delicate tracery of pale green high overhead, the promise that somewhere, the sun still shone. That somewhere was too far away, and too faint — unreachable. The trees were the whole world; she felt it. Tree bark on either side of her scraped her skin as she fumbled her way along. The damp air clogged in her lungs, thick with the reek of rotting leaves and village smoke. In this place without sight or sound, the stench itself became ominous. It crowded at her blinded eyes, her deafened ears, until in her mind the stink took on a shape and sound all its own. It became a living thing that stalked her, that tried to choke her.

Bad! Bad!

Suddenly, there was a round hole of light ahead of her, low to the ground. A tunnel of light, fogged with a swirling haze of thick, sweet smoke — she was distantly amazed that she could see it. Where were Nokar and Kirgen? They'd been ahead of her, and now there was nothing on the path but her and the stink. A gust of air blew in her face from the tunnel, and the stench grew heavier and richer — the world spun slowly around her, and she giggled. It struck her funny that there was no place for her to fall down. The trees held her up. She felt warm and sleepy and woozy. Her fingers scrabbled at the dark rim of the glowing gold tunnel — bark scraped her knuckles — she was aware of the pain of torn flesh, but unconcerned. It felt like somebody else's pain. She knelt and looked directly into the tunnel — into the light — and the light blinded her. Ghost images danced in front of her as she crawled into the narrow, low inlet.

I was born like this once, she thought, and giggled again. *In a moment I'll burst out of the end of the passage, and the Hoos warriors will scream welcome — no, no, no . . . Not Hoos. Wen. I'm going to see the Wen. Wen, Wen, Wen again . . .*

She smiled, and tumbled out of the crawlspace into a blaze of light as bright and hard as a whitestone wall. Her eyes blurred and watered, and for an instant, images resolved into shapes she almost understood. Nokar and Kirgen, Faia, Kirtha, the three outcast Wen children, Thirk — all lying in a heap to one side of her; the faces of staring strangers with angry eyes, strangers who blew smoke into the tunnel with big, silk-sided bellows; trees grown in the form of a city, hung with shimmering silks.

Then, with a terrific crack, darkness descended.

Lost, all lost. Choufa curled in a tight ball in a cranny

formed by the intersecting maze of branches. She beat her fists against the tree and sobbed. The peknu were lost, gone, doomed. Food for the trees. And when they died, her hopes for escape — for herself and the rest of the sharsha, would die too.

She'd felt them coming as soon as they crossed into the Wen territory. The Keyu had alerted her, rousing from their sluggish sated state to greedy hunger in an instant, clamoring for the fresh bodies that soared in their direction. And when the peknu came within range, the Keyu reached out with their god-touch and pulled them in.

There had been an instant when Choufa thought the peknu would escape. They had fought — their own god-touch against the Keyu's grasping, and for a brief moment, something inside the Keyu fought against itself. Dissonant voices screamed for the freedom of the peknu, put their energy with that of the peknu — until those voices were coldly and viciously silenced. And the Keyu won.

The Keyu would always win.

Choufa dried her eyes. She could not doubt anymore what would happen to her. She had no need to hope — hope was dead. She found peace in impending ruin; the future was out of her hands. It wasn't her fault anymore. She stood and walked slowly along the branch, and down into the center of the sharsha tree. No one was visible in the main part of the tree. She didn't wonder where the other sharsha had gone. She was simply glad they were.

Then she heard a soft cry, quickly muffled, and sharp whispers. She followed the noise, down along the maze of intertwining branches, through two of the hollow trunk-rooms, and then up into an offshoot trunk. The other sharsha looked up, frightened, when she crossed the threshold, then turned back to the focus of their attention.

Thedra crouched on the floor, her face twisted with pain, gripping her belly. She rocked back and forth, panting and crying.

"What is she doing?" Choufa whispered to Kerru, who stood by the entryway and watched.

"The baby is coming out of her belly. She said she was inside the Keyu-thoughts. She said the Keyu called more food — then all of a sudden the Keyu felt her in their thoughts, and called the baby to come out. They made her time come. The Silk People will be here soon to take her away."

"The Silk People are busy. They caught the peknu. They used sleep smoke on them —"

"The stupid peknu won't make any difference!" Kerru snapped. "The Keyu called Thedra's baby because they want to eat Thedra now. They will make the Silk People come and get her."

"I just thought maybe the peknu could help us —"

Kerru looked at her sadly. "No one is going to help us."

Choufa nodded. Yes, it was so. There was nothing she could do, and nothing anyone else would do. She watched Thedra, and began to feel sick again. The pregnant girl quit writhing and crying for a moment and just leaned forward on her hands and knees, breathing heavily. Then her huge belly heaved under the dull gray cloth of her tunic, and she screamed and began to rock again.

It was awful. Choufa saw blood and closed her eyes. *I don't want a baby in my belly,* she thought, and started to back away from the scene.

Two green-and-gold men shoved Choufa out of the way, walked up to Thedra, looped ropes around her wrists, and dragged her out of the room and away from the sharsha and the sharsha-tree. Choufa could hear Thedra screaming and fighting long after the older girl was out of sight — crying and begging for help —

Won't somebody save us?! Choufa cried inside. *Won't someone help all of us?!*

<No help there is no help for *we cannot help* you for you are mine you are ours, > said the slimy whispers inside her head. <You will come to me will come to love us come when it when it is your time is your time. >

She became aware of a foul taste in her mouth, and of pain that ripped straight through her eyes to the back of her skull. Red flares flashed behind her eyelids with every beat of the bludgeoning cadence of her pulse. She was lost in darkness, lost inside as well as out. She was unsure of her name, could not remember where she was, had no idea how she came to be there.

Rumblings began softly — then became louder. Where they far away? Did they move nearer? *Storm coming?* she wondered, and "storm" felt wrong but the *feeling* of "storm" — of things brewing, gathering energy, waiting to explode into sudden fury — that was the feeling the rumblings gave her.

To pain and confusion, she added fear. The arrhythmic thundering noise, she felt sure, was tied to the darkness, to the hurtings of her body.

Drumbeats, she thought.

And remembered.

Roba Morgasdotte came fully awake and forced her swollen, matter-crusted eyes open. It was dusk. She lay naked, facedown on hard-packed clay still cold and damp and slimy from the last rain. She was cold; her head hurt; her wrists and elbows and shoulders blazed with agony. She tried to roll over or sit, but couldn't — someone had tied her wrists together behind her and strung them to a tree branch overhead. Every move she made — even something as simple as turning her head from side to side — sent fresh fire lancing from her shoulders up to her fingertips.

If she eased her head carefully from side to side, she

could see Thirk to her right, and the older Wen girl to her left — both of them facedown; naked; tied. It hurt too much to twist any more, but from the groans and labored breathing all around her, she had to assume the rest of the exploration party was there.

"Anybody awake?" she whispered.

"Yah," Seven-Fingered Fat Girl answered.

"Do you know what happened?" Roba rested her cheek on the wet clay and closed her eyes and tried to focus her attention on something besides the pain.

"Yah." The girl's voice was strained. "They used *evastevoffuschrom* — 'smoke to sleep the bad-beasts.' The Wen use it to make sleep the little roshu or kellinks what get on the Path."

Roba groaned. "You're saying they trapped us and drugged us."

"They not nice people," Fat Girl said. "I tell you peknu this — you don't think I tell you true."

Medwind's voice, muffled and edged with bitterness, came from Roba's left. "We believed — we simply didn't think there was anything the Wen could do to us." Roba heard a brief scuffle, then Medwind's muffled swearing. "Damn them — I can't move at all! Lying here flat on my belly and sick as death — and I can't even roll to my side to breathe."

Sick, Roba thought. *That's certainly part of it.* Her mouth had been home to rodents while she was unconscious, she decided; unclean, unhousebroken rodents. They'd left their fur and worse coating her tongue. Her stomach churned on nothing, the world tilted and rocked like a fisherman's boat in stormy seas. She'd never been seasick at sea — she was seasick here on dry land.

"Why will the magic not work?" Roba heard Faia's voice. "I can feel its presence — but I cannot touch it."

At the sound of the young woman's voice, Kirtha wailed, "Mama! Help me!"

Roba's aching hands tightened into fists. The misbegotten Wen had tied even the smallest of the children.

I can get out of this, she thought. *There are tricks for tapping into magic. The magic is here — and if it's here, I can use it.*

She forced herself to relax. She convinced her body that it was floating, free and comfortable in a sea of mud — *warm* mud. She imagined riding a slow spiraling current of warmth down into the mud, until it surrounded her and she became a part of it. She felt good — safe and warm and free. *Earth,* she thought. *Full of energy* —

She reached out, probing through the earth for simple power, for a mere acceleration of a natural process — the process of rotting the rope that bound her. It wasn't even really magic, what she sought to do — nothing more taxing than the spell a farmer might use to sense the character of the next day's weather.

She sent her mind coursing, searching through the earth as far as she could stretch, quartering around her like a fanghare sniffing water in the desert. The power stayed just out of reach, palpable but inaccessible.

Air, she thought, and in her mind re-created herself as a thing of wind and sunlight — she imagined herself drifting free of the muddy earth, free of her bonds, of the towering walls of trees — saw herself drifting formless and free among, then above, tall clouds. *Power,* she thought, and searched for it.

There was no power for her to take from the sky.

Patiently, with enormous calm, she communed with fire, and then with water — and always, the power was close enough that she could feel its presence, but untouchable.

She came back to herself then — back to her shame and her pain and her captivity. Roba let her head drop forward. The elusive, unidentifiable magic defeated her. *Ironic,* she thought. *I am surrounded by some of the greatest magical talent in Arhel, and all that talent isn't going to be able to save my life.*

The drums pounded, incessant noise without rhythm. The Wen sang and chanted. Somewhere nearby a woman screamed, and the first gasping squalls of a newborn baby tore into the air.

Then the chanting grew louder and faster, and the drums were joined by thundering booms so deep Roba felt them before she heard them.

"Now." Medwind spoke, her voice flat and emotionless. "The biggest drums are saying 'Now!'"

"What do they mean?" Thirk asked. "What 'now'?"

"Now we die," Seven-Fingered Fat Girl said. "Now they give us to the Keyu."

The first fat drops of cold rain struck Roba's face and stirred the mud in which she lay, and a flash of lightning and the hard crash of nearby thunder punctuated the Wen drumbeats.

A man with a knife knelt beside Medwind's head and pressed his blade gently against the base of her throat. His green-and-gold silks brushed the ground. He spoke to someone behind her in rapid Sropt. "Beat her around a little. Let her know we're in charge."

"Lizard-humping tree-burner," Medwind snarled, also in Sropt. "Your mother screw with worms — your father was one."

Behind her, the unseen second man laughed and jerked on the rope that held her wrists. In spite of herself, Medwind gasped. Then he dug his heel into the bend at the back of her knee — and she yelled.

"Don't break her," the first man said. "I don't want to have to carry her to the Keyu. She's too heavy." He looked down at Medwind and pressed the knife against her flesh so hard she felt it bite into her skin.

She winced, but held very still.

"So you speak the Tongue of People, hey, peknu? Well, then, you'll take comfort in knowing that you're going to die for a good purpose. You're shit, and we're going to fertilize the Keyu with you." He grinned and with his free hand fumbled under her shoulder in the mud, until he found her breast. He pinched her nipple and twisted. "Tree-food — that's you."

Medwind bit her lip and kept quiet.

"Do we have time to enjoy her?" the second man asked. "I've never had peknu before."

"It wouldn't be worth the cycle of cleansings you'd have to do afterwards." He spat in Medwind's face. "Peknu — pah! That's lower than *dracch*ing corpses."

She heard the other man sigh. "Maybe so — but she looks livelier than a corpse."

"She won't for long." The first man glared at Medwind. "You are going to behave. If you don't we'll slit your belly and pull your entrails out and feed you to the Keyu that way. The Keyu don't care if we rip you into shreds — so long as you're still breathing when they get you."

The second man kept one foot braced on the back of her knee and pulled her upward by tugging on her bound wrists. The pain was incredible.

"You understand me, stinking peknu?" the man asked.

"Yes," Medwind whispered. She glared at him through her haze of pain and added to herself, *You corpse-*dracch*ing tapeworm-abortion. I understand. And if I ever have the chance, I'll make you understand. I'll rip your balls off with my bare hands and stuff them up your nose.*

The second man cut the rope that bound her, while the first kept the knife in her throat. She tried to recall a Hoos grapple that would work with one man standing on her knee twisting her arms behind her and the other one trying to knife her, and she came up empty. The Hoos were not supposed to end up in those positions, she decided.

"Hurry up and retie her," the first man snapped.

The second was fumbling with the rope. Medwind squirmed, and instantly the pressure on both her throat and the back of her knee increased.

"Do not move," the first man said.

Medwind could feel her blood running in warm, pulsing streams down her neck. "Yes," she said, and held her arms out behind her for the second man to bind. She clasped her palms together and interlocked her fingers.

The second man muttered, "That's better." He jerked the coarse vine-rope so tight Medwind gasped, and the bastard with the knife at her throat grinned.

The deepest of the drums were pounding out, "Feed us, feed us!" Medwind found this unnerving.

They pulled her to her feet and dragged her into line. Each member of the exploration team was there. Nokar looked like the very hells — frail and helpless and beaten. And older — she couldn't believe how much older he looked. His naked body seemed to be made of nothing but paper and bones.

The rest were battered and bleeding. Fat Girl fought like one insane — or like a beast, who would rather chew off its leg and die free than face the end its captors planned. The rest struggled at intervals, or went passively. But none of them were Hoos.

As a Hoos, she had duties. The duty to rescue her friends. The duty to escape. The duty to kill her captors or die trying. She'd spent the first years of her life learning her duties and a thousand tricks for carrying those duties out.

She tried to stay calm and to wait for opportunity to present itself. She knew she would only get one chance — if she got that. Any mistake, any prematurity on her part, would be fatal. She watched, and stayed ready.

But the Wen dragged her and her friends over their branching roads carefully. They too knew a thousand tricks. They stayed wary. They didn't make any mistakes. They led the outlanders and the outcasts into a tree-circle, full of drummers and dancers and hellish noise, and Medwind felt the last of her hope evaporate.

The Silk People were taking them all to the Keyu, along aerial walkways worn smooth by the passage of the uncounted sacrifices who'd preceded her.

Her hands were tied behind her back, but Seven-Fingered Fat Girl fought the Silk People with teeth and feet; butted her head into the stomach of one green-and-gold-swathed captor; screamed fury and terror into the noise that surrounded her. Once long ago she had trusted people and had walked quietly beside men like these — and once she was ripped from the arms of her parents, given a pack and a dartstick, and thrown to the jungle to be food for kellinks or roshu or dooru. In spite of the Silk People, she had lived. Knowing she went to her death, she would not go quietly again.

The three men of the Silk People dragged her along the treewalks, up and down the twisting braided branching paths, stumbling as she kicked and fought. She did everything she could to make them lose their balance. If they fell and took her with them, or even if they didn't fall, but dropped her, she wouldn't care. She would rather fall and die than feed the Keyu, she thought. She would rather do anything than become food for the Keyu.

She could hear her tagnu and the peknu behind her, struggling too. She didn't have time to think about the others who shared her predicament — the best she could do was wish them luck, and a quick death.

Ahead, more of the Silk People waited, and beyond them — beyond them squatted the Keyu, as ugly and twisted and malevolent as she'd remembered. The tree-gods thundered their impatience — drummed *Feed us, feed us!* at terrible volume, so that the very jungle seemed to shake.

Seven-Fingered Fat Girl never quit fighting — but the men were used to resistance. They brought her safely down to the ground, between the rows of waiting Silk People, and into the cursed circle of the gods. Then they held her there, twisting one arm behind her back until she fell to her knees. They waited.

More men brought the rest of the group into the circle. They bound Dog Nose tightly — hands and feet. He'd given them a fight, she thought. His nose bled and his face was bruised and swollen, and his chest was scratched and cut and bleeding in two places. The men who carried him in looked equally battered. Dog Nose looked at her from across the clearing.

On her knees, but with her head unbowed, she met his eyes. *You were right,* she thought. *We should not have travelled with the peknu.* She regretted their anger with each other the last few days, and the time she had not spent with him. She regretted holding her position as the band's fat over him. So many regrets.

"I'm sorry," she mouthed.

He shook his head "no" and looked into her eyes. He formed the word "peknu" with his lips, then something Fat Girl couldn't make out.

She moved her head in the tiniest of increments — "no" — and willed him to understand her.

She saw comprehension in his eyes, and he mouthed "in peknu."

This time she understood.

He mouthed the words again. Slowly. "I — love — you."

It was a peknu sentiment — their language had no such words. She nodded, feeling tears starting down her cheeks. "I love you," she told him.

He nodded and looked satisfied. "Goodbye," he mouthed, at the same time that the Silk People noticed the exchange. They dragged Dog Nose out of her line of sight.

She bit her lip and tasted the salt of her tears. *May we meet after death in a place with no gods,* she thought.

The Silk People dragged Nokar beside her, and she felt a moment of dismay. His head hung, and he shuffled when he walked. They had beaten him, too — welts and bleeding cuts stood out from the mud all over his naked body. Even without the bruises, however, there would have been something wrong with him. He looked older than before, though she would not have imagined that was possible. His skin was gray and tight over his bones — and so thin and fragile-looking she thought she could almost see the bones through it. He had not looked like that in the peknu town.

He's dying, she thought, then almost laughed at the stupidity of her concern. They were all dying.

She turned her eyes away from him, and saw Runs Slow, hands tied behind her back, still fighting with the man who restrained her. The man hit her — hard — and she fell forward and lay crying in the dirt.

The green-and-gold-silk man who held Kirtha stood beside the one who held Runs Slow. That man laughed and said something to Runs Slow's keeper, then picked up Kirtha and swung her upside-down by one foot. Kirtha shrieked and her face went red. Immediately, Faia, Medwind, and even Nokar were fighting again. Fat Girl rammed her head into the groin of the man nearest her and broke free — surprising all of them. She was on her feet and charging the man who dangled Kirtha before he could put the child down. Fat Girl got in one head butt to his face before he dropped Kirtha and punched his fist into Fat Girl's belly.

Fat Girl went down, gasping for air — and the first man she'd rammed with her head walked over while she lay there and kicked her in the side. She tried to find some satisfaction in the first man's limp, and the gaping hole in the other man's mouth where his front teeth had been, but pain swallowed that satisfaction far too quickly.

When the first man tired of kicking her, he grabbed

her by one ankle and dragged her back to her place in line. She was too hurt to struggle.

She wished she could kill the stinking Silk People. She'd often wished them dead, but she'd never thought of herself as the weapon that would kill them. At that moment, she wished she were such a weapon.

The last of the spectators filed in. At a signal from the priest, the drums stilled. The chanting stopped.

The biggest of the Keyu spoke.

Give us our offerings, it drummed. *We hunger.*

The Mu-Keyi, chief priest of the village, pranced and strutted like a puffing-krull seeking mates. He drummed boasts to his gods — boasts of the wonderful things he'd done for them, of the grand sacrifices he gave them. While he drummed, the green-and-gold-silk men lined up in some prearranged order, with their victims held firmly between them. Her captors pulled Fat Girl back to her feet. In front of her, two men held a bald, tattooed girl who leaned from side to side, crying. The girl was pale. Blood ran down her legs and pooled at her feet. A sharsha, Fat Girl realized. She'd only seen one before, on her own terrible naming day — the day of her exile. That day, the sharsha had been the only food for the Keyu.

The drums started up again, and the first of the green-and-gold silk men moved forward. He held Kirtha aloft.

The Mu-Keyi drummed and danced and chanted, while Kirtha's guard carried her to the base of the biggest tree and put her down in front of it.

"Kirtha, RUN!" Seven-Fingered Fat Girl screamed, and Kirtha stood and started to run toward her mother.

The Keyu's thick white palps wrapped around the little girl, and the huge tree made a strange, crooning, creaking noise. The child screamed and struggled and kicked. The front of the tree split open from the base

upward, and the palps brought the child forward to
the mouth.

The Silk People drummed and prayed and chanted.
Faia screamed. She kicked at her guards and fought to
get free.

Kirtha stopped screaming and stared at the Keyu.
The tree quit pulling the little girl toward its maw. The
rest of the trees quit drumming for food. The priests
fell silent. Everything stopped.

In the sudden silence, Fat Girl heard Kirtha say,
"Bad tree."

The Keyu's palps burst into flames.

Chapter 8

When first the Wen guards forced Medwind into the tree-circle, she could find no cause for hope. But as the moments passed, and the Wen began their ritual, she sensed something that made her think she and her colleagues might have a chance to survive after all.

Energy filled the tree-circle — the same eerie, inaccessible energy that had dragged the exploratory team off course and made their airbox crash. The clearing was the heart of it — birthing place of a maelstrom of power. Medwind centered herself and reached out magically; she tried to touch it — and as before, the power slipped out of her reach.

She bit her lip, frustrated, and studied her two guards surreptitiously. *I'll fight without magic, then,* she thought. *I've done that before.* But she knew she'd never fought magic without magic.

No sense worrying. Brooding about the things she couldn't change would only waste her time and her energy, and keep her mind from more productive avenues of thought. She worked at the rope that bound her wrists until she was free of it — the trick of clasping her hands together when the Wen tied her worked well enough. She held onto the rope — she decided she'd better look the part of the helpless captive.

And then, free and disguising the fact, she studied her options. The Wen tagnu might consider dying bravely to be a virtue, but winning and living to fight again were the only virtues in the Hoos world of war.

So Medwind Song concentrated on tactics for the coming battle. The terrain in which she would have to fight was a flat, mud-floored basin, ringed on all sides by a circle formed of nine ramets of the largest baofar tree she had ever seen. Baofar genets, the whole of the organism, were usually comprised of hundreds of trunks and could fill an entire valley, but the trunks, the ramets, were quite slender, with thousands of delicate white strands of silk that hung from their bark to the ground and blew in the breeze. In the place of that silk, these ramets of the baofar were the width of row houses in Ariss, and in place of fine silk they grew heavy white limblike palps that writhed unnervingly. She eyed the bloated tree's trunks and its engorged palps with distaste.

It's done well, she thought, *on a sacrificial diet.*

The only way out was the way they'd come in — through the single opening in the circle of trees. Beyond that point, the village became a maze of tree-branch walkways and under-branch paths — one of which would take them out of the accursed Wen village. Medwind had no idea how she could negotiate her way through that maze, but she would concern herself with that problem only when it presented itself.

Inside the circle, about sixty of the Wen observers in their gaudy silks clustered near the exit. She would have to go through them — if she could get past the gods-bedamned guards who held her and her friends — and past the priests.

The guards had knives. She knew how to deal with knives.

The priests carried no visible weapons — they were, no doubt, protected by magic. Therefore, even if she could kill her own guards quickly — and take out as many of the others as she could — she would still probably fall to the priests. She would probably die there, she thought — and the rest of the attack would be for nothing. She tried to think of another strategy.

Then the baofar spoke. *Give us our offerings,* it drummed. *We hunger.*

All Medwind's plans shattered. She stared at the Keyu, horrified. In spite of everything the Wen kids had told her, she had not been able to think of the trees as her enemy. She'd kept believing her problems would come from the people.

She stared at the priests, for one wild instant hoping that somehow one of them had done that thunderous drumming.

But no. The tree had spoken.

The tree was alive with magic. Now that she knew where to look, she could sense the power of the monster baofar, locked into its multiple ramets and buried roots and intertwining, low-hanging, branches; coursing through its twitching, groping white palps; signaling its hunger into the air.

We have to fight that? she thought. *Without weapons, and without magic?*

Despair overwhelmed her. She could win against humans — and even a hundred humans, she thought, could fall to a sufficiently angry Hoos. But a tree? A giant tree? What in the hells . . . ?

Then one of the Wen carried Kirtha up to the the biggest of the baofar's ramets, and it didn't matter anymore what she could or couldn't do. She dropped the bonds on her wrists and snapped her arms out and up into the throats of her two guards. While they were still disoriented from the surprise attack, she pulled both into reverse headlocks. She snapped the neck of the first man — it didn't break cleanly. He fell, convulsing, and Medwind's stomach knotted. She hated to kill — she hated even worse to do it messily. She made sure the second man died quickly, with one clean snap.

One of the onlookers saw what she was doing and shrieked. Heads turned in her direction.

She caught the second man's knife as he fell and started to run toward Kirtha — and suddenly the drumming stopped, and Kirtha said, "Bad trees," and the palps of the baofar ramet that held her burst into greasy yellow flames.

Medwind stared at the little girl, tracing the path of the magic in her mind. *She's touching the tree. Using its own magic against it.*

Then the tree threw the child out of its grasp, and pandemonium erupted in the clearing. One of the Wen priests shouted "Demons! Demons! Throw them all to the Keyu!" The drums throbbed to life, and the guards ran at the trees, dragging the rest of the exploration party and the weird-looking green-striped girl with them.

Medwind ran at a tree herself. There was no time to give the rest of the group instructions. No time, in fact, for anything but running, being caught in the slimy hard embrace of the Keyu, and —

— <*Yes-s-s-s you have come to us come must come to us come to me you are ours (MINE!) ours you will join with us love us you will *fight them, fight them* love ME!*> said voices in her head — echoes and whispers — lovers half-remembered — something embracing her that felt both wonderful and terrible, a violation of her mind and the sweet embrace of a longed-for and only-just-found other part of herself and somehow, somehow, she woke herself a bit from the voices and — though she could still hear them, though she couldn't escape them — she remembered her danger.

All around her, in the physical world, she could hear the screams of terrified people and the madness of the drums. For the briefest of instants, she focused on the people she loved — the people she hoped to save.

Then Medwind let her mind connect with the mind of the tree. She made the tree's structure a part of herself — let its roots become her feet and its branches her arms —

and made its magic her own. And when the accumulated magic of the baofar coursed through her, she circled it back into the tree in the shape of fire.

Heat built around her while part of the tree-voice murmured, <*Love us join us feed us,*> and part screamed, <*No fire don't burn no help me help us!*> and part whispered, <*Yes yes yes-s-s-s YES!!! BURN!*>

The tree tried to fling her away as it had Kirtha, but Medwind held on. She kept forcing the tree's power back on itself, kept burning the huge baofar —

The tree changed its tactics. It wrapped its palps around her face and secreted masses of viscous white slime, dripping it over her eyes and nose and mouth. The stuff stuck and hardened almost instantly, and Medwind began to suffocate. She hacked at the palps with the dead guard's knife, but the knife got stuck in the goo, and her hand with it.

Her lungs, deprived of air, burned. She clawed at her face with her free hand, and that hand, too, stuck to the secretions.

Linked to the tree, dying, she mindscreamed into the void that reached out to envelope her —

Help me!

Choufa heard the drumming start. With her eyes closed, she could follow the progress of the peknu along the sacred paths to the tree-circle. They glowed like torches, the peknu — she and her fellow sharsha were nothing but glow-bugs in comparison.

The Keyu would be pleased, she thought. No doubt the peknu would make tasty treats for them. The last ones certainly had.

She sat alone on the branch. She wanted to be alone — Thedra was going to the Keyu, too. When the trees began to feed, they would draw Choufa in, and she would share their feeding with them. Against her will, in spite of herself, she would share the moment of her friend's death and the hopeless knowledge that soon she would die in the same manner.

And now, too late to tell Thedra, she knew the secret. It would not have made any difference, but she thought Thedra would have wanted to know. Choufa had felt the moment when the girl birthed and noted a sudden brightening of the glow that came from her — and a new, faint glow that came from her newborn baby. Thedra didn't gleam with the brightness of the peknu, but she came very close.

That is the secret, Choufa thought. *The Keyu like us even better after we've had babies. So we have to have babies, who grow up to be new sharsha — and the Silk People tell us that having babies is the only way we can hope to be free. That way, they always have someone to feed the Keyu.*

The Silk People's lies infuriated her, but her fury had no teeth.

She stretched out on the platform of woven branches and closed her eyes tighter. It was starting. The Keyu thoughts began to pull her in.

<Food is there is food it is mine/ours/mine *do not do this!* we want I want food yess-s-s-s that one is mine!>

She felt them hungering, reaching out toward the smallest bundle of light; felt them wrapping their coils around it; and with a sudden shock, felt it merging with them — hearing them as she heard them.

The Keyu crooned their pleasure. *<Come to us come to me little one you are one of us one with us (YOU ARE MINE NOW) *let her go let-her-go!* NO! mine I am hungry let us love you we love I love — >*

The little peknu was frightened — and angry. It touched the Keyu with its mind, and Choufa felt it change something, felt it take the strength of the Keyu and twist it, using all that power to burn the Keyu who held it.

Yes! she thought. *That's it! The little peknu isn't as strong as the Keyu, but she is strong enough to turn the Keyu's power back at it. Even I am that strong, I think.*

The voices of the Keyu cut off, replaced by a mindscream that started in the Keyu circle and spread — spread through the trees around her, and out in a circle to the edge of the village. *Fire it burns fire is burning us fire!* some of the Keyu screamed, and Choufa felt the Keyu that held the smallest of the peknu fling it away from itself.

Choufa crowed. *Again, littlest one!* she thought. *Burn the evil gods again!*

But the littlest peknu was out of their grasp and not vicious enough or angry enough to do what needed to be done — and the Keyu put out the fire she'd started, and began to clamor for other, safer meals.

The babble grew louder and more strident in her mind, and Choufa felt the Keyu wrapping themselves around all of the peknu — and Thedra.

One of the peknu fought, and for a moment Choufa again sensed the Godtrees burning. For a moment, she believed the peknu might win. Then, though, the Keyu did something to the peknu, and her thoughts grew weak and dim, and she thoughtscreamed a plea for help, and grew still and silent.

No, Choufa thought. *No! They have to fight the Keyu — the peknu have to win.*

She threw aside her caution, and willingly embraced the thoughts of the trees, became a part of them, traced with her mind the branching channels of their power until she reached into the source of their strength —

— and then *she* twisted the power back and stung the gods with their own might.

She pulled some of the power to herself. She used it to touch the peknu who was locked in the Godtrees' embrace and turned the dripping, sticky raw tree-silk that covered the woman's face into dust. The woman took a long, shuddering breath, and then another. *Burn them now,* Choufa urged. *Kill the Godtrees.*

She moved away, pulled more strength to herself,

and touched the minds of the tree-voices that called out against the slaughter. *Burn the Keyu,* she begged. *Help the peknu.* And the rebels among the Keyu cried out <*Yes-s-s-s we will help we will kill! burn! kill! us-them-us! I don't want to die better to die than to live this way die free die we will die! Free!*>

The Keyu turned against themselves. The Godtrees fed power to the peknu and stole it back; pulled power from each other; set fires to themselves, put the fires out. Choufa, linked to the Godtrees, felt the pain of burning almost as if it were her flesh that burned; she heard the confusion that raged in the minds of the Keyu and reveled in it. She made herself concentrate on touching the rest of the peknu, the ones the trees were busily devouring even as they fought. *Fight the Keyu,* she urged. *Touch the Godtrees, and burn them!*

Roba, wrists still tightly bound, fell hard against the tree when the Wen threw her to it. Her back scraped down the bark — then the tree's cold white tentacles wrapped around her and dragged her toward a split in the base of the tree that widened into a gaping black maw. She struggled. The tentacles gripped tighter — sticky and horrible.

Then the tree devoured her.

The tentacles tossed her into the maw and released her, and again she fell. The maw snapped shut with a loud "clack."

For an instant, she lay in something soft and dry — something that felt to her like a mattress of spiderwebs. There was no light. The noise outside was muffled — she could hear the screams and the drumming and the shouting, but all those things sounded very far away. The air inside the tree was moist and musty, laced with a faint, sickly-sweet reek of decay.

She struggled to her feet, fought again to free her wrists, and again failed. The stuff she stood in gave beneath her, so that she had to fight to maintain her balance. She peered around the inside of the tree, trying to find even one detail she could use to orient herself, but the darkness was absolute. She took a cautious step forward, lost her balance, and fell.

Hopeless, she thought. *There is nowhere to go inside a tree.* She worked at her bonds anyway. It was something to do.

She became aware of a soft rustling that came from all around her. The sound was so slight — so trivial — that even once she'd separated it from the louder, horrible sounds outside the tree, she didn't attach any importance to it. At least, she didn't to begin with. But the soft, whispery sound — so like folds of cloth brushing against each other — grew in importance the longer it continued.

She managed, after some squirming, to catch the knot at her wrists, and for a long moment, with her hands twisted awkwardly, she worried it between her fingers. She kept at it even when her hands cramped. The knot loosened, then unraveled. The rope fell away into the darkness, and her hands were free.

She pushed herself to her feet — an easier task this time. With her hands held in front of her, she moved forward a finger's breadth at a time. Around her, above her, behind her, beside her, the rustling continued. Soft whispering. Faint sussurations. Something there.

She bit at her lip until the taste of her own blood filled her mouth. She crept forward over the soft material that shifted with every step she took, fighting to keep her balance in the featureless dark. She fell — once, twice — and climbed up to edge forward again. Her outstretched fingertips touched something soft — damp and cold and sticky — something that moved when she touched it — something that reached out and wrapped around her fingers in a chilly, slimy embrace —

At the touch, she heard voices in her head. She felt

wet, probing thoughts sliding through her mind, groping. <*Ours,*> they said, <*We want we love we hunger —
ours.*>

She pulled her hands back and pressed them to her
mouth. The mindvoices vanished. Her heart pounded.
She dropped to her knees and crawled; away, she
hoped, from whatever it was that had touched her.

The whisperings in the dark grew louder.

Something soft and wet draped itself across the back
of her neck — a gentle touch, feather-light. She
brushed at the spot and her hand caught on a sticky,
stretchy tendril, thin as spider-thread. She pulled the
tendril off her neck, but it stuck to her hand. She pulled
it off with her other hand. It stuck to her fingers. In the
meantime, another light, wet touch brushed her back.
Before she could pull away, several more of the tendrils
attached to her arms and her legs. The tendrils
brushed her cheeks and tugged at her breasts. She
swung, fists clenched, and hundreds of the tiny, gluey
threads caught her arms in mid-swing and held them.

An instinct for self-preservation made her keep her
head down. The space around her was thick with
threads that caught and covered every bit of her body
they could reach. They clogged at her ears, covered
her back and the backs of her arms and the bottoms of
her feet in a solid mass. With her head down, at least
she had breathing room.

The mass of threads began to tighten — gently at
first, and then with more insistence. They dragged at
her, pulling her upward. She tried to straighten her
legs, but couldn't. She was careful not to struggle too
much — the hellish tenacious mass would suffocate her
in an instant if she gave it a chance.

Then she bumped against something soft and yielding. She dragged past it, bumped something else,
dragged past it as well, and came to rest with her back
pressed against slime. She felt a quick, burning sting at

the base of her spine, then tingling and numbness at
the spot, and suddenly the voices were with her again.

< — *will help we will kill! burn! kill! us-them-us! I don't
want to die better to die than to live this way die free die we will
die! Free!*> the voices clamored.

She felt the same stinging and numbness along the
bottoms of her feet, which pressed into the goo, and in
her shoulder blades, and along the backs of her arms,
which were spread out high and to either side of her.
She would have screamed, but she didn't dare.

The decaying stench grew stronger. Suddenly she
caught a faint whiff of smoke, and cutting through the
mindbabble, she heard a familiar authoritative snarl.
*Center on the trees as if you were grounding to them. Then pull
magic from them, and turn it back on the* stekkonks. *Burn
them!*

Medwind! Roba thought. The Hoos warrior was alive
somewhere in the mess and fighting. Roba followed
her instructions and found, to her amazement,
incredible power within her grasp. She shaped it carefully and burned into the tree that surrounded her —

— and screamed. Searing white-hot agony ripped
through her body, as if she were the one on fire.

<*Yes! Yes-yes-yes-(NO!)-yes!,*> the voices in her head
begged. <*Better to die than live better dead this way than live
like this better dead (DON'T! NO FIRE!) free dead is free is
dead!*>

Pain. It flowed into her, its conduits the points on her
body where she joined the tree. She didn't know if she
was brave enough to burn the tree again. She didn't want
to hurt like that again, and she didn't want to die — no
matter what the voices in her head told her. Better live
than die — it was always better to live than die —

The tree began to burn again, the fire initiated somewhere else, by someone braver, or stronger — or by
someone who couldn't feel the pain. The tree-voices
fought in her head while the pain grew. They screamed

and cried out, their anguish echoing hers. Agony — she writhed, tossed, squirmed, and lightless fire blazed through her body. She forgot herself, and screamed, and when she did, she threw her head back—

The mass of tree-stuff filled her mouth and her nose and stuck on her open eyes, and stopped her breath.

Her mind swarmed with panicked thoughts. *I don't want to die,* and *Kirgen, gods I'm going to miss Kirgen,* and, with the desperation of a drowning woman, while she drew in all the magic she could hold, *Get this stuff AWAY from me!*

The result was instantaneous — and impressive. The massed stuff vanished from her nose and her mouth and her eyes, and the tangles that held her lost their grip. Once again she fell to the ground. All around her, she heard the tremendous ripping sound lightning made when it struck a tree and exploded it into splinters. And the lesser darkness of night in the Wen jungle replaced the total darkness of her prison in the tree.

She could breathe. She was free. The frantic babbling voices of the tree were gone from the inside of her head.

She lay on the ground, mostly hidden inside what remained of the tree-stump. Flickering green faeriefires and hell-red magefires cast long, jerky shadows, and threw the Wen, her colleagues, and the hulking, malignant trees into high relief. The noise of the fighting was immediate again — close and terrifying. Wen ran by her, so close she thought they might have touched her. She didn't know for certain. Her arms and legs wouldn't move. She couldn't feel them at all. She could turn her head from side to side, but she was afraid to. If she moved, someone might notice and realize she was still alive. Then they would kill her, and she couldn't fight back. She couldn't even tap back into the tree's power to hold them off. The magic had slipped from her grasp the instant she shattered the tree.

She was helpless.

Medwind fell to the ground, and drew in a long, shuddering breath. *Burn them now,* the new voice in her head insisted. *Kill the Godtrees.* The urgent mindspeech came from whoever or whatever had saved her life.

Yes, she thought. The power was there. And the network of the baofar tree ran farther than she'd suspected. She'd felt the mass and range of the thing when she'd been trapped in its grasp. Now she had an idea of how to kill it. She forced herself to her feet and ran between two of the huge ramets, burning the tentacles when they reached for her. Outside of the circle and out of reach of the tentacles, amid trees that grew in orderly ranks, she sank to her knees and dug her fingers into the soft, moist loam.

She gathered the night's darkness around her and inhaled through her teeth; soft hissing — the Hoos mantra for quick, deep trancing. She let her eyelids lower, forced the air out. She dug her bare toes into the earth, pulled the air in. Forced the air out, and with it, visualized her fingers and toes putting out roots and spreading them deep into the ground. Hissed the air in, and pulled after the magic bound into the baofar the way rootlets probed after water. Nothing, nothing, but her rootlets told her the power was close. . . .

Exhale, grow deeper — inhale, pull in the strength —
Exhale — inhale —

She had it! Inhale — deeper, fuller; her lungs were near bursting with air; her body overflowed with magic. She held her concentration and twined the rootlets her mind created into the baofar's deep-buried, far-reaching, tangled network of roots and ramets. She took in its shape, its extent, the myriad branchings of its form and fixed those paths in glowing traceries in her mind's eye. She paused — breath caught — shaped the magic into slow-burning magefire that was impossible to put out; that would burn under the ground; that would, eventually, reduce the monstrous baofar to cinders.

She touched the familiar shapes of minds she knew — Faia and Nokar, Thirk's less familiar thoughtforms, and the mind of the stranger who had saved her life. She couldn't find any of the rest in the mindnet — but she pushed worry away. Later, later.

Join with me, she whispered into the minds she recognized. *Draw strength from the tree you touch and feed it into me.*

She felt their surprise, then their elation — and then the incredible surge of magic that flowed into her and almost overwhelmed her. She exhaled slowly, and slowly fed the magic in the form of magefire into the baofar's roots. She felt the roots catch, and traced the dying of the tree by the blacking out, one by one, of the glowing rootlines drawn in her mind.

She came to the end of her breath, held the magic tightly, inhaled and filled again. The baofar attacked — sent surges of its magic against her. She caught them, changed them, turned them — exhaled. The tree-death spread.

Inhale and fill. Exhale and burn.

In her mind's eye, the center of the baofar's rootsystem was gone — a circle of spreading darkness. Inhale. Exhale.

She felt hot. Ignore it. Inhale. Exhale.

One edge of the uneven circle of roots disappeared — the remainder, still glowing behind her half-closed eyelids, looked like a skeletal drawing of the Tide Mother, waning, its cup tipped and spilling fire.

Chill bumps raised on her arms, and the hair stood on the back of her neck. The omen she'd seen that morning — bad omen. She pushed it out of her thoughts.

Inhale. Exhale. Sweat dripped from her hair, along her neck, down her back. Ran off the tip of her nose and down her arms and thighs. The heat became terrible, the world around her changed from darkness to the light of first dawn. In her mind's eye, the last tiny remnants of the baofar's roots blinked away to nonexistence.

Dead! The tree was dead.

She hung her head, gasping and exhausted. The backwash of energy escaping from the dead baofar drained the strength out of her. *Rest,* she thought. *Gods, I need to rest.*

Medwind opened her eyes.

"Oh, farkling gods!" she yelled. Tiny magefires trickled out of the ground all around her. They licked at the bases of the orderly rows of slender ramets and flickered up the giant ramets that formed the heart of the baofar. People screamed. The air was scented with smoke and a few stray ashes that caught in the nose and stung the eyes.

The whole of the keyunu village had been one tree — one overgrown, twisted baofar, with ramets that formed the tree-circle, the houses, the walkways — *oh, no — even the paths!* she realized. The whole village was starting to burn. And, even though magefire burned slowly, if they didn't get out soon, Medwind and her colleagues would be trapped in the center of it.

She kept low and ran between the giant, predatory ramets of the baofar. The palps twitched and spasmed as she passed. The movement seemed to her more death-throes than any sign of awareness in the baofar. The Wen ignored her. They beat at the flames, stamped the little blazes with their feet, flapped their robes — they used anything they could get in hand; a few got too close to the fires and ignited into greasy, shrieking human torches.

Meanwhile, her people — where were they? As it died, the baofar was releasing the magic it had trapped. Medwind could feel power again within her reach. She centered and caught it — shielded herself as best she could, and peered into the otherspaces for some sign of Nokar, Faia, Kirgen, or Kirtha, Roba, or Thirk or the tagnu kids.

Faint familiar glows came from inside several intact ramets and from the blasted remains of a trunk on the other side of the circle. Medwind ran to the nearest of the ramets — she could feel Nokar inside it. She shoved the frenzied Wen out of her way, and when they tried to attack her, blasted them with a bolt of faeriefire. The Wen retreated. As a precaution, she created a shield around herself — just in case they changed their minds. Then she pressed her palms against the tree-mouth, and channeled energy into the closed aperture until the wood burst apart in a shower of splinters.

"Nokar!" she yelled over the riot of noise surrounding her. "Nokar — get out of there!"

She didn't see him — but she could *feel* him. Movement caught her attention. A white man-shaped sac glistened in the dim firelight. It was suspended at her eye level and attached to the far wall of the trunk — at the sound of her voice, it writhed and shuddered weakly. Her breath caught in her throat. "Nokar!" she screamed. She recalled the magic the stranger had used to save her life — *Dust,* she thought. *Turn the stuff into dust.*

The sac shifted — she could tell Nokar was trying to turn his head toward her, though his features were unrecognizable beneath the coating. He twitched — his body was attached to the tree-wall at belly and knees and feet, palms of hands and chest.

She ran to him, pressed her hands against the tough silk membrane, closed her eyes, and let energy race from her fingertips into the web. *Dust,* she thought. *Be-*

come dust. She felt the tingle of magic surging through her and sensed success. Drained, she sagged against the tree-wall.

Flakes and strips of the stuff began to peel away from Nokar. The fibrous bands that attached him to the tree broke one by one. His hands came free, then his feet and legs, and then the band fixed to his belly broke, and he dropped. She blocked his fall with her body, and let him slide to the tree-floor. His head lolled back and forth, and he blew a long, slow breath that sent a stream of white silkflakes out of his mouth into the air.

"Nokar! Up!" she shouted.

His eyes stared at her, unblinking. He didn't move.

Her lungs ached from the smoke that collected in the confines of the hollow trunk. Every breath burned her. She sobbed, and grabbed the old saje and dragged him out of the baofar ramet. She left him on the ground, but formed a magical shield around him that would keep the Wen away and protect him temporarily from the magefires, then ran to the ramet that held Faia.

When she blasted it open, she found the hill-girl leaning against the inside wall, spitting dust and gasping. Faia had freed herself — though shreds of silk tattered from her bare skin so that she looked like a corpse escaped from its mouldering shroud. Thin trails of blood ran down the girl's left arm and leg. As Medwind helped her out of the ramet, she saw more blood on the girl's back.

"Hurts," Faia said, and sagged against the Hoos mage. She, too, stared blankly in front of her and made no move to protect herself. Medwind dragged her to Nokar's shield and shoved her inside.

She didn't know how she was going to get the rest of them out. She was so weak, so close to exhaustion. Thirk was still trapped — Kirgen was, too. And Roba . . . there was something wrong with Roba. The tagnu kids were safe—Kirtha was with them. She could sense the little cluster of them hiding nearby.

And she was running out of time. The fires were spreading. The tree-path out of the circle already glowed in places with the red gleam of magefire.

<*I'll help you — if you'll help me,*> a voice whispered in her head. It was the voice of the stranger who'd saved her life. <*I'll give you more strength. But you have to take me with you.*>

<*Agreed.*> Medwind didn't know who spoke, or where the voice came from, or how she would keep her promise. She didn't, at the moment, care.

Then energy came to her, energy she didn't have to fight for. She let it flow through her, into the tree that held Kirgen. It was raw power, unshaped, and with it, she split the ramet open at the base — as the power poured through her, the tree kept on splitting. The magic grew stronger as it flowed. Strength added to strength, as small energies within the tree itself combined their magics with Medwind's and the stranger's.

She was shocked. She'd thought the baofar completely dead — but there was still some life in it, and at least part of that life was trying to suicide.

The ramet twinned, and the two sundered halves toppled away from each other in slow, graceful arcs that seemed immune to gravity. Both halves hit the ground and bounced and shuddered — one half outside the circle, and one half into the clearing, where it crushed several of the hapless Wen who had not yet fled beneath its huge branches. Flames from the bases of the other trees licked at the downed treetop, and it ignited.

Medwind called a faeriefire to light the interior of the ramet — it was hollow, as the others had been, and full of white, squirming shapes from bottom to top — and she wondered where in that mass of heaving tree-silk Kirgen might be.

The faeriefire appeared — a small, pale green light that flickered into existence in front of her, and moved, at her direction, to the center of the fallen baofar ramet. It cast soft green shadows down into the deep crevasses in the wood and made eerie shadowshapes among the many shifting forms inside. Medwind moved closer, looking for a human form within those oddly mottled bulges of silk.

Then one rounded bulge turned toward the light, and Medwind recognized it for what it was — a human face — eyes blinded by a coating of silk, half-opened mouth filled with rootlets. She could suddenly make out the lines of the body — palp-pierced, silk-coated, child-sized — and saw that it was marked beneath the silk with bands of dark and light. Medwind's breath caught in her throat. *Still alive*, she thought. *Oh, dear gods, it's still alive.*

Other bulges shifted; turned toward the light as best they could; opened mouths in silent cries. Most were small forms — the Wen were small people — but the bodies in the trees were smaller than any adult. *Surely*, Medwind thought, *they didn't sacrifice children to their Godtrees.*

But the evidence, the hundreds of little forms among bigger bodies grown into that single ramet of the baofar, said otherwise. The wriggling bodies looked like kittens newly born, still wrapped in birthsacs, helpless. When she touched the wood, she could hear their faint, fading mindcries.

<— feel light I/we feel light there was no light no light for so long now (I WANT TO LIVE!) die we can die let us die *save me!* — > they mewled.

Medwind pulled her hand from the wood as if burned. *These* were the gods of the Wen — these sacrificed children who had spent years, perhaps centuries, in deathless, grisly captivity. And she had nearly joined them.

She moved to the base of the ramet and climbed into the split. She found Kirgen, not completely silk-covered nor grown through with palps and roots as the Wen children were, but suspended from one side of the ramet. His arms were wrapped around another form in a gesture of protection.

Medwind used the stranger's energy to change the silk covering him and the other form into dust. Kirgen struggled out of the ramet. The other person, who Medwind realized was the tattooed Wen girl, didn't move.

"She's dead," Kirgen said. He leaned against the ramet. "She was dying when they brought her here."

Medwind hardly heard him. She stared at the twitching bodies in the ramet. Near the base there was one adult-sized body — a body with one gold-banded braid not coated by the silk wrapping.

"A saje. One of Praniksonne's party," she whispered. She stared at him. His body was pierced at a dozen key points by tendrils of the ramet. The tendrils grew completely through him, linking his spine and his vital organs directly into the structure of the tree. She tried to imagine changing not only the silk that coated him, but also those linkages, into dust.

He would die instantly, she realized. His heart and kidneys and liver were all punctured, and from the look of him, the tree had laced itself in and out of his spinal column as if it were running a seam. That series of tendrils probably terminated directly in his brain. He was a dead man — then or later. If she released him to speed his death out of misplaced mercy, she was afraid she wouldn't have the energy she needed to free Thirk and do whatever had to be done for Roba and the tagnu.

The magefires will give them all grace soon, she thought. *That will have to be good enough.* She turned her back on the saje.

Kirgen was up and moving under his own power. She saw him at the shattered ramet. She moved to the trunk that imprisoned Thirk. *Kirgen will take care of Roba,* she thought. With the last of her energy, and the last of the stranger's magic, she blew open the trunk. She ran through the circle of fire; she avoided looking around her beyond what she had to do to find Thirk. She didn't want to see any more of those pitiful child-shapes.

Once freed, Thirk was groggy and very weak. She hoisted him onto her back and staggered with him to the shielded circle where Nokar lay. The last Wen kept a respectful distance. *Couldn't do a damned thing to save myself at this point,* she thought. She bared her teeth at them, and they backed further from her. *Lucky, lucky they don't know that.* She pushed inside, and turned back to help Kirgen — but he had Kirtha riding on his shoulders and the tagnu kids trailing at his heels, and he was carrying Roba in his arms.

The Wen didn't have the respect for Kirgen they had for her. They attacked — and he blasted the attackers into cinders. He trudged through their smoking remains without seeming to notice, and as he got nearer, Medwind could see tear streaks channeling the soot on his face.

Medwind dissolved the shield. Faia was still bleeding, and she looked sick and weak. But the hill-girl crouched over Nokar, fingers rested on his chest, and Medwind could sense the healing magic that ran from her to him. Faia looked up when the shield dropped and brushed her tangled hair from her face. "He's dying, Medwind. We have to get him out of here."

Medwind stared around the clearing. The magefires were spreading inexorably. The smoke was chokingly thick; the sky rained ashes. "Yah," she agreed. "Now would be a good time. Except I don't know where in the hells to go."

Through the thick smoke, several small, quick forms approached. One of the smallest ran straight to the exploration party. She was nearly bald, and every visible fingers' breadth of her skin was a mass of intricate, interweaving tattoos. In heavily accented Sropt, she said, "Quick, follow us. We will lead you out of here, but you must take us with you."

"Who are you?" Medwind asked.

"I saved your life," the skinny child said. "I will save it again. And then you will save mine."

Medwind helped Kirgen position the unresponsive Roba on his back. Faia and Dog Nose propped Nokar up between them. Seven-Fingered Fat Girl put Kirtha on her shoulders and held Runs Slow's hand. Medwind helped Thirk up, and he leaned on her.

Medwind told the little girl, "Let's go."

The skinny girl led them out of the circle and into the midst of a herd of children — about fifteen of them, all tattooed, one boy, the rest girls (and some of those very pregnant). *What in the hells are we going to do with all these kids,* Medwind wondered. But where the kids led, she followed. They trotted along a ground path, one that twisted and tangled through the tree-maze. Several times, the whole crowd of them had to backtrack, stopped by flames or desperate Wen. One of the older tattooed girls fell, transfixed by a spear. Faia caught one of the big stone knives in her thigh, and bled and swore. The smoke was a bigger danger than the Wen, however, and Medwind crouched as best she could to stay beneath the worst of it.

They reached a wall of flames — the tiny aperture that entered onto the tree-path blazed with magefire.

Medwind clenched her fists in frustration. She didn't have the strength left to pull in magic to fight the fire. She was too weary even to shield effectively. She stared at the burning tree-wall, powerless.

The skinny little kid and her friends, though, were doing something. They all touched hands and stared at the flames. The magefires slowly dimmed, then backed away from the aperture that led into the long and twisting path. Medwind yelled, "Get through fast," and she and the staggering Thirk made a clumsy run at the smoking, charred wood.

They would have to go through one at a time. Medwind knelt to go through first. Thirk stumbled and fell heavily against her, and she tripped into the red-glowing wood. The coals seared into her left shoulder, and she jerked away, hissing from the pain. She scooted through and turned and pulled him in after her. She could see Kirgen, with Roba on his back, coming in as she and Thirk started down the path.

The tattooed children held back the live flames, at least from the first part of the passageway. Nevertheless, the heat in the tree tunnel was unbearable. Every breath she took burned her lungs. She would have given anything she owned for a cloth to hold over her nose and mouth. Her eyes watered from the heat and the smoke and the ash that blew in the hellish firewinds. Coals fallen to the forest floor burned her bare feet when she misstepped. She ached for a single wisp of cool air, or the touch of fresh water to her cracked, blistered lips. She hobbled forward, praying to all the gods whose names she could remember for the safe passage of the people she loved and dragged the whimpering Thirk behind her.

The path widened much faster than she remembered and was much shorter. She thought she recalled the passage taking hours, through convoluted, narrow tree-walls — but with a few steps, she was to the point where she and Thirk could once again move side by side. And after a single turn in the passageway, she could see the end of the twin rows of trees. Her mind refused to accept this, even when she made out, in the deep gloom of the jungle's daybreak, the forms of the airboxes hunkered down in the small clearing ahead.

It's a trick — or a trap, she thought. *One last Wen ruse.* But the airboxes remained solid and unchanging as she and Thirk drew near.

They used drug-smoke on us on the way in, she remembered suddenly. *But the roshu were real.* She stopped and looked around the clearing from the relative protection of the tree-walls. She could see none of the huge beasts. She moved forward again as Kirgen caught up with her and bumped into her.

She and Thirk staggered forward again, in a gross parody of a run. They moved out of the tree-tunnel — and the faint cross-breeze of cool, clean air brushed against her skin and trickled into her lungs. She moved faster, crossed the clearing, and stumbled up to Nokar's beautiful carved airbox, now scarred by roshu claws and with the door ripped completely away from the frame. She fell into the airbox interior, and she and Thirk lay on the cool wood floor for an instant, panting and weeping. Kirgen joined them and placed his burden carefully along the aisle between the rows of high-backed benches. The rest of the troop caught up in ones and twos. The horde of tattooed kids brought up the rear in a solid, screaming, cheering clump. Everyone crowded into the battered airbox.

Faia and Dog Nose placed Nokar beside Roba.

"They need healing," Faia said.

"Yah," Medwind agreed, "but not here. We need to get to safety first."

Kirgen, who was kneeling at Roba's side in the narrow aisle, gripped the unconscious woman's hand and looked up at the Hoos woman. "I don't know what's wrong with her — but she may not live until we find a safe place."

Medwind nodded. She stared pointedly at Nokar and, when Kirgen's gaze followed hers, answered softly, "I know. But we have more than two lives to think of. We need to use whatever energy we can muster to fly out of here. When we get someplace secure, then — well —" She shrugged.

The muscles in Kirgen's jaw clenched. "I could fly us

out now — but I'm too drained. It will be hours before I can summon and control sufficient magic to lift us off — and you're in worse shape than I am."

In her own language, the homely little tattooed leader of the Wen pack asked Medwind, "Why do you not take us out of here now? We saved you, just as we promised."

Medwind sighed. "We need the — ah — the Keyu-strength, but we are too tired to bring it to us."

"There are no trees in the sky for you to touch," the girl objected. "How can you use Keyu-strength there?"

Faia, cradling Kirtha on her lap and hugging the little girl, said in Sropt, "Same strength is in sky and earth, wind and fire. It come from everything around us."

The skinny girl tipped her head to one side and said, "If it is there, we can get it for you. Show us how to find it; then take us out of this place."

Medwind's eyebrows lifted. She translated what the girl said to him, and the two of them exchanged looks. "What do you think?"

"Fine with me. Show her how to tap the ley-lines if you have the strength."

Medwind demonstrated, trying not to think of the fire that moved ever closer to their downed airbox, or of the horrors she'd just survived. She taught the Wen children the rudiments as quickly as she could, and thanked every god she could think of when the first thin trickles of channeled energy bubbled to life in their cupped hands.

Then she showed them how to direct it into the control bar — and explained that, once the airbox was off the ground, they couldn't stop bringing in the energy until they were safely back on the ground. Everyone's life depended on them — one more time. She made *sure* they understood that.

"Are they ready?" Kirgen asked. He tugged on his

singed beard and shifted in the pilot seat. "As soon as they're ready, I'll lift us off."

Medwind asked them, and one by one, those tattooed kids who could channel magic nodded their readiness.

Their leader, the same skinny little girl who'd saved Medwind's life twice already, said, "We can do this. We won't fail."

Without further discussion, the kids crouched in a line down the aisle, and started pulling in power and feeding it through each other and into the control bar. Their magic was neither neat nor pretty, but it was enough.

Kirgen leaned on the control bar wearily and began to shape the raw energy — and slowly but steadily, the airbox lifted out of the clearing and away from the burning Wen village.

¤ *Chapter 9*

Seven-Fingered Fat Girl and Dog Nose crowded together onto the airbox's eagle-seat so they could be together while Fat Girl directed Kirgen. Wind roared in through the opening left by the missing door; Fat Girl's throat was sore from shouting over it. She was stiff from sitting in one place for so long. But she didn't care. Beneath her, the flat blanket of jungle changed to deep green, crumpled folds of earth, and in the distance she saw the jagged blue lines of a range of mountains.

Home, she thought. *We're almost home.*

Not without cost.

She ignored the burns on her back and sides. She and her people were better off than the peknu; the Keyu had shoved Dog Nose, Runs Slow, and her out of the way and refused to eat them. *Once tagnu, always tagnu,* she decided. Her blisters and raw, red patches hurt, but they looked less awful than the open, bleeding sores the Godtrees had left on the peknu.

She touched Kirgen's shoulder, near one of those sores. "Hurt you?" she asked.

He winced. "Like fire. And part of my hand is numb. Damn trees dug holes in all of us." He glanced back at his woman, lying in the aisle, and she could see terrible fear and sorrow in his eyes. Fat Girl imagined how she would feel if Dog Nose were hurt, and maybe dying, and she wished she hadn't said anything. The young peknu looked so sad.

She pointed at the mountain range. "We get there soon? Yes?"

Kirgen nodded.

"Good. We are almost past the place where the Silk People live. Where the trees are thinner, they don't live there."

Medwind leaned forward and shouted, "I imagine the Silk People are trapped in low-lying regions where baofar grow."

Kirgen yelled back, "You think the Wen are tied to the Godtrees?"

The Hoos woman nodded. "I'd hate to make any more wrong assumptions. The last one almost got us killed — I don't think I'll ever assume we can handle anything the world throws at us again — but I think so."

"That would be good," the saje yelled. "Seven-Fingered Fat Girl and Dog Nose have pointed out three more Keyu-villages that we've passed. I wonder why those Keyu didn't attack."

Fat Girl was pleased with how well she had followed most of the conversation. When Kirgen asked that, though, she decided she hadn't understood as much as she thought.

She and Dog Nose exchanged puzzled looks. Fat Girl phrased her question carefully in the saje's language. "You ask why rest of Godtrees not attack us?"

"Yes," Kirgen said.

Seven-Fingered Fat Girl raised her eyebrows and shrugged. "You killed gods. You think other Godtrees want you to come and kill them? The Keyu know we are near — they always know everything. But they not touch us. Gods not like to know they can die, I think."

Kirgen laughed. "That makes a lot of sense."

Medwind moved forward, keeping well clear of the gaping hole in the airbox side and out of the way of the tattooed Wen children. She crouched between the three of them, in front of the control bar. The warrior woman asked Fat Girl, "Where is the closest place we can land and make camp? Right now, we need to take care of our wounded more than we need to find the city."

Fat Girl remembered the battle with rival tagnu that had cost her most of her band. "We must go far as the first mountain valleys, because tagnu not go into the mountains."

She saw Medwind frown. "The Wen children are tired, and the rest of us are not strong enough yet to wield the magic in their stead. And more than anything, we must tend to Roba and Nokar."

Seven-Fingered Fat Girl rested a hand on Medwind's sooty shoulder. Earnestly, she said, "Until we reach mountains, tagnu got Paths everywhere. If we bring airbox down near Path, tagnu of that Path attack us quick-quick. Maybe we able to kill them all. Maybe not. We all tired and we hurt. Maybe we not fight so good. So we go to mountains now."

Medwind leaned forward and rested her hands on her bare, dirt-coated knees. She sighed. "This is your world, Fat Girl. You're in charge."

Fat Girl nodded, satisfied. That was the natural order of things, after all. She led and others followed.

Choufa focused on the yellow metal bar in front of her and pulled in the power the dying Keyu released. It became more difficult the farther she got from the burning Wen village. Only some of the other sharsha could help — only some of them could feel the power that flowed from the earth and sky — and from the slaughtered Godtrees. Those who could not help sat with their hands clasped, waiting. Their eyes told Choufa they were waiting for the Keyu to reclaim them all.

It wouldn't happen. No matter how tired she got, she wouldn't let it.

The airbox passed over other Silk People places, and briefly, as they flew over, she could hear the frightened voices of the Keyu.

<— not food we do not want I/we/I do not hunger for that lifefire do not catch do not bring them pass let them pass don't let them hurt us —>

And Choufa smiled, and whispered in the mindspeech of the Keyu, *<Pay us with your strength. If you don't, we will come and take it, and we will burn you. We burned the other Godtrees, and now those gods are dead.>*

She heard the panic in the Keyu voices and felt them scrabbling after power to send — then energy flowed into her and into the other working sharsha as well. Their eyes went wide with surprise. A few of the children whispered cheers.

The sharsha who couldn't feel the Keyu-strength enter the airbox didn't know what had happened. For all of them, stocky, dark-haired Maari asked, "Why do you smile, Choufa?"

Choufa bared her teeth in a wicked grin and hissed, "The Godtrees fear us. They cry out when we pass and beg for their lives. They gift us with their power, so that we will go away and leave them alone."

Maari grinned in return. "We should burn them anyway," she said.

Choufa shook her head. "We will take their power and fly to places with no gods. And none of us will be food for the Keyu."

"Yah," Maari said after an instant. "That is good enough."

The airbox settled in a meadow at the mouth of a deeply cut valley; the valley angled back into the high ridge and vanished between the bulky shoulders of sister peaks.

Medwind and Kirgen pulled out the few provisions the roshu hadn't gotten. They distributed clothes from the packs and set up shelters for everyone. The tattooed Wen kids refused to sleep in tents — they insisted that when the time came, they would sleep on the floor of the airbox. They gave Medwind bitter little smiles when she offered them help and said that sharsha didn't need help. She noticed that they and the tagnu kept as far from each other as work and the confines of the clearing allowed. She wondered at that, but didn't ask.

When camp was set up and the walking injured were being treated for their wounds, Medwind knelt by the bed she'd made for Nokar. He was protected by a felt tarp and wrapped in blankets and spare clothes to ward off the mountain cold. He lay, breathing shallowly, his face pale and waxy. His eyes were closed. He hadn't responded to anything since she pulled him out of the baofar ramet.

"You saved my life once, old man," she whispered. She traced his soot-grimed, age-crinkled eyelids with a finger. "Are you going to let me return the favor?"

Nokar didn't respond.

Faia came up and squatted beside her. "I have been doing what I can to heal the burns and tree-wounds, Medwind." The girl picked a stem of grass from the meadow and absently chewed on its base. "Most of the damage will heal on its own. Only some of the wounds will require the intervention of magic — herbs and roots took care of the simple things."

"That's good news. Who will need the healer-magic?"

"Kirgen has some damage to one hand; I have the hole in my leg from the knife; Roba is terribly injured; and Nokar . . . well . . ." Faia looked away, back over the endless expanse of greenery that rolled to the west. "Well . . ." she said again.

The hill-girl tore the remainder of the grass stem into long strings. Her fidgeting was making Medwind nervous.

Faia put down the shreds of grass and sighed. "There are things I have to take care of very soon. Right now Roba is caught between waking and sleeping — trapped in the world of feverdreams. I have done what I can for that. Tomorrow, perhaps she will recognize people. We will see. However, she cannot move her arms or legs, either. The baofar bored its rootlets straight into the whitecord that runs through the spine. Something ripped the rootlets out of her. That destroyed most of her whitecord. It is because of the whitecord damage that her breathing is very weak, and she cannot move, and she has so many bad burns. She could not escape the magefires."

"Can you heal her?"

Faia closed her eyes and exhaled slowly. "I do not know. I have several problems. First, the whitecord is complex — every bit of it has to be restored exactly right or the result will be a disaster. Second, I have not repaired whitecord damage on people before — only on sheep. Third, I will not be able to heal her from outside. To fix the cord, I will have to become part of it."

Medwind raised an eyebrow. "That's dangerous."

Faia looked down at her hands. "I know. If one of the sajes were in any shape to transport, he could go get someone with experience. If we could wait a day or two, Kirgen might be able to go. But I am afraid she will die before then. And . . ." The hill-girl faltered and stared into Medwind's eyes with a worried expression.

"What's bothering you?"

"She does not like me. She is jealous because of Kirgen and Kirtha. If everything does not go well, I am afraid she will blame me — and that Kirgen will blame me, also."

"You will be risking your life to save her."

Faia's mouth twisted into a half-smile. "People seem to only remember that when the results are good."

The Hoos warrior nodded slowly. "You are right, of

course." She stroked her fingers along her husband's face and waited for the hill-girl to continue. When she said nothing, Medwind sighed and asked, "And what of Nokar?"

There was a moment of uncomfortable silence. "His condition is worse than Roba's, although the baofar damaged him only a little," Faia said. "From the injuries the tree caused, he might have some weakness in his legs — especially his left leg — but that is all."

Medwind's stomach twisted. "Then why do you say his condition is worse than Roba's?"

"Because magic seems to be the cause of his injuries." The hill-girl stared down at the old man and slowly shook her head. "None of his worst symptoms were caused by the baofar. The problem is, I think, that he is so old. There are spells on top of spells to keep him from aging — all of them buried very deep. You knew of this?"

Medwind was startled. "No" she said. "He did a lot of his work alone at night. So did I. There were things both of us did that we simply didn't talk about. We gave each other that privacy."

She thought of her vha'attaye, with their skulls still stored in the back of the airbox. All Nokar knew of the vha'attaye were those things non-Hoos could rightfully know. And he knew nothing of the rituals to Etyt and Thiena. It unnerved her to realize she didn't know all of his secrets, either.

So Nokar was older than he looked. *That* was hard to imagine.

Faia said, "From the spell-shards and echoes, I would guess he had an entire set of spells set one inside another to ward off aging. They seem to have invoked each other to respond to changing situations."

Medwind frowned and stared at the old man. "Those are called nested subroutines — they're very elegant when done well, but they're *hrun*ing complicated to set up, and they eat enormous amounts of power." She glanced down at the old man, surprised. "He might have earned the *Eye of the Infinite* with real magic after all."

Faia reached out and touched Nokar's unmoving hand. Medwind saw tenderness and worry in the girl's gesture.

The hill-girl said, "When we went into the magicless areas, his spells collapsed in on each other. He got much older, very fast. Without any magic, he would have caught up to his real age and died in just a day or two. I think the baofar actually saved his life — at least for a while."

"But not for very long."

"Not now. Nothing can reverse his age —"

Medwind cut Faia off. "The Time River —"

Faia shook her head. "You barely survived that, from what you told me, even though you were young and strong. You went back, what — four hundred years? But you only seem to have gotten fifteen or twenty years younger in the process. I do not think fifteen or twenty years would do anything for him — even if he could survive the Time River."

Medwind stared down at her hands, turning them over and over. Finally she clasped them together and looked back up at the hill-girl. "How much time do you think he would need?"

"I can't tell. Not at all."

Nokar turned his head and opened his eyes. "I'd need at least a — hundred years, Med," he croaked. "I'm well past — two hundred by this time."

Medwind's shoulders sagged. "There's no way, then."

"No." Nokar stared into her eyes. "I'm going to die. But if you can — buy me some time — I want to see the — City of the First Folk. I can die happy then."

Medwind looked at Faia. "Is there anything you can do?"

"I do not think so. His are not injuries sheer magical strength can repair. His spells within spells need to be reformed — and I do not have the art for that." The girl's voice cracked.

Medwind saw the brightness of unshed tears in Faia's eyes. Her own throat was tight. "*Kyadda*, Faia. You take care of Roba. I'll do what I can for Nokar."

The girl nodded and got up and walked away, head down and shoulders slumped.

As soon as Faia was out of earshot, Medwind turned her attention back to Nokar. "I can give you almost forever, old man," she whispered.

He smiled weakly. "Dear love of mine." He reached out with difficulty and patted her hand. "I wish that were true."

She leaned closer and stared earnestly into his eyes. "It is true, Nokar. The vha'attaye don't die."

"They don't live, either. If I were vha'attaye, I couldn't smell — the sweet smell of your hair — or taste your salty kisses — or roll over in the bed at night and — squeeze your very fine breasts." He gave her another gentle smile. "I've lived long, Medwind. Those are — my principle pleasures now."

"But I don't want to lose you."

"Life is like that, Medwind. Eventually, we lose — everything we love. What you must do is — love many things — so the process takes longer." The old man attempted a wheezy chuckle that became an ugly cough.

She leaned over and kissed him firmly on the lips. Her tears mingled with her kisses. "Get some sleep, old man," she said. "I don't want to find someone else to love today."

Choufa curled with her back against the airbox wall, and stared over the lumped forms of sleeping sharsha. The look-holes framed a lonely, star-filled sky. Her burns ached, but the tall, red-haired peknu woman had smeared a sweet-smelling mash of plant-leaves on them. That took the worst of the pain away.

It was not pain that kept her awake. It was fear.

She wriggled upright, and crawled cautiously over the oblivious sleepers. She peered out the opening.

The air was bitterly cold, and thin. Gusts eddied around the airbox and blew through her coarse, tattered robe, raising bumps on her skin and causing her nose to run. Her teeth chattered. She wrapped her arms around herself and rubbed them against each other. For the chance to view the weird landscape in front of her, she had suffered far more than cold.

To one side of her, huge black walls of stone, bigger than the biggest Keyu, crawled up to the sky. They were so tall and mighty, even trees were afraid to climb to their peaks. She could make out, in the darkness, the silhouette of the line beyond which the trees would not go. That was the place Choufa thought she would like to reach.

How wonderful it would be to live in a world without trees. Without trees, nothing would scare me.

In front of her, dark lumps clustered close to the airbox. The peknu had such ugly little cloth houses; but Choufa recalled the beautiful silk hangings that had always surrounded her before and decided there was much to be said for some kinds of ugliness.

Beside the folds of one of those little houses, a tiny fire glowed. The peknu woman she'd saved sat by it, awake as Choufa, staring back the way they had come. The fire cast the sharp planes of her face in ruddy hues and gave some color to her star-white hair. The woman looked worried and sad. Suddenly she appeared to realize someone was watching her. She looked over at the airbox. Her pale eyes gleamed in the firelight. She smiled and said, in soft, oddly accented Folk-Speech, "If you already awake, you can come and company me."

Choufa climbed out of the airbox and walked over.

The woman handed her a heavy blanket. "Here. Take. Is Keyu-ugly cold this night. Sit by the fire. You can tell me your name and tell a story."

Keyu-ugly cold. Funny words, but Choufa liked them. "Keyu-ugly cold," she agreed, and took the blanket, and took a seat near the woman, out of the wind. "My name is Choufa. What story do you want?" she asked.

"Hai, Choufa. I called Medwind Song. Sometimes just Medwind. You save me, save all of us." The woman grinned at her. "Tell me why *you* need us save you."

Choufa laughed bitterly. "Not a big story there. I'm sharsha."

Medwind Song wrinkled her forehead, and shrugged. "Sharsha. You say that before. What that mean?"

"We are the people the keyunu kept to feed the Keyu. The Silk People kept us until we had babies — to make new sharsha — and then they fed us to the Godtrees." Choufa looked out into the darkness, into the place that was so far from her destroyed home, and pulled the blanket tighter around herself. "If we did not come with you, where would we go? After the Keyu were dead, the Silk People would have killed all of us, I think. They hated us."

"Sometimes, people fear what they not understand. They hate what they fear. That the way of some people."

"It's a bad way."

Medwind Song nodded. "Yes. You right." She placed a few more twigs and broken branches on her fire and sighed. "You out of that place, safe from those people. Now what you want to do?"

That was the source of Choufa's new fear. She had no idea what would happen next. She and her fellow sharsha were away from the hated Keyunu — but they had no place to run. "I don't know," she admitted. "Where are you going? Can we go there?"

"We hunt lost City of First Folk. Tagnu lead us there."

Choufa made a face. The other woman noticed and cocked her head to one side.

"You and tagnu, you no like each-each?"

Choufa shook her head slowly. "The tagnu are bad."

Medwind wrapped her arms around her knees and rested her chin on her forearms. She fixed Choufa with an intense stare. "You think so? Why?"

Choufa squirmed. "They — they had to leave the village."

"Yes. Why they had to leave? You know?"

Choufa licked her lips. Her mouth felt suddenly very dry. "Um — the Keyu made them leave."

The pale-eyed woman nodded, and an expression of satisfaction crossed her face. "Same Keyu who say you bad and had to be sharsha. You really bad? You *should* be tree-food?" she asked.

"No!" Choufa snapped.

"Right. They not really bad either." The pale-eyed woman stared out into the darkness. "I think Keyu picked tagnu because they had no *magic*, and you sharsha because you had lot-lot *magic*."

"*Magic?*" Choufa stumbled a bit over the foreign word.

"Power." Medwind frowned slightly. "How you made the airbox fly today. Tagnu not know that word in your tongue, so I not know it."

"No word for it," Choufa told her. She thought about the *magic* for a moment. "It is what the Godtrees do — and no one could talk about that. We prayed to them and asked them for things, but no one who wasn't Keyunu could say their name. And I don't think even the Keyunu dared to talk about them."

"Feed the *hrun*ing trees little children. I *bet* they not want talk about that." Medwind spat into the fire, and it hissed.

"*Hrun*ing trees?" Choufa asked.

The woman winced. "That a bad word. Forget it, you understand?"

Choufa grinned at her and said nothing. Hru*ning*, she thought. Hru*ning* . . . hru*ning* . . . hru*ning*. "*Magic*" *is a good word, but I bet* "hru*ning*" *is better.* She decided under no circumstances would she forget that word.

They sat together without speaking for a long time, listening to the croaking and buzzing and grumbling of the night things, and the whispers of wind through the grass. Finally, though, Choufa asked, "Medwind Song, can we go with you to this *city*? We could help you."

Medwind gave her a sad little smile. "You can come. *But* — we not know what we find there. First Folk city maybe very dangerous. Maybe you not want come."

Choufa studied the complex patterns of green and tan that curled up both her arms; *keyudakkau*, symbols of everything she hated in the Silk People — and she wanted to laugh. Any situation that contained even a chance of survival at the end of it didn't seem dangerous to her. She didn't doubt for an instant the other sharsha would feel the same way. "We'll come," she said.

Roba remembered fire — red-on-black-on-red, hellish trees, smoke and pain and more pain; drums and chants. She remembered being sure she was going to die. She even thought she remembered dying, but that memory, at least, appeared to be false.

The morning air was cold on her cheeks. Every breath was a new and separate agony, and every word burned in her ruined throat. She could see Kirgen's hand curled around hers — but she couldn't feel it. She couldn't feel anything below her neck. Her body seemed to belong to someone else — someone who had gone away and wasn't intending to come back. The really disturbing thing was, she still felt she had a body — the only problem was that it wasn't the one she could see. Her invisible but tangible body was bathed in amorphous pain. She kept trying to move her hand, to rub away the pain, and although her mind told her the hand had moved, she could see damned well it hadn't.

"I will send my spiritself into the whitecord," Faia said. She sat cross-legged on the floor of the tent on the other side of Roba.

Roba looked at the hill-girl — lean, graceful, young, and very, very beautiful — and she hated her. She hated the girl, and the girl's lithe movements. She hated the compassionate healer smile Faia gave her — and she hated just as much the nervous, uncertain glance the girl threw in Kirgen's direction.

Faia said softly, "I cannot promise this will work right. I cannot promise it will work at all. I do promise I will do everything I can."

Kirgen gave the hill-girl a grateful smile, and for an instant Roba hated him too.

"This thing you must know," the hill-girl said, speaking only to Kirgen. "Once we start, you must not violate the shield or touch either one of us, no matter what you see, or what we say. You understand?"

"No. Can't I even hold her hand?"

"No." Faia looked at him. "You cannot. Not one touch."

Kirgen started to argue, but Faia was already taking a long, slow breath and closing her eyes. She traced an arc around her from the ground to the point over her head. The air inside the sphere she drew began to glow blue.

"Amazing," Kirgen whispered.

Roba found herself impressed even through her haze of pain.

Then the blue glow stretched out and engulfed her. Faia toppled to one side, and Kirgen instinctively moved toward her. At the same instant, Roba heard Faia's voice inside her head.

Do not touch me! the voice demanded.

"Stop!" Roba croaked. "I can — hear her inside me. She says — don't touch."

"Oh. Well . . ." Kirgen sat back and looked anxiously between Roba and Faia. He pushed his hands onto the ground in front of him and chewed on his bottom lip.

Here it is, the voice muttered. Roba felt a few errant tingles at the base of her neck and one sudden blaze of pain in her left hand that immediately vanished back into nothingness. *I have found the top of the whitecord. For a little while, I will be a part of you. Both of our lives depend on how you react — I am matching your whitecord to mine, but if Kirgen or you or anything else causes me to lose my concentration, the whole spell could snap.*

Roba responded directly to the hill-girl for the first time. *And what a pity that would be, I'm sure. Then you will walk away, and I will die, or go on being a cripple — which will leave Kirgen free for you. That's what you want, isn't it? You and Kirgen and Kirtha — and me gone!*

The voice in her head was mild. *Not precisely, Roba. Both of us occupy your body right now. If the spell snaps, then my whitecord will configure itself to yours — and we will both end up dead or crippled.*

The rush of shame that overwhelmed Roba kept her mind occupied through the arduous, painful procedure that followed.

Medwind had spent most of the night in meditation. For a while, the little sharsha kid, Choufa, gave her a diversion from her worries, but when the girl went back to the airbox to sleep, the worries returned to fill the void.

Morning came too soon and offered too few answers. She could feel the edge of Faia's dangerous magic from Roba's tent. She could feel Nokar, hanging on to his life by the thinnest of threads. She could feel her own weakness, and her own inadequacy for the task before her. She sat outside the tent, staring at the last stars as they faded on the western horizon and wished she could take herself and Nokar back in time to a place where they were both young and strong.

She considered what lay ahead. A spell that could give Nokar back his life would be one that required subtlety and enormous skill and incredible amounts of power. She would have to figure out how Nokar had created the spells-inside-of-spells with which he had held back the plunderings of time. She would have to discover how he made those spells call on each other, what each separate spell did, and where each had fragmented when the magic faded. She would have to bring him back to health, rejuvenate his failing organs, and repair the shattered spells —and at her best, in full health, she simply wasn't that good.

In the last hour of night, she'd thought of an alternative. It was clumsy and heavy-handed. More than that, it would cost her, and cost her in such a way that she would never know the extent of the price she paid.

She could give him part of her own life, slice the years off of her own time, and graft those years on his life. By the very nature of the gift, it was something she could give and never miss —

I'll never know how many years I'll have — except I'll know some of them are gone, she thought. *Even so, if I could give him a year for a year, I would not question. I would simply give.*

If only it were so clear-cut.

The magic would not work that way. It would eat up part of the fabric of her life in the removal, part in the transfer, and part in the grafting on, so that a year of her life might only bring him a week, or a day, or an hour.

Or I could give him a year — or ten — and watch him die in the next instant anyway. How much would be enough to save him?

How much am I willing to give for love? she wondered. *How many of my days are one of his smiles worth? How many sunrises can can I willingly forgo to gift him with a glimpse of this city of his dreams?*

She clenched her fists and stared into the dying

embers of the campfire. *How much can I pay, knowing when the time I've given has gone, I'll lose him anyway?* She felt the oppressive weight of guilt. Gifts, she had always thought, would be freely given, and the price never questioned. She stared out across the lands that lay to the west and yearned for a simple answer.

There were none. *But then, in a perfect world the gods would never put a price on love.*

Seven-Fingered Fat Girl and Dog Nose lay in the tall meadow grass, and kissed, and fumbled, and rolled on the ground.

"This would feel better if you took off your myr," Dog Nose whispered. "I'll take mine off, too." He tugged at the front flap of her loincloth.

She pushed his hands away. "I know it would feel better," she whispered back, "but we said we weren't going to do that until we got back to our city."

"We're almost there." Dog Nose's voice was plaintive.

We sure are, Fat Girl thought. Her heart raced, and her lips trembled, and she really, truly wanted to take off her clothes and, well —

But she and Dog Nose had agreed to wait.

She didn't *want* to wait. They were out of the wind, hidden by a little depression in the meadow. The late afternoon sun on her skin was warm. The grass was soft and smelled sweet. Dog Nose pressed against her and wrapped his arms around her, and his skin felt like hot silk where it touched hers.

She wrapped one leg over his back and pulled him tighter to her. He rolled on top of her, and balanced his weight on his arms, and leaned down and kissed her — slowly and gently.

She shivered, and when they finished kissing, she pulled him close enough that she could nibble on his neck. He tasted salty, and felt wonderful — and when she nibbled just right, he groaned quietly.

But they were going to wait.

Dog Nose pressed warm little kisses behind her ear, and into the soft hollow at the base of her neck, and down the line between her breasts. With tiny movements, he nibbled his way to one breast, and kissed and licked and nibbled until she gasped for breath, and dug her fingernails through the grass at her sides to the cool earth beneath.

It feels so good, she thought.

He moved over her again, and pressed his body on top of hers, and this time rested his weight on her so that the lean, hard muscles of his chest crushed her breasts. The rest of the world seemed to vanish — she could hear nothing but their breathing, which grew faster, and the pounding of her heart in her ears.

We were going to wait, one tiny voice in the back of her mind whispered, but she had heard enough of that voice. She tugged at the band of her myr, and pushed at it until it was down out of the reach of her fingers. Dog Nose rolled away from her long enough to pull the myr down her legs and off. He stripped his own off, too, and moved over her again. He smiled shakily, and squeezed his eyes shut as he covered her body with his.

Their skin touched from cheek to chest to thigh to ankle. He slipped his hands under the small of her back and then held very still.

"Oh," he whispered, "you feel so good."

"Yes." She marveled at the pleasure of their bodies so close together, the wonderfulness of skin against skin. She ran her hands in long, slow lines from his shoulders down to the lowest point on his thighs that she could reach. The smooth, hard curves of his body felt so beautiful, and so right.

He slid one knee down between her thighs to push her legs apart, and she moved with him, wrapping her legs around his back and locking her ankles together; pulling him tightly to her —

"Ummm — please forgive interruption," a voice said from right next to them in the grass.

Seven-Fingered Fat Girl yelped. Dog Nose rolled off of her, and over onto his stomach, and sighed hugely. Then he beat his head on the ground.

Fat Girl stared at his antics. She couldn't help herself. She giggled. He looked over at her, and shook his head; then he grinned.

She peeked through the grass toward the sound of the voice. Faia stood politely at the edge of the depression, with her back to them and her hands in the pockets of her tunic.

"It time we go now. Everyone looking for you so we can leave."

Fat Girl sat up and tied her myr back in place. She gave Dog Nose a cockeyed little smile, which he returned. "So we wait until the city after all," she whispered.

Under his breath, Dog Nose muttered the three most terrible swear words Medwind Song had taught him, and Fat Girl laughed again.

The two of them followed Faia back to the airbox, holding hands and trying to act as though nothing out of the ordinary had happened. They took their places in the front of the airbox. Everyone else joined them.

Fat Girl was pleased to see that Nokar was up and walking, though he leaned heavily on a staff and moved slowly. He looked very sick, but Fat Girl decided that, since he was moving around, he would get better with time. Medwind, who got into the airbox behind him, looked exhausted — her skin seemed almost gray. But when she looked at the old man, she smiled. Both of them wore the brightest, gaudiest clothing Seven-Fingered Fat Girl had ever seen. They acted like they were celebrating — and she supposed they were. They were going to get to the city, and get to look at all the rest of those *books*.

Roba and Kirgen climbed into the airbox together. Roba moved with some difficulty and leaned on Kirgen when she walked, but both of them also looked happy. They whispered with their heads close together and laughed frequently. Thirk, who entered after the two of them, glanced in their direction and scowled.

All of the older sharsha kids poured in through the doorway in one mass, their voices high and excited. They crammed into the extra places on the benches, chattering about how wonderful it was to run and be someplace with no trees. Fat Girl nodded to herself. She could certainly sympathize with that.

The little kids were playing in the aisle. They had been even before she and Faia and the rest had climbed in.

Runs Slow had made little people and beasts out of twisted stems of the long grass, and she and Kirtha were busily running those playthings in the aisle of the airbox with several of the youngest sharsha children. The kids squealed with delight and mock terror as several of the grass monsters attacked one of the grass people. The other grass people fought off the attack, and Fat Girl grinned. Runs Slow was directing a repeat of the kellink attack that had brought Four Winds Band to the city in the first place.

Then one of the sharsha kids decided her grass monster was a doori and flew it down and snatched Kirtha's little grass person and flew off with it. Runs Slow yelled, "You can't do that!" at the same time that Kirtha shrieked and the little grass doori burst into flames. Suddenly all the kids were yelling and fighting. Faia waded into the middle of the altercation, pulled Kirtha out, and said, firmly, "No more fires! Not with your friends!" She made the little girl sit with her nose to the airbox wall.

Fat Girl put her hand over her mouth and turned away. It wouldn't do for Kirtha to see her laughing — but it was funny.

Kirgen settled in his seat, and some of the sharsha sat in a line in the aisle again. They all held still and cupped their hands as if they were holding water, and the next instant the airbox lifted off the ground.

"Now where?" Kirgen asked her.

Dog Nose and Fat Girl had conferred at length on that point. They knew the meadow didn't lead into the right valley. They'd tried to decide whether the right valley was to the north or the south. It was so difficult to tell — there hadn't been all that many landmarks as they got closer to the city, and the few landmarks they'd chosen turned out, from the air, to be common features of many of the mountains. So an approach from the valley wouldn't be very helpful.

But if they flew along the ridge, they decided they would be able to pick up the trail they'd followed out. At least the tall, carved standing stones should show up from their vantage point in the sky.

"We have to fly along very top-top of mountain. Rock backbone. There road we can follow," Dog Nose said in the peknu tongue.

"It's hard to fly that high for very long," Kirgen said. "The air is thin and it takes more magic to keep the air-box up."

"Fly fast, then," Fat Girl suggested.

Kirgen grinned and shook his head. "That won't help. But we'll do what we can."

The airbox described a smooth curve and headed straight at the mountain ridge. Beneath them the ground rose into huge, rough folds, and the bare rock jutted out like a sleeping giant pushing through his blanket of trees. Fat Girl saw movement beneath them and, after an instant, realized what she was seeing. A pack of kellinks was herding some big running beast into a cut-off. They streamed across the ground like a river running backwards, splitting into bunches at every obstacle, then reforming. From the air, they were incredibly beautiful. She pointed out the monsters to Kirgen and Dog Nose, and Kirgen dropped the airbox low enough for an instant that everyone could see them. The beasts looked up, then fled down the valley.

The airbox looks like a big hunting doori to them, Fat Girl realized. She grinned. It would be wonderful to hunt kellinks from an airbox — to shoot them from the open door, without having to take a chance at being their prey. If she could, she would kill them all. She knew at firsthand that they weren't nearly as pretty on the ground.

The airbox reached the mountain ridge. Below, Fat Girl could see a thin white line that traced along the mountain's spine. "There," she shouted. "See it."

Kirgen nodded, and screamed, "There it is! Look! Look, everyone. A First Folk artifact! The road!"

Dog Nose pointed out something Fat Girl hadn't noticed. In the long shadows of morning, three standing stones, their heads topped with monsters, clustered together around a flat circle of stone. "We passed that!" he yelled.

Nokar wanted to land the airbox on the ridge and take a look at the standing stones, but Medwind cut him off vehemently. "On to the city!" she shouted.

The air that blew in through the door-hole was incredibly cold. Fat Girl wished for a moment that she'd taken the Hoos clothing Medwind had offered her that morning, but, even as she rubbed the chill-bumps off her arms, she decided she was glad she hadn't. The city was going to be a tagnu city. She wanted to claim it as a tagnu.

Besides, she decided as pragmatism fought with imagined glory in her mind, she could take some of the Hoos warrior's clothes later, when the cold became unbearable.

A cliff edge along the path beneath them looked very familiar. A huge flat stone created a shelf that jutted out over a cliff; the sheer face of the cliff fell away to a

stream far, far below. Fat Girl pointed the place out to
Dog Nose, and he stared, then howled with laughter.
"That's the place where Roshi stood and peed over the
edge," he yelled. "Remember? He said, 'I'm a water-
fall!' —" Dog Nose stopped laughing. His face grew
somber and he stared down at the cliff and shelf again.
"I wish he could be here."

Fat Girl watched the mountains rolling under her,
and the thin, worn white ribbon of the First Folk path. *I
wish he could be here, too. I miss him — I miss all of them.*

The mountain ridge curved down, then up. "I think the
city will be on the other side," Fat Girl yelled to Kirgen.

The young saje nodded. The airbox went over the
ridge, and a valley opened beneath them. The city
unfolded in front of them, built onto the side of the
mountain. The inside of the airbox erupted with
shouts and cheers and screams in three languages.

Seven-Fingered Fat Girl screamed with the rest of
them. "Home!" she yelled. "Home! Oh, Dog Nose,
we're home!"

"Yes!" Dog Nose roared.

"HA!" Kirgen shouted.

"So *land* the damned thing already!" Nokar called
from the back.

Kirgen laughed and circled once. The interior of the
airbox became silent except for the sound of rushing
wind. Everyone held still, and watched out the windows while Kirgen picked out a flat spot for the
landing. He finally chose a point high in the city, near
the top of the mountain but still inside the massive
walls. He dipped the airbox lower, circled tighter and
slowed, until finally he could hover. Then he eased the
crowded airbox onto the narrow patch of browned
grass between two sets of four-spined arches. Nearby, a
huge, two-storied domed whitestone building sat, the
carved face of a monster watching alertly from its side.

The silence broke as the airbox's passengers began

to applaud. Then, like hovies out of a cage, the youngest sharsha kids and Runs Slow and Kirtha shot out the airbox door and bolted across the narrow green. They were halfway up the arches by the time the first adult, Faia, made it out of the airbox. And by the time the rest of the older kids and adults joined them, they crouched atop the twin arches like multiple heads on two giant spiders.

Fat Girl and Dog Nose dropped lightly to the grass and walked across the clearing to the overlook. From there, the rest of the city spread out beneath them, as beautiful as when they left it.

Medwind stood next to Nokar. "Where is the library?" she asked."

"Library?" Fat Girl puzzled over the word.

"Place with books in it," Nokar explained.

"Oh." Fat Girl pointed down over the cliff, to the enormous whitestone building below and almost directly in front of them. She could see the giant carved monsters, still sitting on their stone perches, still waiting by the doors as if they might come to life at any moment and eat any intruders. She pointed. "That one," she said.

"*That* one." Nokar's smile was rapturous. "Is it full of books?"

Fat Girl laughed. "From the floor clear to the top in every room."

"Look, Medwind." The old man pointed at the lines of stone monsters in front of the library and then at others visible through the city. "There has been evidence in other finds that the First Folk had an active cult of saurid worshipers . . ."

Thirk pushed his way through the mob and stood a little apart. He glared at the noisy children, then closed his eyes and inhaled. "He's here," the man said loudly. "Delmuirie's here."

Fat Girl didn't understand that. And she didn't

understand Nokar, who droned on in words equally dull and incomprehensible. She turned away, and wrapped her arms around Dog Nose. They were home! *Home*! In *their* city — their beautiful, giant, *safe* city. And if they worked things right, she and Dog Nose and Runs Slow would never have to leave the safety of those walls again.

Dog Nose hugged her back, and smiled down at her. "We have time to talk to the peknu about bringing our food later," he said. "But we're back in our city now. Let's find someplace nice, and —" He grinned suggestively.

Fat Girl grinned back. "Yes," she said. "Let's."

Faia waved to the two of them as they started away from the group, and impatiently, Seven-Fingered Fat Girl trotted over to her to see what she wanted.

"Drink this," Faia said and handed her an animal-skin flask.

"What is it?"

"Alsinthe tea. I told you about it before. You do not need any babies when you're just getting started." The tall girl grinned down at her and nodded toward the several round-bellied sharsha girls with one eyebrow arched. "Believe me, you do not."

Fat Girl chuckled, and drank the tea. "Is that all?"

"Drink a little every day. Then you will have no worries." Faia winked at her. "And have fun."

Seven-Fingered Fat Girl glanced over her shoulder at Dog Nose, who was shifting impatiently from foot to foot, his thumbs stuck into the band of his myr. "We will," she said.

She ran to Dog Nose's side, and the two of them charged down the hill hand in hand.

Roba went over and stood by Medwind while she set up her tent. The majority of the expedition was setting up camp — and she supposed she should be helping Kirgen, too. The shadows were already long — soon it would be dark and cold, and she and Kirgen would need food to eat and a place to sleep. There was something she wanted to talk to the Hoos about, though.

"She risked her life for me," Roba told her friend.

Medwind looked up from pounding a tent stake into the dirt, and nodded. "I know."

Roba sighed. Medwind saw the obvious, she reflected, but never seemed to look any deeper. It was that barbarian mind-set, she decided. Once the outside of a problem was dealt with, they seemed to think the inside would be fine, too.

"She could have just left me the way I was — and then she could have had Kirgen. I couldn't have done anything to keep him."

Medwind brushed the dirt off her hands and rested them on her thighs. She looked up at Roba and her face wore an irritating expression that suggested she thought Roba was missing something obvious. Roba had seen that expression before — and she hated it.

"Roba." Medwind started using that *voice*, too — the one she'd always used when Roba was particularly obtuse regarding some obvious point in one of their lessons. "This is important. Please pay attention. Faia doesn't *want* Kirgen. I believe she likes him. I truly do. She slept with him once — just once — and Kirtha was the purely accidental result. But Faia doesn't love Kirgen and never did." The Hoos woman stood, and shoved her hands into the pockets of her *staarne*. "She likes him enough that she wants him to be happy — and if you are what will make him happy, she'll like you too. Unless you keep treating her like your enemy."

"But she had his child. How can she not want *him*?"

Medwind said, "You're mistaking your people with hers. She's Kareen. To the Kareen, a woman has her own child. If the father wants to be involved, that's wonderful. If he doesn't, the mother doesn't worry about it."

Roba was appalled. "That's terrible."

"No." Medwind shook her head and gave her friend a wry grin. "That's Kareen. In my tribe, you have to prove you can get pregnant before you can get a husband from the tribe. Which is why I ended up catching all of mine from the ranks of the enemy during battles. Kirgen is Arissonese and in the first generation of academic sajes who will be permitted to marry and still keep full ties to the University. I'm sure his views of fatherhood aren't what you're expecting, either. Before the Second Mage/Saje War, sajes fathered children by women they hired for the night and never knew who their children were—or even if they had them."

"You're saying that I'm being prudish again."

"Inflexible would have been my first choice of words, I think. Possibly obstinate. Maybe even close-minded."

Roba felt her cheeks beginning to burn. "Fine, already. I get your meaning."

Medwind laughed. "But I like you anyway. And so does Kirgen, and so does Faia. That's why she risked her life for you, I suspect. Just remember to thank her when you get the chance."

Roba nodded and glanced across the green to where Faia stood, looking down into the city and talking to Thirk with animated gestures. It wasn't going to be easy to say "thanks" adequately for what Faia had done.

But she'd find a way.

¤ *Chapter 10*

The camp came to life at daybreak the next morning. After a hurried breakfast of grains and dried vegetables from the meager remaining supplies, everyone went in separate directions.

Most of the sharsha children took off exploring. The two older Wen kids were once again — well, Medwind decided, "exploring" would be a good word for what they were doing, too. Runs Slow and Kirtha and Choufa tagged along with the scholars as they descended into the main part of the ruins and headed for the library.

From above, the library was shaped like the Arissonese letter "entreg" — a staff with two horns that jutted out and upward to either side. In the midst of fallen and shattered buildings and piles of rubble that marked sites where buildings had once stood, the library was remarkably intact. As they descended into the lower city, Medwind could see that it was built to follow the contours of the cliff — it sloped downward as steeply as the side of the mountain on which it was built.

The stone road that meandered down the cliffside and through the city was harder to walk on than the grass-covered cliffs to either side. The scholars and the children abandoned it quickly, and struggled down the steep hill, hanging on to tufts of grass to keep from falling to the bottom. Medwind stayed with Nokar and helped him down the rugged incline. He was excited as a child — and his limited stamina seemed only to frustrate him.

The city was oddly laid out — the roads led near things, but not actually to them. Instead, they terminated in large stone circles. And even down the steepest of inclines, there were no steps. Medwind shook her head, bemused. The First Folk must have had a reason for such odd design, but for the life of her, she couldn't see it.

As they neared the front of the library, even the limited and slightly breathy conversation among the scholars faltered and finally stopped. Enormous obsidian-eyed saurids, bone-white and alert-looking, perched on either side of the broad walkway that led up and into the library, watching. Medwind counted over forty of them before she gave up counting entirely and just looked. The craftsmanship of the statues was extraordinary. Their wings were semifurled, their bodies crouched in attitudes of readiness, their long, narrow faces displayed toothy, hungry grins.

Medwind had to give the Wen kids credit for getting into the library. Those uncannily lifelike statues gave *her* second thoughts.

Medwind Song walked between the twin rows of saurids that towered over her and felt their eyes follow her. Hair rose on the back of her neck. All the scholars stayed together, moving in awed silence through the ruins. None of them could find the right words for the place they had reached at such cost.

The First Folk were supposed to have been a backward, primitive culture, but these buildings and artworks rivaled the finest current civilization had to offer — and as Medwind stared at the graceful, decidedly eccentric curves of the arches and domed roofs, she wondered if current civilization had not even been surpassed.

She stopped at a particularly fine statue of a lean, graceful beast perched on the body of a beheaded kellink. The stonework was magnificent — the beast seemed almost to breathe. The saurid's wings were partially unfurled, and the underparts, in the deep crevasses, still bore faint traces of color. Paint flakes of red and black reminded her of hovie colors.

Impossible that paint has survived out here, she thought. *Rain, cold, freezing, and thawing; all the elements should have scoured paint off this stone ages ago. Either this site was occupied recently — or some other force is involved.* She closed her eyes and felt for the touch of magic.

Somewhere nearby, a wellspring of energy waited. So — that would serve as a satisfactory explanation for the paint chips, and the remarkable preservation of the library.

"Nokar, look!" she said, and pointed to the paint chips.

The rest of the scholars looked, too. With enthusiastic murmurs, her colleagues ran from statue to statue, checking for paint traces on the other saurids. Most were bare — still they found a few traces of brown, copper, bright yellow, tan, gray — and more of that vivid scarlet.

Nokar laughed. "These must have been incredibly gaudy when the First Folk still lived here. Can you imagine these statues, painted all over like giant flocks of hovies?"

Medwind studied the long line of gleaming white statues, and colored them in her mind's eye. "Yes," she murmured at last. "It would have been lovely — like a festival."

"Typical barbarian approach to art," Thirk commented, and sniffed. "Slather anything that doesn't move or can't fight back with eight colors of clashing paint, hang it all over with bells and tassels and trinkets until you can't even see what's underneath — and call the resulting mess beautiful. Ornamentation is the death of true art."

Medwind muttered, "I'll give *you* the death of true art, you *hruning* little *d'leffja* . . ." *Haven't even thanked me for saving your obnoxious carcass, and you have the kead-daba to look down your nose at the Hoos.*

Nokar rested his hand on her arm and said, in a soft voice that was meant to carry, "Ignore him, dear. He's a Delmuirie scholar. Don't expect words of wisdom from him."

Everyone laughed — everyone except Thirk.

"True." Medwind grinned and enjoyed the expression of fury on Thirk's face, and amused herself briefly with headhunter thoughts. Then she walked up the broad ramp and under the huge, arching doorway into the library.

A flock of little brown birds scattered, screeching, in front of her, flying up through the light-ports carved in the upper reaches of the walls and out in a steady stream.

Behind her, she heard Thirk mutter, "You'll regret mocking Delmuirie."

She was tempted to turn and laugh at him — silly little man with his ludicrous dedication to fringe scholarship and his dark and toothless threats. But she decided she would not deprive the man of his last shred of dignity, no matter how tattered it might be.

There were, in any case, other things to think about.

The library spread before them all — a vast wonderland of unread works, endless rows of luminous white tablets waiting on shelves that reached to the ceiling, probably four stories above near the front, and much higher the further back she looked. The floor stayed level while the ceiling rose, reminding Medwind of a mammoth man-made cavern.

Shelves curved around out of sight to either side of her; doorless arches beckoned from both sides of a corridor that stretched a daunting distance in front of her, promising more rooms of books. Forests of central pillars became arches that rose and met, and amusing painted monsters peeked out from the interstices, wearing bird-nest hats and long stripes of white droppings; or did vaguely obscene things inside of stonework niches high overhead. Light streamed in from huge circular openings just beneath the domed roof of the structure — they were similar in form to openings in the smaller domed buildings Medwind had seen throughout the ruins. The shelves in front of her were carved from pale green trevistone, engraved on the ends with pictures of plants that twined and flowered, with hovies and sea-monsters — inscriptions along the edges told undeciphered secrets, and First Folk numbers marked each set of shelves.

Nothing was broken. Nothing was falling in. Aside from a general coating of dirt and the obvious signs of habitation by generations of small animals, the building could have been new.

Wonderful, she thought. *A gift of the gods.*

She pointed out the angled slashes and dots that were the First Folk numbers. "They've evidently got these divided into categories of some sort." Her whisper echoed through the massive structure.

Behind her, Roba whispered, "Gods, wouldn't you love to find the directory?"

There was a moment of silence. Then Kirgen said, "What a terrific idea. I bet we could find one if we looked."

Nokar rubbed his hands together. "Oh, I concur. With an index, we could, perhaps, decipher categories, determine First Folk logic and values, learn a few words — by all means, let's go after the directory."

Thirk kept back and looked vaguely superior and amused by the rest of the scholars' enthusiasm. No doubt he would have been bounding about in wild abandon if they had been on the trail of the nonexistent Delmuirie, Medwind thought. But a library directory wasn't important enough for him.

The rest of them discussed what form such a directory might take, then split up. Faia and all three kids took off toward the back, Roba and Kirgen went left, and Thirk, after a moment's hesitation, followed Faia down the corridor. That left Nokar and Medwind to take the right branch. They went past more of the beautiful, carved green shelves, past a huge circular pit carved into the bedrock floor, and through a massive arched doorway.

On the other side of the arch, the character of the library changed completely. The shelves inside the next chamber were of palest blue seraphine, polished to a high gloss. No carvings decorated their sides, and even the indexing numbers were discrete and placed unobtrusively on shelf corners. The rows of pillars and arches were of the same glossy seraphine. No funny gargoyles adorned the high places. Medwind found the room serene and ethereal — but lacking the charming personality of the green room.

Nokar, however, wandered along the rows of shelves, touching the cool stone and smiling like a saje who discovered he had escaped all the saje hells and found himself, improbably and unexpectedly, in his own idea of heaven. From time to time he would pull out one of the glossy white tablets and run his fingers along the indented text.

"Oh, Med," he whispered finally. "This is better than I could have imagined in my finest dream."

She gave him her brightest smile — her pain she hid inside.

She had managed to hide from him the price she had paid for this dream of his — and she would not see an instant of his happiness spoiled. Whenever his death came, it would take him by surprise, and quickly — and when it was over, she would consider *vha'atta*, and Nokar's wishes, and weigh one against the other. She thought by the time he'd looked around the library, he might be amenable to something that would buy him time in any form.

Roba and Kirgen appeared in the dividing doorway, laughing.

"Medwind, Nokar, you just have to *see* this," Kirgen said.

Roba was wiping tears of laughter from her eyes. "Really, you do," she agreed. "Come see." She glanced around the pale blue spaces. "This is really different," she said. "Built by somebody with the opposite opinion of proper library design."

She and Kirgen burst into laughter again.

"I take it you haven't found the directory," Medwind said dryly.

"Not yet," Kirgen agreed. "Though it doesn't look like you two have, either. But this is better. By Wilmer, this is better. These lizard-worshipers had some really *twisted* ideas."

Medwind and Nokar exchanged glances, and Nokar's eyebrows rose. "By all means, Medwind, dear. Let's go take a look at this jewel of strangeness."

They followed Roba and Kirgen across the lovely green chamber and into the other side arm of the building. Through the arched doorways, the mood changed again. This time, every fingers' breadth of wall space was covered by brilliantly colored mosaics. The room's pillars were carved bloodstone, the arches black marble inset with obsidian and semiprecious stones.

The mix of colors was breathtaking — gaudy beyond belief; vibrant; joyous. It was only when Medwind could pull her attention away from the overall impact of the room to take in the details that she discovered the cause of Roba's and Thirk's amusement. The subjects of all those murals ranged from the erotic to the graphic to the downright pornographic — except that the artists had chosen to portray all their fanciful positions with various saurids, hovies, kellinks, and other "survival" fauna as the models. The results, from romantic two-beast encounters to some really bizarre multispecies orgies, became simply hilarious. The beasts' facial expressions were delightful. Medwind, looking from scene to scene, found herself laughing along with her colleagues.

"We can probably guess the subject matter of the books in this room," she said.

"Truly," Nokar agreed. "Such a pity there are no beds here. I think we would find — ah — sleeping here an inspiring and perhaps even educational experience."

"You, love, are a dirty old man," Medwind whispered.

"*You* spend over two hundred years in celibate study, analysis, and work and see how you turn out," he retorted. "Especially when a lovely young headhunter proposes marriage to you after you are well into your dotage."

Medwind forced herself to keep on smiling. But his words only reminded her that time was wasting — and she wanted him to see and do everything that could possibly be done in the First Folk ruins.

"Well, this is remarkable," she said finally, "but it isn't finding the directory. And there doesn't appear to be anything in here that comes close to resembling one of those."

"Point well taken," Roba said. "With deep regret, I suggest we move onward."

They met Faia coming back. "Incredible rooms," she said in greeting, and all of them laughed.

"What did I say?" she asked, her voice plaintive.

"We're beginning to suspect *all* the rooms are incredible," Medwind said. "So what did you find?"

"The next section is a series of six smaller rooms, each in a different kind of stone, with metal decorations. I could not make any sense of the artwork in that section — there was nothing recognizable. The section following has buildings and diagrams and things of that sort carved on the walls. It is all in plain whitestone.

Compared to the rest of what I have seen, it seems dull. But the last section is wonderful. It has no books in it. Instead, it is full of statues like the ones at the front of the library — except all of these still have their paint on. The kids are playing back there now." She turned to Medwind. "You will love it," she said. "It is simply beautiful."

Medwind discovered Faia was right. The statues were stunning. They stood in long rows in four different rooms at the back of the library, seeming to have stopped, for just an instant, to pose for the absent artist. The First Folk had brilliant artists among them. Medwind ran her fingers along one statue, and the coldness of the rough stone startled her. The statues should have been warm, she thought.

"What are they?" she asked. "The styles vary from statue to statue, but the structural details of all the beasts are the same."

Nokar shrugged. "Gods, perhaps. Guardians. Personifications of various religious or philosophical ideals. We never have gotten a good grasp of First Folk theology — we've never had enough data." The old man smiled and looked around him. "We do now, of course. Though this library alone will take at least a hundred years to catalog and translate." He sighed. "I wish I were going to be here to do the work."

Medwind nodded with satisfaction. *You can be,* she thought, but she said nothing. She would let him grow hungrier for the idea of continuing scholarship before she broached the topic of vha'atta again.

Thirk joined them, a smug smile on his face.

"I found the directory," he said.

"Really!"

"You jest!"

"— Oh, that's wonderful!"

Nokar asked, "Where?"

"Considering the general rudeness I've had to put

up with, I don't know that I ought to tell you — but I'm a better man than that. I'll tell. You all walked right past it to get here."

Medwind frowned, trying to remember anything that had even vaguely resembled a directory. They'd seen the green room . . . the seraphine room . . . the bawdy room . . . the metal-sculpture rooms and the whitestone ones with the buildings and roads — and then this place with its beautiful painted sculptures.

Nothing, she thought. *There was nothing that held lists of numbers in order with writing around them. Nothing like that at all.*

"Can't figure it out, can you?" Thirk asked and laughed.

"No," Nokar said. "I saw nothing that might be a directory."

"Then the despised Delmuirie scholar makes the first major find, hey?" He chuckled. "Look at the designs on all those buildings on the central room — the one you can see from everywhere in the library. The designs are rows of numbers, with writing beside each number. There's your directory."

The scholars went back to look. Sure enough, the carvings of buildings were covered with rows of First Folk script.

"That certainly appears to be a directory," Medwind said. "Now we only have to figure out what in the hells it all means."

Choufa and Kirtha and Runs Slow stayed in the largest of the four statue rooms after the adults left. All three girls clambered over the stone monsters and sat on their backs and pretended to ride them. Kirtha tired of the game quickly and got down and walked from monster to monster and began talking to them. Choufa, however, imagined that the beasts were like airboxes that could carry her back into the sky and take her wherever she wanted to go. She had been very impressed by the airbox.

Runs Slow, on the back of her beast, played out a scene of bloody revenge. "My monster flies down on the people of Blue Circle Silk! I throw my hurlstick and hit them all! They fall down dead!" she shouted.

This seemed a very good idea to Choufa. She elaborated on it. "Yes!" she yelled. "*My* monster takes me to every Keyi in the world! They cannot hurt me because I have *magic*! I burn them with *magic* fire and they burn and die! There are no more Keyu in the whole world!" She remembered the look and the smell of the burning Keyu, and she smiled.

"Good!" Runs Slow pretended to fly her beast, kicking its sides the way she'd seen peknu riders kicking their groundbeasts. "I am going to the peknu town. The peknu will give me much food and many pretty things because I have killed all the Silk People."

That seemed like a good idea. Choufa liked food, and she certainly liked pretty things. "I'm going to the peknu town, too. They will give me even more food and more pretty things because I have killed all the Keyu," she bragged. "It is more important to kill the Keyu than to kill the Silk People."

"Then I'm going to kill the Keyu, too!"

"You can't. I already killed them all."

"I can if I want to. You just *said* you killed them all — but you didn't really."

"Did so."

"Did not, *sharsha*."

"Did, too, *tagnu*." Choufa glared at Runs Slow, and Runs Slow glared back.

Runs Slow narrowed her eyes. She took a deep breath, then whispered, "That green stuff all over you looks ugly."

It was a telling blow. Choufa had nothing to come back with. She stared at the tattoos on her arms and hands and knew that every inch of the rest of her was covered with equally hideous designs, and her eyes filled with tears.

She climbed down off her beast while hot tears blurred her vision and rolled off her cheeks and walked away from the monster room. She heard quick, light footsteps behind her. She kept on walking.

A hand rested on her arm. "I'm sorry," Runs Slow said. "I didn't want to make you cry."

Choufa sniffled but didn't say anything.

Runs Slow said, "I think your decorations are pretty. I just wanted to make you angry."

Choufa bit her lip. "The Silk People hurt me. You know how they made these pictures?" She held out her arms and stared at them with loathing. "They stabbed me with sharp needles. It hurt so bad I wanted to die. They did it so I would be ugly — and I am." In spite of herself, she started to cry again.

"No. You're still pretty. I think so. Kirtha thinks so." Runs Slow turned and called back into the monster room with a rapid chaos of words Choufa didn't understand. "I asked her didn't she think you were pretty."

There was silence from the room.

Kirtha was talking to the monsters the last time I saw her, Choufa thought. *But was she in the room when I left?*

Both girls exchanged puzzled looks. "Was she in there when you came out?" Choufa asked.

"I thought so. She was talking to the monsters."

"I thought so too."

They walked back into the biggest monster room.

"Kirtha!" Runs Slow called.

Choufa began looking down the long rows of statues. She couldn't see the little girl. "Kirtha?" she yelled.

"Kirtha? Where are you?"

Both girls stood quietly, listening. Silence. They shook their heads. *If we lose her, the peknu will kill us,*

Choufa thought. *Or at least throw us out of the city. That would be the same thing.*

"We have to find her," she told Runs Slow. "Terrible things will happen to us if we don't."

Runs Slow nodded. "There is a door at the back of this room. We should check in there."

They ran through the door. The room behind was dusty, dimly lit by what appeared to Choufa to be circles of clear stone — and filled with stacks of dust-covered white tablets. There were no little footprints in the dust.

"She hasn't been in here."

"No," Choufa said. "She hasn't."

"Then where?"

Standing at the door of the empty room, Choufa suddenly heard the low, heavy grating of stone against stone. The noise was coming from nearby.

"The next room," Runs Slow whispered. "Run!"

Choufa could imagine terrible things — a statue fallen on the little girl, or stones broken loose from the wall, even the huge roof overhead collapsing. She didn't trust all that stone above her. But when she and Runs Slow charged around the corner and into the next room, nothing was out of place.

There were only six statues in the room, which was much smaller than the one they'd just left. The room was dimly lit by more of those clear stones in the ceiling. Even in the dim lighting, though, Choufa could see Kirtha wasn't in there.

"The sound . . ." Runs Slow said.

"The next room?"

"Maybe."

They ran to the third monster room, then the fourth. Kirtha was nowhere to be found.

"We need to check the rest of this place," Choufa whispered, "but we need to make sure the peknu don't see us until Kirtha is with us again."

Runs Slow nodded vigorously. "We must find her fast."

Both girls took off at a run, racing down the aisles, darting quietly into side rooms if they spotted any of the peknu, looking into each cranny and hideaway provided by shelves. The building was huge, but by moving quickly and splitting up, they managed to cover it all. They met back at the first monster room, breathing hard and thoroughly scared.

"Nowhere," Choufa said.

"I couldn't find her, either."

"She has to be here. There is only one door, and that is clear at the front. Somebody would have seen her."

Runs Slow crossed her arms over her chest and shook her head. "If we couldn't find her, she isn't here."

"Well, she has to be *somewhere*!"

"Yes. But not here."

Choufa buried her face in her hands. "The peknu will be so angry."

"They will probably make us leave," Runs Slow offered. "They will probably make us be tagnu again."

Choufa looked up. "Think. She was talking to the monsters. Do you think one of them could have eaten her?"

Both girls eyed the statues doubtfully.

"Maybe," Runs Slow said. "I hope not."

"Well, what about that noise we heard in the next room. Do you think that was the sound of a monster eating her?" The more Choufa thought about that possibility, the more likely it seemed. The monsters stared at her with their beady black eyes, and grinned wicked grins with their long, sharp teeth showing.

"Maybe because she was all alone," Runs Slow said. Her eyes were huge and round. "Maybe they haven't tried to eat us, because we are together. But if she was alone ..."

"You're right," Choufa agreed. "Maybe we should tell the peknu."

"No. We have be sure first."

"But if the monsters ate her —"

Runs Slow held out her hand. "We'll look together."

Choufa took her hand, and trembling, both girls walked back into the second room. Knowing what she knew, Choufa realized that these monsters' smiles were much more wicked. They looked hungrier than the monsters in the first room, and their eyes watched her more closely. She shivered — and only part of that shiver was because the room was cool. Her fingers instinctively tightened around Runs Slow's.

"How will we know which one ate her?" she asked.

Runs Slow gave her an odd look. "We'll check the teeth. We'll be able to tell from the teeth."

Choufa looked at all those very sharp, very white teeth, and her heart pounded so hard she was sure it would burst from her chest. "I don't want to," she whispered.

"I know. But we have to."

"I know."

They walked forward, slowly, taking tiny steps that got smaller the closer they got to the first monster.

"Nothing on those teeth," Choufa said.

"We have to look closer than that." Runs Slow climbed up on the base and stared at the teeth with her face right next to them. Choufa thought she was very brave — but crazy. "Nothing on those teeth but dust," she reported, and jumped off the base.

They crept to the next one.

"You have to look this time," Runs Slow said.

Choufa nodded, and swallowed hard. She licked her lips, and very, very carefully, she climbed up onto the base. She stared at the monsters' teeth. Like the last monster, this one had a mouth full of dust.

"Not this one," she said. Her voice came out as a funny croak.

They worked their way to the back of the room,

taking turns. Runs Slow checked the giant red-and-black monster, Choufa checked the tan one with big blotches of dark brown, Runs Slow checked the pale blue-green one with thin black stripes. That left the last monster for Choufa.

It was bigger than the rest of them, she realized. It gave her a knowing smile as she approached. She was almost certain she could see it breathing.

Please don't eat me, she thought. *Oh, please, please, please don't eat me.* She was shaking so hard she was afraid she would fall off the base, but she climbed up anyway, ready to look at the monster's teeth.

The moment her feet touched the base, the room came alive with the grinding sound of stone against stone. *Oh, no!* Choufa thought. She shrieked, and fell off the pedestal, trying to back away.

Runs Slow grabbed her shoulder as she scrabbled backward. "Stop," she whispered. "Look at the wall!"

A section of it was sliding up — a single band of greenstone in the striping of green and white stone that made up the room was crawling into the ceiling high over their heads. Behind the opening, darkness waited.

"She's in there," Choufa said.

"Should we go in, or should we tell the peknu?"

The stone came to a stop high over their heads, held still for the briefest of instants, and then began to descend.

"Let's go," Runs Slow said. "Hurry! Before it shuts!"

They ran under the closing stone door, and it slid smoothly shut behind them. The darkness surrounded them.

Then Choufa's eyes began to adjust. "Look," she whispered. "There's light ahead."

They walked toward it, down a gentle slope. The stone beneath their feet was smooth. They reached the light and found that it came from overhead, a single circle of the clear stone, carved to throw light in six triangles to all sides of them. They stared at it for a moment.

"Pretty," Choufa said. She thought she would like one of those lightstones to keep where she slept at night, so the darkness would never frighten her again.

"Kirtha," Runs Slow called softly. "Kirtha!"

The little girl didn't answer.

They walked on, away from the light, farther down the slope. In a short while, they reached another spot of light and left it behind, then reached another. Choufa noticed that the ground beneath her feet no longer felt like stone. She bent down and touched it. It was soft and grainy. She scooped up a handful of the stuff and it ran through her fingers.

"What are you doing?" Runs Slow asked.

"Touch the ground. What is this?"

Runs Slow crouched and picked up a handful. "Sand," she whispered. "It is a kind of dirt that grows near the salty lakes."

"Are we near a salty lake?"

"We might be."

Choufa noticed, when they reached the next light in the tunnel, that one small set of footprints preceded them, going in the same direction they travelled. The rest of the sand had been carefully swept smooth in huge semicircles. They followed the footprints.

"Kirtha!" Choufa called. "Kirtha! Come here!"

They listened to their cries echo away to nothing.

Then they heard a faint, answering call. "Come see!" the high, piping voice shouted, and the echoes of that shout whispered past their ears and came back to them again.

"YES!" Runs Slow shouted.

"She's not hurt!" Choufa yelled.

They both broke into a run, keeping their eyes on the faint trail of tracks in the sand. They passed two more lighted areas, and then the path leveled out and turned abruptly to the right.

They raced around the corner and came face to face

with Kirtha, who sat cheerfully beside one of a multitude of large, round boulders that covered the floor of the cavern. She played in the sand under the sad eyes of yet another of the giant painted monsters.

Choufa looked up. Tens and tens of tens of the sparkling lightstones dotted the roof of the cavern. They made the room bright as outside, and lit the rows of big white boulders. All the boulders were covered with the funny lines and dots the peknu got so excited about. Around the room, more monster statues sat, and the expressions on all their ugly faces were sad.

There were two arching passageways out of the cavern besides the one the girls had come through. Choufa, no longer frightened by the monsters or worried about Kirtha, found that she was curious. She trotted across the warm sand to the first, which lay to the right side of the cavern. She peeked down it.

At the end of a short, dark tunnel, she could see the lights of another cavern, full of more round boulders just like the ones behind her. She went to the other passageway.

Like the first two, it held the carved boulders. But a brighter, yellower light emanated from around the corner and out of sight. Choufa called to the other two girls, "Come down this way! There's something here!"

Runs Slow hurried to her side. Kirtha dawdled behind, playing in the sand until Runs Slow called her in that other language. Then she came quickly enough. They walked down the passageway together, noticing that the light grew more and more brilliant the closer they got.

It's beautiful, Choufa thought. *Light yellow as the taltiflowers that grow in the tops of trees —*

They reached the end of the short passageway and peeked to one side.

There, caught up in a pillar of the yellow light, a man knelt on one knee, held his sword in one hand and raised a giant stone cup aloft with the other. He didn't move — didn't even seem to breathe.

Choufa looked at his handsome face and fell in love. She thought she had never seen anyone so beautiful.

Thirk waited until everyone was busy doing sketches of the site or taking rubbings of the directory before he interrupted Roba. She tried not to show her annoyance, but she wished she could just tell him to go away.

"I need to talk to you," he told her, and his voice was urgent.

She suspected she knew what he wanted to talk about. She was going to have to deal with it sooner or later — later would have been much more pleasant, but —

"Fine," she said. "Let's go somewhere else to talk."

She led, and as her site, chose one of the giant, sunken circles that were a feature of the green room. She sat down on the edge of the circle and waited for Thirk to join her. *We're far enough from everyone else that they won't hear what we say,* she thought, *but close enough that they can get here fast if he takes this worse than I'm expecting.* She wasn't sure how Thirk would take her news of her defection from the Delmuirie cause — she didn't know him that well. Her caution seemed necessary.

Thirk sat beside her, and got right to the heart of his concern. "Why didn't you defend your paper — and why did you let them laugh at Delmuirie without saying anything?"

How badly do I need my job? she wondered. It was a thought that had crossed her mind frequently — and as she sat in the midst of the most incredible archaeological find in the history of Arhel, she decided, *Not very badly at all.* As codiscoverer of the site — and with priority access to everything in it — her future was guaranteed. She would be able to claim a senior mage post in the historical department of any university in Arhel — including Daane. She smiled as she thought of returning to her alma mater in triumph.

She decided she could afford to be brutally honest. She thought after an instant's further reflection that she would probably even enjoy it.

"Thirk," she said, "you have to realize that I wasn't making enough money as your assistant to keep up with rent on a single-room apartment in the Hout-Cadhay Quarter. I was eating badly once a day and hiding from my landlady. I couldn't afford ghostlights. I was heating and cooking on dried dung. When you made any possibility of a raise contingent on my becoming a member of the Delmuirie Society, I had no choice but to become an enthusiastic supporter of Delmuirie."

"So you're saying that you took advantage of my generosity by pretending to support the aims of the Delmuirie Society—"

Roba cut him off. "I'm saying I did what I had to do to put food on my table. This isn't a question of how much I do or don't believe in the contributions of Edrouss Delmuirie to society. For the record, I doubt that there ever was an Edrouss Delmuirie, and I think the Delmuirie Society is composed mostly of lunatics, fanatics, and romantic fools dreaming big dreams." Roba caught her breath, and clenched the muscles in her jaw and went on. "This is about my survival. I had two options. I could starve — or I could do something that I found repugnant. And while I had quite a few options in the repugnant category, yours was the one that didn't have acquiring a social disease as a probable outcome."

She locked her fingers together and glared at Thirk. "So I joined your stupid society, and when you asked me for a theory for presentation, I gave you a theory."

Thirk's face was a mask. He nodded once, curtly. "Tell me how you came up with your theory, won't you?"

"Kirgen and I dug out every old historical myth we could find that dealt with Edrouss Delmuirie. We scrounged out every piece of tripe we could find in

Faulea's library, then went over to the Daane library
and pulled out records so ancient we had to scrape the
dust off them with a knife blade — we took legends
from every discredited historian Ariss ever produced.
We didn't hide our sources — you saw them. I gave you
plenty of time to check them."

He nodded and his mouth thinned to a grim line.
"So you intended your theory to make fools of the
Society members."

"I intended it to keep my job for me. *Which*," she
added with a snarl, "I don't need anymore."

"Of course." Thirk Huddsonne looked down at his
hands and sat motionless for a moment. Finally he
looked up. "You don't have your job anymore. That
can only be what you expected. However, you are quite
correct, I'm sure, in assuming you will have more
offers than you could possibly accept. Your association
with this find will almost certainly guarantee that — in
spite of the references you'll get from me. They won't
be good," he said softly, "but I'm not foolish enough to
think that will make any difference.

"You've put me in a bad position, Roba." Thirk
played absently with the fringe of his belt. "I'm left
having to find Edrouss Delmuirie's final resting place
by myself. I *thought* I had someone who would help
me." He looked at her sadly and slowly shook his head.

Roba couldn't believe what she was hearing.
"Weren't you listening, Thirk? There is no 'Delmuirie's
final resting place' — certainly not here, and probably
not anywhere. That theory we put together was *worth-
less*. Just do First Folk research here with the rest of us.
You can come out of this with extra funding for your
department, recognition by your colleagues; gods,
man, this place can *make* your career. You could be Saje
Primus of Faulea by next year."

Thirk gave her a strange little smile. "I can be
anyway — but on my terms. You discredit your theory.

I don't. I believe the gods who guide all things bring Truth to the fore in their own time and their own way. I believe the gods have worked through you — in spite of you." His voice got louder and took on a ringing quality. "And when I go back to Faulea, it will be to restore Edrouss Delmuirie to his rightful place in history. I'll change Arhel." He stopped, and his face grew pale, and suddenly he hung his head. In a softer voice, he said, "No. That is boasting. Through me, Edrouss Delmuirie will change Arhel. Remember, when that time comes, that you could have been at my side. That will be punishment enough for your faithlessness."

Roba stared at Thirk. Then she gave him a little half-smile and clicked her tongue against the roof of her mouth. "I guess it will be," she said. She stood and slowly walked back to the directory, where the rest of her colleagues were still hard at work.

That man, she thought, *has transported body without brain.* She shoved her thumbs into her belt and looked back to where the saje sat and stared off into nothing. *He's communing with the Mocking God. He's drunk from the Well of Delusion. He's insane,* she decided as she reached Kirgen. Of all the ways she had thought Thirk might take her news, going mad hadn't even occurred to her as a possibility.

She knelt beside her young saje and rested a hand on his shoulder. "Come see something," she whispered. "And tell me what you think."

* * *

It had been an exhausting day, and Medwind felt drained. Worry about Nokar took most of the pleasure out of the discovery of the library. Other concerns combined to distract her, too, until at last she found herself, not cataloging numbers and headings, but simply staring at the directory and tracing the First Folk symbols with one finger.

When she realized she was in the way of people getting real work done, she excused herself and climbed up the side of the mountain back to the airbox. Once there, she rummaged around through the back storage compartment until she located the large padded leather bag that held her dearest possessions. She removed the bag along with a bedroll that held the rest of her gear, and carried her things to the nearest of the First Folk buildings.

The building she chose was large—round, two-storied, and domed. The central room was bright and covered with charming mosaics. But a bright room wouldn't meet her needs. She went through the rounded doorway into the adjoining room. There, too, the walls were covered with mosaics—but the room itself was suitably dark.

She made herself a place to sit and an altar, unpacked her vha'attaye and reverently set them out. Then, following the ancient ritual, she began to call forth the waking dead. Incense smoke coiled out from the painted skulls' nose holes and grinning mouths. Her tiny travel drum pittered like rain on a *b'dabba*. She hummed and stared into the light of her two little candles, and began to sing. And as she sang, the darkness that surrounded her grew darker, and the hair rose on her arms and the back of her neck, and cold walked through her body and ached in her bones. Thick emerald tendrils of light began to coalesce around first one skull, and then all but one of the rest. Joy filled her. Most of her vha'attaye had found their way home. The file-toothed skull of Troggar Raveneye, best enemy, remained dark and empty. Medwind channeled more of her magic into the summoning—to no effect.

Perhaps he is still lost, she thought. *Perhaps he will soon return, as the others have returned.*

The ghostflesh finished forming over the bones of the vha'attaye, and the ghosteyes lit with their uncanny fire, and the ghostmouths opened and closed, clicked and skritched. But though they muttered among themselves, the dead gave her no greeting.

Medwind pressed her forehead to the floor, then rose slowly.

"I come to honor you," she whispered to the impassive faces of the waking dead. "I come to cherish you, and to give you my love."

Still the vha'attaye withheld their greetings.

"Please speak with me," Medwind pled. "I have longed for the voices of my loved ones."

"Don't waste your love on the dead," Rakell Ingasdotte whispered. Her bonevoice scraped like claws on dry wood — a cold parody of the warm, vibrant voice Medwind remembered. "We are greedy, but not for love — only for life. The little driblets you feed us when you call us forth make us hungrier for what we cannot have. We dried bones have forgotten love."

Medwind stared into the ghostly eyes of her dead friend and colleague and said, "That isn't true. You remember our friendship as well as I."

"The place between the worlds is a poor place for remembering friendship," the vha'attaye said. "It is a better place for learning want." The ghosteyes narrowed while ghostflesh twisted into a semblance of a leer. "I *want* more life. If I can't have mine, I'll take yours!"

The green glow around the skull blazed brighter; it grew, like a well-fed flame; it pulled and drew energy and life from the Hoos warrior.

Medwind hadn't been prepared for an attack. She'd trusted Rakell, and it took her an instant to realize what was happening, and another instant to shield herself. When her shield went up, the Mottemage's attack stopped, but Medwind could feel the toll Rakell's assault had taken from her flesh and her bones and her breath. She was exhausted; her strength was gone. The attack had been powerful — with a shudder, she realized she could have died.

She stared into the glowing eyes of her dead friend. "Why did you do that?"

The Mottemage laughed — a hideous sound. "I want life. Or death. Not this horror in between."

Medwind clenched her hands into fists. "You wouldn't have killed me — not really."

"No. Of course not. So why don't you put down your shield? We're friends, after all."

The mocking in the vha'atta's voice felt like a knife in Medwind's heart. "You *are* my friend," she whispered.

The other vha'attaye laughed — hissing, scraping dead-thing laughter. "Friends," they hissed. "We are all friends."

Rakell's eyesockets gleamed brighter in the darkness. "I *was* your friend," she whispered. "But you treated me the same way you treated your enemy — look what happened to him."

Medwind looked at Troggar Raveneye's dark, empty skull. "What happened? Where is he? I believed he was still lost —"

The Mottemage laughed again. "Not so. He was devoured by the things that hunt between the worlds. His soul was ripped to shreds. There is nothing left of him now. Any hope he might have had — of another life, another chance — is gone."

Medwind remembered the pitiless cold thing born of void and hatred that had come bearing down on her out of nowhere. She remembered her fear — and she felt anguish for Troggar Raveneye, best enemy. She felt a grief at news of this passing that she had not even felt at his death. She pressed her face to the floor and wept.

Living, he'd been so young — so beautiful, with muscles that flowed beneath smooth copper skin, eyes black as night. He had not conceded defeat when she cornered him in battle, had not consented to be her husband to buy his life. He'd fought on, and nearly won. She'd been enchanted by his courage and his grace — and she had not meant to kill him. To the last, she meant to spare him — for her *b'dabba* and her bed.

She would have loved him; for those few minutes, she did. But he got through her guard and wounded her. She parried, an instinctive move that she followed with a stop thrust —

— he fell, dying, and smiled at her, and touched his forehead once —

— honor among warriors, the concession of defeat by a superior —

— then he died.

She did vha'atta — Huong Hoos honor, reverence for skill and knowledge worth saving. Yet she had failed to save him after all. She had cost him instead — cost him his life, and then his soul. Twice he had paid her, and paid too much.

Above her bent neck, the voices of the dead mocked her, mocked her tears and her weakness, mocked her love. They were her past, her family, her memories — they were the part of her that made her Hoos. Yet they hated her; they despised her. She was imperfect, and they — distant and unchanging — had no tolerance for her imperfections. She was living — and they envied her life.

She banished them, then — blew out the candles and scattered them away from her; chased them back into the cold and the dark and the emptiness. She heard the echoes of their sobbing cries, soft hisses, high screeches as they fled down the path that led between the worlds. She sat and stared at the hollow bones, cold bones, bones with the smoke of incense still curling out of the nose holes and the grinning jaws.

How could she send Nokar to such a fate? she wondered. How could she stand to hear hate and envy in his voice, where now she heard only love?

But how could she let him die? How could she say goodbye, knowing she could hold back the moment of final goodbye — perhaps forever?

The memories of the Wen Godtrees rushed back to her, unbidden. She relived the moment she first saw the struggling forms pinned to the tree-flesh and recognized them for what they were — and she felt again her revulsion. But at that moment, her mind drew an ugly parallel, one she hadn't seen before. The Wen worshipped trees animated by the trapped souls of their undead children — and the Hoos communed with the caged spirits of their long-dead parents. No matter that the Wen sacrificed their living offspring where the Hoos preserved the souls of those who had died. At that moment, she could not see where one sacred rite was any less hideous than the other.

She had never thought of vha'atta as something wrong before. She stared into the darkness, into the bony faces of her ancestors. Was vha'atta wrong?

And if it was — how could she save Nokar?

She stretched out on her bedroll then, grateful for the darkness that swallowed her, and sought the temporary oblivion of sleep.

Chapter 11

A soft voice outside the doorway called, "Please come to the library as soon as you can. Some of the children are missing."

Seven-Fingered Fat Girl had been lying with Dog Nose on a shared blanket, holding him close in drowsy contentment. The past with all its horrors was behind her and could not hurt her ever again. The future waited, full of work and probable hardship. But the present — that had seemed perfect.

Some of the children are missing.

She was on her feet, fists clenched, her stomach twisting in a frightened knot, before the echoes of that soft voice died away. She was weaponless — the Silk People had stolen her dartstick and her darts along with her peknu clothes. Dog Nose, beside her, pulling his myr on, had suffered the same fate. His hurlsticks were burning in the Silk People village too.

No matter. The two of them would go and help search, and if they could not kill whatever had stolen the children, at least they might distract it while the peknu did.

But how could the children be missing?

As she considered, a handful of ways sprang to mind. They could have climbed over the wall — some doori might have picked them off the top of it, or kellinks could have caught them on the other side. They could have wandered into one of the many caves that dotted the cliffside of the city. They could have fallen into the

lake, they could have become trapped in a ruined
building —

"Which children?" Dog Nose asked as they ran
toward the library.

"Don't know." Fat Girl was hoping, however, that the
missing children were all sharsha. She wouldn't say
that out loud, and she didn't wish the sharsha any ill —
she would feel sorrow at the loss of any of the little
strangers. But she never wanted to lose another friend.

They met up with the peknu in the library. Faia sat,
covered by a ball of blue light that sank into the library
floor, her eyes closed. Medwind Song, her face red and
puffy, sat at some distance from her and stared into a
black bowl filled with water. Nokar leaned on his staff
between the two of them and watched them both.
Everyone else waited in silence.

Fat Girl inventoried the watchers, and her pulse
sped. One of the sharsha kids was missing — but so was
Kirtha. And worst of all, so was Runs Slow. She looked
over at Dog Nose. From his horrified expression, she
knew he had reached the same conclusion she'd
reached.

"We promised Roshi we'd take care of her," Dog
Nose whispered.

"We weren't watching her. We didn't keep her with
us." Fat Girl hung her head. "If she is lost, how do we
repay our broken promise?"

Dog Nose whispered, "Broken promises cannot be
repaid."

"Shhh!" Kirgen glared at them, and she and Dog
Nose fell silent.

Faia lifted her head and opened her eyes. "They are
that way," she said, and pointed toward the back of the
library, and down. *Down?* Fat Girl, bewildered, thought
something must be wrong with the peknu *magic*. The
mountain went up.

At almost the same instant, Medwind said, "I can see

them — but only barely. Only enough to know that they are still alive. They seem safe enough. They are in a large open space, and there is a — a well of a sort — a source of enormous power."

Medwind pulled her gaze away from the bowl. "Unexpected."

"What is?" Nokar asked.

"The power well — I know of no magic that could make it — its power hides its nature — some form of magic disguises its location —"

"How do we find the littlest ones?" Dog Nose asked.

Faia drew in the sphere of light that surrounded her, and for the briefest instant, she glowed. Then the glow vanished, and she stood. "I sense them beyond the back of the library."

At the back of the library, Fat Girl explored the four rooms filled with monster statues — she and Dog Nose had not ventured back that far their first time in the library. She touched some of the brightly colored beasts and shuddered. They looked too much like kellinks with wings to suit her. She could imagine them racing down out of the sky and snatching her up in their toothy jaws and swallowing her whole. They frightened her.

I don't need to be afraid, she told herself suddenly. *They are stone. They are* nothing. She smacked one in the nose and made a face at it — she would have spit in its eye, but the peknu might have noticed and laughed at her. Feeling better, though, she continued her search.

Everyone went through the rooms quickly the first time, then more slowly the second.

"We need to start looking through the other buildings," Kirgen said. "Outside, along the walls — there are so many places they could be —"

"I said from the beginning this was no sort of trip for children," Thirk announced. "Perhaps now you can see the Delmuirie scholar is right again."

Fat Girl looked at the rest of the peknu to see what they would say. They ignored the man.

"The children are here," Faia insisted after they'd finished the second tour of the rooms. "They are *here*."

Medwind said, "Perhaps if we went outside the library, we could find something that would tell us why your Searching indicates they are in here — when it's obvious they aren't. Maybe they've gotten into a building or a cave behind the library."

Faia sighed. "That isn't the feel I get, but you might be right. Searching for my daughter is much more frightening than Searching for sheep ever was."

Thirk had been wandering around the room, studying the monster statues. He spoke up. "I'll wait in here, and let you know if they somehow show up.

Medwind's face showed her annoyance. "Why don't you make yourself useful and search for the children with the rest of us? You can admire the statues later."

"Let him stay," Faia said. "There is some important fact I'm missing. Perhaps he'll find it."

Seven-Fingered Fat Girl didn't like Thirk. He reminded her of the man who stole her tablet in the marketplace. He dressed the same, he looked very much the same, and at that moment, she sensed a similar lying tone in his voice. She made a tagnu hand-signal to Dog Nose — the one for "quiet and hide," and he nodded slightly and carefully drifted out of the room. The peknu and the sharsha headed toward the front of the library.

Fat Girl ducked behind a statue and crouched out of sight.

Something about Thirk's attitude struck Roba as strange. She didn't think for an instant he intended to wait for the children — he'd made it clear all along how he felt about them. No — he was up to something, and she intended to find out what it was. She told Kirgen to go along, that she'd catch up with him in a minute. Then she pressed herself against the wall just outside the door and hoped Thirk at least intended to stay in that room.

For a moment, the only sounds she heard were those of the rest of the team and the sharsha kids going outside — talking, occasionally calling for one or another of the missing children — and then she heard nothing at all.

Dog Nose appeared by her side, fingers to his lips. She nodded. Apparently she wasn't the only one suspicious of Thirk. The two of them waited together. Then she heard the scuffling of feet in the other room and Thirk's mutter.

"Fine," he whispered, and the whisper echoed through the room and out into the corridor, "now let's see what you do."

She heard a brief, scraping sound — and then a heavy, rolling grinding — stone against stone. At the same time, she heard Thirk's delighted "Aha!" She peeked carefully around the edge of the doorway, and saw one panel of the back stone wall rising up into the ceiling high overhead. *Incredible*, she thought. She held her breath. Another corridor appeared behind the moving stone slab, leading down.

That's where the kids are, she thought. *Down that corridor somewhere.* She waited. She wanted to run out and shout, "Thirk found where they went," but something about the man's actions stopped her. He was staring down the dark passage. The stone panel came to rest near the ceiling, held its position for an instant, and began to return to its initial place. Suddenly, Thirk conjured a faeriefire and sent it down the secret tunnel, and hurried after it. The heavy stone door slid shut behind him.

Seven-Fingered Fat Girl materialized from behind one of the statues and ran to the back of the room. Dog Nose ran after her, and Roba followed.

"He pushed this," Fat Girl said. She pointed to a stone panel carved to look like a part of the base of the statue.

Once Roba knew what to look for, she didn't have any trouble seeing the press-bar. She could tell its makers had tried to keep it inobtrusive, but not to hide it. That said something about the purpose of the place at the other end of the passageway, she decided. She wasn't sure what — but it said something.

She told Seven-Fingered Fat Girl, "Go get everyone else and bring them down the tunnel. I'll go on ahead with Dog Nose." She gave the boy a questioning look, and he nodded. "I don't know what Thirk is doing — but I don't trust him."

"I go right now," Fat Girl agreed, and raced off.

Roba watched the girl until she disappeared around a curve, then turned back to the press-bar. Her heart raced, and her pulse pounded in her ears. She wished she knew what Thirk intended. Why hadn't he told everyone of the press-bar? Did he think he would get additional fame as the discoverer of the secret passageway? That seemed likely to her. But she wished she could be sure. She'd expected him to be angry at her and at Kirgen. They'd mocked him and his grand passion — his scholarly pursuit of Edrouss Delmuirie. But instead of anger, he'd responded with some mystical nonsense about signs and portents and the will of the gods regarding Delmuirie. And he'd said nothing else about her — or to her, for that matter.

What was he thinking?

She pressed the bar — it moved with startling ease, and the panel slid up again. She and Dog Nose entered, and moving as quietly as they could, crept down the dark passageway.

They linked arms to stay together in the darkness. At several points, Roba noted areas of lesser darkness. When she looked up, she could see faint circles of dark blue against the black. She wondered briefly if they were windows into the night sky — but there would be time later to explore.

They heard a voice echoing back through the passageway. "Here you are, little ones. I've come to save you." Thirk's voice, distorted by the passageway, sounded hideous to Roba.

She tugged at Dog Nose to make him walk faster. She kept her fingers on the smooth side of the wall and felt it change in small degrees to rougher, less finished stone. The texture of the floor beneath her feet changed, too. And then she saw the first gleamings of light ahead.

Thirk's faeriefire, she thought. *I wish I dared summon one — but I don't want him to know I'm here. Not yet, anyway.*

Thirk's voice suddenly filled the tunnel. "By all the gods," he roared. "It's Delmuirie! I've found Delmuirie."

A child screamed.

He's lost his mind, Roba thought, and broke into a run —

Behind her, she heard the stone passageway moving again, and in front of her she heard Thirk chanting. She heard no further childish screams — in fact, she heard no sounds from the children at all. She burst into a sand-floored cavern, covered with carved boulders — Thirk wasn't there. The light came from a doorway to the left. She and Dog Nose ran toward the light, dodging the boulders.

Shouts echoed down the corridor behind her — *Help is coming,* she thought — and she noted the sound of running feet, and she came through the doorway to find Thirk holding Kirtha down on another of the boulders, in front of a pillar of light that contained a kneeling man.

Thirk had a knife in his hand — a stone Wen knife with bright eyes and sharp teeth inlaid in the blade. Choufa and Runs Slow were frozen in one corner, caught in mid-stride — held by a stop-spell of some sort. A man, frozen in a golden pillar of light, knelt behind Thirk, a sword in one hand and a chalice in the other. Roba warded herself instinctively, something the children had not known to do. Kirtha was staring at Thirk, her eyes wide with terror — but the stop-spell held her, too.

"Thirk, no!" Roba screamed.

He seemed not to hear her. He kept chanting, with the knife at Kirtha's throat. Then, like a man wakening from a dream, he looked up, and a vicious smile crawled across his face. "This is the will of the gods," he said. "The gods have given me suitable sacrifice to raise the magic that will set Edrouss Delmuirie free. I was right after all, wasn't I, Roba? Delmuirie is here — you see? You mocked me — all of you mocked me. You scoffed at me for believing Delmuirie created the Barrier. You scoffed at Delmuirie. Now you can see him, standing in front of you, waiting in a pillar of magic for me to come to him and release him into the world of the living again. He'll set us free, Roba. He'll release the Barrier, and give us the rest of the world, and the universe beyond. He'll set all of Arhel free."

Thirk frowned and pressed his knife against Kirtha's throat. "But you were right, too — the children did have a reason for being on this expedition. I simply failed to realize the gods would provide all I needed to work their will in this manner —"

"No, Thirk! Let the children go. The dark magics are never the will of the gods!"

"Not so," he said. "The gods created both light and dark, and all things work their will. The power grows in me — from the fear of this child, from the pain she will soon feel, and ultimately from her death. At the moment of her death, I will break the bonds that hold the great Delmuirie prisoner, and he will go free."

There was a rustling behind Roba in the doorway, and others crowded around her.

"You'll die first," Faia said.

"No. My death is not the will of the gods." He smiled, and made a quick cut along Kirtha's arm. Blood spouted from the wound.

Every magician in the room attacked instantly — with faeriefire, with stop-spells, with anything they could throw — and the column of light bent the magic toward itself and drew it all in. It didn't touch Thirk.

Thirk smiled, and pressed the knife to Kirtha's throat. "You see," he said. "The will of the gods." He began to chant. A reddish glow grew around him — Roba saw it at the same moment she and Kirgen and Faia all charged at the madman. His hand flashed, and blood spurted from Kirtha's other arm —

Roba was closest. She got there first.

My debt to Faia, she thought. And — *I'll kill him!* — as she drove her head into his side. He fell backward against the pillar of light. She saw it enfold him — but she fell with him. The glows of red and yellow fire mixed, and behind her children started to scream —

Stop-spell broken, she thought. *Good*.

She twisted as she fell, and the brilliant yellow light surrounded her. Her fall slowed, and she realized she could hang there, in mid-air, and never fall. She floated, surrounded by the light, and watched Thirk's knife.

How very strange, she thought. *Look at how it floats*. The knife was spinning upward in slow, lazy spirals. Sounds dimmed and distorted; the voices of her friends seemed to come to her through miles of water.

"Get out," they were yelling. "Get out, Roba!"

Silly of them, she thought. *Why would I ever want to leave?*

Peace enveloped her — but someone was pulling at her ankle. She wished whoever it was would quit. She was becoming part of the universe — and that distraction would not let her forget the outer world so that she

could join completely with the mind of the magic
around her. Thirk was with her in that mind — rapturous and repentant. Delmuirie's thoughts met hers
in joyful merging. Peace became one with her, and a
presence that was more than Thirk, more than Delmuirie — that was wisdom and life itself — filled her,
and she suddenly understood *everything*.

Still, she couldn't take her eyes off that knife. For an
instant and an eternity, it hung in mid-air, suspended
up among the carved spirals and stone knotwork.

Then another incredible burst of magical fire
poured itself into the pillar, and someone screamed,
"Come on, Roba! Help me!"

The knife sped up at once and fell very fast to the
floor, and Roba finished slamming to the ground with a
painful thud. She was able to move her eyes. Kirgen
was leaning over her and looking down at her. "Roba,
can you hear me?" he asked. "Speak to me."

She felt an incredible sense of loss. The wisdom was
gone. The warmth and the peace were gone, the
understanding of all the secrets of the universe — all gone.
She frowned at Kirgen. *If he took me away from all that, I'll
never forgive him,* she thought. And she said, "Of course I
can hear you. Why wouldn't I be able to hear you?"

Kirgen started to answer.

He didn't have the chance. From the other chamber,
a ululating cry began. It was a heathen sound, primitive, heartrending; it was the sound of grief too great
for words.

Fat Girl had appeared out of the gathering darkness,
frantic. "Come," she had gasped. "Hurry. Children are
found."

Medwind and Kirgen had automatically scooped
Nokar into the Hoos carry and run after Fat Girl back
into the library.

Medwind worried while she ran. *Found? In the*

library? she had wondered. *How can that be? And if everything is as it should be, why are we running?* Then Fat Girl revealed the hidden tunnel, and Medwind's concern grew. Thirk was not in the room waiting for them. So apparently he was down the tunnel —

A scream echoed out of it, cut short. The exploration party charged in —

Something wrong, terribly wrong, she kept thinking, and indeed, it was. Thirk stood at the side of a man held motionless in a column of light and enacted some ritual in which Kirtha appeared to be slated for role of main sacrifice; the other children were frozen in their places; Roba was trying to reason with the lunatic —

She and Kirgen put Nokar down at the same moment Thirk made his first cut. The room erupted with magic — she and Roba and Kirgen and Faia and Nokar attacked — the man should have fried where he stood.

That wasn't what happened. The column of light reached out and bent all that magical fury toward itself and *swallowed* it.

Thirk cut Kirtha again, and everyone ran forward. Roba got to him first, and butted into him with her head; he fell sideways into the column, and she fell, too. Then everything happened at once.

Faia grabbed Kirtha, who'd started screaming at the top of her lungs.

The column grew brighter, and, almost as if it were a living thing, it reached out and enveloped Thirk, and began to swallow Roba as well.

Kirgen tried to pull Roba out of the devouring pillar of light.

A stream of pure white fire shot from behind her and poured into the column, and the encroaching light receded enough that Kirgen could pull Roba to safety.

Medwind turned as that white bolt faded, to see that it had come from Nokar — and to see Nokar draw in on himself and crumple to the ground. She ran to his side, dragged him out of the archway into the other room so she could have enough space to revive him, and reached out with her magic to touch him and feed him her strength.

His body rejected her magic. He was dead. There was no cell of him that was intact — he had poured every bit of his lifeforce into saving Roba. Medwind couldn't give him back his life — he had given it away too completely. Not even years of her own life would revive him.

He was lost to her — and as she stroked his paper-thin skin and brushed closed his still-warm eyelids over his clouding eyes, she thought of the skulls on her altar. She thought of Nokar as a painted skull, a green ghostflesh face that whispered at her in anger, and that cowered in the dark, endless horror of the place between the worlds. *No,* she thought. *I love him — and because I love him, I will not give him over to that place.* She would lose him entirely before she would let his soul huddle in fear of the things that hunted between the worlds.

He would go on, his soul would go free — and whatever life there was at the end of the darkness, she hoped that he would find it. If the saje hells awaited him, she hoped he found himself in one he liked, full of bookish friends and bawdy women.

And if there was nothing beyond, as she sometimes thought, she hoped that at least there had been enough goodness in his life to make up for the long darkness.

She threw back her head then and cried out; gave tongue to the Hoos cry of mourning, gave voice to her howling grief and loss. He was the first love she'd lost, and she was losing all of him. She cried, and thought even as she did that the gods had never seen so many warrior's tears.

She stood at last, ignoring the hands that touched her shoulders, the voices that murmured sympathy.

She dragged him over and propped him against one of the boulders — Hoos custom, that the dead should not enter eternity lying down. She pulled off one of her war-necklaces and draped it over his neck — Hoos honor, to tell the gods that here was a warrior's spirit. She pulled from her waistbag a bit of jerky, and ripped a piece from it, and placed it on his tongue — Hoos duty, that the dead should not go hungry.

Then she knelt and kissed him once. Around the lump in her throat, she whispered, "I love you, old man. Find safe passage to whatever fate awaits you. Remember me if you can."

When she stood straight again, she set her jaw and wiped the tears from her eyes. She took Nokar's sturdy wood staff, and, with the voices of the not-Hoos calling after her, she walked away, through the boulder-strewn room and up the passage. There was something yet that she had to do — one final duty she owed the dead.

Kitchkithn, Hoos faeriefires, lit her way. Behind her she heard footsteps, but she did not care. She wanted no company for the task that awaited her. So she walked faster.

At the top of the passage, she could not find any latch that led out. Impatient, unwilling to search, she made a *vodrono*, a "far hand," to push the press-bar on the other side. The panel rose, and her *kitchkithn* raced in front of her through the library and back up the hill to the building that housed her altar.

She did not release the light until she faced the skulls of her vha'attaye. Then she let it go, and with the weight of darkness around her, she knelt, and placed Nokar's staff on the ground in front of her, and lit the candles and the incense, and took up her drum.

The vha'attaye came — all but Troggar Raveneye, who by her hand was destroyed for all eternity.

She pressed her forehead to the floor and

whispered, "I come to honor you." Tears started down her cheeks again — the pain of parting was too much. But she had her duty to the dead.

The vha'attaye hissed and creaked and began their whispery speech, but she held up her hand and stopped them. "Waking dead," she said, "spirits of the people I will always love, who are those people no more — I have come to say goodbye. Nokar told me to love many things, so it would take longer for me to lose the things I loved. But of those I have loved, all are gone — beyond my reach in one way or another. Except you. And you do not want my love.

"I've brought you to me to give you your freedom. I would not — trap you in the p-p-place between the worlds. I would — know your sp-sp-spirits were safe."

She was crying so hard the ghostly faces were mere blurs in front of her.

"Find glory, and n-n-n-new life," she sobbed, and took up Nokar's stick and smashed it down on the skull of Inndra Song, grandmother's grandmother. Bone shards flew, and flecks of fire from the burning incense blew in the wind and winked out.

"Find glory, and new life." She smashed the skull of Haron River, grandfather's father.

A wind rose up around her — the magical fury of Rasher the Hunter, who tried to fend off her staff. She ignored the buffetings of the wind and held her staff steady.

"Find glory, and — and new life." She smashed the skull of Rasher the Hunter.

"I'm s-s-s-sorry," she wept, and smashed the empty skull of Troggar Raveneye, best enemy and Advisor.

She stood then, with the bone shards surrounding her, and stared into the eyes of Rakell Ingasdotte, once friend, once Mottemage, now angry and unappeased spirit waiting freedom. "Once you t-t-truly loved me, as I still love you," Medwind whispered. "You were my teacher and my champion; we were friends and colleagues. I gave up my husbands and my herds to learn from you; now I give up my people and my past to set you free. I did not ever want to hurt you, Rakell. I did not ever mean to cause you this pain. I did not want to lose you — and when you were killed, I never got to say goodbye."

She clenched the stick tighter in her hands. "Goodbye, Rakell Ingasdotte. Find glory and new life. I hope someday you will find a way to forgive me, too."

She raised the staff.

Rakell spoke. "Goodbye, warrior and friend. Thank you."

Medwind closed her eyes and swung her stick. The skull of Rakell Ingasdotte, Mottemage of Daane University, teacher and best friend, shattered — and the spirit it had chained flew free.

Medwind pressed her face to the floor. It was cool and hard and somehow soothing. She stayed like that until the crying passed, until she could breathe normally.

Then she pushed herself upright, and kneeling, faced the shards of the vha'attaye. She sang the warrior's song that summoned the gods, and when she was finished, she stared at the darker swirls of black that hung between the glowing candles.

She spoke in the GodTongue:

"Etyt, Thiena,
Know I have failed in my duty
To preserve and protect,
To honor and keep the vha'attaye.
The spirits entrusted to me
Are lost by my hand.
I have failed in my duty
To have husbands,
For I am husbandless.
I have failed in my duty
To have children,

For I am childless.
The bones of my enemies do not
Hang at my belt;
My heart holds no joy.

"I am unworthy; I am no fit Hoos.
I relinquish my *b'dabba*.
I relinquish my people.
I relinquish my place in Yarwalla —
My spirit will wander without rest.
Turn your faces from me,
Gods of my better days.
I am none of yours."

She lifted the remainder of her war-necklaces and laid them on the altar. She pulled the *sslis* from her nose and threw it to the floor and crushed it under her boot.

She turned — and saw the silhouette of someone crouched in the doorway. In the darkness, she could not make out who it was, until she realized the stranger had been — still was — touching her mind.

"I followed you," the voice said in the darkness, lilting in its soft, accented Sropt. "You looked so sad." The voice belonged to the Wen sharsha, Choufa.

Medwind waited, still feeling the touch of their minds linked by the girl's magic.

The girl's mindvoice whispered through her thoughts. *I heard you,* she said. *You gave up everything you had to save your friend. I understand.*

Choufa stood and walked to her and said softly in her Wennish tongue, "Now you have no people. I have no people. You have no child — I have no mother. But we have saved each other's lives. We are bonded. If you will take me as your daughter, I will take you as my mother, and then at least we will have each other."

The slender girl stopped a short distance from Medwind.

So brave, Medwind thought. *She would have made a glorious Hoos.*

Medwind closed the distance between them and opened her arms and embraced the child.

"You are my daughter," she whispered, and pulled the girl close, and held her tight.

"It's hard to believe that really is Delmuirie," Roba said.

Kirgen had been staring at the two men encased in the pillar of light. He looked at her when she spoke, and gave her a wry half-smile. "Nearly impossible," he agreed. "You're certain it is?"

"Yes." Roba shivered, remembering her plunge into the pillar of light and her eager embrace of the self-dissolving consciousness existing inside of it. "I have no doubt. Thirk has joined his hero."

"That's fitting, I suppose. I wish the bastard was dead, though, instead of Nokar." Kirgen stared into the shimmering light to the two forms inside. "It galls me to see that stupid smile on his face."

"Not me." Roba shivered. "He could be in there forever, beyond time — he can't move, he can't do anything. Forever in prison." She turned her back on Thirk and Delmuirie.

Behind her, Kirgen muttered, "Forever isn't half long enough."

Roba wanted to think of something else, anything else — and the bright-painted statue in the corner near her caught her attention.

She walked over to it and brushed the cool, smooth stone form with her fingertips. "Look at it," she said. "It almost seems to weep." She studied the way the monster bent over the tablet clutched in its talons, and sighed. "Look at how its head hangs, and how its wings droop. And its face is so sad."

Kirgen joined her, and wrapped his arms around

her waist. "Every one of them down here looks the same," he remarked. "They seem appropriate for this place and all that's happened."

He hugged her hard. "You nearly gave your life saving the life of my daughter — and if old Nokar hadn't done what he did, I would have lost you. I owe you both everything I have."

Faia had finished healing Kirtha's wounds. She sat across the cavern from the pillar of light, holding the little girl. "I also give you my thanks, Roba. What is mine is yours, in thanks for my daughter's life. We will be going back to Omwimmee Trade as soon as we can find a way — I was wrong to bring her here. I thought nothing could hurt her with me to protect her; I am fortunate to still have her. But before we go, if there is anything I can do for you, or anything I could give you, you only have to ask."

Roba sighed. "You saved my life first. We are now merely even. But if you don't mind, I would ask you a question."

"Ask."

"Do you love Kirgen?"

Faia smiled sadly and shook her head in a slow negative. "Kirgen and I met at a terrible time, and found some comfort in each other, and went our own ways. We did not love each other then, and we do not love each other now." The hill-girl brushed a lock of hair out of her daughter's eyes. "We share our child — but you and Kirgen are free to take public bond — or whatever is the custom of your people. I will wish you only happiness and health."

"Thank you. I will wish the same for you."

Roba looked around her, at the sharsha children who were tangled together in little lumps on the sand, sound asleep. They were safe, she thought, and free from the horrors they'd endured. Dog Nose and Seven-Fingered Fat Girl curled in a tight ball with Runs

Slow tucked between them, acting like a tiny new family. They had a home at last, and each other. She studied the body of the old man sitting by the doorway in the next room. She would miss Nokar, she thought. She had been fortunate to know him.

Medwind would be back soon — Roba supposed once her friend had a chance to deal with her grief, she would take over the expedition.

In the meantime, it was warmer in the cavern than it was at the campsite, and Roba could see no purpose to be served in waking sleeping children. So she would wait for Medwind's return — or morning, whichever came first.

She thought perhaps she ought to rest. The day had been long and hard, and her body ached with weariness. But too much had happened, and the excitement had not yet worn off. Too much strangeness still beset her. From the meeting in Medwind's house to the terrors of the Wen tree village to her near-death and healing to the incredible library filled with mysteries — and finally to this seeming burial ground where so much had come to pass — she could not take it all in.

She looked from dead Nokar to Thirk embedded in the light like a bug in amber to the sad-faced drooping monsters who clutched their tablets. Too much. She couldn't believe she was still alive. By all rights, she shouldn't have been.

Kirgen sat in the sand, exhausted. Roba paced. After a while, Kirgen's head dropped to the sand and he slept. Roba still couldn't rest. She traced her fingers over the inscriptions on the luminous white boulders. She wandered over to the nearest monster. She touched its face — cold stone, lovingly carved, lovingly painted. She studied its downcast eyes and looked down at the tablet it seemed to be staring at. It held the tablet in one huge, taloned forefoot. It seemed to be pressing the claws of the other forefoot into the tablet itself—

"Kirgen!" she shrieked, waking all but the dead in the cavern. "Oh, my gods, Kirgen, you have to see this!"

Kirgen leapt up, groggy and awkward, and ran to her side. He stared around the room; then, when he could find no impending danger, looked at her as if he suspected the stress had been too much for her. From the expression on his face, she suspected he thought he was watching her lose her mind. "What is it, Roba?" he asked. His voice was rough from sleep.

She pointed at the monster's left forefoot. "Look at that," she demanded.

He looked at the tablet, and shrugged, and looked at her, his eyes questioning.

"No. I mean really look at it. Look at the claws. Look at what they're doing."

Kirgen looked — and Roba could almost see the instant when he woke completely up. He gasped. "It's pressing the First Folk letters into the tablet with its claws. By the gods, Roba — its claws are made just right to form the First Folk alphabet — three on the top, one on the bottom! Dots and slashes — of course. What else could it make with those claws but dots and slashes?" He stared at the monster and whispered, "But then — then could it be that the First Folk weren't human?"

Roba wrapped her arms around herself — excited beyond all imagining at the bizarre possibilities. "This is almost certainly a burial ground, Kirgen. Why don't we dig up one of whatever's buried here and find out?"

Kirgen stared at the rows of carved boulders. "Let's see if we can even move one of those," he said. "I don't see how we can. They're huge. We'll probably have to wait until tomorrow and dig under one."

They walked to the nearest boulder. They pushed on the side — and it rolled over instantly. It was hollow, and Roba realized it was made of the same stuff as the tablets. Beneath it, lying on the sand, was something dark. A mummy bundle, she thought, wrapped in glossy black wrappings. She and Kirgen exchanged uncertain glances and began to tug at the wrappings.

Roba heard a thin, sticklike snap, and the "wrapping" pulled back, and back, and still further back — it was not a wrapping, but a huge wing. Beneath it, sunken in but still covered with tight black skin, was a face very much like the faces of the statue monsters.

She and Kirgen stood a long time staring at that face. Roba was faintly aware that she heard the rumbling of stone and footsteps coming down the corridor. She realized, in a dim way, that Medwind had come to stand beside her.

"What is this?" The Hoos woman's voice cut across her reverie.

"One of the First Folk."

"No — one of their pets or sacred beasts, more likely," Medwind said.

"One of the First Folk." Roba knelt and pulled the mummified wing away from the foreleg. "The incised writing on the tablets is theirs. Look at the claws." She pointed to the curled forefoot with its huge, sharp talons. "Three on top, one on the bottom. Pressed into whatever medium they used for their tablets, those claws would create exactly the impressions we've found."

"But they're saurids. Beasts. Survival creatures, like the hovies or kellinks."

Medwind knelt beside Roba and touched the mummy. She touched the stone bracelet it wore high on its huge foreleg, and the rows of metal rings that pierced the edges of the creature's neck-rilles. She reached a tentative finger out to brush against one of the huge, pointed teeth that showed through cracking, flaking flesh.

The Hoos woman pulled her finger back, and crouched, staring at the giant monster. She asked aloud the question that already nibbled in the back of Roba's mind.

"If these are the First Folk, from which folk are we descended?"

Medwind hugged Faia, then Kirtha. "There should be enough money left to keep you and Kirtha for a long time, even if business is bad. You know where we kept it —" she said, and Faia laughed.

"I know. I remember. You have told me a dozen times."

"I don't want you to lack for anything." Medwind smiled at the hill-girl. "Take a husband or two," she suggested. "Have more children—you can, after all. Be happy."

"I would rather only take a husband if I can find a man I honestly love. But Kirtha and I will be fine. And we will be happy. You and your daughter do the same."

They hugged again.

"Are you sure you will not be coming back?" Faia asked. "If you even doubt, I will tear up the letter of possession for the house." She looked uncertain.

Kirtha watched Medwind and her mother, wide-eyed. "Home now?" she asked.

"I won't be coming back," Medwind said. "That house has too many memories and too much of the past for me. I'm done worshipping the past. I'm done carrying its bones around on my back. I won't even be staying here in the First Folk City after the Wen kids are settled in. Others will have to decipher Arhel's past." She looked down at her feet. *It is hard to describe freedom to one who has never suffered bondage,* she thought. "Kirgen and Roba have high hopes for research here, but Choufa and I will be moving on."

"What will you do?"

"I don't know yet. I'll find something."

Faia gave Medwind a wistful smile. "Will I see you again?"

Medwind shrugged. "Someday, perhaps. If not in this world, then maybe in the next."

Kirgen joined them, and asked Faia, "Are you ready? I need to start transporting the Wen kids' food — so we need to be going soon."

Faia nodded. "Gentle winds, warm hearth and dry roof wherever you travel, then, Medwind."

"Happiness, Faia. Happiness, Kirthchie."

Kirgen, Faia, and Kirtha vanished from the ruins in a cloud of smoke that the day's gentle breeze quickly dispersed. Medwind watched the last wisps and tatters vanish. Then she turned away.

The future waited, wide open, uncertain, full of promise. And for the first time in her life, she was free to walk toward it.

THE END

Glossary of Odd or Foreign Terms
(Including Several Words Your Mother Won't Approve Of)

Baofar — (Arissonese) Name for any member of the class of trees made up of multiple *ramets*, or individual trunks, connected by a complex underground network of roots. The entire organism is referred to as a *genet*. The majority of Arhel's baofars produce both an edible fruit and a short, round seed-pod from which long, trailing silklike threads depend at maturity. The individual ramets are usually small, but the genets can grow quite large. Of course, there are always exceptions.

Braxille — Largest city in the Fisher Province of Arhel. Built mostly underground. Subject to severe cold and months of darkness at mid-winter. Has the reputation, possibly deserved, of being the most miserable "civilized" spot in Arhel.

D'leffja — (Huong Hoos) (n. pejorative) A goat-molester. The verb is "d'leffik."

Dludergaad — (Huong Hoos) 1. A member of the Dludergaadar, the association of Huong Hoos thieves. 2. A term of admiration bestowed upon successful goat-thieves or horse thieves in a Huong Hoos tribe.

Dooru — (Wen) Any of four varieties of large, saurid flying predators that still inhabit the area above the Wen Tribes Treaty Line. Below the Treaty Line, such beasts have been extinct at least since the Second Purges.

Drum-Tongue — (Wen) Version of *Sropt* that can be "spoken" by playing a tuned drum. The method long-distance communication used by the Wen Tribes.

Easho — (Huong Hoos) Unit of measure equal to the length of the thighbone of a tall man. Not standardized.

Entreg — (Arissonese) Fifteenth letter of the Arissonese alphabet. Sound is "nt."

Etyt — (Huong Hoos) God of war. Consort of *Thiena*.

Evastevoffuschrom — (Wen) Literal translation is "smoke-monster- sleep"; a hypnotic agent released into the air by burning the ground seed pods of the split-leaved baofar.

Fanghare — (Arissonese) Small, predatory ground marsupial common to the desert of the Fey Plateau. Has very large ears. Is nocturnal, a mammal, and four-limbed.

Farsight — (Arissonese) Term used to describe the magical arts of future prediction or prediction of concurrent events in far-off places. Little discrimination is used in separating the two meanings.

Fern-madness — (Wen) A form of insanity brought on by ingestion of fronds of the rare white fern. Intensity of the madness varies with dose, and sufficiently large doses can cause death.

Fnaffigchekta — (Wen) Sropt — literally "drum-trade."

Fnaffigglotim — (Wen) Sropt — literally "drum-speaking."

Genets — see *Baofar*.

Gornat Wilds — (Fisher) Village near Big Tam. Very small and primitive.

Grum — (Arissonese) Esp. saje. One of the Seven Ugly Gods thought to inhabit the lowest and most horrible of the saje hells. The others are Makog, Dramfing, Shelfud, Torling, Keknok — and Wilmer, The God Whose Name Is Not Spoken.

Hai — (Hraddo) Pronounced *hay'-eye*. The word of common greeting in Hraddo, the Trade Tongue, which bears overtones of both "stay and talk a while" and "I mean no harm" — it has made its way into common speech in other languages in Arhel.

Hekpeknu — (Wen) Sropt — literally "woman-thing-that-looks-like-people."

Hout-Cadhay Quarter — The cheap-rent quarter in one of the outer circles of Ariss, home of whores and thieves and poor scholars and equally poor writers and far too many mediocre musicians.

Hraddo — The official trade tongue of polyglot Arhel. An extremely limited artificial language made up only of those sounds pronounceable by all the peoples of Arhel, uninflected, lacking all articles and pronouns, and with a grammar that changes tense by tacking the word "yesterday" or "tomorrow" onto the end of the sentence. Even so, fifty-seven of the roughly one thousand words of Hraddo are profane, and wars have been fought over misunderstandings the language has caused.

Hrogner — (Arissonese) Esp. saje. Chief Saje god of Mischief. Also the name of Faia's handed cat.

Hrun — (Huong Hoos) *Extremely* pejorative. The verb is *hrunik*, the noun *hrunja*. The base word refers to the act of kakophagery. The subject is one of the few taboos in the Hoos culture, which views all thirteen of its official sexual orientations as completely normal and considers religion a weird but unavoidable obligation.

Imitation-Proageff artwork — Arissers have an appalling admiration of the artworks of Shumt Proageff, a Ralledine artist who lived during the House Five Renaissance. Proageff's subjects during his entire prolific career were the same five women, who, from the record his paintings left, appear never to have owned or worn a stitch of clothing in their lives. But while Proageff was prolific, demand for his works far outstrips supply. Thus, there is a brisk market for cheap reproductions of his more famous works — especially the ones that also include the horses.

Keaddaba — (Huong Hoos) 1. Large or sturdy bones. Rare usage. 2. Unmitigated arrogance, gall, insolence, chutzpa, or nerve. Definitely the more common usage.

Keyu — (Wen) Sropt — 1. God. 2. Tree.

Keyunu — (Wen) Sropt — Literally "tree/god-people."

Kranjakken — (Huong Hoos) Exclamatory (Warning — literal meaning pejorative in most languages or cultures.) One of one hundred sixty-nine specific Hoos words relating to the physical act of human copulation.

Kyadda — (Huong Hoos) A sort of useful linguistic noise, the specific meaning of which is difficult to pin down. Can mean "yes," "thanks," "everyone is still breathing," "everything will be all right," or even "this isn't perfect, but it will certainly serve for the time being." Has spread from Huong Hoos to other languages which lacked such a broad verbal burp, and retained its same meaning — or lack thereof.

Peknu — (Wen) Sropt — Literally "things-that-look-like-people."

Prembullin Sajerie — (Arissonese) More progressive of the two saje schools of thought. Following the Second Mage/Saje War, the Prembullin Sajerie opened the doors of Faulea University to women, in positions both as scholars and as instructors, and permitted the sajes within its membership to enter public bonds with women. Slightly the larger of the two schools of thought, and with fractionally more power at the time of this writing.

Prodictan Era — (Arissonese) Period of severe censorship between the First and Second Purges, when all historical records were subject to extreme revisionism by whichever fanatics were in power at the time. The result is that all historical records written during the Prodictan Era are subject to wild inaccuracy. Unfortunately, because the First Purges destroyed all available historical records, and the Second Purges destroyed all records that didn't suit the tastes of the parties in power, Prodictan History is the best available for many time periods.

Puffing-krull — (Wen) Small green six-limbed jungle saurid that has bright red bladders behind each of its legs. When posturing to attract mates, it inflates each of these bladders to such huge proportions that it can then only waddle with difficulty until the bladders deflate. Male puffing-krulls tend to congregate on fallen logs and large rocks during the mating season, where they are entertaining to watch.

Ramet — See *Baofar*.

Raouda — (Wen) 1. Small, pulpy succulent with attractive flowers that grows as a parasite on rain forest trees. 2. Deadly neurotoxin made from the pressed leaves of that plant.

Schkavak — (Huong Hoos) Pejorative. 1. Thief, specifically, a thief who is not a member of the Hoos association of thieves, the Dludergaadar. 2. Any thief who steals from oneself.

Sharsha — (Wen) Sropt — Literally "a sacrifice."

Sheshrud — (Huong Hoos) 1. The small slimy softbodied white grub that feeds on the dung of large mammals throughout Arhel. 2. Pejorative term for an outlander.

Skeruekkeu — (Wen) Pejorative. Biologically impossible. Skeru are little smelly insects.

Stekkonks — (Huong Hoos) Another specific pejorative phrase of extreme (and unfortunately unprintable) rudeness.

Tagnu — (Wen) Sropt — Literally "not-people."

Temrish — (Arissonese) Archaic. Term for a form of contractual bondage, the specifics of which are no longer known. Term originates from at least the Prodictan Era, and probably before.

Tethjan Sajerie — (Arissonese) The reactionary "old guard" school of thought in Faulea University. Still proscribes any meaningful contact with women, still abhors the presence of women on the Faulea campus, and refuses to recognize the contributions of women in general or the Magerie in specific to the practice of magic.

Thiena — (Huong Hoos) Goddess of war. Consort of *Etyt*.

Transport — (Arissonese) Proprietary saje form of magical transportation. No saje may reveal the art of teleport to anyone not a saje and a sworn member of either Prembullin or Tethjan Sajeries. No saje may reveal the art of teleport to any mage especially. Even after the opening of the Mage and Saje Universities to members of the opposite genders, this rule remains firm.

Tree-Naming — (Wen) The ceremony that serves to mark the coming of age of Wen children of both sexes. Generally occurs between the ages of ten and twelve, and always near the onset of puberty.

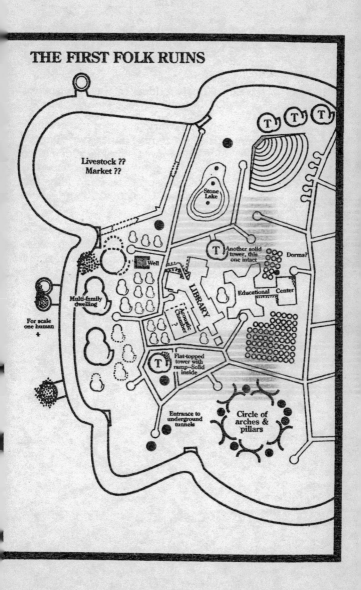

THE FIRST FOLK RUINS

Livestock ??
Market ??

Stone Lake

T T T T

Another solid
tower, this
one intact

Dorms?

Well

LIBRARY

Educational   Center

Multi-family
dwelling

Acoustic
Chamber

For scale
one human
4

Flat-topped
tower with
ramp—Solid
inside

Entrance to
underground
tunnels

Circle of
arches &
pillars

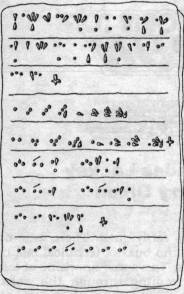

- ONE OF THE BEST
EXAMPLES SO FAR
OF A BEGINNER'S
WRITING TABLET—
THE FIRST SECTION
IS THE ALPHABET IN
CORRECT ORDER (AS
YET, WE ARE UNABLE
TO DETERMINE THE
SOUNDS THESE LETTERS
REPRESENT.) THE (+)
SEEMS TO MEAN
COMPLETION, THOUGH.

- SECOND SECTION TO
(+) ARE NUMBERS 1-16.
NOTE THAT COUNTING
IS DONE IN DOUBLE-
BASE · FOUR.

- THIRD SECTION MAY
BE SPELLING OR
WRITING PRACTICE OR
BOTH. NOTE TEACHER
CORRECTIONS OF (··)
SYMBOL, AND PRACTICE
OF THIS SYMBOL AT
BOTTOM OF TABLET.

- ADULT TABLETS USE
NO LINES.

<u>FIG (e)</u> — STUDENT TABLET
FIRST FOLK — WEN RUINS
(FROM CLASSROOM III-B-WEST)

There Are Elves Out There

An excerpt from

Mercedes Lackey
Larry Dixon

The main bay was eerily quiet. There were no
screams of grinders, no buzz of technical talk or
rapping of wrenches. There was no whine of test
engines on dynos coming through the walls.
Instead, there was a dull-bladed tension amid all
the machinery, generated by the humans and the
Sidhe gathered there.

Tannim laid the envelope on the rear deck of
the only fully-operated GTP car that Fairgrove had
built to date, the one that Donal had spent his
waking hours building, and Conal had spent track-
testing. He'd designed it for beauty and power in
equal measure, and had given its key to Conal, its
elected driver, in the same brother's-gift ceremony
used to present an elvensteed. Conal now sat on

its sculpted door, and absently traced a slender finger along an air intake, glowering at the envelope.

Tannim finished his magical tests, and asked for a knife. An even dozen were offered, but Dottie's Leatherman was accepted. Keighvin stood a little apart from the group, hand on his short knife. His eyes glittered with suppressed anger, and he appeared less human than usual, Tannim noticed. Something was bound to break soon.

Tannim folded out the knifeblade, slit the envelope open, and then unfolded the Leatherman's pliers. With them he withdrew six Polaroids of Tania and two others, unconscious, each bound at the wrists and neck. Their silver chains were held by some-*things* from the Realm of the Unseleighe—inside a limo. And, out of focus through the limo's windows, was a stretch of flat tarmac, and large buildings—

Tannim dropped the Leatherman, his fingers gone numb. It clattered twice before wedging into the cockpit's fresh-air vent. Keighvin took one startled step forward, then halted as the magical alarms at Fairgrove's perimeter flared around them all. Tannim's hand went into a jacket pocket, and he threw down the letter from the P.I. He saw Conal pick up the photographs, blanch, then snatch the letter up.

Tannim had already turned by then, and was sprinting for the office door, and the parking lot beyond.

Behind him, he could hear startled questions directed at him, but all he could answer before disappearing into the offices was "Airport!" His bad leg was slowing him down, and screamed at him like a sharp rock grinding into his bones. There was some kind of attack beginning, but he had no time for that.

Have to get to the airport, have to save Tania

from Vidal Dhu, the bastard, the son of a bitch, the—

Tannim rounded a corner and banged his left knee into a file cabinet. He went down hard, hands instinctively clutching at his over-damaged leg. His eyes swam with a private galaxy of red stars, and he struggled while his eyes refocused.

Son of a bitch son of a bitch son of a bitch. . . .

Behind him he heard the sounds of a war-party, and above it all, the banshee wail of a high-performance engine. He pulled himself up, holding the bleeding knee, and limp-ran towards the parking lot, to the Mustang, and Thunder Road.

Vidal Dhu stood in full armor before the gates of Fairgrove, laughing, lashing out with levin-bolts to set off its alarms. It was easy for Vidal to imagine what must be going on inside—easy to picture that smug, orphaned witling Keighvin Silverhair barking orders to weak mortals, marshaling them to fight. Let him rally them, Vidal thought—it will do him no good. None at all. He may have won before, but ultimately, the mortals will have damned him.

It has been so many centuries, Silverhair. I swore I'd kill your entire lineage, and I shall. I shall!

Vidal prepared to open the gate to Underhill. Through that gate all the Court would watch as Keighvin was destroyed—Aurilia's plan be hanged! Vidal's blood sang with triumph—he had driven Silverhair into a winless position at last! And when he accepted the Challenge, before the whole Court, none of his human-world tricks would benefit him—theirs would be a purely magical combat, one Sidhe to another.

To the death.

*   *   *

Keighvin Silverhair recognized the scent of the magic at Fairgrove's gates—he had smelled it for centuries. It reeked of obsession and fear, hatred and lust. It was born of pain inflicted without consideration of repercussions. It was the magic of one who had stalked innocents and stolen their last breaths.

He recognized, too, the rhythm that was being beaten against the walls of Fairgrove.

So be it, murderer. I will suffer your stench no more.

"They will expect us to dither and delay; the sooner we act, the more likely it is that we will catch them unprepared. They do not know how well we work together."

Around him, the humans and Sidhe of his home sprang into action, taking up arms with such speed he'd have thought them possessed. Conal had thrown down the letter after reading it, and barked, "Hangar 2A at Savannah Regional; they've got children as hostages!" The doors of the bay began rolling open, and outside, elvensteeds stamped and reared, eyes glowing, anxious for battle. Conal looked to him, then, for orders.

Keighvin met his eyes for one long moment, and said, "Go, Conal. I shall deal with our attacker for the last time. If naught else, the barrier at the gates can act as a trap to hold him until we can deal with him as he deserves." He did not add what he was thinking—that he only hoped it would hold Vidal. The Unseleighe was a strong mage; he might escape even a trap laid with death metal, if he were clever enough. Then, with the swiftness of a falcon, he was astride his elvensteed Rosaleen Dhu, headed for the perimeter of Fairgrove.

He was out there, all right, and had begun laying a spell outside the fences, like a snare. Perhaps in his sickening arrogance he'd forgotten that Keighvin could see such things. Perhaps in his insanity, he no longer cared.

Rosaleen tore across the grounds as fast as a stroke of lightning, and cleared the fence in a soaring leap. She landed a few yards from the laughing, mad Vidal Dhu, on the roadside, with him between Keighvin and the gates. He stopped lashing his mocking bolts at the gates of Fairgrove and turned to face Keighvin.

"So, you've come to face me alone, at last? No walls or mortals to hide behind, as usual, coward? So sad that you've chosen *now* to change, within minutes of your death, traitor."

"Vidal Dhu," Keighvin said, trying to sound unimpressed despite the heat of his blood, "if you wish to duel me, I shall accept. But before I accept, you must release the children you hold."

The Unseleighe laughed bitterly. "It's your concern for these mortals that raised you that have *made* you a traitor, boy. Those children do not matter." Vidal lifted his lip in a sneer as Keighvin struggled to maintain his composure. "Oh, I will do more than duel you, Silverhair. I wish to Challenge you before the Court, and kill you as they watch."

That was what Keighvin had noted—it was the initial layout of a Gate to the High Court Underhill. Vidal was serious about this Challenge—already the Court would be assembling to judge the battle. Keighvin sat atop Rosaleen, who snorted and stamped, enraged by the other's tauntings. Vidal's pitted face twisted in a maniacal smirk.

"How long must I wait for you to show courage, witling?"

Keighvin's mind swam for a moment, before he remembered the full protocols of a formal Challenge. It had been so long since he'd even seen one. . . .

Once accepted, the Gate activates, and all the Court watches as the two battle with blade and magic. Only one leaves the field; the Court is bound to slay anyone who runs. So it had always been. Vidal would not Challenge unless he were confident of winning, and Keighvin was still tired from the last battle—which Vidal had not even been at. . . .

But Vidal must die. That much Keighvin knew.

From Born to Run *by Mercedes Lackey & Larry Dixon.*

*   *   *

Watch for more from the SERRAted Edge:
Wheels of Fire by Mercedes Lackey & Mark Shepherd (October 1992)

When the Bough Breaks by Mercedes Lackey & Holly Lisle (February 1993)

MERCEDES LACKEY:
Hot! Hot! Hot!

Whether it's elves at the racetrack, bards battling evil mages or brainships fighting planet pirates, Mercedes Lackey is always compelling, always fun, always a great read. Complete your collection today!

Urban Fantasies

Knight of Ghost and Shadows (with Ellen Guon),
69885-0, 352 pp., $4.99 ☐

Summoned to Tourney (with Ellen Guon), 72122-4,
304 pp., $4.99 ☐

SERRAted Edge Series

Born to Run (with Larry Dixon), 72110-0, 336 pp., $4.99 ☐

Wheels of Fire (with Mark Shepherd), 72138-0,
384 pp., $4.99 ☐

When the Bough Breaks (with Holly Lisle), 72156-9,
320 pp., $4.99 ☐

High Fantasy

Bardic Voices: The Lark and the Wren, 72099-6,
496 pp., $5.99 ☐

Other Fantasies by Mercedes Lackey

Reap the Whirlwind (with C.J. Cherryh), 69846-X,
288 pp., $4.99 ☐
Part of the Sword of Knowledge series.

Castle of Deception (with Josepha Sherman), 72125-9,
320 pp., $5.99 ☐
Based on the bestselling computer game, *The Bard's Tale.*™

Science Fiction

The Ship Who Searched (with Anne McCaffrey), 72129-1,
320 pp., $5.99 ☐
The Ship Who Sang is not alone!

Wing Commander: Freedom Flight (with Ellen Guon),
72145-3, 304 pp., $4.99 ☐
Based on the bestselling computer game, *Wing Commander.*™

Available at your local bookstore. If not, fill out this coupon and send a check or money order for the cover price to Baen Books, Dept. BA, P.O. Box 1403, Riverdale, NY 10471.

Name: _____

Address: _____

_____

I have enclosed a check or money order in the amount of $_____